COWE

CA

AND

THE RESCUE PILOT
BY
RACHEL LEE

COWBOY DEPUTY

BY

CARLA CASSIDY

THE RESCUE PILOT

BY

RACHEL LEE

COWBOY DEPUTY

BY
CARLA CASSIDY

First published in Great Britain 2012
by Mills & Boon, an imprint of Harlequin (UK) Limited,
Eton House, 18-24 Paradise Road, Richmond, Surrey TW9 1SR

© Carla Bracale 2011

ISBN: 978 0 263 89495 0

46-0112

Harlequin (UK) policy is to use papers that are natural, renewable and recyclable products and made from wood grown in sustainable forests. The logging and manufacturing processes conform to the legal environmental regulations of the country of origin.

Printed and bound in Spain
by Blackprint CPI, Barcelona

Carla Cassidy is an award-winning author who has written over fifty books. Carla believes the only thing better than curling up with a good book to read is sitting down at the computer with a good story to write. She's looking forward to writing many more books and bringing hours of pleasure to readers.

Chapter 1

It was only when she saw the dancing swirl of cherry-colored lights in her rearview mirror that Edie Burnett glanced down at her speedometer. She was going forty miles an hour. As she eased off the gas pedal and pulled to the side of the street in front of a little dress boutique, she caught sight of a sign that indicated the speed limit was twenty-five.

Muttering a curse beneath her breath, she came to a stop at the curb. This was just the icing on the cake of crud that had become her life.

The official car pulled up behind her and she watched in her rearview mirror as the driver got out. Tall and lean, his khaki shirt tugged across broad shoulders as he walked toward her driver window with purposeful strides.

An errant curl of dark hair flopped onto his broad forehead and it only took that single glance in her mirror to know that the man was a hot piece of hunk.

Still, at the moment she didn't much care what he looked like. She needed to figure out the best way to talk him out of giving her a ticket. She wasn't sure she could afford lunch, much less a fine for speeding.

Cute or pathetic? She quickly decided to reach for cute and clueless and then resort to crying if necessary. It had worked for her more than once in the past.

"In a hurry?" His deep, pleasant voice resonated inside her and she looked up to see long-lashed eyes the color of rich, dark chocolate gazing at her.

"Oh, wow, I'm so sorry. I had the radio on and it was a really good song and I guess my speed just kind of got away from me." She gave him a bright bewildered smile. "I didn't notice the speed limit sign until I saw your lights flashing in my rearview mirror."

"But surely you noticed you'd entered the heart of town," he countered.

"I'm such a dunce," she agreed, once again giving him her friendliest grin.

"Driver's license please," he said, no returning smile curving his sexy lips.

Her own smile faltered as she dug into her oversize purse for her wallet. Damn. He was obviously going to give her a ticket. She handed him her license and watched in her mirror as he returned to his car, unable to help but notice that he looked just as good going as he had coming.

Now was the time she'd usually summon up fake tears and hope she could find a soft spot in his heart. But as she stared blindly out the front window the tears that blurred her vision were achingly real.

The past seven months of her life had been an utter nightmare, culminating in the call from somebody here in town that her grandfather needed help.

It had been two years since she'd last seen her grandfather, Walt Tolliver. At that time she'd come back to the small town for her mother's funeral. That particular trip back had been brief and so filled with grief she now scarcely remembered it. Since that time she'd tried to call the old man every weekend, yet in the past six months with her own life falling to pieces, Edie hadn't talked to her grandfather.

A sob escaped her and was quickly followed by another. By the time the deputy returned to her car window, she was blubbering like a baby.

"Hey, there's no need for that," he exclaimed as he held her license out to her. "I'm just going to issue you a warning."

"It's not that," she replied, the words choking out of her between sobs. She grabbed the license and tossed it into the dark recesses of her purse. "It's my life. It sucks. A year ago I was too stupid to live. I thought my creep of a boyfriend loved me and I wanted to do something special for him for his birthday so I gave him my credit card and told him to buy himself the stereo system he'd been drooling over. He bought the stereo all right, and half the store. He maxed out my card and disappeared.

I used most of my savings to pay off the card and then I lost my job."

The words tumbled from her lips as if of their own free will as tears continued to cascade down her cheeks. "Then this morning as I was packing up to drive here, my landlord appeared with a thirty-day notice for me to get out. He's selling the house where I rent an apartment and I have to go."

She suddenly looked up at him, appalled by the gush of her personal problems to the handsome stranger. God, how embarrassing was this? She swiped her cheeks with the back of her hands. "I'm sorry, this isn't your problem. I'm sorry I was speeding and I appreciate you just giving me a warning."

"Are you okay to drive the rest of the way to Walt's house?" he asked.

She nodded. "I'm fine."

He stepped back and motioned for her to pull away from the curb. It was only when she was back on the road that she wondered how he knew she was headed toward her grandfather's place.

How embarrassing, to totally break down in front of a stranger and spill the sordid details of her life. She hadn't cried a tear with each bad thing that had occurred over the past year. It seemed unfathomable that she'd had a mini-breakdown in front of a stranger.

At least she hadn't told him everything. She hadn't told him that the credit card debt Greg had left her with had been the least of the heartache he'd left behind.

She dismissed both Greg and the hot deputy from

her mind as she turned off Main and onto a tree-lined residential street. Black Rock was typical of many small Kansas towns, with the business section taking up two blocks of the main drag surrounded by picturesque side streets lined with mature trees and pleasant, well-kept homes.

When she'd been young she and her mother had often visited her grandparents for a week or so each summer. Her mother and her grandmother would spend much of that time in the kitchen and Walt would entertain Edie by teaching her to play chess, bird-watching in the backyard and gardening.

Those had been some of the happiest days of Edie's life. But when she'd been a teenager, she'd opted for spending time with her friends instead of visiting grandparents. Then the years had slipped away and everything had changed.

Her grandmother had passed away, her mother was gone and now the only family she had left was her Poppy, and according to the brief phone message she'd gotten from somebody here in town, he needed her. The problem was she wasn't in a place where she could be much help to anyone.

As she pulled up in front of the familiar two-story house, her heart fell. Even the forgiving glow of the late afternoon sun couldn't take away the air of neglect that clung to the place.

The lawn needed a good mowing and the house itself screamed for a fresh coat of paint. Weeds had choked the last of the fall flowers in the beds that lined the walkway to the front porch.

She got out of her car and tried to ignore the sense of being overwhelmed. Was he ill? Poppy was seventy-one years old. Was he too old to be living on his own? How was she going to help him when she could barely help herself?

She knocked on the door, hoping he was at least well enough to open it. "Who is there?" The deep voice resounded with energy from the other side of the door.

"Poppy, it's me, Edie."

The door flung open and Edie breathed a sigh of relief at the sight of her grandfather, looking older, but robust and healthy. "What a surprise! If it isn't my favorite girl in the whole wide world." He pulled her into the foyer and into the loving embrace of his arms.

He smelled of cheap cologne and menthol rub, of early autumn air and sweet childhood memories, and as she hugged him back she wondered why she had stayed away for so long.

He finally released her and motioned her to follow him inside. "Come on, then. I need to check on my dinner."

As she followed behind him toward the kitchen she noticed that the inside of the house was neat and tidy and the scent of a roast cooking emanated from the kitchen.

Maybe it had been a cranky neighbor who had called her because of the condition of the exterior of the house and the yard. She couldn't remember the caller giving his name but it was obvious that he had overreacted. Thank God her grandfather seemed fine.

She'd take the next couple of days and mow the lawn, weed the flower beds and maybe get a couple gallons of paint to spruce up the place. She made a commitment to come visit every two months and resume her weekly phone calls.

"Got roast and potatoes for supper," he said as he went to oven and opened the door. "And green beans from the garden. Go on, sit down while I stir these beans and add a little bacon grease."

"Are you expecting company?" she asked, noticing that the table held two place settings. Unless Poppy had suddenly become a psychic, the extra plate hadn't been set for her.

"Benjamin is coming over. He stops by two or three times a week for dinner and some chess." Walt smiled at her. "It will feel like a regular party with you here." He finished stirring the beans and then grabbed a plate from the cabinet and added it to the table.

"I was beginning to think you'd forgotten all about your Poppy," he said with a touch of censure in his voice.

"You know the phone lines go both ways," she replied.

"I know, but I figured if a young girl like you wanted to talk to an old coot like me, you'd call." He eased down in the chair next to her at the table. "What are you now, twenty-three or twenty-four?"

"Twenty-nine, Poppy." Although the past year of her life, she'd made the mistakes of a teenager and suffered a woman's grief.

One of his grizzly gray eyebrows lifted in surprise. "Twenty-nine!" He swiped a hand down his weather-worn face and shook his head. "Seems the past couple of years have plum gotten away from me. That means it's been almost ten years since I lost my Delores and over two years since we lost your mama." For a moment he looked ancient, with sadness darkening his blue eyes and his paper-thin lips turned downward.

The sadness lasted only a moment and then his eyes regained their usual twinkle. "I hope you're going to be here long enough for me to teach you a lesson or two in chess."

She laughed. "I'm not leaving here until I win at least one game."

"Good," he said, obviously delighted. "That means it's going to be a nice long visit."

Although Edie was glad she was here, again she was struck by the thought that he seemed just fine and whoever had called her saying he needed help had definitely overreacted.

He jumped out of his chair and walked over to the oven and opened the door. "Benjamin should be here soon and we'll eat. Are you hungry?"

"Starving," she replied. Her lunch had been a bag of chips she'd eaten in the car. "Is there anything I can do to help?"

"There are a couple of nice tomatoes in the

refrigerator. If you want to, you can slice them up and put them on the table."

As she sliced the tomatoes, they chatted mostly about the past, playing a game of *remember when* that created warm fuzzies in Edie's heart.

She shouldn't have stayed away for so long. Poppy was the only family she had left in the world. Her home in Topeka was just a three-hour drive to Black Rock but somehow her personal drama and heartbreak had taken over and the last thing on her mind had been her Poppy.

"You'll like Benjamin," Poppy said as he took the roaster out of the oven and set it on hot pads in the center of the table. "He's a good guy and a mean chess player."

And probably eighty years old, Edie mentally thought, although she was grateful her grandfather had a friend for company. Maybe this big house was just too much for Poppy. Maybe it was time for him to think about an apartment or someplace where he didn't have to worry about maintenance and upkeep. Time to talk about that later, she thought as the doorbell rang.

"That should be Benjamin," Walt said and left the kitchen to get the door.

Edie wiped off the countertop and then pasted a smile on her face as Walt came back into the kitchen. The smile fell as she saw who followed at his heels, not an old, gray-haired man with stooped shoulders and rheumy eyes, but rather the very hot deputy who had pulled her over and witnessed her mini-breakdown.

"Edie, this here is my friend, Benjamin Grayson. Benjamin, this is my granddaughter who surprised me this evening with a visit," Walt said.

"Hello, Edie, it's nice to meet you." He stepped forward and held out a hand, obviously deciding to play it as if he'd never seen her before.

He'd looked great earlier in his khaki uniform but now with worn tight jeans hugging his long lean legs and a blue cotton shirt clinging to his broad shoulders, he was pure sin walking.

"Nice to meet you, too," she replied as she gave his hand a short, curt shake.

"Go on, sit down," Walt said. "Let's eat before the roast gets cold."

Edie slid into a chair at the table and tried not to notice the clean, male scent mingling with a woodsy cologne that wafted from Benjamin.

He might have smelled good and he might have looked great and in another place and time she might have been interested in him. But Edie had sworn off relationships and men and sex for the rest of her life. Besides, her intention was to be in Black Rock for only two or three days.

As the men joined her at the table and filled their plates, Walt and Benjamin made small talk about the weather and the forecast for a harsh winter to come.

Although Edie was glad she'd gotten the phone call that had prompted her to come for a visit, she still didn't see any real issue where her Poppy was concerned.

"Any word on that missing girl?" Walt asked.

Benjamin shook his head. "Nothing. It's like she vanished into midair."

"Missing girl?" Edie looked at Benjamin curiously.

"Her name is Jennifer Hightower, a twenty-two-year-old who went missing three weeks ago," Benjamin replied.

"And she's not the only missing girl in town," Walt said. "Benjamin's own sister went missing over two months ago."

Edie saw the darkness that crawled into Benjamin's eyes as he nodded. "That's right, but surely we can think of something more pleasant to talk about while we eat." There was a note of finality in his tone that indicated this particular subject was closed.

Walt immediately began to talk about the fall festival the town was planning in the next month. As Edie ate, she found that her focus tugged again and again to Benjamin.

His face was tanned as if he spent a lot of time outdoors rather than inside at a desk or seated in a patrol car. He had nice features, a no-nonsense slight jut to his chin, a straight nose and lips that looked soft and very kissable.

There was no question that she was curious about his sister, felt a tinge of empathy as she imagined what it must be like to have a family member missing.

Edie didn't know about missing family members, but she was intimate with grief, knew the sharp stab of loss, the ache that never quite went away.

She could only assume that Benjamin wasn't married

and she questioned why a handsome man like him would choose to spend a couple nights a week playing chess with an old man.

"How long are you planning to visit?" he asked.

With those gorgeous, long-lashed eyes focused intently on her, a small burst of unwanted heat ignited in the very pit of her stomach.

"Just a couple days or so," she replied, grateful her voice sounded remarkably normal. "I need to get back home and take care of some things." And he knew exactly what those things were because she'd spewed them out in a mist of tears when he'd pulled her over.

"You still managing that restaurant?" Poppy asked.

She hesitated and then shook her head. "Unfortunately a couple weeks ago I showed up at the restaurant and found a padlock on the door and a note that said the place was out of business." She tamped down the residual anger that rose up inside her each time she thought of that day. There had been no warning to any of the employees, no hint that the place was in trouble.

"So, have you found a new job?" Poppy eyed her worriedly.

"Not yet, but when I get back home I'm sure I won't have any problems finding something," she assured him with a quick smile. The last thing she wanted was for him to worry about her.

Thankfully dinner went quickly and as Poppy stood to clear the table, Edie shooed him away. "You two go on and play your chess. I'll take care of the cleanup."

"I won't argue with you. I like the cooking but hate the cleanup," Poppy said.

"I could help. It would only take a minute," Benjamin said.

Edie shook her head. "I've got it under control." The last thing she wanted was to be butting elbows with him over the sink. He was too big and too sexy for her and she didn't want him close enough that she could smell him, feel his body heat.

She breathed a sigh of relief as the two men left the kitchen and disappeared into the living room. It took her only minutes to store the leftovers in the refrigerator and then stack the plates for washing.

There was no dishwasher and as she got the dish drainer rack from the cabinet, she remembered all the times she'd stood at this sink and helped her grandmother wash dishes.

It hadn't been a chore; it had been a chance to talk about the day, about the weather, about life with a woman Edie had considered wise and loving.

The last time Edie had been here she'd been thirteen years old and madly in love with a boy named Darrin. It had been a case of unrequited love. Darrin had preferred video games to girls.

"It's not a mistake to love," her grandmother had told her. "But you need to love smart. Choose a man who has the capacity to love you back, a man who can make you feel as if you're the most important person in the world."

As Edie washed and rinsed the dishes, she wondered

what her grandmother would say about the mess Edie had made of her life. She had definitely loved stupid, choosing to give her heart to a man who not only didn't have the capacity to love her back, but also had all the character of a rock. The price she'd paid for loving stupidly had been enormous and she'd been left with the determination to never put her heart in jeopardy again.

A burst of deep male laughter came from the living room as she placed the last dish in the drainer. It sounded like the two of them were enjoying their game.

Darkness had fallen outside and Edie realized she hadn't brought in her suitcase from the car. As she entered the living room both men looked up from the chessboard. "What are you doing, girl?" Poppy asked. "Come sit and watch a master at work." He gave her a grin that twinkled in his eyes.

She returned his smile. "I gather from the smug look on your face that you're winning."

"I've been playing him a couple nights a week for the past six months and I have yet to win a game," Benjamin said.

His gaze slid down the length of her, the quick once-over that a man might give a woman he found attractive.

She felt the heat of his gaze and quickly moved toward the front door. "I'm just going to get my suitcase from the car."

"Need any help?" Benjamin asked.

She quickly shook her head. "Thanks, but I can get

it." She scooted out the front door and into the cool September evening air.

For a moment she stood on the porch and stared up at the night sky. Here in Black Rock the stars seemed brighter, closer than they did in Topeka.

"Make a wish, sugar," her grandmother would tell her whenever the two of them had sat on the porch and gazed upward.

Edie reached up and grabbed the small charm that hung on the gold chain around her neck. The gold was cool in her fingers but warmed quickly as she held it tight.

There was only one wish she'd like to make and she knew it was one that could never come true. She released her hold on the charm and headed to her car in the driveway.

Behind her car was parked a large black pickup she knew must belong to Benjamin. Funny, she would assume he was more the sweet little sports car type than the big, bruising truck.

She'd packed light and grabbed the small suitcase and overnight bag from her backseat, then headed inside the house. She heard no sound from the living room. Apparently the current chess game was intense enough that both men were concentrating.

She carried the suitcase up the stairs, the third and seventh steps creaking beneath her weight as they had when she'd been a child. She entered the last bedroom at the end of the hall, the room where she'd always stayed when she and her mother had come for a visit.

The dusty pink paint on the wall and the pink floral spread covering the double bed brought another wave of memories.

Every night that she'd slept here she'd been tucked into bed lovingly not only by her mother, but also by her grandmother. And often Poppy would come upstairs to sneak her a cookie or a little bowl of popcorn. In this house, she'd always felt loved like nowhere else on earth.

It took her only minutes to stow her items in the dresser and closet, then she headed back downstairs where it sounded like the chess game had ended.

As she entered the living room, Benjamin and Poppy got up from the small game table. "He beat me both games," Benjamin said. He smiled at Edie, a warm, sexy smile that once again fluttered a faint heat through her veins.

"Maybe you and Edie could play a few games together, you know, practice so eventually you can beat the master." Poppy grinned.

Benjamin laughed. "I'd love to hang around and play a game of chess with Edie, but unfortunately I've got some reports that need to be written before morning."

The twinkle in Poppy's eyes faded as he looked at Benjamin seriously. "You know how to find those girls. Find the aliens and you'll find out what happened to that Hightower young woman and your sister."

"Aliens?" Edie looked from her grandfather to Benjamin with curiosity.

Poppy nodded. "Space aliens. I keep telling Benjamin

and his brothers that they've landed here in Black Rock and until we get them rounded up, nobody is safe."

A sick feeling swept through Edie as she stared at her grandfather, hoping to see the familiar twinkle of a joke in his eyes. But there was no twinkle—only a faint tinge of fear coupled with the determination of an intergalactic warrior. And then she knew why somebody had called her to check on her Poppy. It was because he was losing his mind.

Chapter 2

Benjamin saw the dismay that swept over Edie's features at Walt's words. She was a pretty woman and he knew her statistics from looking at her license. She was five foot four and weighed 117 pounds. Her hair was auburn and her eyes were green.

But those statistics didn't begin to really describe the woman who stood before him. Yes, her short curly hair was auburn, but it shone with a luster that made his fingers itch with the need to touch. *Green* was too ordinary a word to describe her eyes, which sparkled with tiny shards of glittering gold.

The orange sweater she wore complemented the burnished highlights in her hair and intensified the color of her eyes. Something about her stirred him in a way he hadn't been stirred in a very long time.

"I'll walk you out," she said, casting a meaningful look at him.

"Walt, as always, thanks for the meal and the chess game," Benjamin said.

"Thanks for the company," Walt replied, obviously unaware that his previous words had upset his grand-daughter. "Edie, you can pull your car into the garage. I sold my car a year ago. I got tired of paying for insurance."

Edie nodded. "Thanks, Poppy, I'll do that."

As Benjamin walked out with Edie, he caught a whiff of her perfume, something subtle and spicy that reminded him of tangy fall air and cinnamon.

"I'm the one who called you," he said when they were far enough away from the front door that Walt wouldn't hear. "I've been worried about him."

In the illumination from a nearby streetlight, he could see the confusion on her pretty face. "I didn't catch the name of the person who'd called me and once I got here I thought maybe it was just a cranky neighbor upset because the yard needs some work. He seemed so normal."

"He appears to be normal in every way except for the little issue that he thinks space aliens are trying to take over Black Rock. It wouldn't be a big problem but he's often out in the middle of the night alien hunting and I'm afraid he'll get hit by a car or fall down someplace where nobody will be able to help him."

"How long has this been going on?" she asked. She still looked overwhelmed by this news and as he remembered the things she'd told him when he'd pulled her over for speeding, he had a crazy desire to take her into his arms and assure her that everything was going to be all right.

Instead he rocked back on his heels and frowned thoughtfully. "About six months. My brothers and I have tried to assure him that there are no space aliens in town, but he's adamant in his belief and gets downright cranky when you try to tell him different. Look, I'd recommend you take him into his doctor and get a full checkup done. Maybe this is some sort of a medical issue."

"I guess that's as good a place to start as anywhere," she replied. "Well, thanks for all your help with him. I guess I'll see you around over the next couple of days, but hopefully not in my rearview mirror with your lights spinning."

He grinned at her. "As long as you're not a fast woman, we won't have any problems in that area. But I can't promise I won't follow you just because I think you're pretty." Someplace deep inside he recognized he was flirting a little bit.

She must have realized it, too. But her eyes cooled and she took a step back from him. "I am a fast woman, probably way too fast for a small-town deputy."

He wasn't sure who was more surprised by her response, him or her. Her lush lips compressed as she frowned once again. "Thanks again for you help. See you around."

She turned and headed back to the house in short quick steps that swayed her shapely hips. Benjamin watched until she disappeared behind the front door and then released a sigh as he got into his truck.

He had no idea what had possessed him to attempt a little flirt with her. It was obvious by her response he wasn't very good at it. Still, her cool response had surprised him.

Since his brothers Tom and Caleb had hooked up with their soul mates, Benjamin had become the toast of the town when it came to the single women. But all the women who were interested in him left him cold.

He'd been cold since his sister, Brittany, had disappeared over two months ago. Tom, his oldest brother and the sheriff of Black Rock, still held out hope that she would be found alive and well, but even though Benjamin never said anything out loud, as each day had passed with no word from her, he'd lost hope of ever seeing his little sister again.

As he backed out of Walt's driveway, he tried to ignore the stab of grief that always pierced his heart when he thought of his missing sister.

And now they had another one missing. Tom was reluctant to tie the two disappearances together, but Benjamin had a bad feeling about the whole thing. He was afraid Black Rock was in for dark days, and the darkness had nothing to do with Walt's imaginary space aliens.

As he headed for the ranch his thoughts returned to Edie Burnett. For a minute as he'd seen her tears after he'd pulled her over, he'd thought she was faking them to get out of a ticket.

Old Mabel Tredway did it on a regular basis. The eighty-two-year-old woman shouldn't be behind the wheel of a car and whenever Benjamin pulled her over for crossing the center line or going a little too fast, she wept like a baby. But the one time he'd given her a ticket, the fake tears had stopped on a dime and she'd cussed him, his dead mama and all the cattle on his ranch.

However, Edie's tears had been real and as she'd burped up the details of her life with each sob, he had decided not to write the ticket.

She had enough to deal with in deciding what to do with Walt. Benjamin and his lawmen brothers had come to the end of their rope with the old man. Nobody wanted to see anything bad happen to him, but they all felt it was just a matter of time before he got hurt.

As he pulled into the gates that led to the family homestead, he felt the familiar sense of peace the place always brought to him. The house itself was an architectural anomaly. What had started as a simple two-bedroom ranch had become a sprawling complex as rooms were added with each birth of a child.

There was also a small cottage just behind the house where Margaret Kintell, a sixty-eight-year-old widow, lived. Margaret had worked as a housekeeper for the Grayson family for as long as Benjamin could remember. Her husband, John, had worked as a ranch hand until he'd passed away several years ago, and even though Benjamin had encouraged Margaret to retire she insisted that her job was still taking care of the Grayson children.

Unfortunately Benjamin was the only Grayson child still living in the family home and he wasn't exactly a child at thirty years old. His brothers Tom and Caleb lived in town. Brittany had been living in town at the time of her disappearance and Jacob was holed up in a small cabin nestled in a grove of trees on the ranch property.

The porch light was on so he knew Margaret was probably still in the house rather than in her little cottage. As he walked through the front door, the scent of apples and cinnamon filled his nose and Tiny came running toward him, barking a happy greeting.

"Hi, Tiny." He bent down on his haunches to pet the mixed-breed mutt who had stolen his heart six months ago. "Margaret?" he called as he stood. As he walked through the living room toward the kitchen, Tiny followed close at his feet.

She greeted him in the doorway and gestured him into a chair at the table. "Go on, now, sit down. I made fresh apple cobbler and I know that nutcase Walt probably didn't feed you good and proper."

Benjamin smiled and eased down at the table. "Actually, he had a very nice roast and potatoes for dinner." Margaret had been mad at Walt since last year's fall festival when his apple pie had beaten out hers for a blue ribbon.

She harrumphed as she scooped up a healthy serving of the cobbler into a bowl. "Probably got the recipe from one of those space aliens of his. I don't know why you have taken that man under your wing. You're too soft,

Benjamin. That's always been your problem. All Walt Tolliver needs is a stern talking-to." She placed the bowl in front of him and then went to the refrigerator and pulled out the jug of milk.

"Maybe his granddaughter can talk some sense into him. She arrived in town today."

"Really?" Margaret placed a glass of milk in front of him and then sat across from him. "That would be Julie's girl."

"Edie," Benjamin replied. "Her name is Edie Burnett."

"That's right. Julie married that no-account Kevin Burnett. He was a drinker, that one, and a womanizer. The marriage lasted just long enough for Julie to get pregnant. It was a shame, her dying like that in a car accident. So, what's Edie like?"

Hot. With tantalizing eyes and a body that could make a man weak in the knees. He spooned some of the apple cobbler in his mouth in an effort to think of a more reasonable response.

"She didn't seem to know what's been going on with Walt and when she realized he thought Black Rock was being invaded by space aliens, she seemed a little overwhelmed by it all," he finally replied.

"She in town to stay?"

"No. I imagine she'll just be here long enough to figure out what needs to be done with Walt and then she'll go back home."

"What's she like? Julie was a pretty woman and sweet as that cobbler."

"She's nice-looking," Benjamin conceded, "but I think she might have a little bite to her." He thought about how her gaze had frosted over when he'd attempted a little light flirtation.

If he were a man who liked a challenge, he might have pursued a little more flirting just to see if he could melt that frost. But Benjamin was a man who'd never felt enough passion to work too hard for anything. Except this ranch.

"She's got her work cut out for her in straightening out that old man," Margaret said as she rose from the table. "I'm going to head to my place. It's time for this old broad to call it a night."

Benjamin smiled. "Good night, Margaret." The old woman had the heart of an angel and the saltiness of a sailor, but she helped to keep the ranch and Benjamin's life running smoothly.

Once she was gone the silence of the house pressed in on him. Growing up with all his siblings in the house, he'd longed for silence.

But lately the silence in his life had felt oppressive, ushering in a loneliness he'd never felt before. His brother Jacob had closed himself off in the cabin in some form of self-imposed isolation. Brittany was missing and Tom and Caleb now had beautiful bright women to fill the silences in their lives.

He got up from the table and carried his bowl and glass to the sink. As he rinsed the dishes and placed them in the dishwasher, he thought of all the things he needed to get done in the next couple days while he was off-duty.

Of course, the law enforcement team in Black Rock was so small that all of the men were often called in on their time off. He left the kitchen and doused the light, then headed toward the master bedroom.

As always, when the silence pressed in the heaviest, his thoughts turned to Brittany. A little over two months without a word, without a clue as to what happened to her. They'd found her car hidden in an abandoned barn a month ago and it was at that moment that any hope he might have entertained in seeing his sister alive again had died.

With intentions of rising before dawn to start the catch-up on chores around the ranch, he shucked his jeans and shirt and got ready for bed. Tiny sat next to the bed and looked up at him expectantly.

"You know you have your own bed to sleep in," he said to the dog, who cocked his head as if he didn't understand. Benjamin pointed to the dog bed in the corner. "Go on, get to bed."

Tiny remained in place for a long moment and then finally slunk slowly to his bed. He got in and then looked at Benjamin with mournful brown eyes.

"I don't know why you look so sad," Benjamin said. "We both know you'll be curled up in my bed at my feet before morning."

Minutes later, as he eased down onto his king-size bed, his thoughts returned to Edie Burnett. She'd been quiet during the meal but he had a feeling quiet wasn't really in her character.

He burrowed down and closed his eyes. It was just his luck that the first woman in a long time who had stirred something inside him was only in town for a couple days.

From what she'd told him, she'd have a mess on her hands when she got back home. She had to find a new job and another place to live. He didn't want to think about what she was going to do if Walt's problem wasn't a quick fix.

He drifted off to sleep with visions of lush lips and green eyes playing in his dreams and was awakened some time later by the ringing of his phone on the nightstand.

He was awake instantly, his heart drumming a rapid beat. He glanced at the clock as he fumbled in the dark for the receiver. Just after midnight. Nothing ever good came from middle-of-the-night phone calls.

"Yeah," he answered as he sat up.

"It's me," his brother Tom said. "I'm at the hospital. Somebody beat the hell out of Walt Tolliver and he won't talk to anyone but you."

"I'm on my way." Benjamin hung up as he climbed out of bed. As he pulled on his clothes he wondered what the hell had happened to Walt and where the hell Edie had been.

Edie rolled over and looked at the clock next to her bed. Just before midnight and she still hadn't managed to fall asleep. When she'd come back into the house after Benjamin had left, she'd grabbed her keys and then moved her car into the garage. When she'd returned she'd wanted to ask Poppy more questions about the space aliens he thought were trying to take over Black Rock, but she was afraid to indulge the delusion. She was hoping to talk to his doctor and ask how she should handle the situation.

Even if she'd wanted to talk to him about it, the opportunity didn't arise. Immediately after, Poppy had gone to sleep in the bedroom just off the living room.

She'd climbed the stairs to her room, but knew that sleep would be elusive. She'd taken a long hot shower and tried not to think about Benjamin Grayson. But thoughts of the man kept intruding.

She'd been rude to him with her little remark about being too fast for a small-time deputy, but even though she'd just met him, she'd felt an inexplicable need to distance him from her. His smile had been far too warm, his eyes had been too brown and for just a moment, she'd been afraid that he might make her forget that she'd sworn off men for the rest of her life.

She'd been an accident waiting to happen when she'd met Greg. Reeling with grief over her mother's unexpected death, she'd met him in a bar two weeks after the funeral. It had been love at third drink.

They'd dated for two months before he'd moved in with her and she realized now she'd been far too naive, hadn't asked enough questions and instead had believed everything he'd told her about himself.

They'd talked of marriage and children and he'd filled the loneliness that the absence of her mother had left behind. He'd told her that he was an entrepreneur between projects and that his money was tied up in his latest endeavor. God, she'd been such a fool.

One thing was clear, she didn't need anyone in her life. When she got back home she'd focus on finding a new job, a new place to live and cleaning up her messes. She would be just fine all alone for the rest of her life.

She must have fallen asleep because she knew she was dreaming. Pain ripped her body, but it was a pain tempered with a sense of joy. A bright lamp nearly blinded her as the pain intensified. A murmur of voices took on an urgency that was suddenly terrifying and at the same time a bald-headed man wearing a doctor's mask glared at her with accusation and a phone began to ring.

She awoke with a gasp, the taste of overwhelming grief and crushing guilt thick in her mouth. Disoriented for a moment, she looked around the moonlit room. Then she remembered where she was and that the phone she'd heard in her dream was actually the phone ringing in the house.

As it rang again…and again, she realized Poppy either didn't hear it or didn't intend to answer it. She looked at the clock. Twelve forty-five. Whoever was calling was persistent, for the ringing didn't stop.

She jumped out of bed and left her room. Flipping on the hall light, she ran down the stairs and grabbed the receiver of the phone in the living room.

"Hello," she said half-breathlessly.

"It's me, Benjamin." His deep voice sounded irritated. "I'm here at the hospital with Walt."

"What?" Confusion sifted through her as she looked at the closed door of Poppy's bedroom. "But he went to bed earlier."

"Apparently he went out. Somebody beat him up and he managed to flag down a car that brought him to the hospital. He's going to be all right, but I think you should be here."

"I'm on my way. Where is the hospital?"

"Go straight down Main to Chestnut and turn left. It's about halfway down the second block. You can't miss it."

She murmured a goodbye and then raced back up the stairs to get dressed. Her heart beat an uneven tattoo as she thought of somebody beating up Poppy.

Why, oh, why, had he left the house in the middle of the night? This delusion of his about space aliens obviously had a dark undertone.

Within minutes she was dressed and in her car creeping down the darkened Main Street, seeking Chestnut. Benjamin had sounded angry, as if it were somehow her fault that Poppy had been out wandering the streets. What did he expect her to do? Strap the man into bed at night?

She found the hospital, a two-story brick building with a large parking area near the emergency room entrance. She easily found a parking space, and as she hurried into the door she prayed that Benjamin was right and Poppy was going to be okay.

Once again she kicked herself for staying away for so long. She didn't need Poppy, but it was obvious he needed her. The first person she saw when she walked into the waiting room was Benjamin.

His dark, thick hair was tousled as if he'd just climbed out of bed, making him look even sexier than she remembered. He jumped up from the plastic chair he'd been in as he saw her.

"Where is he?" she asked.

"Where were you?" he countered, his shoulders rigid with tension. "Didn't you know he had gone out?"

"He went to bed just after you left. I went upstairs to go to sleep, as well. What was I supposed to do, tie a little silver bell around his neck so I'd know if he was on the move?" she asked belligerently.

The tension slid off his shoulders and he smiled. "You'd need a ball and chain because I'm afraid he'd be able to get a little silver bell off." He rocked back on his heels and slid a hand through his unruly hair. "Sorry, I didn't mean to come at you like that."

"And I'm sorry I didn't have a ball and chain on Poppy," she replied, reluctantly charmed by his apologetic smile. "How is he? Can I see him?"

Benjamin nodded. "He's been waiting for you. He refused to talk to me until you got here. Come on, I'll take you to him." He placed his fingers just beneath her elbow, and she felt the warmth of the touch burning her through the sweater she'd pulled on. She tore her arm away from him.

What was it about this man that made her feel defensive and prickly? Maybe she was overly sensitive to him because he was the least of her problems. She had a life in Topeka that was in complete and total chaos and a crazy grandfather in Black Rock that she somehow had to fix before she could go home.

She heard Poppy before they reached the exam room. "I'm fine. I just need to go home and rest a bit." His voice held the raspy edge of frustration.

As she and Benjamin stepped into the exam room Edie's breath whooshed out of her at the sight of Poppy, who sat upright on the examining table. One of his eyes was blackened and swollen shut and his jaw held a massive bruise that appeared to grow darker as she stared at him.

"Oh, Poppy," she exclaimed, her heart squeezing tight in her chest. "What happened?"

He shifted positions and winced. "One of the bastards caught me."

"Where were you, Walt?" Benjamin asked.

The doctor, an older man with a receding hairline and a kind smile, held up a hand to halt any questioning. "Before we get into that, I'm Dr. Drake. I've been Walt's doctor for the past twenty years." He held out a hand to Edie, who introduced herself.

"Other than what's obvious, what are his injuries?" she asked.

"A couple of cracked ribs and a lot of bruising along

his left side. I'd like to keep him here under observation for a night or two."

Edie breathed a sigh of relief at the doctor's words, but Walt took exception. "I don't need to stay overnight. I want my own bed in my own house."

"Walt, as your doctor I'm afraid I'm going to have to insist," Dr. Drake said firmly. "You took quite a beating and I wouldn't be doing my job if I just let you out of here without running a few more tests."

The mutiny on Poppy's face eased into something resembling resignation. "I'm not going to wear one of those damn gowns and this place better have cable television. And I want a pretty nurse."

Dr. Drake smiled. "I think we can handle all that. Now I'll just get out of here and let Benjamin conduct his investigation."

"Dr. Drake, before I leave, I'd like to have a word with you in private," Edie said.

He nodded. "I'll be in my office at the end of the hall, and if I'm not there just grab a nurse and have her hunt me down." He left the room and Edie turned back to Poppy as Benjamin stepped closer to the bed.

"Where were you, Walt?" he asked again.

"Out by the cemetery. I thought that might be a hot spot for those creatures and damned if I wasn't right. I was only there about an hour when one of them showed up. Either I made a sound or those suckers have some kind of extrasensory stuff 'cause even though I was hiding behind a bush, he came tearing after me." He looked from Benjamin to Edie. "I think it's best if you leave town, Edie. Those creatures are violent and this town isn't a safe place anymore."

"I'm not going anywhere, Poppy," she replied. "At least not until I know you're safe and well."

"This space alien, what did he look like?" Benjamin asked.

"Like an alien," Walt exclaimed, seeming to get more agitated with each question.

"Poppy, you need to be more specific," Edie replied. "Was he little and green?"

Poppy shot her a look as if she'd lost her mind. "He wasn't some damn cartoon Martian. I couldn't tell much what he looked like. He was wearing all black. His face didn't have a nose or mouth, just big eyes."

"Where exactly in the cemetery were you?" Benjamin had pulled out a small notepad to jot down the pertinent information.

"I was hiding behind that big burning bush at the entrance and the alien was just inside the gate."

"What was he doing?" Benjamin asked.

"Just walking," Walt replied.

On and on the questions went. To Benjamin's credit he didn't lose patience even when Walt got cranky and insisted they needed to call in more law enforcement for the small town.

When the nurse came in to move him from emergency into one of the regular rooms, Edie and Benjamin were shooed out. Edie gave Poppy a gentle kiss on the top of the head and after promising to visit him the next morning, she and Benjamin left the room.

"You didn't get much to go on," she said to Benjamin as they walked down the hall toward the doctor's office. Nervous energy jangled inside her. She'd managed to hold it together in front of Poppy, but she felt perilously close to losing it now.

"I'm sure it wasn't a space invader on a nefarious mission, but *somebody* hurt Walt and I intend to find the person responsible," he said with an intensity that somehow calmed her.

"Why would somebody want to hurt him like that? He's an old man. He's not a threat to anyone." She was horrified to feel the ominous burn of tears in her eyes. God, she'd only been with Benjamin three times and she refused to be in tears yet again.

"Are you all right?" he asked. There was a softness in his eyes, a gentle but steady light that made her want to fall into it. He raised a hand, as if to touch her hair or cheek, but dropped it as she stiffened her back and took a step away from him. Someplace buried in her mind she recognized that this man was definitely dangerous to her.

"I need to speak to Dr. Drake. Please keep me updated on the investigation." Without waiting for his reply, she turned and hurried down the hall, away from him…away from temptation.

Chapter 3

The Black Rock Memorial Cemetery was located about two miles from Walt's home. It was a peaceful plot of land, shady with large trees and with several stone benches amid the headstones.

The grass was neatly mown and the flower beds without a weed. The place was maintained by Josh Willoughby who lived in a small house next to the cemetery. He was an affable man who worked at the feed store and took care of the cemetery on the weekends and on his days off.

Benjamin's parents were here. They'd been killed in a helicopter accident six years ago and as Benjamin approached the front gate, he made a mental note to stop by their graves before he left.

The bush that Walt had told him he'd hidden behind

was next to the front gate, a burning bush that had fully flamed into red leaves with the fall air.

The grass was too short and dry to show any signs of the struggle that had taken place between Walt and his space alien. He bent down on one knee next to the bush and began to comb the grass with his gloved hand, looking for some sort of evidence that might help identify Walt's attacker.

As he worked he couldn't help but think about Edie. She'd been foremost in his thoughts since he'd left her at the hospital near dawn.

He'd been impressed by how she'd handled the situation at the hospital. She'd remained calm and patient with Walt even when he'd gotten downright cantankerous.

It was only as they'd stepped out of the room that he saw a crack in her composure. She'd looked small and lost and overwhelmed by everything that was going on. Benjamin had fought the impulse to pull her into his arms and hold her until somehow her world was magically set right.

His family teased him about his penchant for picking up strays. Dogs and cats and people needing help always seemed to find their way to Benjamin.

But his crazy attraction to Edie Burnett had nothing to do with his desire to help her through a tough situation. The very scent of her excited him, her nearness half stole his breath away and her mouth seemed to beckon for a taste. He was like a teenager in heat and wasn't quite sure what to do with his desire for her.

He'd wanted to kiss her, right there in the hospital hallway. He'd wanted to pull her up against his body and wrap his arms around her and hold her until that frightened, lost look in her eyes changed to desire.

It was a new feeling for him, the instant chemistry he felt toward her and one he was reluctant to deny.

All thoughts of Edie flew out of his head as his hand touched something metal. He pulled the item from the grass and gazed at it thoughtfully. It appeared to be part of a key chain, a flat black circle with the initial *A* in silver in the center.

He placed it in a small evidence bag. There was no way of knowing if it might have come off Walt's attacker or had been dropped by somebody else at another time.

"Problems?"

The deep voice coming from just behind Benjamin spun him up and around, his hand automatically reaching for his gun. "Jeez, Josh, you scared the hell out of me," he said as he relaxed. "I figured you were at work."

"It's my day off. I saw you skulking around and wondered if there was a problem."

"Walt Tolliver got the tar beat out of him here last night."

Josh frowned and hitched up his jeans around his bulging belly. He was a big man, an inch taller than Benjamin's six feet and at least fifty pounds heavier. "I've been trying to keep an extra eye out here lately but last night me and the wife went to bed early."

"So you didn't see or hear anything?"

"Only thing I heard was Marylou's snores. The woman sounded like a freight train with brake problems last night, not that I'd like you to mention it to her." He gave Benjamin a pained smile.

"Why have you been keeping an extra eye out here?" Benjamin asked.

"A few times over the past couple weeks I thought I saw lights. I figured it was probably kids fooling around. There was never any damage or any sign that they were there in the mornings so I wasn't sure if it was just my imagination."

"The next time you think you see something, you call the sheriff's office," Benjamin said.

"Is Walt okay?" Josh asked.

Benjamin nodded. "Banged up, but he'll survive."

"He wasn't able to tell you who attacked him?"

"Don't ask," Benjamin said darkly.

A slow grin swept over Josh's broad face. "Let me guess, it was a space invader."

Benjamin nodded. "I'm headed over to the hospital from here to see if he can give me more details this morning than he was able to last night."

"Good luck with that," Josh said. "I'm going back home. Just call if you need anything else from me."

Benjamin watched as the big man lumbered back in the direction of his house, then Benjamin walked toward his parents' graves.

He didn't visit here often. In truth Benjamin had been closer to his siblings than he had been to his mother and father. His parents had loved to travel and once their kids all got old enough to fend for themselves, they were often away on one adventure or another.

He stood at the foot of their graves and wondered if they were both whirling around in spiritual unrest with Brittany's disappearance and Jacob's isolation from life.

Brittany's case had come to a painful standstill due to a lack of leads. As far as Jacob, Benjamin held out hope that eventually Jacob would tell him why he'd quit his job with the FBI and closed himself off from the world.

It was just after noon when he left the cemetery and decided to stop for lunch before going to the hospital. As he walked into the café he spied his brothers Tom and Caleb in one of the booths.

As he walked toward where they were seated, he nodded to Larry Norwood, the town's newest vet, and raised a hand to Billy Jefferson, a neighboring rancher.

"We were just sitting here wondering if our resident alien buster had been successful in his hunt," Caleb teased as Benjamin slid in next to him. "Any sight of the little green men?"

"I'll have you know that Walt specifically said that the alien wasn't a cartoon Martian. He wasn't sure what planet the aliens are from."

"It was somebody from this planet who beat him up," Tom said, his features stern. "And I want that person found and charged. I don't like things like that happening in my town."

Benjamin knew how personally Tom took the safety of the residents of Black Rock. It was what made him a respected and beloved sheriff. "I spoke to Josh," Benjamin said. "He mentioned that he thinks maybe kids have been hanging out at the cemetery after hours."

"I'm not surprised," Caleb said. "Halloween is only weeks away. There's nothing better than taking a girl to the cemetery and scaring her with ghost stories that make her squeal in fear and jump right into your arms."

"Does Portia know you hang out in the cemetery and scare girls?" Benjamin asked with a wry grin.

Caleb smiled. "She was the girl I was scaring in the cemetery."

Portia Perez and Caleb had been high-school sweethearts who had broken up when Portia had gone to college. Recently the two had gotten back together again and seemed more in love with each other than ever.

"What about Walt's granddaughter? What's her name?" Tom asked.

To Benjamin's surprise he felt his cheeks warm. "Edie. Edie Burnett."

"What's she like?" Caleb asked curiously.

Benjamin shrugged. "Attractive. Overwhelmed. She's pretty much alone in the world other than having Walt."

"Uh-oh," Caleb said. "Sounds like a perfect candidate for the Benjamin-to-the-rescue club."

Tom grinned as Benjamin shot his younger brother a look of irritation. "It's not like that at all," he protested.

"She's only in town for a few days and she doesn't seem like the type who would want a man to run to her rescue. Is there anything new on the Jennifer Hightower disappearance?" he asked in an effort to change the subject.

"Not a damn thing," Tom replied.

As the three brothers ate their lunch, they discussed the latest disappearance of a young woman. Jennifer Hightower had gone to work at the convenience store on the edge of town as usual and had been scheduled to work until closing time at midnight. Her car had been left in the parking lot at the store, but she was nowhere to be found.

"The interviews with her friends have yielded nothing. We got nothing from her car. The surveillance tape from the store showed that she was alive and well at midnight when she closed up the place." Tom listed the facts one after another, his voice deep with frustration.

"She doesn't have a current boyfriend and her ex has a solid alibi," Caleb added. "It's like she vanished into thin air."

"Or somebody was waiting just outside for her," Tom said. "Too bad the convenience store doesn't have cameras outside."

"Have we decided that this case is connected to Brittany's?" Benjamin asked. It was the question that they'd all danced around for the past couple weeks.

Tom frowned, as if in pain. "There's no real evidence that they're connected. Jennifer doesn't look anything like Brittany. But the fact is we have two missing women.

I don't want to believe they're connected, but I guess we have to consider the possibility."

His words caused a knot of anxiety to form in Benjamin's chest. If the disappearances were connected, then that meant there was a possibility that somebody in town was kidnapping pretty young women. What he was doing to them was anybody's guess. Until a body was found it was impossible to speculate about what had become of the victims.

All he knew was that there was a new pretty young woman in town and the fear of an unknown darkness walking the streets of Black Rock.

Edie cursed beneath her breath as the lawn mower died for the fifth time in the past hour. She was exhausted, but wanted to get the lawn finished before calling it a day.

She'd been working at it for the past two hours. The problem was twofold: the lawn mower was an antique and the grass was so tall it kept gumming up the motor and conking it out.

Deciding to take a break, she eased down on the top stoop of the porch, thirsty but too tired to walk inside and get anything to drink.

She'd spoken with Poppy several times during the day. He wasn't a happy camper. "The nurse isn't pretty and I think she might be a vampire," he had groused. "Every time I turn around she's taking blood from me."

Edie had soothed him, grateful that the doctor had

agreed to run a battery of tests to see if Poppy's delusion was somehow a medical issue.

And if it wasn't? A little voice nagged in the back of her head. What did you do with somebody who thought they were seeing space aliens? Send them to therapy? Somehow she doubted that Black Rock had a resident therapist who might specialize in alien delusions.

All she could hope for was that Dr. Drake would find something with his tests that would account for the delusions and that whatever it was could be fixed with a pill.

All thoughts of her grandfather fled from her head as a familiar black pickup pulled into the driveway. Instantly her heart did an unexpected tap dance as Benjamin got out of the driver's seat.

Surely it was just because she'd been alone all day, she told herself. It had nothing to do with the fact that he was clad in a pair of killer jeans that hugged the length of his long legs and emphasized his lean abdomen. It had nothing to do with the glint in his eyes that perfectly matched the sexy, lazy grin that stretched his lips at the sight of her.

"Who's winning? You or the grass?" he asked as he drew closer.

"Definitely the grass," she replied as she got to her feet.

"It's too tall and the lawn mower is too old and I'm exhausted," she admitted. "What's going on? Did you find the person responsible for beating up Poppy?"

"I wish, unfortunately I don't have much to report."

He stepped closer to her, close enough that she could smell his cologne. "I went out by the cemetery and looked around. The only thing I found was what looks like a part of a key ring bob. It's engraved with the letter *A*, but I can't know if it had anything to do with the attack on Walt or not."

"Don't tell him what you found. He'll swear that the *A* stands for *alien*," she said drily.

Benjamin laughed.

He had a nice laugh, deep and robust, like a man who enjoyed laughing.

"Actually, I just came from a visit with Walt."

"I spoke to him a couple hours ago and he wasn't too happy." She was overly conscious that the knees of her jeans were grass stained from weeding and she was wearing one of Poppy's oversize flannel shirts over her T-shirt. She didn't have on a stitch of makeup and the fact that it bothered her, bothered her.

"He's still not happy. He wanted me to stop by and pick up a pair of sleep pants that he says is more civilized than the ones at the hospital. He said they're in his top dresser drawer."

"Come on in and I'll get them for you." He walked too close behind her, not stopping in the living room but rather following her into Poppy's bedroom.

She hadn't been in this room for years and it was nothing like she remembered. When her grandmother had been alive the room had been a typical bedroom with the bed covered in a floral print spread and matching curtains at the window. The nightstands had held dainty little lamps and a trunk at the foot of the bed had contained a variety of sofa blankets that her grandmother had crocheted.

Now the bed was shoved against one wall and the nightstands and trunk were gone. A large desk took up much of the room. The top of the desk was cluttered with maps of the galaxy and of the town, notes jotted in Poppy's nearly illegible hand and an instant camera.

"It looks like headquarters for an alien hunter," Benjamin said as he picked up one of the maps of the stars.

"I'm really hoping the doctor will be able to find a medical reason for this craziness." Edie pulled open the top dresser drawer and found the pair of plaid sleep pants Walt had requested. She leaned her back against the dresser, every muscle in her body sore from her fight with the lawn mower.

"Too bad Walt didn't have this camera with him when the attack happened. He could have taken a picture of his assailant." Benjamin looked up from the desk. "You look tired. Why don't you let me finish up the lawn in the morning and you go take a shower and come with me for dinner at the café?"

"The grass isn't your responsibility. I couldn't ask you to finish," she replied.

"You didn't. I offered and you'd be a fool to turn me down," he said lightly.

"Okay, I'll let you finish the lawn in the morning, but I can just grab a sandwich here for dinner." She didn't want to think about going out to dinner with him. It would feel too much like a date and she had no intention of dating ever again.

"Edie." He took a step closer to her. "A nice hot meal will do you good. Besides, the special tonight is lasagna and it's terrific."

Lasagna definitely sounded yummy, and she was starving. She hesitated a beat and then nodded. "Okay, I'll meet you at the café," she finally said. At least that way she could eat and run.

He looked at his watch. "It's four-thirty now. Shall we meet in an hour?"

"Sounds perfect," she said as she followed him out of the bedroom. When they reached the front door, he turned back to look at her.

"You aren't going to stand me up, are you? I really hate when that happens."

She doubted that this man had ever been stood up in his life. "I'll be there," she replied.

The moment he left she raced up the stairs for a long hot shower, already regretting the agreement to meet him. She should have just stayed home and eaten a sandwich. There was something about Deputy Sheriff Benjamin Grayson that definitely put her on edge.

At five-twenty she drove slowly down Main Street looking for the café. She found it nestled between a taxidermy business and a veterinarian's office. As she pulled into a parking space down the street, a knot of nerves twisted in her stomach. *It's ridiculous to be nervous about a quick meal,* she told herself. She'd just eat fast and then get back to Poppy's house.

The evening had cooled a bit as the sun began to sink and she was grateful for the gold sweater she'd pulled on over a clean pair of jeans.

As she walked by the taxidermy store she shivered slightly at the animals in the window. A stuffed wolf looked ready to pounce on prey and a squirrel stood on its haunches with a nut between its paws. She'd never understood the desire to hang a deer head on a wall or stuff Fluffy to keep forever.

Dead was dead and no amount of stuffing and saving could change that. Her hand slid up to grip the charm around her neck. As always an edge of grief threatened to swell inside her, but she shoved it away, refusing to give it power.

Before she opened the café door she smelled the savory scents of frying onions and sweet tomato sauce and her stomach rumbled in response.

The minute she walked in the door, she saw Benjamin leaning against the long counter and talking to an attractive blonde waitress.

At the sound of the bell tinkling above the door with her entrance he turned and smiled at her, that sexy grin instantly heating places in Edie that hadn't been warm in a very long time.

He murmured something to the waitress and then approached Edie. "You came."

"I told you I would. I always do what I say I'm going to do. I'm hungry and too tired to fix something at home. This seemed like the most convenient thing to do." She was aware she sounded not only defensive, but more than a little bit cranky, as well.

It didn't seem to bother him. His eyes twinkling with good humor, he took her by the elbow and led her to an empty booth toward the back of the busy place.

As they made their way through the tables, he was greeted by everyone they passed. It was obvious Benjamin was well liked in the town he served. Not that she cared. He was just a hot, sexy blip in her radar who would be nothing but a distant memory weeks from now.

Once they were seated in the booth she picked up the menu, needing something to look at besides him. But the food listings were far less appealing than Benjamin.

She closed the menu and shoved it to one side. "Don't you have a wife or a girlfriend you should be having dinner with?"

"Don't have either," he replied and then grinned. "But thanks for being interested enough to ask."

"I'm not really interested. I was just making casual conversation." Awkward, she thought. This whole scene felt awkward. She should have made herself a sandwich at the house and called it a night. But the truth was the house had felt far too quiet without Poppy there.

"So, tell me something about Edie Burnett," he said.

"You know more about me than I'd intended for anyone to know," she replied darkly.

"All I really know is that you've had a run of bad

luck lately, but I'm sure there are far more interesting aspects to you."

She leaned back in the booth. "Why are you doing that?" she asked flatly.

He frowned in confusion. "Doing what?"

"Flirting with me." Although she wanted to look away she boldly held his gaze. "I don't know what you're looking for but you won't find it with me. I'm only in town for a short period and, besides, not only am I never going to date again, but I also intend to stay celibate for the rest of my life."

His eyebrows rose and then fell back into place. "A lot of men would consider that a real challenge," he said with that wicked glint in his eyes. The glint dimmed and he shook his head. "He must have hurt you very badly."

"It doesn't matter now, that's so in my past." She was grateful that the waitress appeared at that moment to take their orders.

They both ordered the lasagna special and when the waitress left, Edie took the reins of the conversation. "I pretty well spilled my life story to you when you pulled me over for speeding. Why don't you tell me something interesting about you?"

"Probably the most interesting thing about me is that I have three brothers and one sister and all of us went into law enforcement."

"Was your father a cop?" she asked.

"No, Dad was a genius when it came to buying and selling stocks. He worked the ranch and invested and did very well. When all of us kids got older, he and my mother traveled a lot."

"I know that one of your brothers is the sheriff. What about the others?" She began to relax a bit with the conversation steered away from her.

"Tom is the oldest and he's the sheriff. Then there's Jacob, who became an FBI agent. Caleb is a deputy like me and so was…is Brittany." He winced as he caught himself, but it was obvious to Edie that he wasn't expecting a happy ending where his sister was concerned.

"I'm sorry about your sister," Edie said softly.

"Yeah, so am I. And I was sorry to hear about your mother's death. My housekeeper told me that your mom was not only pretty but also a nice woman."

"She was the best," Edie said, then picked up her glass of water to take a sip and swallow her grief. "You've told me an interesting thing about your family. But tell me something about you personally." She was determined to keep the conversation on him, to focus on anything but herself and all the challenges she faced.

"Let's see." He leaned back against the booth and gave her that lazy smile that never failed to light a tiny fire inside her. "I like a horseback ride at sunset and big juicy steaks cooked outside. Green is my favorite color and I've got a dog named Tiny who thinks he's master of the world. I've never had a broken heart and I don't think I've ever broken one. How's that?" he said.

"Unbelievable," she replied. There was no way a man

who looked like Benjamin Grayson could have gone through his life so far and not broken a heart or two.

At that moment the waitress arrived with their orders and their conversation moved to more general things. He was pleasant to talk to and for a little while, she forgot all that was facing her. But she remained on edge, far too conscious of the allure of his flirtatious eyes and the warmth of his smile.

When her plate was empty she was ready to run. He offered to pay for the meal and after some argument, she accepted.

As they walked out of the café and into the deepening twilight of evening, he insisted he walk her to her car. "It's really not necessary," she protested. "I'm only parked down the street a little bit."

"I know, but it's a gentleman's duty to see a woman to her car," he replied lightly.

When they reached her vehicle, she pulled her keys from her purse, ready to bail and get away from Benjamin. "Thanks for dinner," she said as she unlocked her car door and then turned back to face him. "I appreciate everything you've done, but I can handle things now and you can get back to your own life."

"You aren't getting rid of me that easily," he replied. "I'll be over first thing in the morning to finish mowing the lawn. That was our deal."

She hesitated, not wanting to take anything more from him. He took a step closer to her. "Edie, you don't have to be in this all alone." He reached up and gently pushed one of her errant curls away from her forehead. "Walt is my friend and I'll do whatever I can to support you."

He dropped his hand back to his side but didn't move away from her. She felt as if she'd stopped breathing the moment he'd touched her and she forced herself to breathe now. "I appreciate that. Okay, then I guess I'll see you in the morning."

She'd let him finish the lawn and then she'd have nothing more to do with him. The last thing she needed in her life at the moment was another complication and Benjamin definitely felt as if he could be a big complication if she'd allow it.

For a moment he stared at her lips, as if he wanted to kiss her, and for that same amount of time she almost wished he would. Instead she jerked open her car door and wondered when she'd lost her mind.

"Edie, before you go take this." He pulled out a card from his pocket. "This has my personal cell phone number on it. Don't hesitate to use it if you need anything."

She took the card and dropped it into her purse and then slid in behind the steering wheel, eager to make her escape from this man who made her think about hot kisses and the sweet sensation of skin against skin.

She drove away without looking back, knowing that it was going to take her all night long to forget the feel of his warm fingers against her forehead, to get the very scent of him out of her head.

When she got back to Poppy's place, she called to check in on her grandfather, who was as cranky as she'd ever heard him, then she decided to vacuum and dust the living room.

She needed some sort of activity to occupy her and hopefully keep thoughts of Benjamin from her mind. But he was difficult to cast out of her head.

He was nice. He was definitely sexually drawn to her. She knew it by the look in his eyes, by the fact that he seemed to have trouble keeping his hands off her. Was he only being nice to her because he wanted to get her into bed?

Somehow he didn't strike her as that type and that was what worried her. She reluctantly had to admit that she liked him and that was on top of the wild physical attraction she felt toward him.

By the time she'd finished with the housework she was exhausted and she'd finally managed to banish thoughts of Benjamin from her mind.

She locked the front door and then headed upstairs for bed. Tomorrow she intended to call Poppy's doctor and get an update on the tests they had run on the old man. She prayed that Dr. Drake would be able to find an easy fix for Poppy's obsession and that Benjamin and his brothers would find and arrest whoever assaulted her grandfather.

Even though she was exhausted, once she was in bed her mind whirled with all the things waiting for her when she got back to Topeka. First and foremost on her list of things to do was find another job.

She'd loved managing the restaurant, but wasn't sure she wanted to go back into the same field. In truth she didn't know what she wanted to do with the rest of her life. A year ago she'd thought her future was all planned out. She'd marry Greg, be a wife and mother and decide on a career when their children went off to school.

Greg was on board right up until the time he disappeared from her life. Just like her father. She punched the pillow and closed her eyes, determined to get a good night's sleep without any more thoughts of betrayals from men.

I deserve it, a little voice whispered in her head. *I'm not good enough to be with anyone.* Emotion swelled up inside her but she steadfastly shoved it back down and squeezed her eyes more tightly closed.

She awoke suddenly, her heart pounding with unexpected adrenaline and her body tensed in a fight-or-flight response. Immediately she knew something had awakened her and as she remained frozen in place, she heard a faint noise coming from downstairs.

Somebody was in the house. The thought thundered in her brain. She knew she'd locked the front door before she'd come upstairs. But as she heard more noise she knew with certainty that somebody was there.

She swung her legs over the side of the bed and stood, then quietly crept to the top of the stairs. The noise was definitely coming from the direction of Poppy's bedroom.

Was it possible Poppy had somehow managed to talk the doctor into releasing him? She glanced at the clock on the nightstand, the luminous dial letting her know it was after one. Surely nobody would have released him in the middle of the night. It was more likely that Poppy had left on his own, slinking out like a thief in the dark. He could be so bullheaded at times.

She ran lightly down the stairs, aided by the bright moonlight that flooded in the living room windows. As she gazed toward Poppy's bedroom, she frowned in confusion. There were no lights on, but she saw the faint glow of a flashlight.

"Poppy?" The single word fell from her lips.

The flashlight whirled toward her, blinding her as it hit her eyes. She raised a hand in defense, but gasped as a big body collided with hers.

The force of the collision lifted her off her feet and as she fell, the back of her head slammed into the floor and she knew no more.

Chapter 4

Benjamin sat in his easy chair in the living room and channel-surfed. It was late and he should be in bed, but he was too restless to sleep and it was all thanks to Edie Burnett. Something about the woman had him twisted in knots.

He'd hated to tell her goodbye after dinner and was already eagerly anticipating going to Walt's in the morning to see her again.

It was a new feeling for him, this sweet anticipation, and one he'd never felt for a woman. It had heartbreak written all over it, but knowing that didn't seem to make him cautious.

He'd dated plenty over the past couple years but none of the women he'd seen had shot him full of the simmering excitement like Edie.

But she claimed she wanted nothing to do with men. Or sex. He'd never met a candidate less likely for celibacy. Those lips of hers were made for kissing and her curves were meant to be stroked and loved.

She definitely had some sharp edges that he guessed disillusionment had formed in her. It was that sharpness she used as a defense whenever he got too close.

As they'd eaten dinner, more than once when she got uncomfortable with the conversation, she'd reached up and touched the charm hanging on a gold chain around her neck. The charm was a pair of angel wings that he guessed was a symbol of the mother she'd lost.

He stroked Tiny's soft fur as he changed the channel for the hundredth time and realized that television in the middle of the night sucked. Tiny released a long-suffering sigh, probably wondering why they were in the chair and not in bed.

The ring of his cell phone jerked him upright. He fumbled in his pocket, pulled it out and answered.

"Benjamin, can you come over here?"

It took him a moment to recognize Edie's voice. She sounded strange, stressed to the max and needy. "What's wrong?"

A small burst of laughter escaped her. "I think the aliens have landed."

His stomach clenched with nervous energy. "I'll be right there." He didn't bother to ask her any more questions but instead hung up and was in his truck and headed to Walt's within minutes.

There was no question that something had happened,

something that had her spooked enough to call him. He tightened his hands on the steering wheel as he sped down the dark deserted streets.

At least he knew that whatever had happened, she was physically all right, at least enough to make the phone call to him. But emotionally she'd sounded fragile and he couldn't get to her fast enough.

When he pulled up the driveway, he saw her standing in the doorway. As he got out of his truck, she stepped on the porch. She was clad in a navy nightshirt that barely skimmed the tops of her thighs and her face was as pale as the moon overhead.

"What happened?" he asked as he reached the porch.

"Somebody was in the house, in Poppy's bedroom. I was in bed asleep and I woke up when I heard the noise. I thought it was Poppy, that maybe he'd left the hospital." She frowned and raised a hand to the back of her head.

He took her by the arm and led her into the house and to the sofa. "Are you hurt?" he asked, a new knot in his chest growing bigger. Her skin was cool and her arm trembled beneath his hand.

He wanted nothing more than to pull her against him and hold her tight until she was warm. But his first role was as a responding officer to a crime scene.

"I hit my head," she said. "He shoved past me and knocked me down and I hit my head on the floor."

He reached up and felt the back of her head and muttered a curse as he fingered the goose egg there. "We need to get you to the hospital and have that checked out," he said as she waved him away from her.

"It's fine. I'm fine. I was just out for a minute or two."

"Out? You mean like unconscious?"

She winced. "Stop shouting. I said I was okay."

Benjamin took a step backward, shocked as he realized he had been shouting and he'd never been a shouting kind of man in his life. He sat on the sofa next to her. "Tell me exactly what happened."

He listened and took notes as she told him about waking up and thinking Walt had come home. As she told him about seeing the intruder in Walt's bedroom and that person slamming into her, his blood went cold.

Thank God the intruder hadn't used a gun. When he thought of all the horrible scenarios that might have occurred, he went weak in the knees with relief.

"Did he take anything?" he asked.

"I don't know. I didn't go into the bedroom. When I came to, I just grabbed my purse from the kitchen counter and found your card."

He was grateful to see that some of the color was returning to her cheeks. "I'm going to call my brother and get him out here," he said. "And I'll see if I can rouse Dr. Drake to come over and examine you."

"That's really not necessary," she protested.

"I think it is. It's either see Dr. Drake here or head to the emergency room at the hospital. You were knocked unconscious. You need to be checked out."

She managed to glare at him. "You sound pretty bossy."

"At the moment I'm feeling pretty bossy." As she leaned her head back and closed her eyes, he made his phone calls. When he was finished she raised her head once again to look at him.

"Maybe it was somebody who heard through the grapevine that Poppy was in the hospital and decided to take advantage of the situation by robbing the place," she said. "My car is in the garage. I don't think the person knew I was here."

"That's possible," he agreed. "I'm going to check out Walt's bedroom. I'll be right back."

"I'll go with you." She jumped up off the sofa and a flash of pain momentarily twisted her features.

"Why don't you sit and relax? It's obvious you have a headache." Once again he fought the impulse to take her into his arms.

"I'd feel better staying with you."

Her words let him know just how spooked she still was. She followed close behind him and together they went into Walt's room. "Don't touch anything," he cautioned as he used his elbow to turn on the light in the room.

"Don't worry," she said drily.

Two things struck Benjamin as he looked around the room. The first was that all the windows were still intact and locked, indicating the point of entry had been someplace else in the house. The second was that it was obvious somebody had been in the room. The papers that had been on top of the desk were now strewn across the floor. Drawers hung open with clothes spilling out and boxes had been pulled off the shelves in the closet.

"If they were looking for something of value, they came to the wrong house," Edie said.

"Can you tell if anything is missing?" he asked.

He watched as she gazed around the room and frowned. "Nothing that I can see. Wait…remember the camera that was on the desk? I don't see it anywhere now."

He walked around the desk, checking the floor to see if perhaps the camera had fallen off, but it was nowhere to be seen.

"What on earth has Poppy gotten himself involved in?" Edie asked softly.

"I don't know, but somehow we're going to figure it out," he replied.

At that moment Tom arrived at the scene, followed closely by Dr. Drake. As the doctor examined Edie, Tom and Benjamin got to work processing the scene.

The entry point was the front door, which held an old lock that had been jimmied open. Whoever had come in had apparently gone directly to Walt's bedroom, for there was no indication that anything else had been disturbed.

Dr. Drake pronounced that Edie probably had a mild concussion and would be fine and then he left. By that time Tom had dusted the front door for prints and Benjamin had dusted the bedroom. Benjamin had little hope of lifting anything. Whoever had broken in was probably smart enough to wear gloves.

Edie had nothing to offer as far as what the person had looked like. It had been dark and everything had happened too fast. All she could be sure of was that he'd been big and dark and had hit her like an NFL tackle.

It was after three when they had done all they could for the night and Tom left. Edie was curled up in one corner of the sofa, looking small and exhausted.

Benjamin sat next to her. "How's your head?"

"Better than it was. At least now it's down to a three-piece band instead of a full percussion orchestra." She released a weary sigh.

"You need to get a new lock on the front door. It probably wouldn't hurt to put a new one on the back door, as well. I'll get somebody to take care of it first thing in the morning."

"Thank you," she replied. "I have to confess, I'm a little bit nervous about staying here all alone for the rest of the night without the locks fixed."

He knew better than to think she was issuing an invitation for him to spend the night with her, but he couldn't stop the slight flush of heat that filled him at the very thought.

"I guess you have two options," he said, pleased that his voice sounded normal. "I can either take you to a motel for the rest of the night or I could stay here until morning."

She shot him a narrowed glance and he did everything possible to keep his features without any expression.

The last thing he wanted her to think was that he was somehow taking advantage of the situation.

Releasing another deep sigh, she sat up straighter. "I guess it would be stupid to go to a motel at this time of the night. I'll get you some blankets and a pillow so you can bunk here on the sofa."

"Or, just for your information, I've been told I make a terrific snuggle buddy."

"Deputy Grayson, surely *snuggle buddy* isn't in your job description," she said as she rose to her feet.

"It could be," he replied as he also stood.

"That's so not happening," she said. "But I might share a little conversation with you over a cup of tea before I turn in."

"Sounds like a plan," he agreed easily. As he followed her into the kitchen, he admitted that he'd much prefer a place in her bed, but as she'd reminded him moments before—that was so not happening tonight.

The hot tea didn't quite banish the chill that had taken hold of Edie since the moment she'd come to on the living-room floor.

"Talk to me, Benjamin, tell me more about the ranch where you live," she said, needing something, anything to take her mind off the fact that somebody had been in the house while she'd been asleep and vulnerable.

What might have happened if she hadn't awakened when she did? Would the intruder have eventually crept up the stairs and found her? Would a simply robbery have escalated to something worse—her rape? Her murder?

As Benjamin began to talk about his life at the ranch, his eyes took on the sparkle of a man who loved that life and his deep voice filled with a vibrancy that was vastly appealing.

As he talked of cattle and horses and his daily routine when at home, she felt herself begin to finally relax. There was something solid about Benjamin and the life he led, something that reminded her of all the hopes she'd once possessed, all the dreams she'd once had for herself.

She'd once wanted the kind of life he was describing, one of normal routine and peace, filled with the love of family and the kind of happiness that came from knowing where you belonged.

It had been a long time since she'd felt as if she belonged anywhere. Looking back now, she recognized that there had always been a little part of her that had suspected Greg wasn't the man for her. But she'd been desperate to be loved, tired of being alone and had clung to him despite her reservations.

Greg hadn't been her first mistake. Before him had been Charles, a man she'd dated for almost a year, a man who hadn't known the meaning of fidelity. Loving stupid, that was what she was good at, and it was better to never love again than continue making the same mistakes.

Her head began to pound again as if in protest of her thoughts and exhaustion slammed into her with a force that made her long for the comfort of bed. "I've got to go to bed," she said as she pushed back from the kitchen table. "The extra blankets are upstairs in the closet. I'll just get what you need for the sofa."

He got up, as well. "I'll follow you so you don't have to make an extra trip down the stairs."

"Thanks," she replied and wondered if he was always so nice. She was far too conscious of him behind her as she climbed the stairs.

"Blankets in there?" He pointed ahead of them to the hall closet. "I'll take care of myself," he continued as she nodded. "Let's get you tucked into bed."

She walked to her bedroom doorway and then turned to face him. "Thank you, Benjamin, for agreeing to stay here for whatever is left of the night. I'll be fine once the new locks are installed."

"It's not a problem." He took a step closer to her, so close she could smell the scent of him, feel the heat that radiated from his body. "You had a scare and I'm glad to do whatever I can to make you feel safe."

She felt wonderfully safe and intensely in danger with him standing so close to her. "I guess I'll say goodnight."

"Wait, there's just one thing I've been wanting to do all night." He reached out and pulled her against him, close enough that she could feel his heartbeat beneath the solid wall of his chest.

She held herself stiffly but as his hand slid up and down her back as if to comfort, she allowed herself to relax against him. She hadn't realized just how badly she'd needed a hug until now.

The feel of him against her, so warm, so strong, finally banished the last of the chill that had resided in her since the moment she'd awakened and realized somebody was in the house.

Moments passed and the slide of his hand over her back slowed and instead of being comforted, Edie felt a new tension building between them.

She raised her head to look at him and saw the flames that filled his eyes. Instantly she knew that she should step out of his arms, gain some distance from him.

She did neither.

As his mouth descended toward hers, she opened her lips to welcome the kiss, telling herself she could always justify the madness by claiming brain numbness from her fall.

His mouth plied hers with a welcome heat, his tongue touching hers as he tightened his arms around her. *Falling,* she felt herself falling into him, consumed by him as all other thoughts fled her mind.

She tasted his desire for her, a desire tempered with a tenderness that threatened to be her undoing, and that was ultimately what made her halt the kiss.

A small groan escaped him as he dropped his arms from around her and took a step back. "Are you sure about this celibacy thing?" he asked with a teasing grin.

"One little kiss isn't about to change my mind," she replied. "Good night, Benjamin." She escaped into the bedroom and closed the door behind her, needing to gain some distance from him.

She fell into bed, exhausted by the events of the night, but sleep refused to come easily. The kiss. It was that kiss that haunted her. And the man.

Benjamin Grayson was like no man she'd ever known before and he scared her. She needed to keep her distance from him until she left Black Rock to return home.

But how soon could she get back home? With Poppy getting beaten up and the break-in tonight, how could she possibly consider leaving? She wasn't sure what worried her more, the mess of Poppy or the insane attraction she felt for Benjamin.

She fell asleep with the taste of him on her lips and awakened with the sun streaming through her window and the sound of the lawn mower growling from the front yard.

By the time she'd showered and dressed for the day, the noise outside had stopped. She found Benjamin in the kitchen, seated at the table and sipping a cup of coffee. The very sight of him brought back the memory of the devastating kiss and an irritation surged up inside her.

"Shouldn't you be at work chasing bad guys?" she asked sharply. "This town is obviously infested with them."

One of his dark eyebrows rose. "Sounds like some-body got up on the wrong side of the bed." A blush warmed her cheeks as she headed for the coffee. "I contacted Ed Burell, the local locksmith. He'll be here in the next half hour or so to take care of changing the locks."

"Thanks, I appreciate your help," she said as she joined him at the table. It was impossible to be cranky with him when he was going out of his way to make her life easier.

"My brother Caleb is already out interviewing the neighbors to see if they saw anyone or anything suspicious last night. Tom has been talking to some of the high-school kids to see if they know anything about Walt's attack and I've already alerted everyone in town who processes film to give me a call if somebody brings in an instant camera. There's not much else that can be done at the moment."

"I didn't mean to sound like I thought you weren't doing your job," she replied. "I just wish we could figure out what's going on."

"We will." There was a fierce determination in his voice. "Sooner or later the person who attacked Walt will be caught and charged with the crime. This is a small town and eventually somebody will say something and we'll have our man."

"And hopefully the doctor will tell me all Poppy needs is a pill to fix him right up and I can get back home."

"Now, I've got to admit I'm not in any hurry to see you go." He stood and carried his cup to the sink. "But speaking of going, I need to get out of here." He turned back to face her. "Do you want me to wait with you until the locksmith arrives?"

"No, I'll be fine," she assured him. "I do appreciate everything you've done. Just keep me informed about the investigations and that's all I really need from you." It was an obvious dismissal. "An occasional check-in phone call would be great."

Once again that well-shaped dark brow rose and a twinkle filled his eyes. "That kiss was either very, very bad or very, very good."

The familiar warmth of a blush heated her cheeks. "That kiss was stupid, the result of a head injury that didn't have me thinking clearly."

He laughed. "If that's what you need to tell yourself to get through the day, then so be it. I'm sure I'll talk to you later."

She remained seated at the table as he left the house, trying to ignore the slow burn that he created inside her. Okay, she could admit that she was intensely physically attracted to him, but the kiss they had shared was the beginning and the end of acting on that attraction.

She'd only been seated at the table for about ten minutes when Ed Burell arrived to change the locks on the doors. He left after handing her the new keys.

Edie left soon after that, deciding a visit to Poppy was in order. As she drove down Main Street, she found herself looking at the various businesses.

There was a cute little dress boutique, the Canyon Pizzeria, the café and dozens of other businesses. Unlike many small Kansas towns that had fallen on hard times,

Black Rock seemed to be thriving despite the current economic climate.

Edie parked on the street next to the small hospital. She walked inside and headed to the second floor where Poppy's room was located. When she entered his room, she was surprised to see him dressed and seated on the edge of his bed. A plump nurse with a pretty smile greeted her.

"I just tried to call you," Poppy said. "I can go home. Fit as a fiddle, that's what I am, other than my black eye and cracked ribs. Dr. Drake gave me all kinds of tests and says he wishes he was as healthy as I am."

Edie looked at the nurse, who nodded in affirmation. "He's good to go," she replied. "Dr. Drake should be in any moment if you have any questions."

Moments later a talk with the doctor in the hallway let Edie know he'd found no medical reason for her grandfather's delusion. There was nothing more he could do but release him.

A half hour later they were back home. As Walt prepared lunch, Edie sat at the table and listened to him regaling his hospital adventure to her.

She tried not to be depressed as she realized she was no closer to solving the problem of Poppy than she'd been before his attack. Granted, somebody had beaten up the old man, but it definitely hadn't been a space alien.

As they ate she brought him up-to-date on the break-in and the new locks on the doors. When she told him that the only thing that had been missing was his camera, he blew a gasket.

"The bastards knew I had pictures of them. The night before you arrived here." He got up from the table with jerky movements that spoke of his irritation. "I was going to take that camera down to Burt Smith's discount store to get the pictures developed."

"Poppy, you have to get this idea of aliens out of your head," Edie exclaimed.

"Out of my head? I'm not about to get those bastards out of my head. Tonight I'm going hunting again and this time I'm going to take my gun."

Edie stared at him appalled. Just what Black Rock needed, a crazy man with a gun out in the middle of the night.

Chapter 5

It was just before midnight when Edie and her grandfather left his house. Edie knew it was madness but at least she'd managed to talk Poppy into leaving his gun at home. The good people of Black Rock should give her an award.

"Where are we headed?" she asked once they were in the car and pulling out of the driveway.

"Go south on Main Street, I'll tell you where to turn off when we get there," he replied. He was clad all in black, like a ninja warrior ready for battle.

"Are we going back to the cemetery?"

"Nah, lately on Friday nights they've been in Devon Moreland's clearing," he replied.

Not for the first time since agreeing to this madness, Edie's thoughts turned to Benjamin.

Edie had considered calling Benjamin to ask him to come over and help her change Poppy's mind about going out tonight, but after some thought she'd decided against it.

What worried her was the idea that perhaps she wanted to call Benjamin not because she needed his help with Poppy, but just because she wanted to see him again.

Earlier she'd listened to Poppy talk about his time in the hospital and while he'd napped she'd watched television, but no matter how she tried to keep her mind occupied, thoughts of Benjamin and the kiss they'd shared kept intruding.

He'd kissed her as if he'd meant it, as if it were a prelude to something hot and wild, yet something tender and enduring. She didn't want to believe in the promise of his kiss and if what he'd told her about himself was right, she didn't want to be the first woman in his life to break his heart.

And she would break his heart if he tried to pursue anything with her. Even if he thought he might be the right man for her, she definitely knew she was the wrong woman for him.

At this time of the night the streets were dark and deserted. Edie drove slowly, wishing they were back at the house and not on some crazy hunt for aliens.

"This is the kind of night they like," Poppy said, breaking the silence. He leaned forward to look up at the sky through the windshield. "See them clouds chasing across the moon? They like cloudy nights. Turn left up ahead."

She made the turn and tried not to feel as if she were indulging Poppy's fantasy. They both should be home in bed, but she was hoping that she would see whatever it was that made the old man insist there were aliens in town. Then maybe she'd be able to make him understand that he'd been mistaken.

"How are you doing with that boyfriend of yours?" Poppy asked.

Edie tightened her hands on the steering wheel. "We broke up," she said, pleased that her voice remained neutral.

"Turn left here," he said. "So, does that mean you have a new beau?"

"At the moment I'm footloose and fancy-free, and that's just the way I want it," she replied as she focused on the narrow road they traveled.

"Turn right up ahead," Poppy said.

She felt as if they'd entered a forest. Trees crowded together so closely that the moonlight was obscured overhead. "You can park right up there under that oak tree and we'll walk the rest of the way."

"How did you find this place?" Edie asked as she parked her car and shut off the engine.

"I didn't find it, the aliens did and I found them. It took me a couple months to figure out their routine. Some nights they're in the cemetery and then some nights they're out here." He grabbed the flashlight he'd brought with him and opened his car door. "Come on,

I've got a perfect hiding place where you'll be able to see them."

Edie left the car and followed close behind Poppy as he took off walking through the thick woods, his flashlight beam bouncing in the darkness with each step he took.

No wonder Poppy was in such good physical shape, she thought. On the nights he went alien hunting he must walk miles. They didn't go far before he gestured her down behind a large bush.

"See that clearing?" He pointed the flashlight beam forward to reveal a small break in the woods. "That's where I've seen one of them several times before." He shut off the flashlight and sat in the grass, indicating that she should do the same. "Now we wait and see if one of the bastards show up tonight."

Edie settled in next to Poppy and for the next few minutes the only sounds were those of a soft breeze stirring the leaves overhead and insects buzzing and clicking their night songs.

"You know you won't find a better man than Benjamin," Poppy whispered, breaking the silence.

Startled by his words, she tried to see his face in the darkness. "I'm really not looking for a man, Poppy."

"I'm just saying. Most of the women in town seem to find him attractive, but he's not a trifling man. Out of all the Grayson men he's always been my favorite. Tom is a take-charge kind of guy and Caleb is impulsive and easy to rile. Jacob was always a loner but Benjamin is solid as the earth and has a good heart."

As Poppy continued to extol Benjamin's virtues, all Edie could think about was the dark chocolate color of his eyes as they filled with desire and that crazy hot kiss they had shared.

"I keep telling him he should forget his deputy job and work full-time at the ranch. That's what he loves, working with the animals and the land."

Edie remembered the passion that had filled his voice when he'd talked about the ranch. "If that's what he loves to do then why isn't he doing it full-time?"

"Don't know. I can't ever get a solid answer from him."

They both fell silent once again. The minutes ticked by in agonizing slowness. After half an hour of sitting, the ground seemed to grow harder beneath Edie and sleepiness began to creep in.

They both should be home asleep, not sitting outside in the brisk autumn night air waiting for aliens to appear. She should especially not be out here thinking about Benjamin Grayson, warmed by the memory of the kiss they had shared.

"Poppy, let's go home," she finally said when another fifteen minutes or so had passed. "It's really late and I'm tired."

He sighed, obviously disappointed. "I wanted you to see one of the aliens. I want you to know that I'm not crazy. I know everyone in town thinks I've done gone around the bend, but I'm not nuts."

"Poppy, I don't think you're nuts," she protested softly.

"You're just like your mama, Edie girl. You have her good heart," he replied, a smile obvious in his voice. "I've missed you, Edie. I've missed your phone calls. You're the only family I've got left."

Edie's "good" heart squeezed tight in her chest. Was it possible this whole alien thing was nothing more than a manifestation of Walt's loneliness?

"I've missed you, too, Poppy. And I promise I'm going to be better about keeping in touch with you," she replied.

Before he could answer, the sound of a low motor filled the air. "Here they come," Poppy exclaimed.

Edie peeked through the brush and in the distance saw a small lit vehicle approaching the clearing. It took her only an instant to realize it was an off-road ATV, but with the lights radiating out from it, she could easily see how a confused old man might think it was some kind of a space terrain vehicle.

"Poppy, keep down and keep quiet," she said as the vehicle came to a stop. Her heart slammed against her chest in a frantic tattoo. What would somebody be doing on an ATV in the middle of the woods at this time of night? Certainly nothing good, she thought.

The ATV shut off and Edie gripped Poppy's arm tightly, hoping and praying the old man didn't suddenly jump up to confront the driver.

Her curiosity turned to fear when the lone man stepped off the ATV and she realized he wore some sort of full hazmat suit. No wonder Poppy had thought the aliens had landed.

With the moonlight playing on the silver suit and reflecting off the mirrorlike face of the helmet, the man looked not only otherworldly but also ominous. What on earth was going on?

He carried with him a small spade and some sort of bag that held an eerie yellow-green glow. As Edie and Poppy watched, the man quickly dug a hole and dropped the bag inside.

"I'll bet that's the one who beat me." Poppy's voice was far too loud for the silence in the clearing. The man's head lifted as Edie held her breath and squeezed Poppy's arm even harder.

The man raised a high-beam flashlight and began to shine it in their direction as he pulled a gun with his other hand. Edie gasped as the light found them.

"Poppy, run," she said urgently. She got to her feet and yanked up the old man by his arm.

At the same time she heard the crash of brush ahead and knew the man was coming after them. A scream released from her as the crack of a gun splintered the air.

Thankfully Poppy was spry and seemed to know the woods. They held hands and ran as fast as their legs would take them. In the distance she heard the whine of the ATV and knew their pursuer had stopped his foot chase but intended to continue on the ATV.

The lights from the all-terrain vehicle bounced off the trees as the engine whined and crashed through the brush. With each step she took, Edie feared a bullet in her back.

Poppy's beating had obviously been some sort of warning, but the fact that the man had shot a gun at them let her know he wasn't warning anymore.

She nearly sobbed in relief as they made it back to her car. Poppy fell into the passenger seat while she threw herself in behind the steering wheel and punched the key into the ignition. As the engine roared to life she slammed the gear shift into Reverse.

The tires spun as she wheeled the car around for a quick escape. At the same time the ATV burst through the trees just behind them. Edie screamed and Poppy cursed as their back windshield shattered.

"Drive, girl!" Poppy yelled. "Put the pedal to the metal!"

Edie did just that, flooring the gas pedal and praying that the old clunker didn't pick this particular time to conk out. She flew down the road, barely making the turn that would eventually lead them back into the heart of the town.

"Yee-haw," Poppy yelled. "We lost him."

Edie looked in her rearview mirror and released a shuddering sigh of relief, but there was no relief from the fear that still torched through her. There was only one man she wanted to see, one man who could make her feel safe in what had become a crazy world.

"Tell me how to get to Benjamin's," she said. She wasn't sure what bothered her more, the fact that some crazy man in a hazmat suit had tried to kill them or her desperate need to be with a man she knew she shouldn't want.

* * *

He was dreaming about her. Somewhere in the back of his sleep-addled mind Benjamin knew it was a dream and that he didn't want to ever wake up.

Edie was in his arms, her green eyes glowing with smoky desire. His head filled with the scent of her, that slightly wild spicy fragrance that drove him half-wild.

Her skin was warm and silky against his and he wanted to take her, possess her in a way he'd never possessed another woman.

He was just about to do that when a loud banging broke the dream. Tiny began to bark and jumped off the foot of his bed and raced out of the room.

As the last vestige of the dream fell away, Benjamin leaped out of bed and grabbed the jeans he'd shucked off before going to sleep. As he yanked them on, the knocking at the front door continued. He grabbed his gun from the nightstand and then hurried out of the bedroom and down the hallway, turning on lights as he went.

What the hell? As he pulled open the door Edie and Walt tumbled inside. "He tried to kill us!" Walt exclaimed as Tiny's barks grew sharper. "The bastard shot out the back window of Edie's car."

Benjamin had no idea what was going on or what had happened, but Walt's words ripped a surge of unexpected protectiveness through him as he looked at Edie.

Her eyes were wide, her face pale and he quickly placed his hands on her shoulders and then ran them down her arms, ending with her trembling hands in his. "Are you all right?"

She gave a curt nod of her head. "I'm okay, and it wasn't a space alien, but it was a man in a hazmat suit on an ATV."

"A hazmat suit?" Walt looked as bewildered as Benjamin felt at the moment.

"Come on, let's all go into the kitchen and you can tell me what's going on." Reluctantly Benjamin released Edie's hands and they headed toward the kitchen.

Once there Benjamin gestured them into chairs at the table and as he sat, Tiny curled up at his feet, obviously exhausted by his earlier frantic barking. "Now, start at the beginning and tell me exactly what happened."

As Edie told him the events of the night, a hard knot of tension formed in his chest, first that she and Walt would be foolish enough to venture out in the middle of the night and second because something terrible was obviously going on under the cover of night in the small town he loved.

"Where exactly did this happen?" he asked.

"That little clearing on Devon Moreland's land," Walt said with a frown. "So, they aren't space men?" He looked at Edie and for a moment appeared older than his years.

She reached out and covered the old man's hand with one of hers. "No, Poppy. The man in the woods was definitely human."

Walt frowned and shook his head. "I feel like such a damned old fool."

"He looked like a spaceman. Anyone might have made the same mistake," Edie said gently and then looked at Benjamin. "He was burying something in the clearing. When he saw us, he pulled a gun and shot at us, then chased us on his ATV. He stopped chasing us when we hit Main Street."

"But not before he blew out the back window of her car," Walt added.

"I don't suppose there's any way you could make an identification?" Benjamin asked, although he knew the answer even before she shook her head.

"Impossible. With that suit on I couldn't even swear that it was definitely a man and not a woman," she replied.

Benjamin scooted back his chair from the table. "I don't want you two going home tonight. Why don't I get you settled in here and we'll talk more in the morning."

"I am tired," Walt agreed as he also got up from the table. "I don't like putting you out, but I have to confess I'd feel more comfortable at your place tonight."

"I'll just wait here while you get him settled in," Edie said.

It took only a few minutes for Benjamin to make Walt comfortable in one of the guest bedrooms. As he headed back into the kitchen, his head reeled with all the information he'd heard. The idea of how close Edie and Walt had come to disaster horrified him.

He found her still in the chair at the table with Tiny

in her lap. "What a sweet baby," she said as she stroked Tiny's dark fur.

"Don't let him fool you. Beneath that goofy grin of his is a mutt determined to rule the world." He was glad to see that she looked better than when she and Walt had initially flown through his front door.

"I hate to even ask this, but do you think you could take me back to where you and Walt were tonight? It's been years since I've been anywhere near Devon Moreland's property."

"I think so," she replied.

"I need to make some calls, get things lined up and then we'll head out." Although the last thing he wanted was to drag her out of the house once again, he needed her to show him exactly where all this had gone down.

He wasn't worried about Walt somehow sneaking out again. As he prepared to leave he checked on the old man, who was snoring up a storm. Besides, if he awakened, the ranch was too far out of town for him to try to walk anywhere.

The first thing he did was call Tom and fill him in on what had occurred then made arrangements to meet both Tom and Caleb at the sheriff's office in thirty minutes.

He pulled on a shirt and a jacket, checked on Walt one last time and then he and Edie got into his truck to make the drive back into town.

"I'm sorry you got involved in all this," he said.

"Me, too. Although I'm more than a little curious to

see what *all this* is," she admitted. "That scene in the woods tonight felt like something out of a science fiction movie."

"You and Walt could have been killed," he said with a touch of censure.

"I know, we shouldn't have been out there, but Poppy's original plan was to take his gun and go alien hunting. I got him to agree to leave his gun at home by going with him."

Benjamin fought a shudder as he thought of the old man armed and running amok in the darkness. "I guess I should thank God for small favors."

She released a sigh. "I was hoping that I would see something that had a logical explanation, something that would make me able to convince him there were no aliens in town."

He glanced at her and then back at the road. "I don't want you out again that late at night."

"Don't worry. I can say for sure that tonight was the first and the last of my alien hunting," she replied drily.

"I'd also like for you and Walt to stay at the ranch until we figure out what's going on," he added.

"Surely that isn't necessary," she protested.

"I think it is," he replied smoothly but firmly. "Those were real bullets that were fired at you tonight. We have to assume that the break-in at Walt's is related, and that means he knows who you are and where you live. You saw him doing something he obviously didn't want anyone to see and now he'll see you as a real threat."

As a deputy sheriff he wanted her at his place because he thought it was the best place for her to be. But his desire to have her stay at the ranch transcended his role as a deputy.

As a man he needed to protect what was his and even though he'd only known her for a couple days, somehow in that span, he recognized that he'd claimed her as his own.

He glanced at her again and saw the frown that whipped across her features. She sighed with weary resignation. "I guess I'd be a fool not to stay here."

At that moment they pulled up in front of the sheriff's office where Tom's car was already parked. "I sent Caleb over to the fire department to pick us up a couple suits," Tom said after he'd greeted them. "I figure if the perp felt the need to wear a hazmat suit when he was disposing of whatever he had, it's best if we have them on when we dig it up."

"Good idea," Benjamin replied with a reassuring glance at Edie. She offered him a weak smile and at that moment Caleb arrived and they all headed to the area where Edie and Walt had encountered the man.

Tom and Caleb rode together in Tom's car and followed Benjamin and Edie. "It sounds like Walt stumbled on some sort of illegal dumping," he said as they left Main Street.

"At least we've solved the mystery of the space aliens and I know Poppy isn't crazy." She reached out and directed the heater vent to blow on her face.

"Cold?"

"Just chilled by everything that's happened. Turn left ahead."

He made the turn and checked his rearview mirror to see his brother's car right behind his. "I suppose with everything that's happened lately now wouldn't be a good time to ask you if you've considered moving to Black Rock."

"Why would I consider doing that?" she countered.

So I'd have the opportunity to see you every day of my life. The words played in his head but thankfully didn't make it to his lips. "I know you're going to be looking for a new job and a new place to live. I'm sure Walt would love having you here in town."

"Maybe, but that's not in my plans. We parked up there next to that tree." She pointed ahead.

Benjamin pulled to a halt and cursed himself for being a fool. He seemed to be suffering his first major crush on a woman and other than her response to his kiss, she appeared fairly oblivious to his charms.

He only hoped that this crazy, giddy feeling he got whenever he was around her would fade as he got to know her better.

They all departed their vehicles and it was quickly decided that Benjamin and Tom would don the hazmat suits and go into the clearing while Caleb stayed with Edie.

The minute Benjamin was suited up all thoughts of romance and Edie fled from his mind. This was business and the fact that he and his brother wore hazmat suits meant it was serious business.

Together he and Tom made their way slowly into the clearing, their high-powered flashlight beams leading the way. The woods were still, as if any creatures had long left the area and were afraid to return.

Benjamin had his gun in hand, although he didn't anticipate any trouble. Whoever had taken a couple shots at Walt and Edie from this clearing would be long gone.

Tom carried a metal container specifically designed to transport anything toxic they might find and in his other hand he carried a shovel. Edie had indicated that the person had buried something in a bag, so they weren't looking for some kind of dump of liquid chemicals.

Once they reached the clearing, Tom set down the container and shovel and shone his flashlight on the ground. Benjamin did the same, seeking evidence of a burial site.

It didn't take them long to find not one, but three different areas where it looked as if the ground had recently been disturbed.

Tom picked up his shovel and approached one of the areas. As Benjamin kept his light focused on the ground, Tom began to dig.

He'd removed only three shovels of dirt when Benjamin saw the glow Edie had told him about, a faint yellowish-green glow that definitely looked otherworldly.

He exchanged a worried glance with Tom. What in the hell was going on out here? What on earth could be the source of the weird glow?

His chest tightened with tension as dozens of crazy speculations raced through his head. There were no factories in town, no businesses that might generate any form of glowing toxic waste.

Another swipe with the shovel exposed a white plastic shopping bag with the name of the local grocer printed on the side. It was loosely tied at the top and together the two brothers crouched down to get a closer look.

It was obvious that the glow was coming from whatever was inside the bag. With a dry throat, Benjamin leaned over and untied the bag. As he looked inside a gasp of horror spilled out of him.

An arm.

An arm complete with a hand.

A tattoo of a snake decorated the skin just above the wrist, a tattoo Benjamin immediately recognized. The arm belonged to Jim Taylor, a seventy-eight-year-old man who had finally lost his battle with cancer two weeks ago, a man who had been buried in the cemetery about ten days earlier.

Chapter 6

"Walt Tolliver, what in blazes are you doing in my kitchen?"

The strident female voice pulled Edie abruptly from sleep. She remained buried beneath the blankets, reluctant to rise since she'd only gone to bed a couple hours before. A glance at the window let her know the sun was just beginning to break over the horizon.

"What do you think I'm doing? I'm looking to make myself some breakfast," Walt replied.

As their voices grew softer, Edie closed her eyes once again, but sleep refused to immediately return. It had been after three when Caleb had finally driven her back to the ranch. Benjamin and Tom had remained in the woods and all Caleb would tell her was that the clearing was officially an active crime scene.

She had no idea what kind of crime had occurred there, but the thought that she'd seen part of it in progress chilled her to the bone.

She must have fallen asleep again, for when she next opened her eyes, the sun was shining fully into the room and she felt rested.

Sitting up, she looked around the room where she had slept. Caleb had told her that Benjamin wanted her in the guest room with the yellow bedspread. It was on the opposite side of the house from the bedroom where Walt had slept and across the hall from the master bedroom.

She knew it was the master bedroom because when she'd been looking for her room she'd gone into it first. The king-size bed looked as if somebody had jumped up in a hurry, the blankets and sheets tossed carelessly aside. The entire room had smelled of him and for just a minute as she'd gazed at the bed, she'd wanted to crawl into it and be enveloped by his scent.

The room where she'd slept was pleasant enough, with buttercup walls and yellow gingham curtains at the window. She had no idea what to expect from the day, but was eager to hear from Benjamin about exactly what they had discovered in the clearing.

She got up and went into the bathroom across the hall for a quick shower. As she put on the same clothes, she made a mental note that if they were going to stay here another night she needed to go to Poppy's place and pick up some clothes for both of them.

She left the bathroom and headed down the hallway

and into the living room, where she looked around, interested in the place Benjamin called home.

The requisite flat-screen television hung above the stone fireplace and the sofa was a brown and black pattern. She knew instinctively that the black recliner would be Benjamin's seating of choice. She could easily imagine him there, his long legs stretched out before him and Tiny on his lap.

Thinking about the dog, she wondered where he was this morning. When she entered the kitchen she got her answer. Poppy sat at the table eating what smelled like a freshly baked blueberry muffin and Tiny sat at his feet, obviously waiting for any crumb that might fall to the floor.

The dog wagged his tail at the sight of her and at the same time a gray-haired older woman who stood at the stove turned and smiled. "There she is," she exclaimed.

She bustled to Edie's side and led her to a chair at the table. "I'm Margaret, honey, not that your grandfather would think of making an introduction."

"Hell's bells, Margaret, you didn't give me a chance to introduce you," Walt grumbled. "She can talk a body to death, that one can," he said to Edie, but he had a distinct sparkle in his eyes.

"Don't listen to him," Margaret said. "How about I whip you up some breakfast? Maybe some pancakes or eggs and toast?"

"If Edie wants breakfast I'll be more than happy to fix her something," Walt said as he began to rise.

"This is my kitchen," Margaret said in a huff. "I'll do the cooking around here."

"Poppy, finish your muffin, and thank you, Margaret, but I'm really not hungry. However, a cup of coffee would be great," Edie said.

Margaret got her the coffee and then sat at the table across from her. "You look just like your mama, God rest her soul," she said. "A sweet girl she was and I was sorry to hear about her death."

"Thanks," Edie replied. "Is Benjamin home?"

"No. That poor boy isn't home yet. Walt told me some of what happened last night." She cast the old man a begrudging glance. "Guess he's not as crazy as we all thought he was."

"Just stupid, that's what I was," Poppy exclaimed. "Thinking a hazmat suit was some sort of a space suit."

"It's a mistake anyone could make," Margaret said gruffly as a faint pink stained her cheeks. Poppy looked at her with surprise and then down at his muffin as a slight blush colored his cheeks, as well.

Edie sensed a little attraction in the air between the two. Good, she thought. If Poppy had a woman friend to keep him company, then Edie wouldn't feel so bad about eventually going home.

And shouldn't she be thinking about going home? Poppy's mental health was no longer an issue. Whatever crime had been committed had absolutely nothing to do with her and there was really nothing else holding her here.

Still, maybe she'd stick around another couple days just until Benjamin thought it was safe for Poppy to return to his own house. Her decision to stay had nothing to do with the fact that Benjamin's chocolate-colored eyes made her yearn for things she knew better than to wish for, nothing to do with the fact that his kiss had stirred her on levels she'd never felt before.

It was just after the three of them had eaten lunch when Edie stepped out the front door and sat in one of the two wicker chairs on the porch. The afternoon sun was unusually warm and the air held the scents of fresh hay, rich earth and fall leaves.

In the distance she could see a herd of cattle grazing and several horses frolicking in circles. Peaceful. The scene, the entire place, felt peaceful and enduring.

It would be a wonderful place to raise a family and it wasn't a stretch to think that Benjamin would make a terrific father.

He'd shown incredible patience with Poppy and his affection of his dog spoke of a man who could love easily. Love and patience, the most important things that children needed to grow up healthy.

She reached to hold the charm that dangled in the hollow of her throat. It was cold, like the shell that surrounded her heart.

He was a man who deserved children and that was just another reason for her to steer clear of him. There would be no children in her future.

As she gazed out she saw a plume of dust rising in the air, indicating a vehicle was approaching. She steadfastly ignored the quickened beat of her heart as Benjamin's truck came into view.

She remained seated as he parked and got out of the pickup, his weariness evident in the stress lines down his face and the slight slump of his shoulders. Still, he offered her a warm smile as he stepped onto the porch.

"Long night," she said as he eased down in the chair next to hers.

"You have no idea." He pulled a hand through his hair, messing it up and yet only managing to look carelessly sexy.

"Can you tell me what you found?" She found it difficult to look at him as the sleepy cast to his eyes only made him look sexier and brought to her mind the memory of the kiss they'd shared.

"You won't believe it. I still don't believe it myself." He drew in a deep breath and released it with a sigh. "We found an arm, a foot and a hand each buried in the clearing and all of them glowing like they could power a car for ten years."

Edie sucked in her breath in shock. "Do they belong to somebody who was murdered?"

"We think the arm belongs to Jim Taylor. He died of cancer and had a proper burial a little over a week ago. We don't know who the other hand belongs to, although it's definitely female. And we don't know about the foot."

She stared at him in stunned surprise. "And you don't know why they were glowing like that?"

He shook his head. "My brother Jacob arranged for a contact at the FBI lab in Topeka and Sam McCain, one of the other deputies, is transporting them there as we speak."

"What do you think it all means?" She fought the impulse to reach out and stroke her hand across his furrowed brow. He looked as if the weight of the world suddenly rested on his shoulders.

"It's too early to be able to tell what any of it means," he replied. "But we're wondering if maybe somebody is conducting some sort of experiments on Black Rock's dead."

Edie fought the chill that attempted to waltz up her back. "Any suspects?"

He barked a humorless laugh. "At the moment, only everyone in town." He sighed again, a weary sound that blew through her.

"Why do you do this?" she asked curiously.

He turned and looked at her. "Do what?"

"Why are you a deputy? It's obvious that your heart is here at the ranch. Even Poppy said he doesn't understand why you aren't ranching full-time."

He gazed out in the distance and shrugged. "Working law enforcement is what we Grayson men do. Sure, I love the ranch, but in this town, people know me as a man with a badge. That's who I am." He said the words almost belligerently, as if he were trying to convince himself of something rather than her. "So, how has your day been?"

"Okay, although there seems to be a territorial

war going on over the kitchen. I thought Poppy and Margaret might come to blows over who was going to fix lunch."

"Who won?" He leaned back in the chair and some of the tension in his shoulders appeared to ease.

"Definitely Margaret. In fact she threatened to blacken his other eye if he touched one of her pots or pans."

He smiled then, a tired smile that erased the worried lines that had tracked across his forehead. "I'm not surprised. She's a feisty one."

"There seems to be some strange energy between her and Poppy. It's like they're kids and he pulls her hair and she kicks him in the shin but beneath all the aggression is some kind of crazy attraction."

"They've both been alone for a long time. I think it would be great if they hooked up."

"I can't believe we're talking about my grandfather *hooking up*," she said drily.

He laughed but quickly his laughter died and he gazed at her with smoldering eyes. "It would be nice if somebody around here was hooking up."

For a moment gazing into his eyes she felt as if she couldn't breathe. It took conscious willpower to force herself to look away from him but it was impossible for her to reply.

"I need to get some sleep," he said. "I have a feeling as this case unfolds it's going to take all the energy we have to give." He stood and once again looked weary beyond words.

"Aren't you afraid of nightmares?" she asked as she also got up from her chair.

He took a step closer to her, so close their bodies almost touched. Once again her breath caught in her chest as he reached up and touched a strand of her hair. "There's only one thing that would definitely keep nightmares at bay, and that's if you were in bed with me as my snuggle buddy."

He dropped his hand and stepped back from her. "But since you've indicated that's not happening, then the best I can do is hope that my dreams are pleasant." He didn't wait for a reply but instead turned and went into the house.

She stared after him and finally released a shuddering sigh. For just a moment as she'd gazed into those magnetic eyes of his, as she'd felt the heat of his body radiating out to warm hers, she'd wanted to be his snuggle buddy. And that scared her almost as much as eerie, glowing body parts buried in the woods.

"Can you tell me where you were Wednesday night around one in the morning?" Benjamin asked Abe Appleton, the local retired chemist. Abe's current claim to fame in the town came from the programs he presented to elementary-school classes about chemistry and physics.

"On any given night at one in the morning I assure you I can be found in my bed," Abe said. "Is this about that mess on Moreland's property? Why on earth would you think I had anything to do with that?"

"We're talking to anyone in town who has a background in chemistry," Benjamin replied. The two men stood on Abe's porch. It was just after eight in the morning.

When Benjamin had arrived in the office that morning, Tom had handed him a list of people he wanted Benjamin to interview. Abe had been the first name on the list.

Deputies were still working the clearing, digging to see if there were any other surprises buried there. It would be days before they heard back from the FBI lab on what exactly had caused the glow to the body parts, but the investigation was ongoing.

The small-town rumor mill was working overtime with the gossip ranging from a serial killer in their midst to a mad scientist conducting unholy experiments on murder victims.

"You want to come in, check my alibi with Violet? She sleeps light and would know if I wasn't in bed on the night in question," Abe said. "Benjamin, I make volcanoes out of baking soda for the kids. I suck a hard-boiled egg into a bottle. I have no idea what happened in the woods."

"You know anyone else who might have a background in chemistry?" Benjamin asked.

Abe frowned thoughtfully. "Not off the top of my head. 'Course I don't know exactly what you found. When Violet and I were at the café early this morning, we heard everything from a leg that got up and danced on its own to a hand that grabbed Tom around the throat."

Benjamin grinned. "Sounds fascinating, but it's hardly close to the truth." His grin faded as he considered the truth. "Still, it looks like somebody was doing some sort of experimenting, somebody who might have a background in either medicine or chemistry."

"Can't think of anyone, but if I do I know where to contact you," Abe replied.

"Thanks, Abe. I may be back with more questions."

Abe smiled. "In that case you know where to contact me."

Minutes later as Benjamin backed out of Abe's driveway, he thought of all the arms this investigation entailed. While he was interviewing potential suspects, Caleb was following up with Josh Willoughby at the cemetery. There was no question that the arm they'd unearthed belonged to old Jim Taylor and that meant, at the very least, that there was some grave-robbing going on.

Tom had another deputy assigned to checking the sales of hazmat suits. The suits were not cheap and hopefully they'd get a lead through that avenue.

A different deputy was assigned to interview doctors and nurses at the hospital. Since they didn't know what they were dealing with there was no way of knowing if they were spinning their wheels or not.

As he headed toward the taxidermy store in town, his thoughts turned to Edie, who was never really out of his mind. He was thirty years old and more than ready to be in love, ready to start a family. He wanted to fill the house with children who he could teach to love the ranch as much as he did.

Edie had asked him why he wasn't ranching full-time and Benjamin hadn't been completely honest with her. The truth was he was afraid of what was beneath his badge, afraid that there might be nothing.

Being a deputy gave him a sense of purpose and more than a little respect in the town. Without that what would he be? What would he have?

He dismissed the crazy thoughts from his head as he parked in front of the taxidermy shop. When they had been making the list of people to interview, Abe's name had come to mind first because of his background in chemistry, and after some careful thought Big Jeff Hudson and his son, Little Jeff, were added to the list. None of the deputies had any idea what kind of chemicals were used in the taxidermy business, but Benjamin intended to find out now.

A tinkling bell above the door announced his arrival as he stepped into the shop. This was his least favorite place in town. Dead animals stared at him from all directions. He found the whole thing rather creepy.

"Benjamin!" Big Jeff greeted him from behind the counter in the back of the store. "What a surprise. I rarely see you in here."

Benjamin made his way around a standing deer to approach the thin, older man. "How's business?"

"Not great, but we'll be swamped soon with deer

season opening. What brings you into my little shop of horrors?"

"I need to ask you some questions. I suppose you've heard about the crime scene on Moreland's property."

"Is anyone talking about anything else?"

"It does seem to be the topic of the day," Benjamin agreed. "Is Little Jeff around?"

"He's in the back unloading some supplies, but he doesn't like to be called Little Jeff anymore. He goes by Jeffrey Allen now. You want me to get him?"

Benjamin nodded and immediately thought about the key fob he'd found by the bush at the cemetery the morning after Walt's beating. *A* for Abe? For Allen? The idea of either man beating the hell out of Walt seemed a stretch, but Benjamin wasn't about to close off his mind to any possibility.

Big Jeff disappeared into the back room and returned a moment later followed by his son. It had been years since the nickname of Little Jeff had been appropriate for the hulking thirty-four-year-old who had been primed to take over the family business when Big Jeff retired.

"Hey, Benjamin," Jeffrey Allen greeted him with a friendly smile. "Dad said you wanted to talk to me. What's up?"

"I wanted to ask the two of you about the chemicals you use in processing animals. Any of them considered toxic?"

"By no stretch of the imagination," Big Jeff replied easily.

"Any of them contain some sort of fluorescent properties?"

Jeffrey Allen laughed. "Not hardly. I don't know one of the local hunters or fishermen who want their prize catch to glow in the dark."

By the time Benjamin left the shop he knew more about taxidermy than he'd ever wanted to know. The rest of the day was more of the same, asking questions of people and getting nothing substantial to help with the case.

It was going to be difficult to pin down alibis of anyone they might suspect for the night that Walt and Edie had been confronted in the woods. At that time of night most people would say they were in bed asleep and that was difficult to disprove.

After talking to the people on his list, he returned to the office, where he was updated by his brother Tom. There had been nothing else found in the clearing and Devon Moreland had claimed complete ignorance on what had been happening there.

The bullet that had shattered Edie's rear window had come from a .38 caliber handgun, definitely common to this area. Tom had assigned one of the other deputies to check gun and ATV owners in the area but it would be several days before he'd have a definitive list.

He'd made arrangements for Edie's back car window to be replaced that morning.

It was just after seven when he finally made his way to the ranch. Weariness pulled at his muscles and hunger pangs filled his belly. Breakfast had been a muffin and a cup of coffee and he'd skipped lunch. He was sure that Margaret would have a plate waiting for him when he got home.

As he approached the house he saw Edie sitting on the porch, the last of the day's sunshine sparking in her hair. Pleasure swelled up inside him, banishing any thought of food or rest.

He could get used to coming home to her. There was no question that she touched him on all kinds of levels. As he parked his truck and got out, she rose from the chair and smiled.

That smile of hers eased some of his weariness and replaced it with a simmering desire to learn more about her, to taste her mouth once again, to somehow get beneath the defenses she'd wrapped around herself.

"Long day," she said. It was a comment, not a question.

"I have a feeling they're all going to be long for a while."

"Anything new?"

He shook his head. "Nothing specific. Let's get inside. It's too cool to sit out here once the sun goes down."

The second he opened the door Tiny greeted him with a happy dance that had both him and Edie laughing. "He's become my buddy when you're gone," she said as Benjamin bent down and picked up Tiny.

"Do you like dogs?"

"I love Tiny," she replied. "Where did you get him?"

"Found him in a box on the side of the road. Somebody had dumped him. He was half-dead and I wasn't sure he was going to make it but all he needed was a little tender loving care."

Edie stepped closer to him and scratched Tiny behind one of his ears. "Poor little thing. I wonder if he has nightmares about the bad things that happened to him before you found him."

"I like to think that with enough time and love, bad memories no longer hold the power to give you nightmares," he replied. It didn't escape his notice that this was the second time she'd mentioned nightmares, making him wonder what haunted her sleep at night.

They walked from the living room into the kitchen, where Margaret and Walt were seated at the table with cups of coffee. Margaret jumped up at the sight of him. "The rest of us already ate, but I've got a bowl of beef stew all ready for you, along with some corn bread that will stick to your ribs."

"Thanks, Margaret." Benjamin set Tiny down on the floor and then went to the sink to wash up to eat. "Walt, that eye is looking better," he said once he was seated at the table. "How are the ribs?"

"Still sore, but not as bad as they were. Have you caught the creep who beat me up yet?"

Benjamin was aware of Edie sliding into the chair next to him, the spicy scent of her filling him with a hunger for something other than beef stew. "Not yet, but we're working on it," he said to Walt.

For the next few minutes, as he ate, he told them what he could about the investigation. He finished eating and

Margaret took his plates away and then announced that she and Walt were going to her cottage to play some rummy.

"I think we'll know more about everything when we get some results back from the FBI lab," he said to Edie once the older people had left the house.

"But that could take a while, right?"

"Unfortunately," he agreed with a nod of his head. "In the meantime we'll keep interviewing people and hope that somebody knows something about what's been going on."

Edie leaned back in her chair. She looked as pretty as he'd ever seen her in a deep pink sweater that enhanced her coloring. "I think it's time I go home."

"Do you really think that's a good idea?"

"Whoever chased us the other night must realize by now that we couldn't identify them. Plus I know that Poppy isn't crazy and he's insisting I go home."

He wanted to protest. He wanted to ask her if she'd stay for him. But they'd shared only a single kiss and he really had no right to ask her to stay.

"So what are your plans?"

"I'll stop over at Poppy's place in the morning and get my things and then head on back to Topeka." She frowned. "I hate to leave him like this and I was wondering if it would be okay with you if Poppy remains here a couple of days. He is healing nicely, but I think the attack shook him up more than he's saying. I tried to tell him I wanted to stay at least until he gets back on his feet, but he went ballistic."

"He's welcome to stay until he feels like he's ready to go home," Benjamin said.

She nodded. "I appreciate it."

"And if I need to talk to you? About the investigation?"

"I'll give you my cell phone number and when I get settled in a new place, I'll let you know my address."

"I'll be sorry to see you go." The words escaped him before he realized he intended to speak them.

Her gaze didn't quite meet his. "You're a nice man, Benjamin, and you deserve a nice woman in your life." She got up from the table. "Believe me, I'm the last person on earth you need in your life in any way. I'm not a nice woman and it's time for me to get back to my life."

Before he could respond she turned and left the kitchen.

Chapter 7

It was after eleven when Edie finally left Benjamin's ranch the next morning. Margaret had insisted she have a big breakfast and it had been difficult to say goodbye to both her and Poppy.

She might have stuck around if she thought that Poppy really needed her, but she sensed a bit of romance taking place between him and Margaret, a romance that could fill any loneliness Poppy might have entertained.

Benjamin had already been gone when she'd gotten out of bed and she'd remained in her room the night before after she'd left him in the kitchen.

She'd been afraid to spend any more time around him, afraid that somehow he'd talk her into staying, afraid that he might kiss her again and made her want him even more deeply than she already did. It was definitely time to get out of Dodge, but her heart was heavy as the ranch disappeared in her rearview mirror.

She could have been happy there, she could be happy with Benjamin, if she deserved happiness. But deep in her soul she knew the truth.

Still, she was grateful she hadn't had to face him one last time that morning. It was easier this way, with no long, drawn-out goodbyes.

By the time she entered the outskirts of town she was thinking of the problems that awaited her in Topeka. Thank God she had a little bit of savings put away, just enough to get her into another small apartment.

She wasn't too worried about a job. She'd flip hamburgers if necessary to get by until she found something more permanent. It would have been nice if she'd gone to college, but there had never been enough money at home, and the minute she'd graduated from high school she'd started working to help out her mother.

When she reached Poppy's place she parked in the driveway and got out of the car, surprised when a neighbor hurried out of his house and toward her.

"Hi," he said with a smile of friendliness. "I'm Bart Crosswell, Walt's neighbor. I was just wondering how he's doing. Me and my wife heard about him getting beaten up but we haven't seen him since then."

Bart was about sixty with a broad face that looked as if it had never held a frown. "He's staying with some friends for the next couple days," she replied, "but he's doing just fine."

"Glad to hear that. And I noticed you cleaned up the yard real nice. We didn't want to complain or say anything, but it was obvious that it had kind of gotten away from him over the past few months."

"I'll try to make sure that somebody is keeping on top of it from now on," Edie said, grateful that the neighbor appeared to be a nice guy.

"I don't mind mowing it whenever I mow my own. I just didn't want to step on Walt's toes," Bart said.

"That's very kind of you. When he gets back home maybe the two of you can work out an agreeable arrangement," she replied.

"Will do." He lifted a hand in a friendly goodbye and then began to walk back to his house.

Poppy would be fine, Edie thought as she let herself into the house. He had friends and neighbors that obviously cared about him. He didn't need her. Nobody needed her and she didn't need anyone, she reminded herself as she climbed the stairs.

She pulled her overnight bag from the closet and set it on the bed. It wouldn't take long for her to gather her things and leave town.

Leave Benjamin. She couldn't help the little pang in her heart as she thought about him. In another place, in another time, she might have allowed herself to care about him. But, she couldn't think about that now.

She went into the bathroom across the hall and gathered the toiletries she hadn't taken to Benjamin's and then returned to the bedroom and placed them in her overnight bag.

Once she had all her clothes folded and packed away, she sat on the edge of the bed and allowed herself to think about Benjamin once again.

He'd asked her if she'd considered relocating to Black Rock now that there was really nothing holding her to Topeka. In the brief time she'd been here as an adult, she recognized that Black Rock was a pleasant town filled with friendly people.

It was easy to imagine living in Black Rock. She could get an apartment close enough to the downtown area that she could walk to the stores on nice days. She could enjoy regular visits with Poppy and build a pleasant life here.

There was only one fly in the ointment: a hot sexy deputy with soft brown eyes and hot kisses that made her want to forget her vow of celibacy, forget that she'd given up on finding any real happiness.

No, she wouldn't even consider relocating here. Benjamin Grayson was too much temptation and believing she could ever have a loving relationship with anyone was nothing but utter foolishness.

She rose from the bed and froze as she heard it—the soft, but unmistakable creak of the third step. Her blood chilled as she realized somebody else was in the house, somebody who hadn't announced their presence but was quietly creeping up the staircase.

Her breathing went shallow as she grabbed her purse and shot a wild gaze around the room, seeking something that might be used as a weapon.

There was nothing. And as she heard the distinct

creak of the seventh step panic clawed at her. There was no question in her mind that whoever it was had no good intentions, otherwise they would have said something to announce their presence.

Clutching her purse, she silently moved across the room and into the closet. She closed the closet door and sat on the floor with her back against it and her legs braced on the other side.

For a long moment she heard nothing but the frantic bang of her own heartbeat. God, she'd been careless. She hadn't locked the front door behind her when she'd come inside. She hadn't thought there was any danger.

If it were Bart surely he would say something. Agonizing moments ticked by and she heard nothing. Her heart rate began to slow a bit. Had she only imagined those creaks? Had it just been the house settling?

At that moment a fist crashed into the closet door. "Come out of there, you bitch," a deep voice snarled.

Edie swallowed a scream and pressed her back more firmly against the door. Help. She needed help. Oh, God, her cell phone.

She wildly fumbled in the bottom of her purse for her cell phone. A deep sob escaped her as she scrabbled to find the instrument that would bring help.

He grabbed the door handle and turned it, then threw himself against the door with a force that shook the door frame. "You and that old man ruined everything! I'm going to make you pay if it's the last thing I do."

Deep and guttural. She didn't recognize the voice.

As he slammed into the door once again she managed to get hold of her cell phone.

"I'm calling the sheriff," she cried out as she punched 9-1-1.

When the operator answered she gave them Poppy's address and then screamed as the door shuddered once again.

"You won't get away from me no matter where you go." The voice shimmered with rage. "I'll find you wherever you are and make you pay for screwing up my life." There was a snap of wood as the frame broke and then silence.

The only noise was her gasping breaths and un-controllable sobs. Was he gone? Or was it a trick? Was he waiting for her to venture out of the closet so he could hurt her? She shoved the back of her fist against her mouth as tears blurred her vision.

Who had it been? And what had she done to warrant such intense hatred? Would she be safe going back to Topeka or would he find her there to merit out some form of twisted revenge?

Benjamin was grabbing a quick cup of coffee in the café when he heard the call for a responder to Walt's address. He tore out of the building and jumped into his car, his heart hammering so fast he could scarcely catch his breath.

There could only be one person who would have made that call. Edie. He knew she'd be stopping by

Walt's on her way out of town, although he hadn't known specifically what time she might be leaving.

If anything happened to her, he'd never forgive himself. He should have talked her out of leaving town, insisted that she stick around until they had a handle on the whole situation.

It took only minutes for him to arrive at Walt's. He went through the open front door with his gun drawn, anticipating trouble.

He heard nothing. The silence of the house thundered in his head as he slowly made his way from room to room. He didn't want to call out. If somebody was inside, he didn't want to announce his presence or exacerbate whatever the situation might be. He damn sure didn't want to force somebody to hurt Edie.

When he'd cleared the lower level of the house he crept up the stairs, wincing as two of them creaked beneath his weight. When he reached the first bedroom, his heatbeat crashed so hard in his ears he feared he wouldn't hear anything else.

He cleared the bedrooms and bathroom until there was only one left at the end of the hallway. His heart jumped into his throat as he saw Edie's overnight bag on the bed. He finally called out, "It's Deputy Grayson. Is anyone here?"

She exploded out of the closet and into his embrace. Trembling arms wrapped around his neck and she buried her face in his chest and began to weep.

He held her tight with one arm and his gun with the other. "What happened?"

"He was here. He said I ruined everything and he was going to make me pay." The words escaped her on a trail of tears as she squeezed her arms around his neck.

"Who, honey? Who was it?"

"I don't know. I didn't see him."

He felt her physically pull herself together. A single deep breath and she moved out of his embrace. But her face was achingly pale and her eyes were wide and red-rimmed from her tears.

"I had just finished packing when I heard somebody on the stairs." Her voice trembled. "I got scared. Thank God I grabbed my purse and hid in the closet." Tears welled up in her eyes once again. "I sat on the floor and braced myself as he started to slam into the door. I thought he was going to get in before anyone got here to help."

"Let's get you out of here," he said. As she grabbed her purse from the closet, he picked up her overnight bag and wondered who in the hell had come after her.

"We're going to the sheriff's office to file a report and then I'm taking you back to the ranch," he said once they were in his car. "You aren't heading out of town by yourself until I'm certain that you're no longer in danger."

"If you're expecting an argument, you aren't going to get one," she replied.

"You didn't recognize his voice?"

She shook her head. "It was just a deep growl." She wrapped her arms around herself as if to fight off a shiver. "He sounded so angry, like he would easily enjoy strangling me to death with his bare hands."

Benjamin tightened his hands on the steering wheel as a rage began inside him. The idea of anyone putting their hands on Edie made a rich anger burn in his gut.

When they arrived at the sheriff's office, Tom sat down with them and Edie told him what had occurred. Tom immediately dispatched two deputies to Walt's house to fingerprint the closet and talk to Bart. They hoped Bart might have seen whoever entered the house.

Confident that the investigation side of things was under control, within an hour Benjamin and Edie were back in his car and headed to the ranch.

"I know you were eager to return to Topeka and get things settled there," he said.

"Funny how somebody trying to kill you can change your mind." She offered him a weak smile.

A healthy dose of respect for her filled him.

"I have this terrible fear that if I go back to Topeka now this creep will somehow find me there and I won't have my own personal deputy to ride to my rescue," she added.

Benjamin tried to find a responding smile, but there was absolutely nothing humorous about the situation. "I shouldn't have let you go," he said. "I shouldn't have let you go to Walt's to get your things alone. I should have been with you or I should have talked you out of leaving altogether."

She reached out and placed her hand on his arm.

"How could you know that I might be in danger? Who could know that he'd be after revenge for me somehow screwing things up for him. I just wish I knew what it is he thinks I messed up." She removed her hand from his arm.

"If we knew that, we'd probably have all the answers." Benjamin wheeled through the entrance that led to the ranch. He didn't want to tell her that the thing that worried him now was that whoever had come after her would eventually know she and Walt were staying here.

If it came down to him doing his job or keeping her safe, the job could go to hell. He'd already lost one woman in his life. Brittany. He had no hope of ever seeing his sister again.

Edie had made it clear to him that she didn't want him in her life on any kind of a romantic basis, but his heart was already taken by her and the idea of anything happening to her nearly shattered him.

"You'll be safe at the ranch, both you and Walt. I'll make sure of it," he said firmly.

"I don't doubt that at all," she replied.

As Benjamin parked in front of the ranch his mind whirled with all the ways he could assure their safety. Tom certainly didn't have men to spare given the magnitude of the current investigation.

Maybe it was time to have a talk with Jacob, see if he could enlist his brother's help in keeping an eye on the ranch.

When they got into the house Benjamin sat down with

Walt, Margaret and Edie and told them how important
it was that the house remained locked at all times, that
they keep an eye out for trouble and that obviously the
threat to Edie and Walt wasn't over.

He didn't anticipate any trouble immediately, so
after making sure all the doors were locked up tight,
Benjamin left to go talk to his brother.

Jacob had holed himself up in a small cabin on the
property almost three months earlier. He'd quit his job
in Kansas City with the FBI and had come home with
deep haunting shadows in his eyes and had refused to
discuss with anyone what had happened to him.

The only thing he'd told his brothers when he'd
arrived in Black Rock was that he didn't want anyone to
know he was back. He lived like a hermit and Benjamin
and Margaret provided the supplies he needed.

It took only minutes for Benjamin to pull up in front
of the cabin that was nearly hidden in a thick grove of
trees. At one time this had been a caretaker's cabin,
but during Benjamin's childhood it had been used as a
guest cottage and an occasional romantic getaway for
his parents.

He found his brother where he always found him, in
the small living room in a recliner with a beer in his
hand and the television playing.

Jacob's cheeks and chin were covered with whisker
stubble and his dark hair was longer than Benjamin had
ever seen it. He looked like a man without pride, a man
who had lost the ability to care about anything.

"You look like hell," Benjamin said as he came through the front door.

"And a good afternoon to you, too, little brother." Jacob gestured him into the chair opposite him and turned down the volume on the television. "What's going on?"

"I need your help." Benjamin eased down into the chair.

Jacob raised one of his dark eyebrows. "I hope it doesn't require me leaving this chair or my beer."

A flash of irritation swept through Benjamin. He'd always looked up to Jacob but the shell of a man who had returned to the ranch was nothing like the man who had left.

"Actually, it does require you getting away from the beer and out of your chair," Benjamin said.

"Then the odds of me being able to help you out are pretty slim."

"For God's sake, Jacob. Pull yourself together," Benjamin exclaimed with a burst of uncharacteristic anger. "I need you to help me keep a woman safe."

Jacob took a sip of his beer and eyed Benjamin with interest. "Something in your voice tells me this is a special woman."

Benjamin felt a faint heat crawl into his cheeks. "She's in trouble through no fault of her own. Somebody attacked her today and I don't think the perp is finished yet. I've got her at the house but I'd like an extra pair of eyes watching things there."

"Does this have to do with the Moreland mess?"

Benjamin nodded. "I've got both Walt Tolliver and his granddaughter at the house." He leaned back in the chair and released a sigh. "I'd assumed since they couldn't identify the culprits that they were safe from harm. But I was wrong." He told his brother what had taken place at Walt's house.

"So he didn't go after her to somehow protect himself. He went after her for revenge." Jacob shook his head. "That's a nasty motive for an attack. I'd say whoever you're looking for has a history of a short fuse, maybe some sort of persecution complex. You know the type, the whole world is against him and whatever troubles he has is always somebody else's fault."

"Not much of a profile to go on," Benjamin said.

Jacob shrugged. "Not much information yet to go on. Tom called me last night to give me the latest on what's been happening with the case."

"Right now my main concern is keeping Walt and Edie safe. I'm hoping Tom can spare me so I can hang out at the house, but I'd feel better knowing you had my back."

Jacob set his beer down and his eyes were as black as night. "I got your back," he said simply. "Just let me know when you need me around and I'll be there."

"Are you ever going to tell me what brought you home?" Benjamin asked softly. Jacob broke eye contact and for a long moment said nothing. Benjamin leaned forward in his chair. "Whatever it is, Jacob, we can help you."

His brother looked at him with a wry smile. "Nobody can help me."

"Just tell me this. Are you hiding from somebody or are you hiding from yourself?"

Jacob's eyes widened and then narrowed into slits. "Maybe a little bit of both." He picked up his bottle of beer once again. "Just give me a call if you need me to keep an eye on the house." He picked up the remote control and turned up the volume on the television in an obvious dismissal.

As Benjamin headed back to the ranch house he couldn't help but worry about his brother. He felt as if they'd already lost Brittany and if something wasn't done, somehow they were going to lose Jacob.

It wasn't right for a man to wall himself off from everyone. It wasn't right for a man to be alone with just his beer and his thoughts. Jacob needed something, but until he asked for it nobody could give it to him.

As he once again parked in front of the house and got out of the truck, his thoughts turned to the woman inside. For some reason he felt as if she and Jacob shared that common trait. He thought that Edie needed something from somebody but was afraid or refused to ask.

He only wished it was him that she needed, that she wanted. But he had resigned himself to the fact that the only thing he could do for her was to keep her safe. And when the danger passed, he would send her off to live her life without him.

Chapter 8

Edgy.

That was the only word to describe what Edie felt as she sat in the kitchen. It had been two days since the attack on her, two days of confinement with Benjamin. He hadn't left the house or her side for the past forty-eight hours.

She'd been in bed, but had gotten up a few minutes ago and decided to make herself a cup of hot tea.

She sat at the table with the hot brew in front of her with only the oven light on. This was the first time she felt as if she could breathe, without his overwhelming presence by her side.

Familiarity was supposed to breed contempt, but in this case that old adage was wrong. The sexual tension between them had grown to mammoth proportions. She felt his hot, simmering gaze on her like a hand on her thigh, a palm on her breast, and with each moment that passed she wanted it, wanted him.

And in the past two days Margaret and Poppy had become best buddies, sharing the kitchen like two top chefs, playing card games and giggling like teenagers.

She felt a desperate need to get out of town, but each time she thought about leaving all she could think about was that man hunting her down and making her pay.

There was no question that being here in this house with Benjamin made her feel safe. He'd even insisted Margaret move into the bedroom across the hall from Walt's for the time being rather than stay in her little cottage behind the house. He didn't want anyone to somehow use her to get to Poppy and Edie.

She leaned forward in the chair and took a sip of her tea that warmed her all the way down to her toes. No matter how she tried to keep thoughts of Benjamin at bay, he continued to intrude into her brain.

As if summoned by her thoughts alone, he appeared in the doorway of the kitchen, Tiny at his feet. "I thought you were asleep," she said.

He moved from the doorway to the table and sat next to her. Tiny curled up on the rug between them. "I was on the phone with Tom getting updates."

"So what's new?"

"Not enough to solve the case," he said with frustration. "We know now that the arm definitely belonged to Jim Taylor, the old man I told you about who died of cancer. The other two body parts still haven't been identified. We haven't heard anything from the FBI lab on what chemicals might have been involved."

"Then there's really no news," she said and lifted her cup for another sip of tea.

He forced a smile. "Nothing concrete but they're all gathering information that hopefully will eventually crack the case."

"You should be back in the office instead of hanging around here with me," she said.

"Right now you and Walt are our best clues to what might be happening. If somebody comes after you here, I'll be ready for them. I'm doing my job by making sure you and Walt are safe."

"How come you don't have any workers around here?" she asked curiously. She'd noticed that she never saw anyone in the yard or in the pastures or corral.

"I'm a small operation. I've been able to handle things myself for the past couple of years."

"Tell me about your sister." She'd been curious about the woman who had gone missing, a woman he barely mentioned. "What's she like?"

For just a brief moment a smile curved his lips and his eyes warmed. "Beautiful, impulsive and headstrong. We all spoiled her terribly. But she's also bright and tough and has a great sense of humor."

His smile fell and his eyes darkened. He placed a hand on the table, his long fingers splayed on the top and stared down. "She was working as a deputy like the rest of us. Initially when she missed work none of us panicked. She'd occasionally oversleep or get screwed up with her schedule and forget to come in until we called her. It wasn't until a full day went by with no word from her that we all started to get a little concerned."

He leaned forward and his fingers curled into a tight fist. "By the time two days had gone by with no word from her, we knew she was in trouble. There had been no activity in her bank account, her cell phone wasn't picking up and that's when true panic set in."

She was sorry she'd asked, saw the pain that radiated from his features and compressed his lips tightly together. Her heart ached with his pain but before she could find words to comfort him, he continued speaking.

"I can't explain to you what it felt like when the realization struck that she had met with foul play. Suddenly every minute that passed was sheer torture. It was impossible to eat, impossible to sleep. I tried making deals with fate. You know, if she'd just show up safe and sound then I could be struck dead. If she would just be returned to us then fate could take this ranch from me and I'd happily live in a hovel for the rest of my life." He released a short, strained laugh. "God, I've never told anyone this stuff."

She reached across the table and covered his fisted hand with her own. "I'm sorry, Benjamin. I can't imagine what it must be like to not know what happened to somebody you love."

He uncurled his hand and instead entwined his fingers with hers. "Eventually the gut-ripping desperation passes and you find that you have to eat, you have to sleep, that life goes on no matter what." He gazed at her with sad eyes. "My brothers all hold on to the hope that she'll eventually be found alive, but not me. The day we found her car hidden in an old abandoned barn, my gut told me she's dead."

For a moment Edie didn't know what to say to comfort him, but her need to take the pain from his eyes was visceral. She understood his grief, awakened with her own each morning and went to bed with it each night. "I'm sorry, Benjamin. I'm so sorry that you're going through this."

He tightened his grip on her hand. "Thanks. It actually helped to talk about it. Now, why don't you tell me what puts the sadness in your eyes?"

She forced a laugh and gently pulled her hand from his. "Life," she said. "My life really started to crumble when my mother died." Edie once again wrapped her hands around her teacup. "We were very best friends. My father walked out on us when I was just a baby and it was always just her and me."

"She never thought about remarrying?" he asked.

"Not that I know of. I don't think she ever dated. She had a circle of girlfriends and when she wasn't with them, she seemed content alone. I met Greg in a bar two weeks after Mom's death."

She paused to take a sip of the tea that was now lukewarm. There was something intensely intimate about sitting at the table with everyone else in bed. In the semidarkness of the kitchen it seemed easier to let her guard down, to open herself up to him.

"I was grieving and vulnerable and ripe for the

picking. He moved in and I became one of those too-stupid-to-live women I abhor. I made every mistake a woman can make. I believed whatever he told me about his money being tied up in some high dollar business. He fed me what I needed to hear but it was nothing but lies." She shrugged and offered him a crooked smile. "It felt tragic at the time he left me, but now I realize he did me a big favor by getting out of my life. I'm like my mother. I'm good alone."

Benjamin's gaze lingered for a long moment on her face. "I wish I'd met you first," he finally said softly. "I wish I'd been the man in your life before Greg ever entered it."

There it was, that deep yearning to fall into his gaze, to feel his strong arms wrapped around her, his heartbeat against her own. It was a palpable want, melting something inside her she didn't want melted.

"It wouldn't have made a difference," she said, surprised that her voice didn't sound strong and sure, but rather breathy and faint.

He leaned back in his chair and released a sigh. "Tell me what gives you nightmares."

She looked at him in surprise and gave an uneasy laugh. "What makes you think I have nightmares?"

"I don't know, I've just had the impression that you do."

"Staying up too late and drinking tea gives me nightmares about tea bags," she said as she got up from the table. She carried her cup to the sink, aware of his gaze remaining on her.

She rinsed the cup and placed it in the dishwasher and then turned to face him once again. "Don't, Benjamin. Don't pry to find out any secrets I might have, the kind of woman I am. Trust me when I tell you that you wouldn't like what you uncovered."

"I find that hard to believe," he replied as she walked toward the kitchen door.

"Good night, Benjamin," she said and then left the kitchen. As she went through the living room toward the hallway she fought against the sudden sear of hot tears at her eyes.

The charm around her neck seemed to burn her skin, a painful reminder of loss and grief. It had been her fault. She should have never gotten pregnant. She obviously wasn't meant to be a mother.

Even though the doctor had told her that sometimes these things happened for no discernible reason, when the baby died Edie had known the truth, that somehow she was responsible, that it had been her fault that her baby had been born dead.

Benjamin deserved better. He deserved more than she'd ever be able to give him. She had no intention of having children. She had no intention of ever loving again.

She would admit it, she was a coward. She didn't want to risk the chance of loss once again. Even with a man like Benjamin. Especially with a man like Benjamin.

As much as it pained her, she had to keep him out of her heart.

* * *

It had been another long day. After the discussion with Edie the night before, Benjamin had gone to bed with a heavy heart.

He felt that over the past several days he'd gotten to know her as well as he'd ever known any woman. She was kind and warm and giving. She had a wonderful sense of humor and was bright and so achingly beautiful. And yet, he sensed a darkness in her that he couldn't pierce.

She'd been distant with him all day, as if punishing him for getting too close the night before. Tension had sparked in the air between them until he'd felt he might explode.

The tension had eased when after dinner the four of them had sat at the table and played poker. The laughter the games created was a welcome relief.

There was no doubt that there were sparks between Walt and Margaret. They had begun to act like a couple who had been married for fifty years, finishing each other's sentences and exchanging warm gazes. He had a feeling when this was all over and done he might just lose his housekeeper, but he couldn't feel bad about it. He was only glad that Walt and Margaret had found each other to share companionship in the golden years of their lives.

He now sat in his recliner, Tiny on his lap. Edie had gone into Walt's bedroom to check the wrap around his ribs and Margaret had gone to bed.

A man needed companionship. Men weren't wired to

be alone and he believed Edie wasn't wired to be alone, either. There was no question in his mind that she was attracted to him, that she had feelings for him. He knew it in her gaze, felt it in her touch, sensed it radiating from her as they warily circled one another.

But he didn't know how to get beneath her defenses. He didn't have the tools to know how to get to her heart. Tiny whined, as if sensing Benjamin's growing despondency.

"Shhh." He scrubbed the dog beneath his ear, which instantly halted the whine. Too bad a scratch behind Benjamin's ear wouldn't solve the depression he felt settling around his shoulders like an old, heavy shawl.

Maybe the problem was a lack of sleep, he told himself. He felt as if he needed to be on duty twenty-four hours a day and he'd only been catching catnaps throughout the long nights.

Most of the hours of the night he wandered from window to window, looking outside, wondering if danger lurked anywhere near.

For the moment the investigation was proceeding without him, although he'd kept in close contact with both Tom and Caleb. It was impossible to trace ATVs through motor vehicle records because they were for off-road use. But Sam McCain had come up with a list of people they all knew had the vehicles in town.

Jim Ramsey, another deputy, was checking gun records and collecting the names of everyone who owned a .38 caliber gun. They were still waiting on results from the FBI lab that would hopefully tell them more about what they were dealing with.

The explosion of gunshots and the shatter of glass lifted him from his chair. Edie's scream ripped into his very heart as he raced down the hallway, Tiny barking wildly at his heels.

He ran into the bedroom where Walt had been staying to see the old man on the floor, his upper arm covered with blood and Edie on the floor at his side. The window was shattered into a hundred sparkling shards on the floor.

"Stay down," he yelled. "Margaret, call 9-1-1." He didn't wait for her response but instead raced out the front door, determined to find the shooter.

Edie would do what she could for Walt until the ambulance came, but this might be Benjamin's only chance to catch the person who seemed intent on destroying Edie and Walt.

Thank God he'd still had on his holster. He drew his gun as he left the house. The night was cold and dark and he ran around the side of the house where the shooter would have had a view of Walt's bedroom window.

He tried not to think about Walt and the blood and prayed that the old man wouldn't die before the ambulance could get here.

On this side of the house there were two structures in the distance, a shed and the barn, both perfect cover for a shooter aiming at the bedroom window.

Benjamin stayed low to the ground, grateful for the

cloudy conditions as he raced toward the shed. But before he was halfway there, he heard the sound of an engine, the tinny whine of an ATV.

He flew around the side of the shed and nearly collided with another figure. "Halt!" he yelled, his finger itching to fire his gun.

"Benjamin, it's me," Jacob said. "I heard the gunshots. He had the ATV waiting. He's gone."

Benjamin cursed soundly. "Did you see who it was?"

"No, he was too far away when I spotted him, but he was a heavyset guy."

"I've got to get back inside. He hit Walt." Benjamin was grateful to hear the sound of a siren in the distance.

"I'm going to check around out here," Jacob said as Benjamin nodded and hurried toward the house.

Dammit. Benjamin's heart raced as he went back inside. He found Edie and Walt and Margaret in the hallway. Apparently the two women had managed to drag Walt out of the bedroom.

"He got me right in the shoulder," Walt said as he saw Benjamin. The old man's face was pale as Edie pressed a towel to the wound.

"He's losing a lot of blood." She looked up at Benjamin with wild eyes.

"The ambulance is on its way." Benjamin felt helpless, filled with a rage barely contained as he crouched down next to Walt. "Hang in there, Walt. I still need to beat your ass at chess."

Walt offered him a weak grin. "Don't worry, I'm not planning on going anywhere."

At that moment the ambulance arrived along with Tom and Caleb. Caleb followed the ambulance with Edie and Margaret in tow while Benjamin remained at the house to explain the events to Tom.

He'd just finished when Jacob came in the door. Tom raised an eyebrow at the sight of his reclusive brother. "First time I've seen you out of the cabin," he said.

Jacob shrugged. "Heard the shots and knew Benjamin might be in trouble. The perp parked the ATV behind the barn. He must have walked closer to the house to fire the shots. When I was running up, I saw him heading for the ATV. But before I could get close enough to get a shot or see who it was, he was gone."

"You get a general impression…height…weight?" Tom asked.

"I'm heading to the hospital," Benjamin said before Jacob could reply. "I didn't see anything, I can't help you here," he said with frustration.

Tom nodded. "Go. Jacob and I can take care of things until you get back."

Minutes later in his truck, Benjamin's thoughts weren't on the perp, but rather on Walt and Edie. He'd let them down. He'd promised he'd keep them safe and he'd screwed up. He shouldn't have been sitting in his chair, he should have been walking the floors, checking the windows and keeping vigil.

He shouldn't be a deputy. It wasn't where he belonged. He'd known it for a long time now, but he'd been so afraid of being nothing, he'd held on to the legacy that his older brother had begun. And people had nearly died. At least he prayed they'd gotten Walt help in time.

By the time he reached the hospital he was sick with worry. He went in through the emergency room doors and immediately saw Edie and Margaret sitting side by side.

"What's going on?" he asked.

"They won't let us back there and nobody has told us anything," Edie said. Anguish was thick in her voice.

"The doctor said he'd speak to us as soon as he could," Margaret added. She reached over and patted Edie's knee. "Walt is strong and he's too onery for the devil to want him. He'll be fine." Although she said the words with a lightness in her tone, her dark eyes were filled with worry.

Benjamin shoved his hands in his pockets and leaned against the wall, anger battling with guilt inside him. "I should have done things differently," he said in frustration. "I thought the ranch would be safe. I thought if you were inside the house nothing bad would happen."

"Don't," Edie said. "Don't blame yourself for this."

"I can't help it," he replied. "It would have been different if we'd had enough manpower to station men around the ranch. I should have realized that I wasn't enough to keep you and Walt safe."

At that moment Dr. Drake came out to speak to them. Edie jumped up from her chair and stood next to Benjamin. "He's fine," Dr. Drake began. Edie sagged against Benjamin in obvious relief. "Thankfully the bullet entered and exited the fleshy part of his upper arm. We're going to give him a blood transfusion and keep him here so we can watch the wound for infection."

"I'll see that a guard is put on him during his hospitalization," Benjamin said. One way or another Tom would have to arrange for protection for the old man.

Margaret stood from the chair. "And I'll be staying with him as long as he's here," she said and raised her chin as if to argue with anyone who might protest. "Nobody's going to hurt him while I'm on duty."

"Can I see him?" Edie asked.

Dr. Drake nodded. "Go on back."

Edie started through the door and then turned to Margaret. "He'll want to see you, too."

Margaret offered her a grateful smile and together the two women disappeared behind the door.

Benjamin raked a hand down his face as Dr. Drake offered him a commiserating smile. "Bad night."

"Could have been worse," Benjamin replied. "If that bullet had hit Walt an inch lower, an inch to the left, then I'd be having a conversation with the coroner right now."

The two men turned as the door whooshed open and Tom walked in. "How's Walt?" he asked.

"A lucky man," Benjamin replied. As Dr. Drake said his goodbye and left, Benjamin looked at his older brother. "I've promised a guard here on Walt for as long as he remains in the hospital."

"Done," Tom agreed. "I'll make the arrangements."

Benjamin frowned. "There is something I don't understand. Whoever is behind this has to know that Walt and Edie are no threat to them. Why the attacks on them?"

"Jacob seems to think we're dealing with somebody who's so angry that the body parts have come to light that it's more about revenge than anything else."

"Whoever it is, he's a nasty piece of work," Benjamin replied.

"I've got several of the men checking out the ATVs in the area to see if any are still warm from riding. Walt should be safe here with a guard at the door, but what are we going to do about Edie?" Tom asked. "Maybe it's time she head back to Topeka."

"She doesn't want to go home yet. She's afraid, Tom, afraid that the person will follow her back there. With what's happened tonight, I don't feel comfortable telling her that's an unwarranted fear." Once again Benjamin raked a hand across his jaw. "I think the best thing to do is to check her into the motel for a couple days. I'll stay there with her and make sure she'd safe."

"She'll agree to that?"

Benjamin hesitated a moment and then nodded. "Yeah, she'll agree to it. What I need is for you and the others to solve this thing as soon as possible."

"Jacob is leaning on his contact in the FBI lab so hopefully we'll get some ID results from those body parts sooner rather than later. And by the way, he said to tell you that you should do whatever you need to do and he'll make sure Tiny is taken care of."

Benjamin frowned, thinking of all the logistics. "Maybe we should leave my truck here, make sure we aren't followed, and you can drop Edie and me off at the motel. That way hopefully nobody will know we're there except Brett, and he won't tell anyone if we ask him not to."

"On another note, I think we might have another missing young woman," Tom said.

Benjamin wouldn't have thought his tension level could climb any higher, but this news sent it through the roof. "Who?"

"Suzy Bakersfield. Her boyfriend called a little while ago and said she should have been home from work an hour ago. I've got Dan Walker checking it out."

Suzy Bakersfield was a twenty-four-year-old who worked as a waitress at Harley's, a rough-and-tumble bar at the edge of town. "Let's hope she just decided to go home with somebody else and didn't want her boyfriend to know." Benjamin shoved his hands in his pockets and stared at his brother. "You think these missing women are tied to whatever else is going on?"

Tom's frown deepened and for a moment he looked older than his thirty-six years. "I don't know what in the hell is going on in this town. It's impossible to know if the two are related until we have more information. All I really know is that I have a terrible feeling that things are going to get much worse before they get better."

Benjamin clapped a hand on his brother's shoulder.

"We'll get through this, Tom. Just like we got through Mom and Dad's deaths, just like we got through Brittany's disappearance. We'll get through it because that's what we Grayson men do."

Tom flashed him a grateful smile as Benjamin dropped his hand back to his side. "Let me know when you're ready to take Edie to the motel. In the meantime I'm going to step outside, get on my phone and make some arrangements."

Benjamin watched him go and then sat in one of the chairs to wait for Edie. It could have been her. That bullet could have easily hit her, killed her.

How could he protect her from an unknown assailant? One who was so filled with the need for some twisted revenge that he'd stop at nothing?

Within thirty minutes Sam McCain walked through the door. His coffee-colored face offered Benjamin a smile. "You okay?"

"As okay as I'm going to get."

"Tom tagged me for the first guard duty on Walt."

"Hopefully it will be a quiet, uneventful shift for you."

"There hasn't been a quiet, uneventful moment in the past couple of days," Sam returned.

"You got that right," Benjamin replied.

As Sam left the room to find Walt, Benjamin returned to his chair. His head spun with thoughts. Who the hell was behind all this? More importantly, would he be able to keep Edie safe until the guilty were behind bars?

Chapter 9

Two things struck Edie as she left Walt's room and returned to the waiting room. The first was that she was filled with a sick adrenaline that she didn't know what to do with and the second was that she could feel a queasy guilt wafting from Benjamin.

He rose from his chair as she entered. "Is he all right?" he asked.

She nodded. "He's going to be just fine, and I have a feeling that if he needs anything at all then Margaret will make sure he has it. What happens now?"

"I've made arrangements for Tom to take us to the motel. We can stay there for a couple days without anyone knowing we're there. I'm confident by then we'll have all this figured out." His gaze held hers, as if anticipating an argument. "Or maybe the best thing for you to do is to find another hotel in a different town."

She considered her options. The idea of running away from danger was definitely appealing, but she didn't want to leave Poppy. Besides, she had a terrible fear that no matter where she tried to hide, she'd eventually be found by the madman who was after her.

"I can't go," she finally said. "I don't want to leave Poppy. At least here I know you have my back."

He frowned. "Yeah, a lot of good that did you tonight."

She grabbed his hand in hers. "Don't do that, Benjamin. Don't blame yourself for what happened. There was no way you could have anticipated this happening." She released his hand. "Let's just get to the motel and get some sleep."

The adrenaline that had filled her from the moment the window had exploded and Poppy had fallen to the floor began to ebb a bit.

She knew she should be terrified that there was obviously somebody who was determined to kill her or Poppy or both of them. She also knew that Poppy would be safe here in the hospital. Deputy Sam McCain had assured her that nobody would get into his room unless they were hospital personnel and even then they would all be scrutinized carefully.

It took nearly an hour for them to finally leave the hospital and get checked into the motel. The room was ordinary with two double beds, a small table shoved against the wall and a wardrobe holding a television.

"Brett Hatcher, the man who owns this place, will make sure that nobody knows we're here," Benjamin said once they got inside.

Edie nodded and sat on the bed nearest the door. She was exhausted and yet keyed up at the same time. Even though it was late she knew she wouldn't be able to sleep for some time.

Benjamin moved to the window and pulled the curtains tightly closed and then turned back to look at her. "Normally I'd have you sleep in the bed nearest the window so that I'd be between you and anyone who might come in that door, but with the events of tonight still fresh in my mind I don't want you anywhere near the window."

"I trust your judgment," she said.

"You shouldn't," he replied with a touch of bitterness as he sat on the bed opposite her. "I should have never put you two at the ranch without a dozen guards on the property."

"Benjamin, I know how small this town is, how many men are working for the sheriff's department. There wasn't the manpower to post guards. You can't beat yourself up about this. It certainly hasn't shaken my confidence in you."

She watched as some of the tension in his shoulders eased. "I swear to God, Edie, I'd take a bullet in the chest before I'd let anything happen to you."

The depth of his feelings for her was there on his face, shining from his eyes and tangible in the air. She felt it wrapping around her and for several agonizing seconds she forgot how to breathe, she couldn't catch her breath.

"I know," she finally managed to say and then jumped up off the bed. "I'm going to take a shower before going to sleep." She escaped into the bathroom where she leaned weakly against the wall.

She'd sworn she didn't want or need anyone in her life, but at the moment her need for Benjamin filled her up inside. She wanted him to hold her, to stroke fire into her veins, to kiss her until she was mindless with pleasure.

She wanted to believe that her need arose from the night's events, from the fact that death had come so close, but she knew the truth. This need, this want of him, had been a slow, steady burn that had been building with each and every moment she spent with him.

Turning on the water in the shower, she tried to tamp down her desire for him. Hopefully in a week or so this would all be over and she would be back in Topeka figuring out her life.

Benjamin deserved more than a temporary woman; he deserved more than her. She stepped into the hot, steamy water and welcomed the relaxing spray that slowly unkinked taut muscles.

She just needed to get into bed and go to sleep. She needed to not think about the fact that Benjamin would be in bed only three feet from her.

At least he'd gotten a room with two beds. Sharing the room for a couple days was going to be difficult enough, but if they'd had to share a bed it would have been nearly impossible.

After several minutes she turned off the water, stepped out of the tub and grabbed one of the fluffy white towels that awaited her. She dried off and then ran her fingers through her wet hair to rid it of tangles.

She hated to put on her same clothes, but had no other choice. When she finally got beneath the sheets she'd take off her jeans and sweatshirt and sleep in her bra and panties.

When she left the bathroom she found Benjamin seated where he'd been when she'd left the room, on the edge of his bed. "At the hospital Tom told me that we might have another missing woman," he said.

"Oh, no! Who is it?" She sat on her bed facing him, so close she could smell his scent, that slightly woodsy cologne that had become as familiar as the beat of her own heart.

"Her name is Suzy Bakersfield. She works as a waitress at Harley's, a bar on the edge of town. She was due home from work a couple hours ago and her boyfriend called when she didn't come home."

"Do you think these missing women are related to the other stuff?" she asked.

He blew a deep sigh. "I don't know. I asked Tom the same question, but we just don't know enough at this point. What worries me is that if they aren't related, then we have two separate criminal issues going on here in Black Rock. I figure now isn't the time to talk to my brother about quitting."

Edie looked at him in surprise. "You're really thinking about it? I hope your decision doesn't have anything to do with what happened tonight."

His eyes were dark as he held her gaze. "It's something I've been thinking about for a long time, but I've been afraid."

"Afraid?" She couldn't imagine a man like Benjamin being afraid of anything.

Once again he released a sigh and averted his gaze from hers. Instead he stared at the wall just to the left of her, a frown racing across his forehead. "I've wanted to ranch full-time for a while now, but I've been scared of what people might think, about what might lie beneath my badge."

"I don't understand," she replied.

"The badge gives me respect in this town. People know they can depend on me and they like me. I've been afraid that if I take off the badge, then I'd be nothing. I'd lose the respect of my friends and neighbors."

"Oh, Benjamin, people like and respect you because you're a good man with a good heart. You're warm and friendly and solid and any respect you've earned has nothing to do with your badge," she exclaimed.

He offered her a smile. "You're the reason why I've decided when these cases are finished, then I'm handing in my badge."

"Me?" She looked at him in surprise. "What did I do?"

His eyes took on a new warmth, a sweet depth that was intoxicating. "I know you're afraid and yet you've handled all this with such courage and grace. Fear isn't stopping you from doing whatever it is you feel you need to do. I figure if you can do that, then so can I."

This time it was she who broke eye contact. "You should do whatever it is that makes you happy, Benjamin. Happiness is so fleeting and when it stands in front of you, you should embrace it with all of your being."

She got up from the bed and pulled down the spread. She needed to stop the conversation, needed to distance herself from him. She didn't want him to admire her. She didn't want him to look at her with his soulful eyes that made her want to fall into his arms and somehow believe that happiness might be hers to embrace.

He seemed to sense her need for distance. "I think I'll take a fast shower," he said as he got up from the bed.

"I'm sure I'll be asleep when you get out so I'll just say good-night now," she replied. She turned off the lamp next to the bed, plunging the room into darkness other than the light spilling in from the bathroom.

He hesitated at the doorway of the bathroom, as if he wanted to say something more to her. She refused to look at him again, afraid that somehow, someway, he'd break down her defenses. He finally murmured a good-night and retreated into the bathroom.

She quickly took off her jeans and T-shirt and got into her bed. With the covers pulled up around her neck, she squeezed her eyes tightly closed and tried not to think about the look she'd seen in Benjamin's eyes.

As she lay in the darkness of the room, she recognized

what she felt from him, what she saw whenever he looked at her.

Love. And it made her realize that no other man had ever looked at her in that way, that she'd never truly been loved by a man before.

She'd thought Greg loved her and she'd believed she loved him. But looking back on that relationship, she recognized it had been emotional need that had driven her into his arms and financial need that had driven him into hers.

In all her relationships before, the missing element had been the kind of love she saw shining from Benjamin's eyes whenever he looked at her.

He'd said he wished he'd met her before Greg and she wished the same. Perhaps then her heart would have been opened to taking what he seemed to be offering her, open to giving back to him tenfold.

But it was too late.

He was too late.

Still, a little part of her wondered what it would be like to make love with somebody who truly loved her?

Benjamin stood beneath the spray of the shower until it began to cool. Somewhere in the span of the events of the past couple days he'd made his decision to turn in his badge. He wouldn't do it now, with Tom so overloaded by what was happening, but within the next few months he would follow his heart and become a full-time rancher.

When he thought about spending all his days and

nights at the ranch in all his imaginings, Edie was there at his side.

He could easily see himself walking up the lane from the pasture and her seated on the front porch waiting for him to return. It was easy to imagine the two of them on horseback, her laughter riding the fresh-scented air and her eyes sparkling with that light that made him weak in the knees.

He'd never felt this way about a woman before, suspected he would never feel this depth of love again. She was a burn in his soul, a song in his heart and he knew that no matter what happened between them, she'd transformed him as a man forever.

He stepped out of the shower and quickly dried off, his head still filled with thoughts of Edie. She'd shown him that he was capable of love, of great passion for a woman. He'd begun to believe that it wasn't in his character to feel those emotions. She made him feel more alive than he had in all his years of life.

He didn't bother putting his shirt back on but pulled on his briefs and his jeans and left the bathroom. The room was dark and silent and he thought she must already be asleep.

He shucked his jeans to the floor and placed his gun on the nightstand, then slid in beneath the sheets that smelled faintly of bleach and fabric softener.

He was exhausted but he instinctively knew that sleep was a long time coming. His mind whirled not only with the shooting of Walt, but also the possibility that another woman had gone missing.

Hopefully Suzy Bakersfield had just gone off with a girlfriend and hadn't checked her plans with her boyfriend. That she was alive and well and would have some explaining to do when she eventually returned home.

But he couldn't dismiss the sick feeling that she was just like Brittany, just like Jennifer Hightower, and she'd somehow disappeared into thin air.

As always thoughts of his missing sister caused a deep grief to rip through his heart. The idea of never seeing her smile again, never hearing her babble about men and work and life, left a hole inside him that he knew would never completely be filled.

"Benjamin, are you asleep?" Edie's voice whispered across the darkness of the room.

"No."

"Me, either," she said and released a deep sigh.

"Things on your mind? Do you need to talk?" He rolled over on his side to face her direction.

She was silent for a long moment. "I'm reconsidering this celibacy thing."

Every muscle in his body froze. He was afraid to speak, afraid to hope what her words might mean. He realized she was waiting for some sort of a response from him. "Oh, really?" he finally managed to utter. "What's changed your mind?"

"You."

He heard her change positions and knew that she'd turned to face his direction. "How did I change your mind?" he asked. His breath was painful in his chest as he tried not to anticipate what might happen next.

"I don't know, you just did," she said with a hint of frustration in her voice. "I want you, Benjamin. I want you to make love to me."

Joy leaped into his heart, but it was a joy tempered with caution. "Edie, I don't want a bullet through the window to force you to make a decision you'll regret later." As much as he wanted her, he didn't want to be just another mistake in her life.

"As long as you'd understand that it's a one-shot deal, that there are no promises or strings attached, then I wouldn't regret it."

Funny, most men would have jumped at the chance for sex with no strings, no commitments, but Benjamin had hoped for more, had desperately wanted more from her.

"Benjamin?" Her whisper held both a wealth of longing and more than a hint of self-consciousness.

He'd take what he could get of her, he thought as he threw back the sheet and got up and then grabbed his wallet from the nightstand. He had a condom tucked inside it, compliments of his brother Caleb who insisted the Grayson men were always prepared.

He was surprised to discover his fingers trembling slightly as he pulled the condom out and placed it on the nightstand next to her bed.

He hesitated, wishing there was some illumination in the room so he could see her face. "Edie, are you sure?"

Her hand reached out and touched his, then her fingers twined with his and she tugged him into her bed. As he got beneath the sheets he felt nervous, excited and as if he were about to make love for the very first time.

He pulled her into his embrace and she came willingly, eagerly. She was all heat and soft curves against him as she hid her face in the crook of his neck.

He stroked his hands up the length of her back, unsurprised that her skin was as silky as he'd imagined. He wanted to say words of love, wanted her to know just how much he cared about her, but he knew that would only drive her away.

She needed this not to matter and so he told himself it didn't, that it was just a hookup for mutual sexual pleasure and nothing more.

Still, when he found her lips with his he drank of her, his heart filling with her taste, the clean soapy scent of her and the warmth that raced through his veins.

"I knew you'd feel so good," she said as he left her mouth and rained kisses down the side of her jaw. She released a small moan as he found a sensitive place just below her ear.

"And I knew the same about you," he murmured.

Her arms tightened around him and she stroked her fingers down his back, increasing the flame that threatened to consume him.

His hunger for her wanted to move fast, to rip the panties and bra from her body and take her with hard, fast strokes. He wanted to possess her in a way she'd never been possessed before, in a way that would make her cling to him now and forever.

But his need was tempered with the desire to go slow, to savor each and every moment that he held her in his arms for he knew this moment probably wouldn't happen again.

He captured her mouth again, their tongues swirling together in a deeply intimate kiss. At the same time his hands moved to her bra fastener. He hesitated, waiting to make sure she wouldn't suddenly protest. When she didn't he unfastened the whisper of fabric.

She shrugged it off and tossed it to the end of the bed, then went back into his arms. His heart banged against his chest at the feel of her warm breasts against him.

She fit neatly against him, as if they were made to fit together. She leaned back slightly and stroked a hand down his chest. "So strong," she murmured and pressed her lips against his collarbone.

He wasn't strong, not where she was concerned. He felt weak and vulnerable and needy as he captured her breasts with his hands. "So beautiful," he whispered. "You make me weak, Edie."

"I don't want you weak right now. I want you strong and powerful."

Her words merely increased his raging need of her. He bent his head and took the tip of one of her nipples in his mouth, enjoying the gasp of pleasure that escaped her.

Her nipple hardened and extended in his mouth as she tangled her fingers in his hair and moaned. She pressed her body into his and he knew she had to realize that he was fully aroused.

Rather than warding her off, his erection seemed to intensify her desire. She grabbed his buttocks, her fingers burning through the thin cotton of his briefs.

He ran a hand down the flat of her belly and slid it under the slick silk of her panties. Hot and damp, she arched up to meet his touch.

A sudden impatience snapped through him. He wanted to be naked and he wanted her naked. He tugged at her panties to remove them and she aided him by lifting her hips.

He then took off his own and pulled her back into his arms, reveling in the feel of bare skin against skin.

Again he touched her damp heat and she caught her breath and then moaned his name. His heart expanded with love for her. Wanting to be the best lover she'd ever had, he increased the pressure of his touch, felt the rising tide of sensation inside her.

He ran his lips across her cheek, down the length of her neck and moaned in pleasure as she reached her climax. She shuddered and cried out his name once more as she went limp.

She didn't stay that way for long. As she reached out and encircled his hard length with her hand, it was his turn to gasp in pleasure.

Control it. He was definitely going to lose control if she continued to touch him that way. He slid away from her and reached for the condom on the nightstand, mentally thanking his little brother for insisting that he be prepared for the unexpected.

When he was ready he crouched over her and framed

her face with his hands. He could easily imagine how her eyes looked at the moment, emerald and glowing with fire. He kissed her lips, her cheek and then her forehead as he slowly eased into her.

Engulfed in exquisite pleasure, he whispered her name again and again and began to stroke in and out of her sweet heat. She gripped his buttocks, drawing him in deep with each thrust.

Lost. He was lost in her and he never wanted to be found. But all too quickly he felt the rise of a tidal wave building up inside him, sweeping him toward completion.

When it came, he took her mouth with his in a kiss that held all the emotions he had inside. And when it was over he slumped to the side of her in awe.

Benjamin had enjoyed sex plenty of times in his life, but never with the kind of love he felt for this woman. His Edie.

No, not his. The deal was that this meant nothing to her. Just physical release without any strings. She'd made it clear in a hundred different ways that she had no intention of loving him back.

But that didn't mean he couldn't try to break through her defenses and win her heart. He rolled over and kissed her, then slid out of bed. "I'll be right back," he said and went into the bathroom.

He washed up and then stared at his reflection in the mirror. He'd never seen her coming. He'd had no way to prepare himself for the tremendous emotion Edie evoked inside him. He'd been utterly helpless to stop himself from loving her.

And he was equally helpless to stop her from leaving him. The sad truth was the people you loved didn't always love you back. But he wouldn't stop trying to win her love until she left town. He'd hold her through the nights, keep her safe and as happy as possible during the days and maybe, just maybe, his love would win.

He turned out the light and left the bathroom. "Good night, Benjamin," she said as he stepped back into the room. Any thought he had of holding her through the night vanished as he realized she didn't want him in her bed again.

"Good night," he replied and crawled beneath the covers on his own bed. He smelled of her and he wanted to keep that scent in his head forever. But, he knew that eventually this case would be solved and just like Brittany, she'd be gone from him forever.

"You have to stop crying," Brittany said to Jennifer Hightower. "You're going to make yourself sick."

"What difference does it make," Jennifer cried. "He's going to kill us anyway."

Brittany snaked her fingers through the bars that separated the two women and attempted to stroke her hair. Jennifer had been crying since their captor had brought in Suzy Bakersfield about an hour ago. Suzy was now unconscious on a cot in the third cell of five in what appeared to be an old, converted barn or shedlike structure.

Brittany had lost count of the days she'd been held captive, although she thought Jennifer had been with her for a couple weeks. She knew from experience that Suzy would remain unconscious for the rest of the night and would awaken sometime tomorrow to horror.

Horror had become an intimate companion to Brittany. When she'd initially awakened in the small cell, she'd screamed herself hoarse and had desperately tried to find a way out, but there was none. The structure was sound, with no apparent weaknesses that could be exploited. Each cell had a cot and a toilet and nothing else that could be used as a weapon or for escape.

They were usually fed a small meal once a day by their captor, but several times there had been nothing for two or three days. Each time he came in, Brittany tried her best to identify him, but he always wore a hat and a ski mask that made it impossible. His voice sounded vaguely familiar but no matter how she racked her brain she couldn't place it.

"Jenny, you didn't eat the food he brought. You need to stop crying and eat. We have to keep up our strength so that if an opportunity arises we can escape." Brittany pulled her hand back from Jenny's head and instead gripped the metal bars that separated the two.

"You can't give up hope," Brittany said, even though she struggled with that, as well.

"There is no hope," Jenny sobbed. She raised her head and looked at Brittany, her eyes swollen nearly shut and her skin splotchy from her tears.

"There's always hope," Brittany said fervently. "As long as we're alive, there's hope."

Brittany had to believe that, she had to believe that somehow her brothers would find them before the last two cells were filled with women, for it was then that she knew their captor intended to begin his game—and the game meant death to them all.

Chapter 10

It was impossible to tell what time it was when Edie awakened the next morning. She knew that Benjamin was already awake. She could hear him in the bathroom and apparently he was talking to somebody on his cell phone.

She'd known making love with him was a mistake, albeit a glorious mistake. Her body still tingled with the memory of his every touch, his every kiss, and there was no way to deny that he was in her heart as deeply as anyone ever had been.

She'd made glorious love with him and she now could no longer deny her love for him and yet really nothing had changed. She couldn't magically undo her past and she refused to let down her guard.

Benjamin was a good man who deserved a good

woman. The charm around her neck suddenly felt as if it burned her skin. She reached up and grabbed it in her hand and for a moment allowed the pain to race through her.

The charm wasn't a symbol of her mother's death, but rather the death of her baby, the daughter who had died without drawing a breath.

A medical mystery, the doctor had said with sympathy in his eyes. A tragedy, the nurse had replied as she'd gently wrapped the perfectly formed infant in a pink blanket.

But Edie had known better. It had been her fault. Somehow she'd done something wrong. She'd been so stressed over the bills and Greg's abandonment. She knew in her heart of hearts it was all her fault.

"They'll be other babies," the doctor had said when he'd signed her release papers. "You're young and healthy and I'm sure there are healthy babies in your future."

But he'd been wrong. The day Edie had buried the daughter she'd named Mary, she'd buried any hope she had, any expectation she might entertain for happiness.

Before the grief could completely overwhelm her, she released the charm and drew a deep breath. This was her secret. Oh, the few friends she had in Topeka knew that she'd lost her baby, but after the birth she'd distanced herself from them all, unable to stand the sympathy in their eyes, the platitudes that rolled so easily off their tongues.

She'd just wanted to be alone with her grief, and there was a part of her that still felt that way. She reached over and turned on the lamp on the nightstand, then got out of bed and quickly pulled on the clothes she'd taken off the night before. She felt better prepared to face the day, to face Benjamin, dressed.

When the door to the bathroom opened, she tensed. The last thing she wanted was a morning after, a rehash of the mistake she'd made the night before.

"Oh, good. You're awake," he said as he came into the room. He walked over to the window and opened the heavy outer curtains, leaving the gauzy inner curtains in place. Sunshine poured in but it was impossible to see out or into the room.

"I was just talking to Tom. He called to tell me the lab report came in." He sat on the edge of the bed and smiled at her and in his eyes, in the warmth of that smile, she saw the memories of their lovemaking.

"Did the results tell you anything about the person responsible?"

"First of all, the good news is that nothing was radioactive. In mixing some of the chemicals a reaction occurred that created the fluorescent glow, but nothing was radioactive. The bulk of the chemicals were ones used almost exclusively by taxidermists, so Tom was on his way to the taxidermy shop to speak to Jeff Hudson and his son, Jeffrey Allen."

"You think they're responsible for this?" she asked. She didn't want to look at him, didn't want to remember the feel of his warm lips against hers, the stroke of his hands across her naked body.

"I think it's a good lead," he replied. "Maybe it won't be long before this is all over." He stood. "In the meantime I called Brett and he's going to bring us some coffee and breakfast in a few minutes."

"Room service? I didn't know motels offered that."

He smiled again, the warm, wonderful grin that made her want to run into his arms, or run as far away from him as possible.

"We've used the motel off and on over the years when we've needed to stash somebody away. Brett is very accommodating when that happens."

As if to punctuate his sentence, there was a knock on the door. Instantly tension replaced Benjamin's warm smile as he drew his gun from his shoulder holster and motioned her into the bathroom.

He peered out the window and instantly relaxed. "It's okay. It's Brett."

He unchained and unlocked the door to admit the older man who carried with him a large shopping bag. He nodded at Edie and walked over to the small table. "Got you some coffee and egg muffins and a couple of sweet rolls," he said.

"Thanks, Brett, we appreciate it," Benjamin replied.

"No problem. Just call the office when you need something else and I'll be happy to do food runs for you." With another nod to Edie he left the room.

Benjamin locked the door behind him as Edie began

to unload the food. Maybe she'd feel better after a cup of coffee. A caffeine rush would surely banish her desire to be back in Benjamin's arms.

They sat at the small table and ate, talking little until the food was gone and they were left with the last of their coffee.

"The good news for the town is that the wooded area where the body parts were found wasn't contaminated and won't require an expensive cleanup," he said. "Something like that could bankrupt a small town like Black Rock."

"That is good news for you," she replied.

"And we'll have good news for you soon," he said softly. "This is going to be over and the person who attacked you will be behind bars."

"From your lips to God's ears." She took a sip of coffee and broke off eye contact with him. It was there again in his eyes, a soft vulnerability, a sweet longing that scared her.

"Edie." The longing she'd seen in his eyes was now in his voice.

She closed her eyes, refusing to look at him. "Benjamin, don't." She was afraid of what he was about to say, didn't want to hear whatever he thought might be in his heart.

"I have to," he said, obviously knowing exactly what she meant. "My lack of real passion used to worry me. I've watched two of my brothers fall in love. I saw the passion in their eyes, heard it in their voices whenever they saw or talked about their women. I thought something was missing inside me. I'd never felt that for any woman I'd dated, until now. Until you."

There it was, out on the table, the one thing she didn't want to hear from him, the last thing she'd wanted to hear. She forced herself to look at him and the emotion in his eyes was raw and open for her to see.

"I love you, Edie. I love you passionately, desperately and I want you to stay here in Black Rock with me. I want you in my life today and forever."

It was exactly what she'd feared. She was going to be his first heartbreak and she hated it; she hated herself for not being the woman he needed in his life.

"Benjamin, you're just feeling that way because of last night," she said. "I'll admit, the sex was great. We obviously have a physical chemistry, but I've told you all along, I'm not looking for a relationship."

"Sometimes when you aren't looking for love it finds you anyway," he countered. He reached across the table for her hand, but she pulled away, not wanting his touch, which would simply make things more difficult. "Edie, I'm a simple man, but I believe you love me. I see it when you look at me, I tasted it in your kisses last night. I've had sex with women before, but last night we made love, both of us together."

She desperately sought the words to deny her own feelings for him, but they refused to rise to her lips. Once again she looked down at the top of the table, finding it impossible to look into his eyes without drowning in his feelings for her.

"It doesn't matter. Don't you see?" She got up from

the table and stepped away from him. "It doesn't matter what you feel, and it doesn't matter what I feel. I'm still going back to Topeka and living my life alone."

A sudden grief clawed up her throat, burned in her eyes, the grief of knowing she was turning her back on love and the darker, deeper grief of overwhelming loss.

She gripped the back of the chair, her knuckles white as she fought for control. But the fight was in vain. Tears began to run down her cheeks as an agonizing pain ripped through her. "Please, Benjamin, leave it alone," she managed to gasp. "I'm not the kind of woman you want. You deserve better than me."

She looked around wildly, needing to escape not only from him, but also from her own dark thoughts, from the incredible pain that threatened to shatter her into pieces.

He got up from his chair and took her by the shoulders, forcing her to look up at him. "What are you talking about, Edie? You are the woman I want and we both deserve to be happy together. I'll ranch full-time and you can do whatever makes you happy as long as each morning I wake up to see your face and each night I fall asleep with the sound of your breathing next to me."

He moved his hand to her cheek and softly stroked there. "We'll build a life together. We'll laugh and we'll love. Each night when the weather is nice, we'll sit on the front porch and watch the horses play as the sun sets. It will be a wonderful life, Edie, if only you'll share it with me."

It was magical picture he painted with his words, one she wanted to step into and embrace and she felt her resolve fading, her defenses crumbling.

"Come on, Edie. You know you love me. Let's raise cattle and children together."

Of all the things he might have said, this was the one thing that exploded apart the picture of happily-ever-after, and her weeping began in earnest.

She didn't want to tell him. She'd never wanted to tell anyone. But she was certain it was the one thing that would turn him away in revulsion, the one thing that would change his mind about loving her.

And ultimately that would make it so much easier on her. If he'd just stop loving her. Then perhaps she wouldn't want him as desperately, as frantically as she did.

"Talk to me, Edie. Why are you crying?" He used his thumbs to wipe at the tears on her cheeks.

She wasn't sure what she was crying for, if it was because she had every intention of walking away from this wonderful man or if she cried for the child who had never been, the sweet baby daughter she'd lost.

He attempted to pull her into his arms, but she whirled away from him, wild with her grief. She headed for the bathroom, needing the privacy, but before she went inside she turned back to face him.

"You don't know me, Benjamin. You don't know what I've done."

"Then tell me. I know nothing you can say will

change the way I feel about you. Nothing that you have done will make me not love you."

He was like a shimmering mirage in the veil of her tears, a mirage that looked like love but she knew if she let him close enough it would disappear.

"I killed my baby, Benjamin. That's what I did." She watched his eyes widen and saw the shock that swept over his features just before she escaped into the bathroom and locked the door.

Benjamin felt as if he'd been sucker punched in the gut. Of all the things he'd anticipated she might have said, there was no way he could have anticipated this.

The one thing he knew was that there was no way Edie could intentionally harm anyone, especially her own baby. He stared at the closed bathroom door, the sound of her weeping drifting through the door.

She'd hit him like a speeding, out-of-control driver and then had left before checking for damage or explaining why she'd been reckless in the first place.

After everything they'd been through he deserved more from her. He knocked on the bathroom door. "Edie," he said, steeling his heart against the sound of her crying. He tried the doorknob, unsurprised to find it locked. "Edie, come out here and talk to me. I haven't asked you for much, but you owe me an explanation."

Her sobs were gut-wrenching. He heard her gasping for air, hiccupping as they began to subside. He remained standing outside the door until there was finally silence on the other side.

"Edie, please talk to me," he finally said. He stepped back as the doorknob turned and the door opened. The ravages of pain were on her splotchy face, in her red-rimmed eyes, and he wanted nothing more than to take her into his arms.

She didn't meet his gaze as she moved past him and sat on the edge of his bed. She stared down at the carpet beneath her feet, her shoulders slumped forward in utter defeat.

"I was almost seven months pregnant when Greg abandoned me." Her voice was flat, as if she'd forgotten all her emotions in the bathroom. "I was reeling with the financial mess he'd left me, still grieving for my mother and wondering how I was going to deal with being a single parent."

He wanted to sit next to her, wanted to pull her into his arms and tell her everything was going to be okay, but he sensed her need to do this alone, to tell her story without the comfort he might offer her.

"For the first couple weeks after he left and the creditors were calling me, I did nothing but cry." She laced her fingers together in her lap, the white knuckles letting him know how difficult it was for her to talk.

"I finally quit crying and decided I was going to be just fine. I'd be a terrific mother and I was strong enough to do it all alone." She raised her head to look at him and in her eyes he saw a woman's grief, a mother's despair.

"Everything seemed normal. I went into labor a week before my due day and got to the hospital. Halfway through the delivery I knew something was wrong. The atmosphere in the room changed and nobody was smiling or joking anymore. Eventually she arrived, a beautiful baby girl who was stillborn."

He could no longer stay away from her. He sat next to her but when he attempted to pull her into his embrace, she jerked away.

"Edie, I'm so sorry for you. I'm so sorry for your loss." His heart ached for her and he wished there was some way he could take away her pain, banish the haunting that darkened her eyes. "What did the doctor say?"

She released a bitter laugh. "That these things happen, that it was a tragic medical mystery that sometimes occurs."

"Edie, you didn't do anything wrong. Sometimes bad things happen for no reason, but that doesn't mean you should blame yourself, that you should punish yourself for the rest of your life."

She jumped up from the bed, her entire body trembling. "But I did do something wrong. In those two weeks that I was so broken, there was a night I thought for just a minute that everything would be so much easier if I wasn't pregnant. I was big and fat and uncomfortable. Don't you see, Benjamin, I wished the baby away and she was gone."

He got up off the bed and pulled her against his chest. She fought him, trying to get away, but he held tight until she collapsed against him as she cried uncontrollably.

He now understood the shadows he'd sometimes

seen in her eyes and the significance of the charm she wore around her neck. What he didn't know was how to take away the misplaced guilt she felt, how to make her understand that to deny herself happiness for the rest of her life wasn't the answer. He simply held her tight, waiting for her storm of tears to pass.

Eventually she stopped crying and simply remained exhausted in his arms. He led her back to the bed and together they sat, his arm still around her shoulder.

For several long minutes neither of them spoke. Her heartbreak hung thick and palpable in the air. He stroked her shoulder although he knew she was beyond the place where physical connection might comfort her.

He drew a deep breath. "The day before Brittany disappeared I had a fight with her. As usual she was late to work and I'd had to cover some of her shift. I was ticked and I told her that there were times my life sure would be less complicated if she'd just get out of it for a while."

He paused to draw another breath, emotion thick in the back of his throat.

Edie was as still as a statue against his side. "What did she say?" she finally asked.

"She laughed and patted my cheek and told me not to be such a grumpy bear. It was the last time I talked to her. Am I to believe that in that moment of anger I somehow made her disappear for good?"

"Of course not."

"Then why would you believe that a moment's

thought had the power to make sure your baby didn't live?"

She didn't answer. Her head remained bowed and her body felt boneless against him and he knew that he hadn't broken through to her.

"Edie, don't throw your life away because of a tragedy. You deserve to be happy, and if it's not with me, then open up your heart to somebody else."

She finally raised her head to look at him and in her eyes he saw the strength of her defenses back in place. She moved away from him and stood, her back rigid and her mouth pressed together in a grim line.

"I'm not strong like you, Benjamin. I can't forget what happened, what I lost." She reached up and touched the charm that hung around her neck.

"I don't expect you to forget," he countered. "Your daughter was a part of you, a part of your heart for nine months. You don't forget those you love and lose. You remember them and sometimes you ache for them, but life goes on and the only way to truly honor their memory is to be happy."

A panic welled up inside him as her walls climbed higher. He was going to lose her before he'd ever really had her. "Edie, for God's sake, let me in. Let me show you happiness and love."

For just a brief moment her eyes shimmered with the love he knew was deep in her heart for him. Hope filled him, but was quickly dashed as she shook her head and the emotion in her eyes vanished.

"I'm sorry, Benjamin, but when this is all over I'm

going back to Topeka. I don't need love in my life. I don't want it. I just want to live the rest of my life alone, without risk."

Once again she headed for the bathroom and disappeared inside. And this time Benjamin didn't go after her.

There was nothing more he could say, nothing more he could do, and for the first time in his life, Benjamin knew the pain of heartbreak.

Chapter 11

Edie would have liked to hide out in the bathroom forever. At least in here she didn't have to look at Benjamin, didn't have to see the love light in his eyes.

It hurt. Her love for him ached in her chest. She'd never wanted anything more in her life than a future with him, a chance to grow old with him at her side.

But she was afraid to love again, afraid to seek happiness. She couldn't forgive herself and she didn't trust that his love wasn't just some illusion to torment her.

She took a shower and lingered after dressing. She didn't want to go back inside the room and see the pain she'd inflicted on him.

She'd never wanted to break his heart. He was such a good man, as solid as the day was long and with a tenderness that was a gift to anyone who knew him.

For a moment if she closed her eyes and let herself go, she could see a future with him, she could hear the days of laughter, feel the love that would fill her world.

The moment was shattered by his knock on the door. "Edie, Tom just called. It's over. Jeffrey Allen confessed to everything."

She sagged against the door. Over. It was all over. Now there was nothing to keep her from going back to her lonely life. She straightened and opened the door. "Good, let's get the hell out of here so I can go home."

"Tom and Caleb are on their way to bring me my truck," he replied. "They should be out front in a few minutes."

"If you don't mind, I'd like to stop by the hospital on the way to the ranch. I need to tell Poppy and Margaret goodbye before I leave."

"You're leaving today?" He looked at her in surprise.

She nodded. "As soon as I get my things at your place I'll be on the road."

"That breakfast we had earlier left me hungry. Come to the café with me and eat a good lunch before you take off. I'll tell you everything Tom told me when he called."

"Only on one condition," she said. "That you don't try to talk me into staying."

The smile he gave her was a weary one with a touch of disillusionment. "I gave it my best shot, Edie. The ball is in your court. I won't try to talk you into anything."

An hour later they were seated at a table in the café.

She'd said her painful goodbyes to Poppy and Margaret and in her mind she was halfway out of town already. She'd only agreed to this meal because she had a long drive ahead of her and had to eat something before taking off. Besides, she was curious about the crime that had kept her in town, the man who had beaten Poppy and terrorized her.

"According to what Tom told me, Jeffrey decided to dabble in a little chemistry and see if he could come up with a way to better preserve flesh," Benjamin said after they'd placed their orders with the waitress.

"Apparently he was hoping to come up with some kind of cream that would work on human flesh, a beauty product that would take the world by storm."

"And so he stole body parts from the cemetery?" she asked.

Benjamin nodded. "That's what he confessed to. From what Tom said, Jeffrey believed that somehow he'd created a radioactive reaction in his experiments, hence the hazmat suit to dispose of the botched batch."

"So, why did he go after me and Poppy? He had to know that we couldn't identify him."

"Interestingly enough, Tom said those two things were what he was most reluctant to admit to. When he did, it was just like we suspected, sheer anger that drove him to attack the two of you. If he'd been successful in his experiments he would have eventually become a very wealthy man. Beauty is a big business these days and he thought he was going to discover a fountain of youth, something that would keep skin from aging."

Edie fought back a shiver as she remembered hiding in the closet while Jeffrey had banged on the door and threatened her.

"You okay?" he asked as if he sensed the fear that suddenly crawled up her back.

"I'm fine, just glad this is all over and I can go back home without looking over my shoulder."

At that moment their orders arrived. Their meal was interrupted several times by people stopping by their table to ask about Walt or talk about Jeffrey's arrest.

Benjamin introduced her to Larry Norwood, the town vet, and to Hugh Randolf, who owned the feed store. She met Karen Patterson, who worked at the bank, and Lisa Rogers, who was a beautician.

Each and every person greeted her with open friendliness and sent home the fact that if she'd chosen differently, Black Rock would have been a wonderful place to call home.

They were just leaving the café when at the door they met a big guy in overalls and a red flannel shirt. Benjamin introduced him as Josh Willoughby, the groundskeeper at the cemetery.

"Hope you're planning on staying in town," he said to Edie. "I know Walt would love having you around."

"Actually, I'm on my way out of town in just a little while," Edie replied. "This was just a visit gone crazy."

Josh smiled. "Seems to me the only one who went crazy is Jeffrey." He looked at Benjamin. "I guess we've solved the mystery of the lights I thought I saw once in a while at the cemetery. Must have been Jeffrey skulking around the newest graves."

"Must have been," Benjamin agreed. "At least this particular issue has been solved."

"Yeah, now all you have to do is figure out what happened to those missing girls," Josh replied.

Edie felt the weight of concern in Benjamin as he released a deep sigh. "Yeah, we definitely need a break where the disappearances are concerned."

Goodbyes were said and then Edie and Benjamin got back into his truck and headed for the ranch. They were both silent for part of the ride. It wasn't a comfortable silence but rather one filled with tension.

Telling him goodbye was going to rip out her heart, but she was determined not to change her course, not to alter her future.

"So, what are your plans when you get back to Topeka?" he finally asked, breaking the miserable silence.

"Find a job, find a new place to live," she replied. "Those are my two immediate concerns."

"You'll let somebody here know where you move? We might need you to come back when this goes to trial."

"You have my cell phone number. That won't change, so you can get hold of me if you need to." As the entrance to the ranch came into view she steeled her heart against a sense of homecoming.

It felt like home. It looked like home, but she reminded herself it was just an illusion. Her grandmother had always cautioned her to love smart, but she'd already made the choice not to love at all. And that was the smartest choice of all.

When they got inside she went to the bedroom where she'd stayed and began to pack her bags while Benjamin headed for the kitchen. She was grateful he didn't hover near her as she placed the few articles of clothing she'd brought back into her suitcase.

She took a clean pair of jeans and a long-sleeve emerald blouse into the bathroom and quickly changed, grateful for the clean clothes after being stuck in the others for two days.

When she left the bathroom she nearly bumped into Benjamin. "I just wanted to let you know that I called Jacob and asked him to bring Tiny back. I thought you might want to say goodbye to the mutt."

A new ball of emotion swelled up in her chest at thoughts of the little dog. She nodded and walked back into the bedroom. She grabbed her suitcase but Benjamin took it from her and together they went to the living room.

At that moment Jacob came in the door, Tiny in his arms. The dog vibrated with excitement at the sight of Edie and Benjamin. As Jacob placed Tiny on the floor he ran first to Benjamin and then to Edie.

She scooped him up in her arms and hugged him as he licked the side of her neck. She smiled at Jacob, noting that the man looked rough with a whisker-darkened jaw and the darkest eyes she'd ever seen. "Thanks for bringing him here for a goodbye."

He nodded and then turned and left the house as Edie placed the dog back on the floor.

"You'll have to excuse my brother. He's not the most social creature on earth," Benjamin said.

"That's okay. Well, I guess it's time for me to get on the road." She didn't quite meet his gaze.

"Edie, if you ever need anything, if you change your mind about me…about us, I'll be here." The yearning in his voice nearly broke her.

She picked up her suitcase and overnight bag and clung tight to the handles so that she wouldn't be tempted to throw her arms around his neck and cling tightly to him. "*Thank you* seems so inadequate for what you've done for me and Poppy, but I'm so grateful, if this had to happen to us, that it happened here with you."

She looked at him then, memorizing his beautiful brown eyes, the strong, handsome features that were permanently etched in her mind. Years from now on cold lonely nights she would remember him and the expression on his face and would be comforted by the knowledge that she'd once been loved.

Together they left the house and he stood next to her car as she stowed her suitcase in the trunk. She dug her keys out of her purse, opened the driver's door and then turned back to look at him.

"Well, I guess this is goodbye." She refused to cry in front of him even though tears began to well up inside her. "I hope you do take up ranching full-time, Benjamin. You come alive when you talk about it."

He nodded, his eyes filled with a sadness it would

take her a long time to forget. "And I hope you find peace, Edie. I hope you find forgiveness for yourself, even though you did nothing to be forgiven for. Be safe, Edie, and try to find some happiness for yourself."

He stepped away from the car and she slid in behind the steering wheel and closed the door. As she started the engine, she swallowed hard against the tears that seemed determined to fall.

Refusing to look in her rearview mirror as she pulled away, she kept her focus on the road ahead. Still, by the time she reached the entrance, her vision was blurred with the tears she could no longer contain.

She believed she was doing the right thing and yet there was a tiny voice deep inside her screaming that she was making the biggest mistake of her life.

"Shut up," she muttered to the voice. Still the tears continued and she angrily swiped at them with one hand. There was nothing to cry about. This was her decision, the right decision.

If you never looked for happiness, then you were never disappointed. If you never sought love, then your heart would always remain intact. It was the safest way to live, wrapped in a cocoon of isolation.

By the time she reached the narrow stretch of highway that would lead out of town, her tears had stopped and she kept her mind focused on all the things she needed to take care of once she got back to Topeka.

She was the only car on the road so it was easy to let her mind wander. She might try the apartments down the street from her current address. She was going to miss that smile of his. She tightened her hands on the steering wheel and consciously forced thoughts of Benjamin out of her head.

She hadn't driven very far when she saw a truck approaching fast behind her. As he got on her tail he honked and then shot into the left lane to pass her.

When he got up next to her she recognized him as the man she'd met earlier at the café. Josh something, the cemetery man. He pointed at the back of her car and gestured wildly as if something was wrong.

Terrific, just what she needed…car trouble that might keep her here for another day or two. She pulled over to the side of the road and Josh pulled in behind her.

He got out of his truck as she got out of the car. "Your back tire is going flat," he said.

"Terrific, and I don't have a spare," she exclaimed. She walked toward the rear of the car and bent down to look at the tire he'd indicated. She frowned. The tire looked fine to her.

Before she could straighten up, something slammed into the top of her head. She sprawled forward to the ground, as pinpoints of light exploded in a growing darkness. Her last conscious thought was that they'd all been wrong.

It wasn't over.

Benjamin wandered the house like a lost man, Tiny at his heels. He'd been alone for most of his adult life but he'd never felt such loneliness.

He'd told Tom he was going to take off the next couple days. With Jeffrey Allen behind bars and that particular crime solved, there were plenty of deputies who could work on the disappearance of the women. He wasn't really needed.

She didn't need you. She didn't love you enough. The words whispered through his brain, bringing with them an ache he'd never felt before.

He'd held out hope until the moment her car had disappeared from his view and it was only then that the last of his hope had died.

He thought about heading to the cabin and talking to Jacob, but realized he wasn't in the mood to talk to anyone, especially Jacob, who seemed to hate life as much as he hated himself at the moment.

There was plenty of work around the ranch that he could do and maybe that was exactly what he needed— physical labor to keep his mind away from thoughts of Edie.

He wanted to make himself so exhausted that when he closed his eyes to sleep that night he wouldn't think of her warm laughter, wouldn't smell her enticing scent and wouldn't remember how she felt in his arms.

As he left the house and headed for the barn, his thoughts turned to his sister. He would always have a little bit of guilt inside him about the last conversation he'd had with Brittany, but he knew it wasn't his fault that she'd gone missing.

Just like it wasn't Edie's fault that her baby had been stillborn. He couldn't imagine the anguish of a woman who had carried and loved her baby for nine months, gone through the agony of childbirth and then ended up with nothing.

An experience like that could definitely scar a heart, but it wasn't supposed to destroy a heart. He shook his head as he opened the barn door. Edie had allowed the tragedy and her misplaced sense of guilt to define her, and there was nothing he could do to change that.

Always before he'd found peace and comfort in the barn where the air smelled like leather and hay and horse, but this time there was no peace, no solace to be found. The only scent he wanted to smell was the sweet fragrance of Edie and she was gone from him.

He pulled out his saddle, deciding to oil the leather. He didn't know how long he'd been working when his cell phone rang. He fumbled it out of his shirt pocket and answered.

"Benjamin, we've got a problem." Caleb's voice nearly vibrated with tension. "Is Edie with you?"

Tension filled him. "No, she left here about an hour ago. She was headed back to Topeka. Why?"

"Her car is out on the highway, but she's not around."

Benjamin's heart crashed to his feet. "I'll be right there." He clicked off and then hurried for the house and his keys.

He was on the road in minutes, telling himself to calm down, that there had to be a logical explanation. She had car trouble or she ran out of gas and took off walking back to town, he thought.

But she had your phone number. Why wouldn't she have called for help? Surely she would have put all personal issues aside if she'd needed help.

By the time he pulled to the curb behind her car, he was half-wild with suppositions. Both Tom and Caleb were there, their cars parked in front of Edie's vehicle.

"There's no damage to the car," Caleb said. "And the keys are in it. I started it up and the engine purred like a kitten, and the gas tank is full."

His words shattered Benjamin's hopeful speculations. His panic must have shown on his features. "There's no blood inside, no signs of a struggle," Tom said.

"There weren't any signs of a struggle in Brittany's or Jennifer's car," he said. Was it possible she'd become the latest victim to a madman who was collecting the young women of the town? "We have to find her," he said with an urgency that made him feel half-sick. He'd lost her because she didn't love him, but he couldn't imagine losing her to this kind of fate.

For the next two hours the three officials walked the area, seeking some clue that might lead to her whereabouts. Tom had people checking in town to see if anyone had seen her. During that time Benjamin's mind raced as his heart grew heavier and heavier.

What were the odds that they'd keep her safe from one madman only to have her fall prey to another? It looked as if she'd pulled the car over on her own. What or who would make her stop?

Was it possible this wasn't another disappearance,

but rather tied to the case they'd thought was closed? But Jeffrey had confessed to everything, he reminded himself.

Dammit, he'd thought she was safe, that the danger was over. He looked at Tom, who hung up his phone and shook his head. "Nobody has seen her in town."

"I want to talk to Jeffrey," Benjamin said.

Tom looked at him in surprise. "Why? He's locked up and couldn't have anything to do with this."

Benjamin frowned thoughtfully. "I know that, but I've known Jeffrey all my life and I've never seen him lose his temper, never seen him hurt a fly." His head was a jumble of thoughts, ones he should have entertained the minute Tom had told him Jeffrey had confessed.

"The beating Walt took was vicious and Edie said the man who tried to get at her in the house was filled with rage. That just doesn't sound like Jeffrey. Besides, you said he readily confessed to the experiments and illegal dumping of the body parts yet was reluctant to confess to hurting Walt and attacking Edie."

Tom raised a dark eyebrow. "Are you thinking about a partner?"

Benjamin nodded. "Maybe somebody he's trying to protect or somebody who scares him more than time in jail."

"Let's go have a talk with him," Tom replied.

As Benjamin got into his truck to drive back to town, he prayed they'd find some answers that would lead back to Edie. He prayed that it already wasn't too late for her. He prayed that she wouldn't become another missing woman, that she wouldn't just seemingly disappear off the face of the earth and he would never know what happened to her.

Chapter 12

Edie regained consciousness in pieces of confusion. She moaned as a sharp pain raged in the back of her head and then realized moaning was all she could do because her mouth was taped closed.

Panic pumped her heart in a frantic rhythm as her eyes snapped open. Her ankles were tied, as were her hands behind her back. She sat on the dirt floor of a small shed and for several agonizing seconds she couldn't remember how she'd gotten there.

Then she remembered being in the car and heading out of town when Josh the cemetery man had caused her to stop. But why had he done this? What did he want with her?

She struggled in an attempt to free her hands, but

they were bound tight and her efforts only made the ties tighter and cut off her circulation.

How long had she been unconscious? Minutes? Hours? Did anyone know she was in trouble? Was anyone even looking for her?

Benjamin. Her heart cried his name. Had Josh taken the other women, as well? Would she become just another woman in the town of Black Rock who had disappeared without a trace?

Tears welled up in her eyes, but she shoved them back, afraid that if she began to cry she'd choke. If her nose stuffed up she would suffocate. She would have laughed out loud at this thought if it were possible. Which would she prefer, suffocation by tears or death at the hands of a crazy creep?

She couldn't wait for help to come. It might never come. She needed to do something to help herself. Wildly she looked around the dim, dusty shed. There were picks and shovels leaning in the corner, but nothing that appeared sharp enough to cut the ropes that held her.

There was a machine standing nearby, bigger than a lawnmower and with a small bucket on the front. Her blood went icy cold as she realized it was probably used to dig graves.

Was that what had happened to those other women? Were their bodies under the ground, hiding in a secret grave that Josh had dug on the cemetery property?

A new panic seared through her. Maybe she could use the blade of one of the shovels to free herself, she thought. At least she could try. She attempted to scoot across the floor but instantly discovered that her hands were not only tied together behind her back but were also anchored to something that held her in place.

Frustration added to her fear as she realized there was no way she could do anything to get out of this mess. She was at the mercy of Josh and fate.

She froze, her heart nearly stopping in her chest as she heard somebody approaching. *Please, please let it be somebody here to rescue me,* she thought. *Please, let it be Benjamin or one of his lawmen brothers who walks through that door.*

The door creaked open and her heart fell as Josh walked in. She raised her chin and gave him her best stare of defiance. He laughed, an ugly sound that twisted in her guts.

"You can glare at me all you want," he said as he leaned against the door and eyed her in amusement. "But the way I see it, I've got the upper hand here and you should be begging me for your life. Not that it would do any good."

His pleasant expression morphed into one of rage as he took a step closer to her. "You stupid bitch, you and that old man of yours ruined everything!"

He began to pace just in front of her. "Jeffrey Allen was on the verge of producing a product that would have set the cosmetic industry on its ears. I was supplying Jeffrey with body parts and he'd agreed to pay me half of whatever he made."

He stopped in front of her, his eyes wild with hatred.

"You know how much they pay me for my work here in the cemetery? Next to nothing. I got to work another job just to put food on the table. I was going to be rich but you and Walt had to stick your nose into things."

He leaned down so close to her that if her mouth hadn't been bound she would have bitten his nose off. In his eyes she saw not only a deep-seated rage but also a hint of insanity.

"You screwed up my plans." His breath was sick, fetid in her face. "And the price for that is death." He straightened and walked back to the door. "After dark tonight I'm going to do a little work in the cemetery. That gives you several hours to think about what it's going to be like to be buried alive."

Horror washed over her, making her slump back against the wall as he left the shed. She wondered what time it was, how many hours she had left before darkness fell.

Her head pounded with intensity and the taste of terror filled her mouth. She should have never stopped the car. But she'd had a false sense of safety and hadn't sensed danger.

Closing her eyes, she realized what she'd heard was true. When facing death your life flashed before your eyes. She thought of those starlit nights with her grandmother and sweet loving moments with her mother.

She regretted all the time lost with her Poppy and hoped that he and Margaret would form a lasting connection that would keep them both company until their deaths.

And she thought about Mary, the daughter she'd lost, the daughter she'd loved. She'd loved her baby and had wanted her no matter how difficult it would be as a single parent.

She'd planned for Mary, had stroked her own fat belly and sung to the baby. She'd never wished Mary away. She'd been beating herself up for something that hadn't been her fault.

In this moment of facing her own death, she realized Benjamin was right. Mary's death was a tragedy, just like Benjamin's sister's disappearance. Both had been tragedies without answers, without blame.

Tears formed in her eyes once again as she realized she'd had happiness right there in her hand. All she'd had to do was reach out and grasp it, grasp him.

Benjamin. Her heart cried out his name. She'd been a fool to let fear keep her from immersing herself in his love, for not wallowing in her own love for him. And now it was too late.

Fate had given her a chance to be with a man who loved her to distraction, a man who made her happier than anyone else on the face of the earth. It had given her the possibility of other babies and beautiful sunsets and a man who would love and support her. And she'd walked away. She'd loved smart and acted stupid and now it was too late to change things.

She looked at the cracks around the door where faint

daylight appeared. How many hours until nightfall? How many hours left before she found herself in the horror of a grave?

Jeffrey Allen Hudson looked like a broken man when Tom led him into the small interrogation room. His shoulders slumped and his broad face was pale, as if some terminal disease was eating him from the inside out.

Tom placed him into a chair at the table and gestured Benjamin toward the chair opposite Jeffrey. Benjamin didn't sit.

"I don't know what you want from me," Jeffrey said. "I've already confessed to everything." He stared down at the tabletop, refusing to look at either man.

"Jeffrey, tell me about the attack on Walt Tolliver's granddaughter." Benjamin placed his hands on the table and leaned forward.

"I already told Tom I did it, so what else is there to say?" He still didn't look up. "Why don't you just leave me alone? I'll face whatever punishment I have to, but I don't have anything else to say."

"If you cooperate with us, maybe I'll put in a good word with the prosecutor," Tom said.

Jeffrey drew a deep breath and finally looked up. His eyes were filled with torment. "What do you want from me?" he asked wearily.

Benjamin ran everything over in his mind as he tamped down the urgency that screamed inside him. "I just need to know one thing. When you stabbed Edie in the leg, did you use a paring knife from Walt's kitchen or was it a pocketknife?" He ignored Tom's look of surprise.

There was no denying the look of confusion that crossed Jeffrey's features. It was there only a moment and then gone as he focused again on the top of the table. "A pocketknife," he mumbled.

Benjamin slammed his hands down on the table. Jeffrey jumped and scooted his chair back an inch. "You're lying, Jeffrey. Who are you protecting? A friend? Your father?"

"No! My dad has nothing to do with this." Jeffrey grabbed the sides of his head with his hands.

"Jeffrey, Edie is missing. Her car was found on the side of the highway and we think she's in trouble. If you know anything, you need to tell us. Jeffrey, you don't want to be a part of her getting hurt or worse." Benjamin wanted to rip Jeffrey from his seat and shake him until the truth rattled out of his teeth.

Tears formed in Jeffrey's eyes. "He told me that he'd kill my dad if I said anything." The words were a mere whisper. "He's crazy, you know. I didn't realize it until we were both in too deep. I promised him half of what I made. He thought he was going to be rich and he was so angry when it all fell apart."

"Who, Jeffrey. Tell me who," Benjamin exclaimed, his anxiety through the ceiling. But before Jeffrey could reply the answer came to Benjamin.

"It's Josh Willoughby, isn't it?" he asked.

Panic swept across Jeffrey's face and Benjamin knew

he had his answer. He looked at his brother. "You'd better send somebody with me to Josh's place, because if I find out he's harmed Edie I'm going to kill him."

He didn't wait for an answer but instead strode out of the room and out of the station. He was on the road to Josh's house when he saw Caleb's patrol car following him.

He'd meant what he'd said. If Josh had hurt Edie... or worse, Benjamin wouldn't blink twice as he beat the life out of the man.

Josh Willoughby. They all should have realized he had something to do with this. He was in charge of the burials at the cemetery. It would have been easy for him to provide Jeffrey with the body parts before the caskets were covered with dirt.

From the moment Benjamin had heard that Jeffrey had confessed, he'd found it hard to believe that he was responsible for beating Walt and attacking Edie. It was completely out of character.

It wasn't out of character for Josh. Josh was known to have a temper and he also owned an old ATV. It made sense that Jeffrey was involved on the science end of the experiments and Josh was the one who did the dirty work.

The day was slipping away, the sun sinking low in the western sky. It would be dark soon and the thought of Edie someplace out there in the dark and in danger was almost too much for him to bear.

You're probably too late, a little voice whispered in the back of his head. He tightened his grip on the steering wheel and tried to ignore the voice. He couldn't be too late for her. He couldn't be.

He'd already lost Brittany. He couldn't lose Edie. It didn't matter that she didn't want to spend her life with him. It was just important that she have a life to live.

The cemetery came into view and just after it was Josh's small house. Josh's truck was parked out front, letting Benjamin know the man was home.

Benjamin parked in front and raced to the door where he pounded with his fist. Caleb parked just behind him and hurried to join his brother.

Josh's wife, Marylou, answered the door. She was a small, mousy woman who didn't socialize and was rarely seen in town. She eyed Benjamin and Caleb with more than a bit of trepidation. "Yes?"

"We need to talk to Josh," Benjamin said.

She didn't look surprised, just weary. "He's out back."

Benjamin leaped off the porch and headed around the side of the house, his heart beating so fast he was nearly breathless. Caleb followed just behind him. "Don't do anything stupid," he said.

"Don't worry, I plan on being smart when I beat the hell out of him," Benjamin replied tersely.

They found Josh in the backyard, a hammer in hand as he worked on a rotting windowsill. "Damn house is falling apart," he said as they approached. "What are you two doing here?"

"Put down the hammer," Caleb said as he drew his gun.

"Hey, what's going on?" Josh asked.

"Where is she?" Benjamin asked as Josh slowly lowered the hammer to the ground.

He straightened back up and looked at Benjamin with confusion. "Where is who?"

Benjamin hit him in the chest hard with both his hands. "You know who I'm talking about. Where is Edie?"

Josh stumbled back a step, his face flushing with color. "Hey, man, what's the matter with you? I don't know what you're talking about."

A white-hot rage flew through Benjamin. He slammed Josh on the chin with his fist. "We can do this the easy way or we can do it the hard way," Benjamin said.

Josh grabbed his jaw. "What's wrong with you? You're crazy, man." He looked at Caleb. "Aren't you going to do something?"

Caleb smiled. "Yeah, I'm going to watch."

Josh dropped his hand from his face and fisted his hands at his sides. "Listen, I don't know what's going on. I don't know what you're talking about." A flicker of rage darkened his eyes. "But if you hit me again, I'm going to sue you and the whole town for abuse."

Benjamin jabbed him in the chin once again. "So, sue me."

"Turn around and put your hands behind your back," Caleb said. "Your partner in crime, Jeffrey Allen, is singing like a canary right now and you're under arrest for assault on Walt Tolliver and a bunch of other crimes that will be detailed later."

"Jeffrey Allen is a lying piece of crap," Josh exclaimed. "He's just trying to get away with everything he did."

"Turn around, Josh," Caleb repeated, his easygoing smile gone.

Josh looked at Benjamin, a small smile curving his lips. "Gee, hope you find what you're looking for." His gaze slid from Benjamin and to the cemetery in the distance.

It was a quick glance, almost imperceptible, but it shot a bolt of electricity through Benjamin, along with a horrifying sense of dread. "Get him downtown," Benjamin said just before he took off running.

"You're too late," Josh's voice rang out. "The bitch ruined everything. She's dead, Benjamin. You hear me? She's dead and buried."

Benjamin nearly stumbled as grief ripped through him. "No. No. No." The single word escaped him over and over again with each step he took.

Too late.

Too late.

The words thundered in his head and his grief was so intense he thought he might puke. The sun had sunk beneath the horizon and twilight had slammed in without warning.

The distance between him and the cemetery seemed agonizingly big. He ran so hard, so fast that a stitch in his side appeared.

Too late.

They'd all been too late for Brittany. They hadn't

known she was in trouble until she'd been gone for too long. They were probably too late for Jennifer Hightower and Suzy Bakersfield.

But this isn't the same case, he reminded himself. Edie wasn't one of the women who had disappeared without a trace. She'd been taken by Josh to punish her for destroying his dreams of wealth.

He released a sob as he flew through the cemetery entrance, his gaze seeking a fresh grave. It was not only grief that ripped through him but also a killing guilt.

They'd all told her it was over, that she was safe. They had taken Jeffrey's confession without asking the hard questions, without doubting the veracity. He'd put her in her car and sent her on her way. This was his fault.

He careened up and down the row of graves, seeking something that looked suspicious as darkness continued to fall. He'd always had a secret fear that he didn't have the capacity to feel deep emotion, to love with every fiber of his being. But as he hurried up and down the feet-worn paths between the graves, tears blurred his vision and he wished he couldn't feel.

He finally reached the end of the graves and didn't know whether to be relieved or disturbed that he'd found nothing. Where was she? Dear God, where could she be? He knew she was here somewhere, knew it with a sickening certainty.

Tom's patrol car pulled up, the lights of the vehicle cutting through the encroaching darkness. "Find her?" Tom asked as he hurried out of his car.

"No." The word worked around the lump in Benjamin's throat.

"Did you check the shed?"

Benjamin stared at him in confusion. "What shed?"

"Beyond that rise there's a little caretaker's shed." He pointed in the direction.

Benjamin took off running. He'd forgotten about the shed, which was tucked out of sight from the cemetery proper. He heard the sound of Tom's footsteps behind him and was grateful when his brother turned on a flashlight to light the way.

The old shed came into view and once again he felt like throwing up. *Please,* he begged. *Please let her be inside there. Please let her be okay.*

He tried not to think about all the places Josh could have buried her body. The cemetery was surrounded by land and he tried not to think about how long it might take before a burial site would be found.

Too late.

The words once again screamed in his head. *Please, please don't let me be too late.* He sent the prayer into the air and hoped that somebody was listening.

Darkness.

It surrounded her and invaded her soul. He'd said he'd come for her when it was dark, when nobody would see him bury her alive.

Her wrists were raw and bloody from working the ropes and the last piece of hope she'd entertained was gone. The darkness had arrived and the monster would arrive anytime.

Edie leaned her head back against the wall. Her head still hurt and she was more tired than she'd ever felt in her life. It seemed ridiculous that all this had happened because Poppy had thought he was seeing space aliens.

It also seemed ridiculous that she was going to be killed not because Josh wanted to protect himself, but because he was angry with her. Killing her was simply about revenge.

People were crazy, but she had been one of the craziest to walk away from Benjamin and love. "Love smart, Edie girl." Her grandmother's voice whispered through her head.

I did, Grandma. I loved smart when I fell in love with Benjamin and now it's too late for me, too late for us.

She stiffened and snapped her head upright as she heard the sound of running footsteps. He was coming. She closed her eyes and tried to become invisible in the darkness. A moan erupted from her as the door crashed open. She opened her eyes and saw only a dark shadow in the doorway.

Death. He had come for her.

"Edie."

She shivered at the voice that spoke her name, a cruel trick for he sounded like the man she loved.

Another body appeared in the doorway and a flashlight beam half blinded her. "Edie!" He rushed toward her and she realized it was Benjamin, not Josh.

She began to cry as he took the tape off her mouth. "It's okay, baby. It's all right. You're safe now. I promise you're safe." He pulled her forward into his arms as Tom got behind her and worked at the ropes that bound her.

"He said he was going to bury me alive," she cried as Benjamin held her tight. "He said I ruined his life so he was going to take mine."

When Tom freed her hands she wrapped her arms around Benjamin's neck, clinging to him as the fear slowly shuddered away.

Tom cut the rope that held her ankles and Benjamin scooped her up in his arms. "Let's get you out of here," he said as she buried her face into his broad chest.

The night was dark and cold, but she felt warm and safe in his arms as he carried her toward the house in the distance where the cars were parked.

"He drove up next to me," she said. "He motioned that something was wrong with my car. I was stupid to stop, but I thought it was safe." She clung tighter. "He told me my tire was going flat and when I bent over to look at it, he knocked me unconscious. I thought I was going to die."

When they reached the car, he placed her in the passenger seat and then hurried around to the driver's door. "Josh?" she asked as he slid in behind the steering wheel.

"Is in jail and I'm taking you to the hospital to get checked out."

She didn't argue with him. Her head pounded and her

wrists were encircled with dried blood from her attempts to get loose. "Why did Jeffrey confess to something he didn't do?"

"Josh threatened to kill Jeffrey's father if he talked," he said.

She leaned her head back against the seat and closed her eyes, trying to process everything that had happened, trying to forget how close she'd come to death. "How did you find me?" she asked, not opening her eyes.

"We leaned on Jeffrey and he came clean about Josh. Then I went to talk to Josh and leaned on him a bit."

She cracked an eye open and looked at him. "Leaned hard, I hope."

He smiled grimly. "I would have killed the bastard if Caleb hadn't been there."

She nodded and closed her eyes, satisfied with his reply. She was exhausted, her emotions a jumbled mess. The taste of horror still clung to the roof of her mouth and all she wanted to do was fall into a deep, dreamless sleep.

Two hours later her wrists had been treated and she'd been checked into a hospital room for a night of observation. "You and Walt are becoming familiar faces around here," Dr. Drake said when she was settled in a hospital bed. "You took quite a hit on the back of your head and I want to check those wrists again in the morning to make sure there's no infection setting in."

At that moment Benjamin appeared in the doorway. "I just brought Walt up to speed on everything. He said it's a good thing we arrested Josh, otherwise he would have had to release himself from here and kick his butt."

Edie gave him a weary smile. "That's my Poppy, ready to take on the bad guys and any space aliens that might invade his town."

"Get a good night's sleep, Edie," Dr. Drake said. "You've been through trauma and rest is the best medicine." He turned and gave Benjamin a stern look. "Don't you stress her with your questions. There's time enough to finish your investigation tomorrow."

"Don't worry, Doc. I'm just going to sit here for a little while until she falls asleep." As Dr. Drake left the room, Benjamin eased into a chair next to the hospital bed.

"You don't have to stay here," Edie protested as she fought to keep her eyes open.

"Yes, I do," he replied. "I need to sit here and watch you sleep. I need to assure myself that you're really okay. I just need to sit here and listen to you breathe." Emotion thickened his voice. "I've never been so afraid as when I saw your car parked on the side of the road. I don't ever want to be that afraid again."

She reached out a hand toward him and he grasped it in his. "I do love you, Benjamin," she said and then fell asleep.

She awakened to a sliver of early morning sun drifting through the window. Benjamin sat slumped in the chair, looking incredibly handsome and equally uncomfortable as he slept.

Her headache was gone and she felt ready to get out

of here, ready to face life with all its joy and with all its heartache.

As she looked at Benjamin her heart swelled as for the first time; she truly allowed herself to embrace all that was in her heart for him. Love. It fluttered through her with sweet warmth, filling up all the cold, empty places in her soul.

She gripped the charm around her neck and held tight. She would never forget the baby girl she'd lost, would always have an edge of grief where Mary was concerned. But she couldn't allow that tragedy to define who she was, to determine her future.

Benjamin's eyes fluttered open and for a moment she wanted to drown in the brown depths as he gazed at her. He straightened in the chair and quickly raked a hand through his tousled hair. "Good morning. How are you feeling?"

"Ready to get out of here and get on with my life," she replied.

"I had Tom take your car back to the ranch," he said as he stood. "I'll just get Dr. Drake in here and see if you're ready to be released."

Before she could stop him, he disappeared out the door. A niggle of doubt shot through her as she got up from the bed and headed for the bathroom.

Maybe he'd decided she was just too much trouble. He'd been emotional last night, but now he'd seemed a bit detached, as if he'd already moved on in his mind.

She changed into her clothes and checked her wrists, grateful that they looked less raw this morning. She finger-combed her hair and rinsed her mouth, then returned to the room to wait for Dr. Drake to come in and release her.

Benjamin came back through the door. "Looks like you're all ready to take off," he said as he leaned against the far wall.

"I told you, I'm ready for a fresh stab at life." She got up from the bed and took a step toward him.

He jammed his hands in his pockets, his expression unreadable. "You should be back on the road within an hour or so."

"Actually, I've been thinking about that. Being locked in that shed for hours, I did a lot of thinking." She took another step toward him, her heart suddenly beating almost painfully fast. "I thought about the fact that we've both suffered from loss, me with my daughter and you with your sister. I grieved for both of us and then realized how silly I'd been to try to protect myself from life…from love. I do love you, Benjamin, with all my heart."

His eyes lightened just a touch and he shoved himself off the wall. "Yeah, you told me that last night but I figured it was the result of whatever drug Dr. Drake might have given you."

She smiled. "He didn't give me any drugs. I meant what I said. I love you, and if it's not too late I want to be a part of your life. I didn't think I needed anyone, but I need you. I need my snuggle buddy."

He seemed to freeze in place. "Are you sure you don't

feel that way because I pulled you out of that shed? Because of some misplaced sense of gratitude?"

"Benjamin, I loved you when I got into my car to leave Black Rock. I loved you the night we made love. I feel like I was born loving you and that when I die, I'll feel the same way." She took another two steps forward, standing close enough to him that she could feel the heat radiating from him, smell the scent that made her think of warm male and home.

"I was afraid, that's why I was running away. I was afraid to believe that I deserved to be happy, but while I was sitting in that shed I knew I deserved happiness, that I deserve you."

He had her in his arms before her heart beat a second time. "I'll make you happy, Edie," he said and his eyes shone with a passion that nearly stole her breath away. "I love you, Edie, and I can't think of anyone I want more by my side for the rest of my life."

His lips descended on hers in a kiss that tasted of shared sunsets and fiery passion and love, sweet love. This was where she belonged, in Benjamin's life, in his strong arms.

When the kiss ended he reached out and touched the charm around her neck. "It's okay if you don't want to have children," he said. "I'll understand if that's what you choose."

He took her breath away. She knew that having a family was important to him and the fact that he was willing to make this sacrifice for her only spoke of the depth of his love.

She placed a hand on his cheek and smiled. "No way. We're going to fill that ranch house full of kids. Mary would have wanted lots of brothers and sisters."

He kissed her again and the kiss was interrupted by a deep clearing of a throat. They sprang apart to see Dr. Drake standing in the doorway. "Well, I guess I don't have to worry about her being in good hands," he said drily.

"Trust me, Doc, she's in the best of hands," Benjamin said as he pulled her against his side.

"Edie, you're good to go," Dr. Drake said.

"Great, then let's leave," she said to Benjamin. She was ready to start a new life with him.

They left the hospital and stepped out into the cool autumn morning sunshine. Once again Benjamin pulled her into his arms, his eyes filled with love and more than a touch of amusement. "I can't believe we owe all this to Walt and his space aliens."

"Maybe that means this was written in the stars," she said.

"So, you're willing to hitch your star to a full-time rancher?" he asked. "I'm not sure what I am without my badge."

She smiled up at him. "Oh, Benjamin, I'd hitch my star to you no matter what you did. I know what lies beneath your badge—a man with honor and compassion, the man I love with all my heart." She backed out of his arms. "Now, are you going to make me stand around in this hospital parking lot all day or are we going to the ranch and start practicing for those babies we're going to make?"

She laughed in delight as his eyes sparked with a fiery need and he tugged her toward his truck and into the future that she knew would be filled with laughter and passion and love.

Epilogue

"I still think we should have done corn bread stuffing," Poppy said as he and Margaret worked to stuff the giant Thanksgiving turkey.

"Sage dressing is traditional," Margaret said, her voice brooking no argument.

Edie smiled as she stood at the window and watched Benjamin as he approached the house from the pasture. It had been two months since the day she'd left the hospital, and in that two months much had occurred.

Benjamin had driven with her to Topeka to pack her belongings and bring them back to his place. Margaret had moved out of the cottage and into Poppy's house and the two seemed satisfied with their slightly contentious, but very caring companionship.

Benjamin still wore his badge, although he'd told his

brother that he was resigning in the spring. For Edie, the past two months had been magic. Her love for Benjamin had simply grown deeper, more profound, with each day that had passed.

All the facts of Josh's crimes had come to light. Jeffrey Allen was cooperating with authorities, hoping to get a lighter sentence when he came to trial.

Josh had provided the body parts for Jeffrey's experiments with the understanding that he would share in whatever proceeds Jeffrey eventually made. It had been Josh who had beaten Walt in the cemetery, an attempt to scare the old man into leaving things alone. It had also been Josh who had shot at them in the woods when he'd been burying the botched experiments.

Pure and simple it had been rage and greed that had driven Josh, and Edie was comforted by the fact that he would be in prison for a very long time to come.

Later this evening Tom and his fiancée, Peyton, were coming for dinner, as was Caleb and his fiancée, Portia. They had invited Jacob, but Benjamin had warned her that he probably wouldn't show up, that he'd prefer his isolation in the small cabin.

The front door opened and Benjamin came in, as always his face lighting up at the sight of her. He pulled her into his arms for a welcome kiss and then smiled as he heard Poppy and Margaret arguing about sweet potatoes. "I hear that our master chefs are at it again."

"At least we can be thankful to know that the dinner is probably going to be amazing," she replied.

"It will be nice to have everyone here," he said,

but his eyes darkened just a bit and she knew he was thinking about the two who would be missing—Jacob, who for some terrible reason that he refused to discuss had isolated himself from life, and of course, Brittany.

The darkness in his eyes lasted only a moment and then was gone, replaced by the light of love as he gazed at her. "I have a lot of things to be thankful for this year, and the main one is you."

As his lips met hers, her heart swelled with her own thanksgiving, happy that she'd been smart enough to open her heart to happiness, to love.

He was escalating his timeline.

When their captor brought in the fourth woman, Brittany realized the last two had been taken within a short span of time. She recognized the latest victim as Casey Teasdale, a young woman who worked as a receptionist in the dental office.

The masked man whistled as he carried the unconscious woman into the cell across from Brittany. Both Jennifer and Suzy went crazy at the sight of the new woman, one begging and the other cursing the man who held them.

Brittany sat silently, watching his every move, looking for something that might help her identify the man behind the mask. But as always, nothing he did led to an identification.

He locked the door of the cell where he'd placed Casey and then headed back toward the door of the barn where they were being kept. He stopped in front of Brittany's enclosure and she felt his sick energy, his excitement as he looked at her.

"Almost time," he said. "I only need to add one more to my collection and then the games will begin." He began to whistle again as he left the building.

Brittany stared after him, knowing that time was running out for her, that time was running out for them all.

* * * * *

THE RESCUE PILOT

BY
RACHEL LEE

All the characters in this book have no existence outside the imagination of the author, and have no relation whatsoever to anyone bearing the same name or names. They are not even distantly inspired by any individual known or unknown to the author, and all the incidents are pure invention.

First published in Great Britain 2012
by Mills & Boon, an imprint of Harlequin (UK) Limited,
Eton House, 18-24 Paradise Road, Richmond, Surrey TW9 1SR

© Susan Civil Brown 2011

ISBN: 978 0 263 89495 0

46-0112

Harlequin (UK) policy is to use papers that are natural, renewable and recyclable products and made from wood grown in sustainable forests. The logging and manufacturing processes conform to the legal environmental regulations of the country of origin.

Printed and bound in Spain
by Blackprint CPI, Barcelona

Rachel Lee was hooked on writing by the age of twelve, and practiced her craft as she moved from place to place all over the United States. This *New York Times* bestselling author now resides in Florida and has the joy of writing full-time.

Her bestselling CONARD COUNTY series (see www. conardcounty.com) has won the hearts of readers worldwide, and it's no wonder, given her own approach to life and love. As she says, "Life is the biggest romantic adventure of all—and if you're open and aware, the most marvelous things are just waiting to be discovered." Readers can e-mail Rachel at RachelLee@ConardCounty.com.

To all the quiet heroes who do whatever is
necessary to care for others

Prologue

Thunder Mountain opened its snowy maw and swallowed the crashing plane. The business jet, its engines dead, not designed to glide without the assistance of power, descended almost like a stone, but the pilot struggled manfully.

The wild creatures, those not slumbering for winter, heard it come in, cutting through the air with a too-quiet but unnatural *whoosh,* heading for the only tree-less space for miles. Those nearby froze and watched the thing slide, burying itself deeper in the snow as it went, metal screaming as it twisted, leaving a trail behind that would vanish quickly as the arriving blizzard blew mightily and dumped its heavy load. Then they turned and fled.

All fell silent. The flakes continued to swirl madly,

the wind to gust powerfully. Wise creatures found hiding places from the storm's fury.

And Thunder Mountain began to devour all the evidence of the crash.

Chapter 1

Chase Dakota stared at cockpit windscreens buried in snow, dirt, rocks and branches. Only the flickering light from his dying console allowed him to see anything at all. Moments later, to his relief, the emergency lights turned on again. Dim but essential.

For long seconds he didn't move, but instead listened. Listened to a world gone oddly silent, muffled by snow and the plane's own soundproofing. No screams reached him. That could be good, or very bad.

He was sweat-soaked from the effort of bringing this damn plane down. The instant the engines had cut out, he'd begun to fly a boulder not a bird, and his battle to optimize the aerodynamics and prevent a fatal dive had been Herculean. Hitting the mountain's downslope had been a boon.

Now he cut off the fuel pumps. Although they'd had a dramatic drop in fuel level, he couldn't be sure something else hadn't caused the dual flameout of his engines and that there might be more than fumes left. Next he switched off everything else that was nonessential now that they were no longer in the air. Mission accomplished.

He took just a moment to do a mental self-check. He wasn't aware of having lost consciousness at any point, but he might not have known it even if he had. Everything still seemed to be in working condition. Good.

He didn't have time for shock. He reached for the buckles of his harness and released them. His first priority was to check on his four passengers. Everything else could wait.

Even as he rose and stepped through the small cockpit, his feet told him the plane had been seriously bent on impact. But looking back through the cabin as he pulled aside the accordion door, he saw with relief that the rest of the plane seemed to be intact. All of it. That meant his passengers were still with him. All of them.

At first all he could hear was panicked breathing. Then a familiar voice said, "That was a helluva landing, Chase."

Billy Joe Yuma. An old buddy.

"Not my preferred type," Chase managed, working his way back through the narrow-bodied business jet. "Anyone hurt?"

"I'm fine," Yuma said. "So's Wendy."

"Ms. Campbell?"

"I…think I'm okay. My sister…"

"I'm checking right now."

He passed the three people, still tightly buckled into their seats, and made his way to the small bedroom in the tail where the sick woman lay. He'd insisted that she be strapped in, overriding the Campbell woman's objections, and never had he been gladder that he'd been willing to go toe-to-toe over something. He grabbed a flashlight from a wall compartment as he passed the small bathroom, and flicked it on.

He saw her, still strapped in place, still too thin to be believed, but blinking. Awake. Aware. Panic filling her face.

"It's okay," he said. "We came down in one piece."

"Fire?" she asked weakly.

"Nope. None. You're going to be okay." An easy, hopeful lie. At this point he didn't have the foggiest idea just how bad this was. He was counting the good things right now, and the good things were that his passengers were alive and his plane intact enough not to present additional problems.

He paused, feeling the aircraft shift a bit as if the wind banged on its side. A quiet groan of metal answered, but nothing more.

"My sister?" the woman on the bed asked, her voice faint.

"She's fine. Everyone's okay. I'll send her back, all right?"

He didn't even have to do that. As soon as he turned around, he was face-to-face with the imperious young woman who had hired him to take her and her sister to Minneapolis. If she weren't so damn bossy, she'd have been an attractive Celtic beauty, with her black hair and deep blue eyes. "Cait," she said.

"She's asking for you."

He stepped into the W.C. to give her room to pass. Then he headed back up the aisle. With every step he felt the torture the plane had gone through as it had slid along the mountain slope. The deep snow had helped, but it wasn't enough to completely shield the plane from the ground underneath, especially boulders. This baby would never fly again.

But now it had one last duty: to help them survive. Glancing out the portholes that weren't yet fully covered by snow told him the blizzard conditions he'd been flying above had begun to reach them. Rescue lay a long way down the road of time and this mountain.

He sat in an empty seat facing Wendy and Billy Joe Yuma. He'd known them both most of his life—the advantage of living in a small town. And he knew he was going to need them both now. They belonged to Conard County's emergency-response team, Wendy as chief flight nurse, Yuma (he hated to be called Billy Joe) as the primary rescue chopper pilot.

Wendy, now a gorgeous redhead of nearly forty, was much younger than her husband. Yuma had learned to fly choppers in Vietnam, and despite the years maintained an ageless appearance. Or maybe he'd done all his aging during the years of war, and afterward when he'd lived in these very mountains with a bunch of vets who couldn't shake their PTSD enough to live around other people.

"You're sure you're both okay?" he asked now.

"Believe it," Wendy answered.

"Been through worse," Yuma replied, "and walked away."

Chase didn't doubt that for a minute. He, too, had flown for the military.

"I'm gonna need you both," he said frankly. "We've got a really sick woman in the tail we need to take care of, Wendy. And Yuma, I need you to help me find out what still works, and how we're going to cope with this blizzard."

He received two answering nods, and both unbuckled their seat belts.

"I'll go back and find out what's going on," Wendy said. "Why do I think it's going to need more than a first aid kit?"

"Because I was supposed to fly them on to the hospital in Minnesota."

"Oh." Even in the poor light he could see Wendy's face darken. "That doesn't sound good." She rose, slipped past the two of them and headed to the rear of the plane.

Chase turned back to Yuma. "We need to make sure we can get one of the exit doors open, and keep it clear. And a walk-around would be good before we get buried any deeper."

"Agreed. Then we'll check the electronics. But first things first."

As they began to pull on their outdoor gear, Chase noted that the air inside was already becoming stale. The downside of having an airtight shelter. He was going to have to figure out how to exchange the cabin air without freezing them to death.

He gave a small shake of his head. As Yuma said, first things first.

Aurora Campbell, known as Rory to family and friends, sat on the edge of her sister's bed in the rear of the plane and clasped her hand as tightly as she dared. Her sister had grown so thin from her lymphoma and the treatments for the cancer that holding her hand was like holding the delicate bones of a small bird.

She hoped her face betrayed nothing of her terror. She'd deal with that later when she gave their pilot whatfor. Right now she only wanted to calm Cait.

"The hard part is over," she lied reassuringly. "Hey, Cait, we were just in a plane crash but we're still in one piece. What are the odds, huh?"

Cait managed a weak smile. Even that simple expression seemed like it wearied her. "Yeah," she said, her voice little more than a whisper. "And people will come to help."

"Yes, they will." Despite the blizzard raging outside, despite the fact that she was fairly certain they were in the middle of nowhere. "And I've got enough medications to hold you until they do." Four days' worth. She had thought she wouldn't need even that much, because Cait had been slated for immediate admission at the hospital they were going to. Had been going to until this freaking jet had crashed on a mountainside in what was starting to look like a damn blizzard.

But for now she shoved her frustration, fear and fury to the background. "Need anything? Maybe I can rustle up some soup…." God, she hadn't even thought about that yet, either. Did this plane have anything on it besides snacks and liquor? Anything that didn't require a microwave to cook it? Because she suspected that was one of the things that probably wouldn't work now.

She didn't know much about planes, but she knew most of their electricity was generated by their engines. And this plane had no engines anymore.

"No," Cait sighed. "As long as we're okay…I just want to sleep a bit."

Rory reached out and stroked the pale fuzz that was all that remained on Cait's head. "You do that." Cait was sleeping more and more of the time. Her heart squeezed, but moments later as Cait slipped away into sleep, she rose and walked out of the little bedroom.

The other woman passenger was waiting for her.

Wendy, Rory seemed to remember. On such small business jets, it was hard not to at least exchange introductions before takeoff.

"I'm a nurse," Wendy said. "Let's sit and talk a bit about your sister so I can help."

"You can't help her," Rory said brusquely. "I have her medicines. What she needs is a hospital, a clinical trial on a new drug. Doesn't look likely right now, does it?" Then she eased past Wendy and returned to her seat, blindly watching the snow build up outside the small window.

She hardly even paid attention to the two men who were forward in the cabin, working to open the exterior door behind the cockpit. She noted that the air was getting heavy, but at the moment she wasn't worried about that.

All she was worried about was Cait, and right at this moment, with the world outside invisible in swirling snow, she was fairly certain there wasn't a damn thing she could do. And she hated, absolutely *hated,* being helpless.

Wendy didn't give her long to sit in hopeless solitude. The woman came forward and sat in the seat facing her. "Cancer?" Wendy asked.

"Non-Hodgkins lymphoma. Aggressive, this time." The words were painful, but she'd never been one to shy away from telling it like it was. No matter how much it hurt.

"This time?" Wendy's voice was gentle.

Rory almost sighed, realizing that she could either choose to be unutterably rude and say nothing, or just dump it out there and shut this woman up. She decided on the latter. "She went into remission four years ago. Unfortunately, she didn't tell me she had a relapse five

months ago. I was in Mexico, and she didn't tell me."
That hurt as much as anything.

"So you came home to find her like this? Why
wouldn't she tell you?"

"She'd given up," Rory said. "Her husband dumped
her the minute he heard and moved in with another
woman. Kinda cuts out your heart, don't you think?"

"It would."

Rory heard the sympathy in Wendy's voice, but she
didn't want sympathy. Sympathy didn't help. All it did
was make her want to cry. She didn't answer.

"You have medication for her."

Rory finally looked at her, her eyes burning.
"Enough for four days. More than enough for a freaking four- or five-hour flight from Seattle to Minneapolis. Only that's not happening, is it?"

To her credit, Wendy didn't offer any false cheer.
"What's she on?"

"Immunosuppressants. Some other drugs. She's been
through radiation, obviously. But as I said, the disease
is aggressive."

"So you're pinning your hopes on a clinical trial of
something new?"

"Yes. I was." That *was* sounded final. But right now
everything felt final.

"They've got some great stuff now, I hear, but I'm
not up on the disease." She leaned forward and laid her
hand over Rory's.

Rory wanted to jerk back, but she couldn't because
that touch somehow didn't offend her. Maybe because
she needed not to feel entirely alone. "That's what they
tell me."

Wendy nodded. "The important thing is to keep her
going right now. Food. Warmth. Keep her resistance up.

I'll help every way I can. But I promise you, I'm part of the Conard County emergency-response team. As soon as this weather lets up, they're going to pull out all the stops to find us."

"Because you're here?"

"Because all of us are here. And we're damn good at what we do."

"How do you know we aren't someplace else?"

"Because Chase was going to drop us at the Conard County Airport on the way to Minnesota. You knew that, right?"

Rory nodded. "A brief fueling stop."

"Well, my husband was looking out the window as we came in. He said this is Thunder Mountain, maybe sixty miles out of town."

It was a slender lifeline indeed, but for once in her life, Rory was willing to grab it. What else did she have?

Turning her head, closing the conversation, she gazed out a window that snow rapidly covered, and fought down the rage, panic and tears.

The exit door behind the cockpit also served as steps. The fact that it opened out and down should have made it easier to move. But the plane's shape had been torqued by the crash, and things weren't meeting the way they used to. And the steps themselves, carpeted for that extra bit of luxury, hampered the effort to shove.

"Maybe we should try the rear exit," Yuma said, wiping sweat from his brow.

"I'd rather not open the door back there if I can avoid it. Any cold air we let in—and there'll be quite a bit of it—is going to hit our sick passenger first. I'd rather let it in as far from her as possible."

"Good point. Well, I doubt the snow is the problem."

"Not hardly," Chase agreed. "Not yet. Not with this."

But the snow was a problem all right, one that promised to grow even bigger in the next few hours. "We've got to get out," he said again. "Find out what our condition is, whether we've got anything else to worry about. And we're going to need to build a fire to heat food."

"In this?" Yuma cocked a brow. "That's always fun."

"I have plenty of alcohol onboard."

Yuma chuckled. "Imagine starting a fire with Chivas. Or Jack."

"I just hope it works. Alcohol burns cold."

"A handful of pine needles" was all Yuma said.

"Sure. I see tons of them out there." But Chase knew that even though the snow buried them, finding them wouldn't be the most difficult task they'd face. But first this damn door. Preferably in a way that wouldn't leave it permanently open to the cold.

"You know," he said as he and Yuma again put their shoulders to the door, "I should have painted this damn plane chartreuse or international orange."

"By tomorrow I don't think it'll matter if it were covered in blinking neon lights."

Chase paused, wiping his own brow. "Yeah. It probably won't."

"Transponder?" Billy Joe asked as they pushed again.

"Damned if I know right now. My instruments were acting like twinkle lights. But first things first. The transponder isn't exactly going to get much attention at the moment."

"That's a fact."

"At the very least we've got to check our situation, make sure we don't slide farther, and then get some hot soup and coffee going. *Then* I'll worry about everything else."

"Agreed."

On the count of three, both men shoved again, and this time the door opened. Not far, just a couple of inches at the top, but enough for Chase to see the problem. One of the heavy-duty locking bolts hadn't slid fully back and it ripped at the door, tearing a small hole but not enough to cause any heartache.

"I need a sledgehammer," Chase muttered. And he needed it right now, because he wasn't going to go outside and leave that door open, freezing everyone in the plane.

He pulled up a service panel in the floor and went hunting. There it was, a heavy-duty hammer. He hadn't ever needed it, but you never knew. He carried a lot of items just for that reason. If he'd learned one thing in the military, it was to be prepared for just about any situation. What you dismissed as unnecessary could wind up costing you a whole lot...like your life.

Yuma leaned back while Chase started hammering on the locking bolt.

"Do you have to make so much noise?" the Campbell woman said sharply. "My sister..."

"Is going to freeze to death if I can't close this door, okay?"

He didn't have to look at her because he could hear the snap of her jaws closing just before he banged again with the hammer.

To his vast relief, it only took a half-dozen blows. He tossed the hammer back in the hatch, closed it and then faced the door with Yuma again. Already the plane was cooling down, but the fresher air was welcome.

They counted to three again and shoved. This time

the door flew all the way down to the packed snow beneath. Another scarcely acknowledged fear slipped away from Chase's mind. They weren't trapped inside. They had a functioning door.

The two men scrambled out quickly over the horizontal steps, which were useless at this angle, then shoved the door up behind them, leaving it open the tiniest crack.

Outside the world looked like a snow globe gone mad. Wind whipped them viciously, howling its fury, and the flakes were becoming icy needles. Chase ignored the discomfort, all his attention focused on finding out how the plane was situated. He didn't want to learn the hard way that they were on the lip of another slide and some little thing could set it off.

He headed straight for the plane's nose. In this heavy snow, it was hard to see very far. He could make out only the faintest of gray shadows of trees around the clearing, but as he approached the front, he saw with relief that there were trees not very far ahead of them. Maybe a hundred, two hundred feet at most. Thick foresting that would stop them if they slid, no dark shadow indicating a deep gorge in the way. Thank God.

The nose was completely buried and he left it that way. Every bit of insulation would do them good until this blizzard passed, cutting the wind, keeping the inside temperature up.

But he felt something very close to sorrow as he walked back along the plane's length. Even with deepening snowdrifts he could see buckled metal on the fuselage, and that the engines had vanished from under the wings somewhere upslope, leaving behind their twisted pylons. Any fuel that was left would be seeping into the snow from broken lines, but he couldn't see any melting to indicate it.

God, what had happened? He hadn't had time to wonder before. He'd gone from half-full tanks to empty so fast it had seemed almost impossible. His fuel pumps must have been spewing precious liquid as fast as they could from somewhere. Just where he wouldn't be able to tell now.

He'd had the damn thing overhauled and checked out last week. That's why he'd been in Seattle. All he could think now was that some mechanic somewhere had failed to do something right. Make some connection. Tighten some clamp, whatever. Somewhere between pumps and engines, there had been a critical failure.

By the time he'd known things were going wrong, they'd been over the mountains with a storm catching up. At forty thousand feet, that was no big deal, but it sure cut his options. He'd had no choice but to hope they'd make it to the Conard County Airport. There was nothing closer that hadn't already been closed by the storm.

He supposed he ought to get down on his knees and thank God they were in one piece. But right now he wasn't feeling all that thankful. He was feeling furious, and worried. Most especially worried about that sick woman in the back of his plane.

Chapter 2

Rory had added more blankets to cover Cait as the cabin temperature dropped a bit because of the opening and closing of the cabin door. She was grateful the air felt fresher now, but worried, too. How were they supposed to keep warm?

Cait barely stirred as Rory tucked blankets around her all the way up to her ears. A knit stocking cap would probably be good, she thought, since Cait didn't have enough hair left to keep her head warm.

She went out to ask Wendy about it. Maybe the other woman had one.

"Actually, I do," Wendy said. "And I'm glad to tell you it's in the overhead bin. Let me get it out. Didn't you bring something like that for when you got to Minnesota?"

"An ambulance was going to meet us. I wasn't expecting Cait to be exposed at all."

Wendy nodded as she rose to open one of the overhead bins. She wore a baggy sweater and jeans, and a very sensible pair of work boots. Just like Rory herself. Accustomed as she was to being on work sites, Rory dolled up only for business meetings, and this trip hadn't qualified for that.

"What about you?" Wendy spoke as she fought with the bin door, at last managing to yank it open.

"I have a parka I dug out before we left."

"Good. I don't usually carry spares of those."

Wendy pulled a thick-knit cap out of a leather duffel and passed it to her. "There you go."

"Thank you so much!"

Wendy smiled, and the expression reached her eyes. "Hey, we're all in this together."

Cait murmured quietly as Rory put the stocking cap on her, but then settled back into sleep. Rory stood looking down at her sister, wishing that for just a few moments she could see that spark again in Cait's expression, but it had vanished long before Rory got home.

Tears pricked at her eyes, but she couldn't afford to let them fall. Not now, not ever. She had to remain strong for Cait's sake, no matter how tough it got. And right now it was tough. All her worst imaginings for Cait's future had just been compounded by a plane crash in the wilderness. In a storm.

Sometimes she thought the gods enjoyed a laugh at human expense. If so, they must be finding this all hilarious.

Time. There was so little time for Cait now. And this accident was eating away at it like a miserable rat. Just enough meds for four days. Then what? Not that the meds were doing much but holding the beast at bay, and not doing a very good job at that. In the days since she'd gotten back to Seattle and had gathered the information and recommendations that had led her to the decision to fly her sister halfway across the country for experimental treatment, she'd watched Cait drift away further and further. Losing even the energy to smile, or whisper more than a few words.

Days, hours, minutes were precious right now. And they were slipping uncaringly between her fingers like the finest of sands.

Her spine stiffened suddenly, and she turned around to march back into the main cabin. There was a pilot who had a lot of explaining to do, and she was going to get her answers the instant he came back inside.

She might not be able to change the situation, but she was sure as hell going to understand it and all that they were up against. She didn't function well in the dark and she refused to be kept there.

Chase and Yuma returned to the plane after a mere thirty minutes. Long enough to assess their situation outside, long enough to dig through the snow at the forest's edge to find some wood and pine needles. They'd even dug a place near the plane to build a fire safely, although that was going to be difficult in this wind.

But Chase had candles onboard, and chafing dishes for those fancy flights where people expected exquisite meals. Plenty of candles. He could heat some soup, maybe even brew some coffee, but open flames in the plane made him uneasy, and they'd suck up the oxygen.

He was holding an internal debate as he and Yuma closed the door behind them. And the first words he heard were:

"Why the hell did this plane crash?"

He turned slowly, his cheeks stinging from the cold

outside. He stared at the Campbell woman, reminding himself that she was undoubtedly edgy because of her sister. And, yes, because of the crash. Plenty of reason to be truculent.

He pulled off his leather gloves while staring at her, and threw his hood back. "Well," he said slowly, "that's the question, isn't it? We ran out of fuel. Unexpectedly, inexplicably. All of a sudden. And since I had the plane in Seattle for an overhaul, I'm going to guess that somebody screwed up. But once that fuel started draining like Niagara Falls, there wasn't much I could do except try to get us down in one piece."

He waited, expecting to get his butt chewed about something, but amazingly, it didn't happen. Then she nodded. "Okay. What now? What are our chances?"

He unzipped his jacket and shrugged it off, tossing it over a seat back. "The charts I looked at before takeoff suggest the storm might last two days. That was then. It wasn't supposed to catch up to us as fast as it did. That's now. It's a helluva blow, and we aren't going to stir from the safety of this plane until it lets up."

"Two days," she said, and sounded almost frightened.

"Two days," he repeated. "If the emergency beacon is working, rescue should come soon after."

"*If?*"

"We didn't exactly make a soft landing. The body of the plane is twisted pretty badly. I don't know how many electrical connections are out, or what hidden damage we have. Just after we crashed, it looked like my sat-nav went out. GPS to you. And the emergency beacon needs that to tell rescuers where we are, after the storm passes. The standard transponder, which I also have, broadcasts from the underside of the plane, so we can pretty much count that out. Regardless, the storm itself will probably interfere with all radio communications, so I can't say for sure whether the problem is the weather or something is broken. I'm going to check on that right now, if you don't mind."

No objection emanated from the beauty, although her expression suggested that she'd have loved nothing better than a fight. Of course. To work off the adrenaline, probably. Or maybe she just hated the sight of him. He didn't care either way. He started to turn but her voice caught him.

"Won't they know where we are from the flight plan? From our last recorded position?"

He faced her again. "We were traveling at over six hundred miles per hour. From the time things started to go wrong, we traveled a long way. And we didn't exactly stay on the flight path while I tried to get us down on some open ground rather than in the forest. So they're going to have to search quite a wide area."

"Then you'd better make sure that beacon is working."

Chase ground his teeth. Now he was absolutely certain he didn't like her. "That thought has occurred to me as well, ma'am."

Stiff now, he turned toward the cockpit. When he got there, he closed the accordion door behind him. *This,* he thought, was not going to make anything any easier.

Rory watched the pilot close the door behind him. What was his name again? She'd paid scant attention… Oh, yeah, something like Hunter. No, Chase. Chase Dakota. He was a large enough man, well-built, with ruggedly chiseled features that hinted just a bit at a possible Native American heritage somewhere in his family tree. Gray eyes that reminded her of steel.

And not especially friendly. Although she supposed she wasn't exactly inviting friendliness at the moment. But why should she? Her sister's life was hanging in the balance, and whether this crash was his fault hardly seemed to matter. Bottom line: They had crashed and they were stuck for two days. At least two days. She would have given her right hand for some assurance that was all it would be.

She realized that Wendy had risen and was moving around toward the rear of the plane, in an alcove just behind the passenger seating but forward of the bedroom in the tail. Rory took a few steps to look and saw the redhead opening lockers above a microwave. The plane's small galley.

Needing to do something, Rory joined her.

"I'm looking at our supply situation," Wendy said, smiling. "Chase always stocks well, but it would sure be nice if I could manage to make us all something hot to drink. Soup, tea, maybe coffee."

"We can't cook. Not without a fire."

"Ah, but we might be able to manage something with candles and these chafing dishes."

"True." Rory allowed herself to be distracted by one of her favorite things: problem solving. She took a quick look at her sister and found Cait still sleeping, and gently breathing. Did parents hover over new babies like this, she wondered, waiting for the gentle rise of a chest to indicate that life continued?

She gave herself a little shake and turned back to help Wendy in the galley. "Coffee might be beyond reach," she said. "How many candles does it take to boil a pot?"

"Darned if I know. But I want my coffee, and there's a whole lot of candles. Besides, we only need to make one pot. I think the guys will build a fire outside soon. We're going to need it."

"That's for sure."

"And I'm sure if we're patient, we can heat a pot of this dried soup." She turned on the faucet and, wonder of wonders, water came out.

"Must be a gravity tank," Rory said.

"Whatever it is, it's a plus. Better to have water right now than have to melt snow on top of everything else."

While Rory worked with chafing-dish holders to elevate them enough to put fat, squat candles beneath them, bending legs and stacking a few of them, Wendy found the pieces of the drip coffeemaker and assembled them, then put coffee in the filter. "First pot of boiling water goes for coffee," she said firmly. "I need a hot drink and some caffeine."

"If you watch it, it'll never boil," Rory remarked, lighting a candle beneath her assemblage. The women shared a quiet laugh at the old joke, then together balanced a chafing dish full of water on the structure.

"I think it'll hold," Wendy said.

"It looks like it, but this time I'm going to watch it boil anyway. Too dangerous to do otherwise."

"I agree. And maybe I should speak to Chase about this."

"Why?"

Wendy tipped her head. "Because we're burning oxygen back here, and this plane is probably pretty air-tight."

Rory hadn't thought of that, but as soon as Wendy spoke, she knew she was right. Planes had air exchangers, but they probably worked on electrical power like everything else. Power they didn't have now. "Go ask. I'll babysit."

Much better to have Wendy ask. Not that Chase Dakota had spared her more than a few words, but she got the feeling he didn't much care for her. Ordinarily, she didn't turn tail in the face of men like that, but right now she was acutely aware that she wasn't the person in charge. That put her on the defensive, and for now that meant stirring up as little trouble as possible.

"Houston," she muttered under her breath, "we have a problem."

Except they weren't halfway to the moon. Although they might as well have been at the moment. She heard some noise from up front and stuck her head out of the galley. Chase and Wendy's husband were pushing the door open a crack. Just a crack. Then they disappeared in the men's compound, so aptly named a cockpit, she thought sourly, and went back to their machinations with the machinery.

No emergency beacon? She refused to believe that was possible. Weren't those damn things supposed to work no matter what? Or maybe that was the cockpit race recorder she was thinking of. All of a sudden she wished she knew more about planes and less about finding and drilling for oil. Or more about cancer and her sister's condition.

She was so used to being on top of things that it killed her to consider all the things she didn't know anything about—like planes and cancer and how long it would take that damn water to boil. Because she sure would like a cup of that coffee.

Wendy rejoined her. "We might get a little chilly. They tried to open the door to a minimum so we don't suffocate, but…" She shrugged. "Nobody said camping in a blizzard in a crashed plane was going to be easy."

"What do you know about the pilot?" Rory asked. "I mean…"

Wendy's face gentled. "It's okay. He's a stranger to you and here we are in a mess. But, trust me, Chase was a military pilot before he started his charter service. He knows what he's doing, and if we lost fuel, then he's right about why. He's not the kind of guy who would authorize any maintenance shortcuts. And, as for right now, I can tell you the military gave both him and my husband a lot of survival training."

"Okay."

Something in Wendy's face changed. "Billy Joe—oh, he'd kill me if he heard me call him that to someone else—"

"Why?"

"He's just never liked his given name. He prefers everyone to call him Yuma."

"I can do that."

Wendy smiled. "I'm sure you can."

"You were going to say?"

"Yuma lived up here in these mountains for a few years after he got back from the war. Post-traumatic stress. He knows how to survive these mountains in the winter."

"That's good to know. That he's experienced, I mean, not the other."

"I understood."

"How did you two meet? Were you just neighbors?"

Wendy smiled again. "Oh, it's a much more interesting story than that. Billy Joe was a medevac pilot in Vietnam. The experience left him with a lot of nightmares, so for years he lived up in these mountains with

some other vets. They just couldn't handle the bustling
world at times. So they kind of built their own hermit-
age."

Rory nodded. "That must have been rough."

"Oh, it was. Anyway, my dad was a Vietnam vet, too,
and when Billy Joe got well enough to try to return to
life, Dad got him hired as our medevac pilot. Our first
one, actually."

"That was nice of your dad."

"He lived to regret it." Wendy laughed quietly, letting Rory know it wasn't a bad thing. "Anyway, I had a
crush on Yuma from the time I was sixteen. He was so
much older and so aware of his flaws that he ran from
me like a scared rabbit. And finally my dad told me to
stop torturing the man."

"Ouch. That must have hurt."

"It did at first. But, you know, it finally got through
my thick head that my dad was right. I was too young,
too inexperienced, and Billy Joe had every reason to
avoid me, and not just because I was a kid."

"So what happened?"

"I went off to nursing school, then worked in a big-
city hospital for a few years until I practically had my
own PTSD. When I came back here it was to become
the flight nurse with the Emergency Response Team."
She gave a little laugh. "You could say I wasn't exactly
welcome on that helicopter."

"But something must have changed."

Wendy nodded, her gaze becoming faraway for a
few minutes. "It was rough, but here we are now...to-
gether forever as Yuma likes to tease me." She turned
a bit. "Is that water heating?"

Rory looked back. "I see a bit of steam on the surface."

"Good, we'll make it yet."

Even the little bit that Wendy had told her had given her an inkling of what her husband had suffered. And some of it, at least, had to be replaying in her heart and mind.

Rory sighed, realizing she wasn't the only person on this plane who had serious concerns. Yes, Cait's life hung in the balance, but surely Wendy must be worrying about Yuma and whether this would affect him.

Yet Wendy soldiered cheerfully on, confident that things would work out. Rory found herself wondering, for the first time, when she had started to lose hope for Cait. Because that's what was going on here: the loss of hope.

Not just the threat of being stranded, but the loss of hope. Did she really think nothing could save Cait now?

The thought appalled her. She shook it away, mentally stomped it into some dark place she couldn't afford to look at. Not now.

Twenty minutes later the four of them were sitting in the passenger lounge savoring hot cups of coffee. Cait still slept, but Wendy and Rory had agreed that their next task would be making soup for her.

"The way I see it," Chase said, "we need to get a fire going outside for at least a little while. We can't keep that door open too long or we'll freeze. And cooking with candles is not only slow but could be deadly."

Rory nodded agreement. No argument with him on that score.

"The wind is a beast, though, so it won't be easy. We'll need to cook, and cook fast before the fire gets buried in snow."

Rory glanced toward one of the few windows still

not covered by snow, and could see nothing but white. "It's that bad?"

"Oh, yeah," he answered her. "I don't want to burn any more candles than we absolutely must because of fire danger, but we're going to have to burn some, obviously. We've got protection against the wind, our body heat will help in a space this small, but it's still going to get pretty cold."

Rory couldn't help but glance back at the tiny bedroom where her sister slept. "I hope she can handle it."

"She's my top priority," Chase said flatly. "Cancer?"

Rory nodded. "Non-Hodgkins lymphoma. NHL for short. She hasn't got a lot of reserves left."

"I can see that. We'll keep her warm and fed if I have to light a fire in the aisle, okay?"

"I'm not sure going that far would help anyone." But for the first time she met his gaze, truly met it, and felt a pleasant, astonishing shock. It wasn't because those gunmetal eyes for the first time looked gentle, though. No, it was something else, something that heated places she was ashamed to even be aware of at such a time.

A sexual reaction at a time like this? She almost wanted to hang her head until a quiet voice in the back of her mind reminded her that adrenaline, shock and danger did funny things to a person. Life asserted itself in the most primitive way imaginable.

Plus, she was dependent on this guy. It was probably a cavewoman response, nothing more. At the same time, it felt good, shocking though it was, so she just let it be. Something in her life needed to feel good.

But it also put her on guard. She couldn't afford to lose her mental footing now—most especially now—and not to a primitive impulse to forget all sense and escape into a few moments of hot pleasure.

"What do you do?" Chase's question shocked her out of her internal dissection.

"What? Why?"

"I'm just wondering if you bring any additional skills to the table here. Yuma and I are trained in survival, and he's a huge advantage for us in that he lived in these mountains during weather like this, without so much as a cabin. Wendy's a nurse and can help take care of your sister. So what do you do?"

For the first time in her life, Rory was embarrassed to admit the truth. "I'm a petroleum geologist. I know about finding oil, and I know about drilling for it. The closest I've ever come to survival conditions was when I told the men working for me to stop drilling because they were going to hit a pocket of natural gas, and they didn't listen. And it wasn't my survival that was at stake."

Chase nodded, but didn't look scornful. Instead, all he said was, "You probably know more than you think."

"Well, I do know the air is getting stale in here and apparently you have to open the door to let in fresh, and that cools us down, too."

He nodded. "We're in a fairly airtight tube. That has advantages and disadvantages, obviously. Something I need to work on."

"And the beacon?"

"Something else I need to work on. But that's not all, Ms. Campbell."

"Call me Rory, please." Formality felt utterly awkward right now.

"I'm Chase then. Anyway, an emergency beacon works great when someone's looking for it. Assuming, of course, it's one of the things on this plane that's still working, and little enough is."

Rory felt her chest tighten with anger and something approaching despair. She had only one goal right now: get Cait into that trial before it was too late. So, of course, everything possible had gone wrong. Listening to Chase, it was hard to remember they were lucky the plane had come down reasonably intact and that no one was injured. Or maybe not just lucky. Maybe she needed to acknowledge this man's piloting expertise. But she wasn't ready to do that. Not with every new bit of information hitting her like a body blow.

Chase continued, his tone quietly emphatic, as if he were determined to make her understand. "Nobody's looking for us right now because of the storm, and we've got an additional complication...we're down in the mountains. That limits range. I don't have a satellite downlink, either, maybe because of the storm, but GPS is down, so that means the beacon can't transmit our location. And with every minute we're getting buried deeper in snow. I doubt the trail left by our slide along the mountain is going to be visible for long, if it even still is."

Her heart knocked uncomfortably. "So we're invisible."

"Right now, yes, and we're also inaccessible, so we need to conserve everything we can. After the storm passes, we might get satellite back, but I'm not going to keep trying until after the storm because I need to preserve what batteries I've got. I'll work on checking the beacon. With any luck it's still working and will work for days."

"And after the storm?" she asked. "I can't just sit here waiting indefinitely for rescue. My sister...my sister only has four days of medicine."

His answer was quiet. "I understand. Believe me.

I understand." Then he dropped another bomb. "I'm going to have to turn off the emergency lighting. That's running on batteries, too."

It was already dark in the plane. And now it was going to get even darker. Rory suppressed a shudder and tried to find the steel will that had helped her rise in what was most definitely a man's world.

Right now, however, it had deserted her. All she could do was look toward the back of the plane and her sick, dying sister, and wonder if she was going to fail Cait.

All because she'd tried to spare Cait a fatiguing, uncomfortable commercial flight. All because she'd wanted to get Cait to the hospital the fastest way possible.

Maybe sometimes fate just wouldn't let you take charge.

Chase watched the expressions play over Rory's face as she absorbed the bad news. It took real effort to read her, as if she practiced keeping a straight face, but her guard seemed to be down at the moment. She truly worried about her sister, of that he had no doubt, and her acceptance of his risk assessments suggested that she wasn't one who argued for the sake of argument. Once she had accepted that someone knew what he was doing, she didn't waste energy fighting it.

That made her fairly unique in his experience. But no less troublesome, because she really was a rare beauty, though she did nothing to enhance her looks. Not even a smidgeon of makeup highlighted her eyes, lips or cheeks. Nor did she need them. And those bright blue eyes of hers appealed to him at a deeper level than thought. A level he told himself he couldn't afford to pay attention to right now. Rescuing passengers and indulging in passions couldn't possibly mix well. Besides, as he ought to know by now, women didn't seem to like him for very long.

He shook himself free of reverie and looked at Yuma. "You said something about the wind when we were outside."

"Yeah," Yuma said. "We need to get ready to build that fire. The wind won't entirely stop, but it *will* change direction after sunset. It always does in these mountains, even in a storm. I don't know why that is, but it'll get calmer for a while and we need to be ready to take advantage of it. Ideally, we should try to make a firebox with metal, if we can find enough in here."

"We can," Chase said firmly. "The galley doors are aluminum. And there are other things, too."

"Good. Let me get one more cup of that coffee before we go out again. Damn, I'd forgotten how cold this mountain can get."

Chase saw Wendy lay her hand on Yuma's forearm, and thought again about how hard this could turn out to be for the man. Not just the plane crash, but all the resurrected memories of his time in these mountains, hiding from the demons of war that wouldn't leave him alone.

The only solution for any of them right now was to keep busy, to feel that they were accomplishing something. First rule: Leave no room for despair. Paralysis would accomplish nothing, and despair could be a killer.

"Okay," he said briskly. "Let's see about making that firebox. A hot meal would do us all some good."

He noted that Rory went first to check on her sister.

Understandable. Unfortunately, the fact that she looked more worried when she emerged concerned him.

"Is she too cold?" he asked.

"I don't think so. It's just that she's sleeping so much. Too much."

"We need to get some calories into her," he said. "Can she hold down food?"

"Mostly liquids."

"Then we'll get her some soup first thing." With that he picked up a screwdriver and started helping Yuma pull down the galley doors.

"What can I do?" Rory asked.

Chase's instinctive response was to tell her to keep an eye on her sister. Then he realized that she needed something far less passive to do. Something that made her feel like she was doing more than holding a death watch.

"There are some aluminum doors up front, too. They're faced with wood veneer, but they're aluminum. There's another screwdriver in the service hatch I left open." He wasn't sure she'd be able to work the screws—they'd been mechanically tightened—but she might surprise him. He and Yuma weren't exactly finding it impossible to loosen the screws in the galley doors.

She didn't say a word as she eased past him, but as his gaze followed her briefly, he could see a sense of purpose in her posture and step. Good.

Then he watched Wendy slip back into the bedroom to check on their patient. Rory, he suspected, hadn't wanted to let anyone else touch her sister. A born guard dog. He liked that.

Chase and Yuma carried the aluminum doors outside into the blizzard to hammer them into the shape they needed. Neither of them wanted to do it in the confines of the plane because the banging would be deafening.

Ignoring the cold and the snow that stung like small knives, they battered the doors into a box with a top. Removing a couple of the inset latches created for air to circulate.

"Instant stove," Chase remarked an hour later.

"Hardly instant," Yuma replied. "I'm soaked with sweat."

"That'll teach you to wear warm clothes in the dead of winter."

Yuma chuckled. "Better than being out here in rags with ratty blankets."

"Guess so." Chase paused after shaking the firebox to ensure it was sturdy. "You doing okay?"

"I'm fine. Yeah, I'm remembering, but the memories of being out here aren't memories of Nam. It's too damn cold."

Chase laughed. "I guess I can see that."

Yuma stood straight and looked toward the almost invisible trees that surrounded the clearing. "Can I be honest, Chase?"

"Hell, yeah." But Chase felt himself tightening inwardly, ready for criticism he felt he deserved.

"You did an amazing job of bringing us down. I'm not sure how you managed it. We're alive because of it."

Chase waited, sure there was more, but it didn't come immediately. Finally, Yuma sighed, the sound almost snatched away by the wind.

"I'm grateful," he said. "More grateful than I can tell you because honest to God, Chase, I'm not sure I could survive without Wendy."

Chase felt his chest tighten in sympathy, but didn't know what to say.

"Do you know I used to be an alcoholic?"

"I was probably too young to hear that rumor."

Yuma chuckled and looked at him. "Yeah, probably. But I was. It was a way to hide. Anyway, I got my act cleaned up before Wendy came back to town to take her second swing at my bachelorhood. Thing was, even then I kept a bottle in my desk drawer."

"I thought you weren't supposed to do that."

"I wasn't." Yuma's mouth tightened a bit. "It was my security blanket. I knew it was right there if I ever couldn't fight off the urge for a drink. For me, anyway, it kept the craving from going over the top."

"I never would have thought that of you."

Yuma shrugged. "It wouldn't work for most folks, I guess, but it worked for me. Never even broke the seal on the bottle. And then Wendy...well, I haven't needed to keep a bottle around since."

Chase nodded, getting the message. Or at least he thought he did. "You've got a lot to be proud of."

"Actually, no, I don't," Yuma said flatly. "Pride doesn't figure into it at all. What I have is a lot to be grateful for, like that woman in there." He paused. "We gotta save Rory's sister, man."

"I know."

"I know you do." Yuma took a step toward the trees. "That's why I respect you. Now let's got get some wood and some pine needles."

Two hours later they had the firebox assembled and working outside. From the window of the plane, Rory watched as the fire burned within the three-sided box.

It had taken some effort to make a chimney so it would draw air up and through, but it was working now.

Dimly in the swirling snow, she could see the men looking for more wood to keep it going. It was getting darker out there now, as night closed in on them.

She ordinarily liked the night, but not this time. The plane had gone dark to save battery power. The only light came from a lone candle sitting on the large work or dining table in the center of four of the seats.

As business jets went, this was a comfortably sized one, capable of carrying twelve or more passengers, with room to move around. She wondered what kind of traffic Chase could carry to pay for a plane like this, then let the thought wander off. What did it matter? There were apparently enough people left in the world who could afford this kind of transportation, and given that it was a plane, being based out of some invisible town in Wyoming was hardly a hindrance to him.

Reluctantly, she tore her gaze from the fire, experiencing a gut-deep understanding of why fire had been so important in times past. Probably since ancient times. It promised life, light, warmth. It held the night at bay.

Nothing inside this plane did that except for a single candle.

It was time to wake Cait and get her to take her medicine. Rory had hoped to feed her soup at the same time, but she couldn't wait any longer. Wendy had heated enough water to make a couple of cups of tea, but no more because they had to be careful.

"Lots of sugar in it," she said to Rory now as she passed her a mug. "And there's another if she wants it."

"Thanks."

She accepted the mug, testing the temperature of the tea with her upper lip. Not hot enough to burn. Good.

Then she grabbed the small nylon bag in which she kept Cait's meds, and headed back, aware that Wendy followed with the candle. A candle in the dark.

Cripes. She needed more than that.

Once in the bedroom, Wendy set the candle on the small bedside table, then slipped away to leave the sisters alone.

"Cait. Cait?" Gently she shook her sister's shoulder. "Cait?"

Slowly, Cait's eyes opened, and she sighed. "Why don't you just let me go?"

Rory's heart stuttered. "Because I can't. Not until we've tried everything."

Cait's eyes fluttered. "I guess."

"Cait, just because Hal left you doesn't mean there's nothing left to live for. You don't need me to tell you that. Now I've got a fresh cup of sweet tea for you."

"And medicine. Always medicine."

"Yeah, medicine. I'm glad I have it. Do you think I can help you sit up a bit?"

"Sure." Cait sounded utterly listless. Rory didn't let that stop her. She lifted her sister carefully, propping her up on pillows.

"Try some tea first," she suggested. "It'll give you energy."

Holding the cup to her sister's lips, she got half of it down her, tiny sip by tiny sip. And as the sugar hit her system, Cait seemed to gain a little energy. Just a little.

Then came the pills. This part sucked, because Cait wasn't finding it all that easy to swallow anymore, not since the radiation treatments. But they got those down, too.

"Great," Rory said, with a smile she didn't feel. Talk about a small handful of pills being an ordeal. "There's another cup of tea for you. I'll go get it."

"I already have."

Rory turned to see Wendy standing in the doorway with another mug in hand.

"Hi, Cait, I'm Wendy."

Cait gave a little nod. "So there are other passengers on the plane?"

"Me and my husband," Wendy said, moving forward to exchange mugs with Rory. "When you get a little more rested, you'll have to join us in the cabin. I'll bet we've all got interesting stories to trade."

Rory expected Cait to decline, but instead was astonished to see her sister smile, however weakly. "Sounds like fun."

"It will be. All of us have had some crazy experiences. I'll bet Rory has had more than her share. And you can keep her honest for us." Wendy winked and slipped out again.

"I like her," Cait whispered.

"Me, too. More tea?"

The second cup went down easier than the first. Unfortunately, almost as soon as it was gone, Cait's eyes fluttered closed and she slipped away again. A few words and a couple of cups of tea had been enough to wear her out.

That was not good, not good at all. Rory had the awful feeling that she could almost see the darkness gathering around her sister, waiting to claim her.

No. God, no. She jumped up, forcing the vision away. She couldn't afford to let such thoughts even cross her mind.

You're not getting her, she thought between anger and despair. *You're not taking my sister away!*

The silence seemed to mock her.

Chapter 3

Dinner worked out quite well, given the arduous conditions outside. At least they weren't going to starve, Rory thought. Cait even managed to swallow a cup of soup and another cup of heavily sweetened tea. This time she asked to join them in the cabin.

Rory's heart swelled almost to breaking. As soon as she bent to lift her sister, Chase appeared and did it for her.

"Nice you can join us, little lady," he said as he carried her, wrapped in her blankets, to one of the chairs near the table. "You get too tired, just let me know, okay? And if you want, the seats recline all the way so you can lie down out here."

"Thanks," Cait managed.

Rory could only look at Chase with gratitude. He had stepped in at the right moment and said exactly the right thing. Not too much, not too little.

And Cait looked content for the first time since Rory had come home to learn how sick she was. These plane seats were wider than normal and deeply padded, so Cait seemed to have no difficulty curling up in a way that made her feel comfortable. She didn't say much, and occasionally she seemed to doze, but she also paid more attention than usual to the conversation around her. She even accepted another cup of tea, and this time held it herself.

There was hope, Rory thought. There was definitely hope. She glanced toward Chase and saw the same expression in his eyes that she was feeling. He, too, seemed to see something promising in Cait's effort.

But the wind and the cold soon reminded them that this was no social occasion. The plane groaned loudly again as a particularly strong gust buffeted it, but nothing moved. They'd be buried by morning, Rory thought. Completely and totally buried in snow. Then what? Panic fluttered through her in a single quick wave.

"Let's get down more blankets," Chase said. "Then I think we should bundle in for the night. I'll take first watch."

"Watch?" Rory asked.

He nodded. "We're going to burn at least one candle all night—more if necessary. Someone has to keep an eye on it. We also need to watch the cabin temperature so we don't turn into popsicles overnight."

Cait had dozed off again. "She'll be warmer here, won't she?"

"Probably," he answered. "As long as she's comfortable, I'd leave her."

"I'll keep an eye on her," Wendy said. "Yuma and I are just going to curl up together on these seats right behind her. Why don't you take the chance to stretch out in the back for a bit?"

"I don't feel sleepy," Rory admitted. Not in the least. Her mind wouldn't stop racing; she had too many worries.

"Fine," Chase said. "You can come up front and keep first watch with me. Make sure *I* don't fall asleep."

She almost offered to stand watch in his stead, but caught herself just in time. He was the captain of this plane, after all, and she suspected that meant pretty much the same thing in the air as at sea. And while she didn't defer to men simply because they were men, she *did* defer to rank unless given good reason not to. There was just no point in stepping on some toes.

"Thanks, I think I will."

Maybe it would ease the terror at the back of her mind, the terror that they wouldn't be found in time to save Cait. She'd seemed better for a while, but Rory knew how illusory that could be.

They settled in the two cockpit chairs with the accordion door closed behind them. There was no light at all, except one small red one.

"What's that?" she asked.

"Control for the emergency lights. I can operate them manually when I need to. Thank goodness."

Thank goodness indeed. She suspected that if all those cabin lights had been left burning, the ones that guided the way to the emergency exits, they'd have gone dark for good by now. "Everything else is down?"

"For now. No point wasting any resources yet."

"I suppose not." Then, "So you really think a fuel line broke or something?"

"Or something," he agreed. In the dark, he kept his voice quiet. "We have wing tanks, but there's a central compartment where the fuel meets and mixes so that the tanks can be balanced. Make sense?"

"Yes."

"We could get in trouble if one tank or the other got used up too fast. We'd not only be struggling to balance ourselves, but we might lose an engine. So everything meets in the middle and fuel is passed back and forth. Considering that we lost fuel from both tanks simultaneously and rapidly, I figure something went wrong in the central holding tank. And at the rate we were losing fuel, I suspect it was being pumped out of the plane."

"There's a mechanism for that, right, to empty the fuel?"

"Yes. We can dump fuel for an emergency landing."

"So that might have gotten screwed up?"

"Maybe. Something sure as hell did, and we won't know until the NTSB takes a look. I know I got no cockpit warning of any kind until the fuel started to get too low. I'd already noticed the gauges were falling too fast, but no indication as to *why*."

"And there should have been?"

"The way these babies are designed, this plane shouldn't hiccup without giving me some kind of alert. What's more, once I noticed the fuel dropping, we were over the mountains, airports behind us were closed and I still thought for a while I'd have enough. I never cut it that close, despite the weight of excess fuel."

"So maybe two things went wrong."

"So it would seem. But it did happen awfully fast. I'm just glad I was able to get us down in one piece. For a while there, I didn't think I was going to."

"I'm glad you did, too."

She heard him shift, and as her eyes adapted to the

near absence of light, except for the tiny bit of red from dash, she could see that he looked her way as he spoke.

"Look, I'm worried about your sister, too. Seriously worried. But if we had to crash in a blizzard, having an intact plane is about as cozy as it could possibly be."

"I guess. Right now it feels like a damn prison."

"That, too." He didn't argue with her, and for a moment she felt a bit embarrassed by her ingratitude. But then she let it go. Right now this plane *was* a prison as much as it was a shelter.

"So what exactly do you do?" he asked her.

"I own a consulting firm. We prospect for oil, and supervise initial drilling to ensure that our clients locate the well optimally. Most of my work these days is in Mexico."

"Do you enjoy it?"

"It's like a great big treasure hunt, in one way. In another it's a pain."

"Why?"

"Because it's a man's world, why else? More so south of the border."

He was silent for a minute. It was a silence so intense she could hear their breathing. Apparently, between the soundproofing of the plane and the mounding snow, nothing else could penetrate this cocoon.

"That would be rough," he said finally. "I watched plenty of women pilots face that stuff in the military. At least they had regulations on their side. You wouldn't."

"And a whole culture against me. Well, not entirely, but you know how that goes. At one job, I had a *curandera* come out and promise to place a curse on anyone who gave me a hard time. It was a last resort, but it worked."

"Can you work anywhere else?"

"Most of the oil in the world seems to be in the wrong places for women to go."

"But you get hired anyway?"

"I'm good at what I do. It may be a boy's game, but I play it with the best. So I charge enough to pay some bodyguards, and sometimes to get a *bruja,* a witch, on my side."

"Sounds almost like being in a war zone."

"Sometimes. It's not the pros who give me trouble, it's the local hires. Usually they settle down with time. They know where the pay is coming from."

"But what about that blowout you mentioned?"

"Ah, that. Well, a couple of guys with more machismo than sense didn't listen when I told them our seismograph readings indicated that we were about to hit a pocket of natural gas. You always hit some gas, and there are precautions to take. I mean, depending on the depth, that stuff explodes out of the well under some huge pressure and a single spark is enough to cause a conflagration. We weren't ready to open the gas pocket, I told them to wait, but they had some kind of incentive or bet on the line and ignored me. I'm just glad I got everybody else out of the area. Then, of course, we had a messed-up rig and a roman candle to put out."

"And the guys?"

"They lived. Nice burns, though. I don't think they'll ignore orders again."

She saw him shake his head, though she couldn't read his expression. "You live an exciting life."

"Sometimes. Ah, I mostly like the people I meet down there. I love the little towns, the pace of life, the color, the music. Roughnecks are just a tough group anywhere. When I'm viewed as a tourist I have a great time. The problem starts when I'm the boss."

"I guess I can see that."

"And it would happen just about anywhere. It's like anything—you take the good with the bad. So you were a military pilot?"

"Yeah. I flew off carriers."

She leaned back a little and twisted, trying to see him better. "I read a story about that once. A true story."

"What's that?"

"It was in Korea, I think. Some navy and air-force pilots were arguing about whether the navy pilots had a tougher landing to make, and the air-force pilots claimed they could land on a carrier no problem."

At that a snort escaped him. "Why do I know how this is going to end?"

"Probably because you've landed on carriers. I guess they went out and drew the outline of a carrier deck and took turns landing. Needless to say…"

"I can imagine. And the navy guys probably crowed that the deck wasn't even moving."

"I believe that was part of it."

"There's a part they probably left out, though."

"Which is?"

"The tailhook."

Rory wouldn't have believed it was possible, but she laughed out loud. "You're right. I don't think that was mentioned."

"Of course not," he said drily. "Look, I won't tell you it's easier landing on a moving deck, but with the navigational aides we've got and the tailhook, it's not as hard as trying to land in that amount of space on flat ground *without* a tailhook."

"I don't need a map to get that one." She hesitated, then asked, "Why'd you leave? You seem too young to have retired."

"I failed my flight physical. And before you get all upset because I'm still a pilot, let me explain. Flight physicals in the military are rigorous beyond belief. Most guys will fail before they reach thirty-five. So some little glitch shows up, one that won't keep you from flying, won't prevent you from getting a job with a commercial airline, but it *will* prevent you from flying combat missions or doing carrier landings. Those are the rules. We're still allowed to fly, to keep our flight status, but we're off the books for actual missions."

"That seems extreme."

"Probably not. We *do* pull a lot of high Gs. Anyway, once I couldn't make carrier landings anymore, I didn't want a desk job so I resigned."

"And built your own little airline."

"One plane and me, a long way from my own airline, but basically, yeah."

"And now your livelihood is lying buried in snow on the side of a mountain."

"So it is." His voice sounded tight, but then he let out a breath. "The important thing is getting everyone out alive. Then I'll deal with the NTSB, the company that did the overhaul and my insurance carrier. By the time all that's taken care of, I would almost bet I'll be ready to kill someone."

"You'll certainly be older."

A quiet laugh escaped him. "Goes without saying."

Concern for her sister, which had been eating her alive for weeks now, cracked open just a little, allowing her to feel for him. "I'm sorry. I know how miserable that crap can be. I went through it on the blowout. I don't know what was worse—dealing with the investigators or dealing with the insurers."

"They were probably both equally bad. They have

the same goal after all—to give somebody *else* a hard time."

Another chuckle escaped her. "Oh, yeah. And to pin blame, preferably somewhere that doesn't cause *them* any problems."

"So what did they decide on that blowout?"

"I feared it was going to be pinned on me as long as the roughnecks stuck together. Easier to blame the *gringa* than the guys you have to work with. I was more than a little surprised to find out that a certain amount of gratitude made them tell the truth, how I had ordered the drilling stopped, and then, when I was disobeyed, cleared the area. At least nobody tried to say I should have halted the drilling myself."

"Could you have?"

"Short of shooting two men, no. And by the time I got back to the site, it was too late. I'd ordered the drilling stopped that morning, then I had to run over to another site where they were complaining that the hole was dry, and by the time I got back…well, we were minutes from disaster. All I could do was tell everyone to clear out."

She paused to sigh. "Oil wells stink when they're pumping oil. Gas is mixed in, of course, but the hydrogen sulfide smell—rotten eggs—is enough to make you gag. There was no smell. They drilled into a pocket of pure methane, and it was odorless. That is so freaking rare. I had no idea they had already broken through when I started shouting for everyone to get away, and screamed again for those guys to stop the drill. No idea. I expected the smell. Maybe they did, too. I don't know."

"So the gas was everywhere?"

"Damn near. It couldn't have been long, though.

Methane is heavier than air. It sinks to ground level. If enough of it had been out there, people would have started getting asphyxiated, and the flash fire would have singed everything at ground level. Instead, we just blew the well."

She twisted toward him. "That's why we have to burn off the escaping gas if we can't manage to capture it. Because it sinks, and when it sinks it's deadly. In the case of that well, we may have been saved by a good breeze. I don't know. I'll never know. I wasn't there when they initially busted into the pocket so I have no idea how much gas just dissipated on the wind or how little escaped right before the explosion."

"But why would those guys press on against orders?"

"Because I'm not the only boss. I'm the geologist. I find the oil, I try to keep them on track until they get the field open. There are other bosses, there isn't anything like unions for those workers, people get paid crap, and if the guy running the drilling operation, say, is getting paid by the well, and not by the hour, he'd have a lot of incentive not to want things to slow down. And he might create incentives for his crews to push on, regardless of safety. I don't know. I really, truly don't know. I know what they want me to know, and I know what I can figure out from my explorations. Beyond that…" she shrugged. "The actual business end of what's happening is opaque to me. I hear rumors, sometimes, but that's it."

"Sounds like a dangerous situation to be in."

"Not usually. Most drillers are cautious and good at what they do. Most of the people working these jobs want to bring in a sound well, not a rocket. We have more problems from faulty equipment than from greedy people. For all I know, the entire thing may have happened because someone didn't want to take orders from a woman."

"Will you be going back when your sister recovers?"

She appreciated the way he posed that question. Her chest tightened a bit, but she squelched the feeling. She'd been alone for a long time, and she could handle this situation on her own. She couldn't afford to show weakness because a stranger was being kind. "I'm not sure," she said finally. "We'll have to see how it goes."

She heard his seat creak as he shifted. "I'm going back to check on the candle, make sure everyone's okay."

"I'll go with you." She couldn't stand the thought of sitting here alone in the dark with that one red, unblinking eye. And checking on Cait had become an absolute compulsion for her.

"How come you have so many candles?" she asked him just before he opened the door.

"I've got even more in my hangar. An errant order got me a lifetime's supply, and the restocking fee was huge beyond belief."

That brought a smile to her lips and lifted her spirits a bit. It seemed that life happened to everyone.

"They make great gifts," he said quietly, a note of humor in his voice. "Well, they did until people started running when they saw me coming."

Everything in the cabin seemed fine. Rory bent over her sister, touching her cheeks, finding them cool but not too cool. She waited a moment, until she felt the flutter of her sister's breath. All was good for now.

The wind's buffeting made the plane creak a bit, but quietly now, not as loudly as earlier. Rory guessed that meant they were getting buried.

"I need some coffee," Chase said. "And since it's cooling down in here, we need to burn a couple of extra candles anyway."

"Oxygen?"

He pointed to the door. "I think enough can get in through that hole the lock left, but if it starts to feel at all stuffy, let me know. The candle seems to be burning normally though, which is a good sign."

Maybe the only sign they'd have, Rory thought. If the candle flames dimmed, they'd know they were in trouble. Like canaries in a coal mine. And a darned good reason to keep watches.

She stepped into the galley and by the light of a freshly lit candle reassembled the stand she'd made earlier from some of the chafing-dish holders. A couple of candles below and soon water was heating.

Rory leaned back against the bulkhead and wrapped her arms around herself. It seemed chillier back here.

"Where's your jacket?" Chase asked.

"In the overhead bin above Cait. I don't want to wake her."

He turned, slipping into the bedroom, and came back a minute later with a royal blue blanket. He draped it over her shoulders and helped tuck it around her. She appreciated the gesture. Maybe not *all* men were meatheads, she thought.

"Doesn't pay to let yourself get cold," he said, and rubbed her upper arms briskly. "It's harder to warm up than to stay warm."

"That's not something I've had to think about the last few years. If anything, I've spent most of my time being too warm."

In the candlelight, she caught the gleam of his smile. It was a nice smile. With that one expression he made her acutely aware that she was a woman and he was a man. And that it had been a very long time since she'd let a man get this close or touch her. She couldn't afford it on the job, or anywhere near the job, and that consumed most of her life.

It also had left her with a less-than-flattering opinion of men. Getting her a blanket, she reminded herself, didn't mean he was any better than the rest.

But then she remembered the way he had carried Cait, as if she were precious cargo, and she felt her heart lurch a bit. He could be gentle. Kind. Concerned. And so far she had to admit he seemed admirably calm and collected considering that everything he had worked for lay in ruins around him. She wouldn't have blamed him for a little display of anger or irritation or *something,* given what had happened to his plane.

Heck, after the blowout, once the injured guys had been removed and the recovery team had come in to try to extinguish the fire, she'd kicked in one of the doors in her trailer. She wasn't proud of it, but sometimes adrenaline and temper got the best of her.

She shivered unexpectedly.

"You're cold," he said.

"I can't be. I'm not any colder than anyone else."

"But you've been living in southern climes. You're going to feel it more than the rest of us."

And without so much as a by-your-leave, he unzipped his jacket, tugged the blanket open and stepped inside it with her. He urged her arms to slip around him inside his jacket, then wrapped his around her.

She sucked a sharp breath, about to protest instinctively. Then, "My God, you feel like a heater!"

"I've been nicely bundled up. And I'm willing to share."

All he did was share. Not by the merest movement did he suggest or hint at anything except that he was giving her his body heat. But he might as well have.

The full-frontal pressure of their bodies immediately unleashed a whole different kind of heat in her. She became all too acutely aware of the hardness of his chest, the flatness of his belly. He managed to keep his pelvis from touching her, so she had no idea if he felt the same response. But she knew what she wanted. She wanted him to bear down on her, make her forget by taking her right here, right now, still fully clothed. A few awkward gropings, some needy pressure…and a rocket trip to the stars would result.

She was that close, and it astonished her that such thoughts should even enter her mind. When she dated, she was a dinner-and-flowers type of woman. She always wanted a courtship, time, a slow progression while she sorted through her feelings.

So much for that. Right now a caveman would have gotten her consent. And all because having Chase Dakota lean against her to keep her warm was suddenly the sexiest damn thing in the world.

She closed her eyes as feelings of desire tormented her. Every nerve in her body seemed to have awakened, become hypersensitive. A heaviness between her legs turned into a slow throbbing, the pulsebeat of need. She heard her breathing deepen and speed up a little all at once, and hoped it didn't betray her.

Heavens, she couldn't remember ever having felt a craving this strong or elemental. It had nothing to do with the kind of person Chase was, and everything to do with the fact that she was a woman, he was a man, and her response was coming from somewhere besides her conscious mind.

Basic. Instinctual. And oh, so good. It was as if she had contained a bottled genie all her life and somehow Chase had just pulled the cork. She didn't recognize the response she was having, but she couldn't argue that it wasn't her.

It was definitely her, as well as something about the man who held her close for no other reason than to make her warm.

"Getting warm?" he asked.

She had to struggle against impulses to answer. "Yes. Thank you." A mere breath of sound.

"Good. We need to keep you wrapped up."

In his arms? Oh, yes. But of course that wasn't what he meant.

"You were colder than you realized," he said. "I felt it."

And what else had he felt, she wondered. Then to her dismay, he was pulling back from her, tucking the blanket around her. She was definitely warmer now, and his action brought her back to her senses. They were making coffee, not a safe process under these conditions, and one they couldn't afford to leave unattended, even supposing he had felt the same shaft of desire she had.

He turned, lifted the lid on the chafing dish and looked. "The water's boiling."

A few minutes later when they stepped out of the galley area with their coffee, Rory immediately noticed how much cooler the cabin was. She looked at Chase over her shoulder and he nodded.

"More candles," he said quietly. "You go sit, I'll get them."

They had made a little pocket of heat in the galley, even though it had no door on it, but stepping into the larger space gave Rory an indication of just how much the temperature was dropping in here.

Chase returned with a bunch of thick candles and set them on the tables that served the passenger seating. Soon they all glowed, driving the night out of the cabin. Rory wondered how long it would take them to drive out the cold as well.

"Now we absolutely can't afford to sleep," Rory remarked as Chase took the seat next to her.

"Nope," he agreed.

Rory watched the flames as she sipped her coffee, trying to imagine the rate at which those candles would use oxygen, and how much oxygen there was in a cabin the size of this plane. She didn't have enough information, of course, but making those mental calculations was a distraction.

Distraction from the hunger she still felt for the man sitting beside her. Even though it had been tamped, wisps remained, reminding her.

She glanced his way. "Do you always wear jeans and sweatshirts when you fly?"

A soft chuckle escaped him. "I was ferrying my plane back from Seattle. I picked up Wendy and Yuma because they were out there for a conference and I couldn't see them taking a commercial flight when I was bringing the plane back anyway. Then you showed up, wanting to go immediately. Sorry, I forgot the uniform at home. I wasn't expecting to need it."

"I was just curious. I've seen plenty of bush pilots dressed like you, but never one running a business charter."

"What I wear depends on the client. Most of them don't see much of me anyway."

"I guess not. So ordinarily you'd have a cabin attendant?"

"Usually a couple of them. People who hire jets for business expect to be treated like precious cargo. There are exceptions, of course. Some people just want to be left alone to work. Or romance each other."

Another trickle of desire warmed her between her thighs. It had been an offhand comment but, like a teenage girl, she responded to it as provocative. She wanted to shake her head at herself. "Must be interesting."

"It can be. But, again, I'm usually at the controls and hear about most of it later. Not that there's usually a lot to hear."

"So you actually are based out of Wyoming?"

"Yes."

"I guess that's not out of the way, when you fly."

"Not really. The bulk of my work is out West. I fly a lot of oil types around the Northwest, into Canada, sometimes to Alaska. Some bankers. Some ranchers, but mostly guys who own companies like yours. Only occasionally do I fly someone back East, but it happens."

"I can't imagine spending my money this way."

"Except this one time."

She looked back toward her sleeping sister. "Except this one time," she agreed. "I'm not rich. I do all right, and I'm not complaining. But I didn't get into this to get rich—I got into it because it fascinates me. It's not every job that can take you all over the world to do the thing you love."

"True."

"And it's not every job that will let you pull out all the stops to help your sister."

He nodded, his expression hard to read in the flickering light. "I kind of mucked that up."

"From what you said, it wasn't your fault."

"Maybe not. But I hired the company to do the overhaul. I picked them."

"Have they worked for you before?"

"Yeah."

"Well then."

He gave a quiet snort. "Yeah. Well then. We'll get Cait out of here as soon as the storm is over. Do you believe me?"

"I have to believe you," she said quietly. "I *have* to."

Chapter 4

The wind blew ice crystals hard against the side of the plane, and even with the soundproofing Chase could hear the *shhh* of it against the metal or windows. A mean night out there, not fit for man or beast. A killer night.

He looked at Rory. "You got enough winter clothes?"

"You mean we may have to hike out of here?"

"I don't know yet. But if we do, what have you got? Boots? Gloves?"

"Yeah. I picked up a bunch of stuff from an outfitter in Seattle. I was promised Minnesota gets pretty cold in the winter, and I figured I couldn't spend every minute at the hospital."

"Where is it?"

"In my carry-on in the overhead bin."

"Which one?"

"Why?"

He sighed. "Because I want to check it out. I want to know everything we're up against. Right here we could make it a few weeks with candles and food. But your sister can't. We may need to make some decisions."

"You want to know if I can walk out of here."

"If necessary."

She shook her head. "My sister can't."

"I know that. I'm already figuring out how to deal with that. But what I need to know is if everyone *else* can walk out of here."

At last she quit questioning him and stood up. She popped the bin open and pulled down a large carry-on. He was just glad she hadn't said it was all in the cargo space below them. First of all, he couldn't get to it, and second of all, it would probably have been flattened like a pancake if not ripped up.

Somebody had advised her well, he thought as he clicked on a flashlight to look at what she had. Waterproof boots with removable liners, great for hiking. A parka for subzero temps with a snorkel hood to protect the face, a thick pair of lined gloves, a pair of ski overalls to protect the legs from cold and wind. Even some Thinsulate undergarments. She'd be okay.

"Good," he said, and leaned back. "I suggest you put those boots on now. You never know. Did you get extra liners for them?"

"Yes."

He nodded. "You got good advice."

"I never settle for less."

He could well believe it. And it also seemed to him that she had come totally prepared for something a lot less civilized than the Minneapolis area. But maybe that was her mind-set after so many years drilling in jungles and on mountainsides. Never cut a corner.

He was a great believer in that himself. He leaned back while she put the boots on. Then she walked quietly down the aisle, just a few feet, to check on her sister. He watched the tender way she touched Cait's cheek and adjusted the blankets around her, careful not to disturb her.

He rose and eased his way back, planning to reheat the coffee. He wasn't ready by any means to change watches yet, and coffee was his second-favorite thing in life, the first being flying.

"She okay?" he whispered before he edged past.

"Fine."

He realized that she had followed him back to the galley only when he turned to face the coffeepot assemblage.

"She seems warm enough, and her breathing is normal for her. No sign of distress."

"That's good. Very good." He lit the candle under the pot, figuring there were maybe two cups left in it. "Want some? Although you ought to think about sleeping."

"Coffee never keeps me awake," she said with a half smile. "Sometimes I wish it could. I'll go get the mugs."

He'd planned to just bring the pot forward, but instead he nodded. Better to have her gone for a minute so he could steel himself again.

Because the simple truth was, hugging her to help warm her up earlier had proved to be a huge mistake. One of epic proportions. You could get kicked to the curb just so often by women before you developed a set of rules to live by.

First rule: If it might last more than a few hours, avoid it. Second rule: Never wake up in anyone else's bed.

Well, he'd screwed up this time, because as soon as

he'd wrapped his arms around Rory, some part of him had realized that a few hours would never be enough, and that he'd probably wake up in her bed if he ever crossed the line.

He couldn't exactly put his finger on why that was, either. He knew he'd had an instantaneous sexual response to her, but that alone meant nothing. Something else had set off the klaxon in his head, and he'd had to fight to stand there holding her rather than skittering away in a quest for self-protection. At least she probably hadn't noticed. Her concern for her sister clearly occupied damn near her entire horizon.

But he had noticed. The response he'd had had remained indelibly imprinted on the most primitive part of his brain, waking every now and then to remind him that Rory was sexy. Sexier than sexy. For some reason she represented a trap, not a fling.

He sighed, leaned forward against the narrow counter and sniffed the coffee. It was just starting to heat.

Rory returned, bearing their mugs. She emptied the dregs into the sink. "How much water do we have?"

"Plenty. If not, look outside."

She pursed her lips at him. "I get that part. I'm thinking in terms of water we need to keep unfrozen. Like for the loo."

"Chemical toilet. I don't know if the collection tank is leaking, but if it is, it won't affect function, although it'll be awful for the environment. I should have enough in the supply tank to last us many, many days. The only water we need is for ourselves."

Just then the plane tipped. Not a whole lot, but Chase felt it in every fiber of his being. Then it seemed to slide, just a little.

He cussed.

"What's going on?" she asked.

"I don't know. If we're sliding, we can't go far. Maybe pressure is melting some of the snow under the plane, lubricating it."

But he wasn't going to guess. He blew out the candle under the coffee and headed forward. He paused just long enough to whisper something in Yuma's ear. Yuma's head popped up, but he didn't move a single other muscle. Wendy remained asleep beside him.

Yuma nodded, then Chase went up front and started pulling out his outer gear.

"I'm coming with you," Rory said, and started pulling on her own gear, including the insulated ski pants.

"It's probably nothing," he said.

"Probably. Then again, you might need help."

His first instinct was to tell her to stay put. But he looked at her again, remembering that she had a rather tough background in her own business. She might be resourceful in a million ways he couldn't even imagine now. So he simply let her finish dressing.

They popped the hatch open, crawled swiftly out, then closed it again.

The night might as well have been pitch. Usually in a snowstorm, the snow magnified just a little light into brightness. But there was no light tonight. Not a moon, not a star, not a streetlamp or house lights. Any candle glow was now completely concealed behind windows buried in snow.

He'd been in darkness like this before, where you couldn't even gather enough light to know where to put your foot, in places he would never name. He hated it.

Chase snapped on his flashlight and instantly the night changed. The wildly blowing snow became visible, but vision hardly got any better. What darkness had hidden before, the snow did now. But not as much.

He could see the fuselage, at least some of it, now nearly hidden beneath snow in some places, blown bare in others. Walking slowly around, scanning the wreck, he heard Rory's boots crunch right behind him. In case the plane was shifting, he took the longer route around the tail section to come up the other side. Then he saw what had happened.

He came upon the wing, and noted that it had opened a crack between the snow beneath it and the snow mounding on the wing.

"There," he said.

"What?"

"The wind must have caught the wing just right and given it some lift." He waited, playing his flashlight over it, giving her a chance to take it in.

"That's what it looks like," she agreed finally.

He glanced toward her, but could see nothing of her face in the snorkel hood.

He squatted down and pulled off his glove, picking up some snow. She squatted facing him.

"Dry," he said. "The snow is so damn dry it's not going to pack. This'll probably happen again."

"Nothing we can do?"

"Nope. Even if we shove snow around the wing, the wind is just going to carry it away again."

"Do we need to get off the plane?"

"It's not like we have anywhere to go. There are trees maybe a hundred and fifty yards in front of us, so even if we're on ice we can't slide far. And trust me, no matter how aerodynamic that wing is, it's not going to be able to carry us far on a wind like this. All it can do is shake us a bit."

"Okay."

"I want to finish looking around, though." Wanted to make sure nothing had changed that he needed to worry about. Besides, doing a visual on his aircraft was a habit so deeply ingrained he couldn't have broken it.

He half wished, however, that he could find something to deal with. Anything. He wasn't accustomed to sitting on his hands doing next to nothing in a situation like this. He needed something to sink his teeth into.

Other than dealing with the crash, the destruction of his plane and the concern about his passengers. Those were all emotional things, and right now he was pretty much putting them on hold. What he needed was some useful action, but the weather right now precluded any kind of action.

"Sure." She followed him around the wing toward the nose.

He stood there, playing the flashlight over the mounded snow that buried the nose and cockpit. It had compressed during their landing, but now he could see that it was beginning to dry and sift away. The character of the snow was changing.

"It amazes me," he said, raising his voice to be heard over the howling wind and the hissing snow, "that when we first landed that snow was packed tight. Now tell me how a storm so dry can keep making snow."

"Maybe it's not. Maybe it's blowing the same stuff over and over because it's so dry."

"Probably. Makes no practical difference, I guess. We still have to wait it out."

"Yeah." Her snorkel turned toward him, her face still concealed. "This has to be awful for you," she said. "Your plane, I mean. I know how I feel when a well blows, and it's not even my equipment."

"That's stuff I can deal with later. Right now I'm more concerned about four passengers—most especially your sister."

She remained silent and still for a beat. Then, "Thank you. She's my foremost concern."

The wind suddenly shifted, blowing crazily from one direction then another until the snow seesawed wildly in the air. "Let's get back inside. Nothing we can do out here right now."

As they crawled back into the plane, icy air snaked down the aisle and carried some snow with it. Just a sprinkling that sparkled in the candlelight. The candles themselves flickered then brightened. Chase was able to bring the door back up himself, and when he turned around, he saw Yuma coming forward with a couple of mugs in his hands.

"Figured you'd be cold," he said.

Rory was already bending over her sister, still wearing her outer gear, but she'd thrown her hood back so she could lean close and check Cait. Chase accepted the mug from Yuma without taking his eyes from her, which is why he caught the way she stiffened.

At once he set the mug on the table, squeezed past Yuma and headed back. "Rory?"

"Her breathing doesn't sound quite right. And she feels warm."

Hoping against hope that it was the contrast after being outside, he touched his own fingers to Cait's cheek. "Hell," he whispered.

Rory turned. "Wendy? Wendy?"

Wendy's eyes fluttered open. An instant later she was fully awake. Chase recognized that response. He had it himself, as did Yuma. Some life experiences taught it to you.

"What's wrong?" Wendy asked. "Cait?"

Rory nodded and stepped back from her sister. "Her breathing sounds funny. She's warm."

Wendy immediately slipped in beside Cait and leaned forward, putting her ear to Cait's lips. Then she touched Cait's forehead and checked her pulse at her throat.

"There's a bit of congestion. It might just be from sleeping too much. The warmth isn't much yet. It could be from the blankets and the hat."

Rory leaned back against the edge of a seat, almost sagging. "What do we do?"

"We're going to have to try to wake her. Get her to cough." Wendy peeled the blankets back from Cait's chest and pressed her ear there, first one side and then the other. "My kingdom for a stethoscope," she muttered as she leaned back, squatting. "It doesn't sound bad, mostly bronchial congestion. I don't hear anything from lower. But she needs to cough. Apparently, her breathing has been too depressed for too long. We need to clear her out."

Rory stripped off her jacket and gloves fast, then pulled the blankets away from Cait enough to grab her under the arms and lift her.

Cait weighed next to nothing, as Chase knew, but he was still impressed with how easily Rory lifted her sister. Then, holding her with one arm, she began to pat Cait's back. "Cait. Cait! Wake up."

Wendy stepped up, fisted her hand and gave Cait a couple of good thumps on the upper back with the heel of her fist.

Cait's eyes fluttered. "Wha—"

"You need to cough, Cait," Rory said firmly. "We're helping you."

Wendy gave her a couple more thumps. Cait's breathing changed, and now even Chase could hear a rattle from where he was standing. "It's coming," Wendy said.

"Should I put her on the bed?" Rory asked.

"Only if this doesn't work. Just make sure you haven't got her so tight she can't draw air deeply."

A couple more thumps, then a cough. A good cough.

"There we go," Wendy said. "Set her on the seat, let her lean forward a bit. I'm going to get her to express some more."

A few minutes later Wendy was happy with the sound of Cait's breathing. And Cait herself was awake enough to show some interest in tea and soup.

Chase quietly let himself into the cockpit and closed the door. He sat in his seat, staring at the red light and the snow in his cockpit windows that reflected it, dim though it was.

He'd understood that they were working with a time frame when it came to Cait. Four days of medicines. He could tell how frail she was. But what hadn't crossed his mind was the fact that she could get sick with something else and die on this damn plane.

He hadn't thought about pneumonia.

There was a helluva lot he hadn't thought about, and right now he wanted to kick himself hard. Instead he opened his toolbox, got down on the deck and used a flashlight to try to see his way around the wiring for the satellite-comm link.

Waiting out this storm wasn't going to cut it. That was now eminently clear.

Winter nights were naturally long, especially this far north, but Rory felt this one dragging painfully. Occasionally the plane juddered from the wind, and once or twice an eerie moan managed to emerge from the twisted metal. But they didn't slide or tip, and beyond that she didn't care.

She cared about only one thing—her sister. She sat across from Cait, watching her constantly, wishing there was anything more she could do right now. The merciless storm continued to howl, however, and it was so dark out there anyway that even if it quieted they wouldn't be going anywhere.

Cait woke periodically, and each time she did, Rory or Wendy encouraged her to cough, and filled her with more tea and soup, as much as they could get her to swallow. Cait's cooperation was frighteningly listless, as if she drank and coughed only because she knew they wouldn't let her refuse.

Rory caught some uneasy, disturbed sleep, waking at nearly every little sound. She heard the murmurs of Yuma and Chase in the cockpit as they worked on the electronics, and wondered how much either of them knew.

Finally, satisfied that Cait had managed to swallow another cup of heavily sweetened tea, and that she had coughed enough to make her breathing sound clear, she watched her sister drift again into sleep and made her way forward. Both men were lying on the cockpit floor, corkscrewed around the seats, with wires dangling from beneath the console.

"Need any help?" Rory asked.

"I wish," Chase answered. "Apart from lack of room, we're looking at spaghetti here."

A flashlight illuminated a number of loose-leaf manuals between them, and the dangling wires.

"Did you find anything broken?"

"Nope. Everything seems to be connected so far, and we're not disconnecting anything. First rule…"

"Yeah," Yuma said. "If it ain't broke, don't fix it."

"There might have been internal damage to some of the units from impact," Rory remarked.

"That's our concern," Chase agreed. "Although you'd think my damn emergency beacon would be up to it. Still, there's the GPS connection. That's a separate unit, and it could have been damaged. Or it may just be the storm. I'm beginning to think we won't know for sure until we get some clearing."

At that moment, Wendy popped her head over Rory's shoulder. "You know, you two... and by *you two* I mean Chase and Rory...you ought to get some sleep. Yuma can watch over things, and I can watch over Cait, but neither of you will be worth a damn when this storm blows out if you haven't slept."

Rory started to argue, but Wendy was having none of it. She tugged Rory's arm and pulled her back to the aft bedroom where the two twin beds abutted the sides of the plane. "Sleep," she said. "It's our watch now. And you don't want to be useless to your sister."

It was that last argument that worked. Edgy though she felt, Rory gave in, removing her boots and snow-pants so she could crawl under the blankets. She was sure she wouldn't sleep, but she began to drift off almost immediately, only vaguely aware that Chase at some point crawled into the other bed.

She was worn out. Everything had worn her out. She hadn't slept well or much since coming home from Mexico to find out how ill her sister was. At least now, with a snowstorm paralyzing them, sleep didn't feel like such a huge waste of time.

When sleep at last arrived, a few rare tears dampened her cheeks.

* * *

Her dreams were disturbed, more memories than dreams, really. She awoke sometime later, while it was still dark, the bedroom illuminated only faintly by the candles that burned in the main cabin.

Back here it had grown cold, so cold that she was curled up in a tight ball with her teeth chattering. She needed to get up, go into the main cabin and seek what warmth she could.

But her mind had hit the ground running, full of thoughts of Cait, of her dire diagnosis, of the fact that the doctors in Seattle could offer no hope this time, except for the trial of a new drug.

Last time had been so different. Nearly four years ago, the doctors had used upbeat words like, *nonaggressive, high cure* and *remission rates*. Yes, there had always been a possibility that the disease could kill her, but their attitudes had been optimistic.

Not now. By the time she had reached the hospital hallways from Mexico, the words that had been flying around were *grave, aggressive, maybe a few months.*

Then one oncologist, a man who never pulled his punches, had said simply, "Your sister's only hope is a trial they're running on a new drug. Do you want me to pull strings and see if I can get her in? I can't make any promises, but they've had some good results with remission."

Because remission was now probably the best Cait could hope for, a few more years disease-free. No one seemed to think there might be a cure anymore. Not now that she had relapsed into an even worse form of the illness.

But Rory wasn't one to give up. She wasn't going to turn precious minutes of Cait's life over to the Grim

Reaper without a fight…even if Cait herself didn't seem to want to fight anymore.

And that son of a bitch Hal had deprived her of hope. He couldn't handle having a sick wife again. At least that was his excuse. Rory suspected he'd been cheating on Cait for a long time, maybe since she first got ill. According to one of the nurses she'd spoken to out of concern for Cait's despair, that wasn't uncommon. Apparently "till death do us part" didn't mean much in the case of lingering illness.

"I see it lots of times," the nurse had said bluntly. "And the ones who stick around ogle me like fresh meat and flirt with me. Right in front of their wives. You ask me, a lot of men just aren't any good for the long haul."

"But you see others who stick it out?" Rory had asked, maybe because she wanted to strangle Hal.

"Sure. There are good men. Just not as many as you would hope. Not when it comes to this."

So Hal was just an ordinary creep, no worse than most of his kind, not as good as some. But part of what maddened Rory the most was the way it had cut the heart out of Cait. No pep talks worked. No desire to get even and show her husband inspired her.

Cait had just plain given up. Life had become a load too heavy to carry anymore. And Rory, who felt an unnatural urge to violence when it came to Cait's husband, restrained herself because even she could see that the damage had been done and there was nothing on earth that would repair the wound.

Except time. But Cait was dreadfully short on time now.

Another tear leaked out from one eye, almost fiery in its warmth against the chill of her cheeks. She couldn't afford this sorrow and weakness—she had to take care of Cait. Later, if nothing worked, would come the time to grieve. But not now, not while Cait still needed her.

Another shiver ripped through her, and she clamped her teeth to still their chattering. It *had* to be warmer in the cabin.

Before she could move, she saw a familiar shape move in the dim glow of the candlelight from the cabin, then Chase bent down near her ear.

"I can hear you shivering. Scoot over."

"I should check Cait."

"I just looked out. Wendy's wide awake, sitting right across from her. Look, your getting hypothermic isn't going to help anyone."

She couldn't argue the basic sense of that, so she scooted over. He'd doffed his jacket and boots, and soon she was cradled against his heat, his strength beneath the blanket. Great strength, she realized as he nestled her head on his sweatshirt-covered shoulder and pulled her close to his chest.

The muscles she felt flexing against her were the hard, flat muscles of hard work, not the bulging carefully cultivated masterpieces some men liked. She'd quit going to co-ed gyms years ago because she had gotten tired of watching men work their pectorals and biceps as if they were the only muscles that mattered.

Of course, when she was in the field, she saw plenty of hardworking muscle, especially on hot days, but she didn't feel it pressed up against her, holding her. Indeed, she'd gotten to where she hardly noticed it. But this was different.

Chase was so warm. Almost too soon, it seemed, his heat began to penetrate her, reaching deep inside, thawing her bones, easing her tension, halting the shivering. Then it filled her not only with comfort, but with a sweet yearning she had almost forgotten existed.

She turned her head a little so she could press her eyes to his shoulder and try to stave off the tears. She didn't cry. She wasn't a crier by nature and hadn't been since childhood. But now she wanted to cry, just sob her eyes out.

She was just worn out, she told herself. It had been a hard few weeks, finding out how sick Cait was, and then trying to find a miracle for her, or at least the hope of one. Exhaustion had weakened her, that was all.

Exhaustion and fear. Because being forced to sit here and do nothing in a crashed plane while her sister's life was waning by the minute was almost more than she could stand. Yet every ounce of common sense argued against every emotion that demanded she do *something*. Doing something right now would be foolhardy.

"You're tensing again," he murmured.

So he wasn't sleeping. Then his hands began to rub her back gently, soothingly.

"Your sister?" he asked.

"Every minute of every day," she admitted.

"Understandable. And being stuck like this has got to be a nightmare for you."

She couldn't deny that, so she didn't bother. It *was* a nightmare, just like the ones she had as a child when something was chasing her and she couldn't move.

"I can't find a problem with the GPS," he remarked. "I don't see any damage, the wiring to it seems fine, so we just have to hope we're not getting signal because of the storm."

"But it could be something you can't see."

She gave him credit for not hesitating. She hated it when she suspected people of trying not to be totally truthful. "It could be. There was a time when anyone who was handy could fix just about anything. Then they came up with black boxes."

She nodded a little against his shoulder, relieved to realize that the urge to weep was fading. Maybe his hand rubbing her back had something to do with that. Or maybe it was thinking about the other problems they faced. She always felt better when she had the true measure of a situation. It always made her feel more in control, and provided an opportunity to think of solutions. She was a born problem-solver.

"Lots of black boxes," she admitted. "Microminiaturization—the curse of modern life."

"Sometimes it is."

"When something breaks, it is. If you can get to a store for a replacement, no problem. On the side of a mountain in a blizzard, big problem."

"Unfortunately. Regardless, I won't be able to say for sure until the storm lets up. With any luck, we'll pick up signal, the beacon will start broadcasting our position, and we'll be airlifted out of here in a matter of hours."

"And if it doesn't?"

"Then we'll damn well start down the mountainside. I mean it, Rory."

"I know you do." She didn't doubt it. "It might be best for me to stay here with Cait if you do. I'm not sure she could survive a trip like that."

"No. Absolutely not. This plane is going to be invisible under the snow. There's no guarantee if some of us start down the mountain that we'd be able to guide searchers back here quickly enough. We go together or we stay together."

"I'm thinking of exposure."

"And I'm thinking of lost time."

Both of which could kill Cait. The ultimate rock and a hard place. "I know. Trust me, I know."

"I'm sure you do. With any luck, we won't have to make the decision either way."

A quiet snort escaped her. "I'm not feeling very lucky right now. Are you?"

A couple of heartbeats passed before he answered. She knew because she could hear the quiet, steady beating of his heart, a reassuring sound. "I wasn't at first. I mean, if I hadn't just had this bird in for an overhaul, I wouldn't feel quite as furious about a mechanical failure. It shouldn't have happened."

"No, it most definitely shouldn't have."

"But," he said, emphasizing the word, "I'm feeling lucky anyway, because given that something went wrong and we lost our engines, it's damn near a miracle no one was hurt."

"True."

"So tell yourself that miracles happen, Rory. And we might be entitled to more than one. Especially given that we shouldn't be here at all."

Her throat tightened and she had to swallow several times before she could answer. Her voice remained a bit husky. "I hope you're right. Are you always so upbeat?"

"The alternative sure isn't any help."

"No." She knew he was right, but at the moment she was finding it hard to feel upbeat about Cait's plight. That would come back as soon as she could take some action again. In the meantime, she wanted to think about something else before the black trickle of despair she felt grew into an ocean. "Was it hard flying without the engines?"

"Not fun," he said, still keeping his voice down.

"We were slightly more aerodynamic than a boulder. Just slightly. Our remaining airspeed was all that gave me any maneuverability and the more that dropped the harder it got."

"But the wings have enough lift that the wind was trying to pick them up."

"That's the wings. And the air has to move across them fast enough to create enough lift for an aircraft this heavy. You remember Bernoulli."

She did, vaguely. "My education has mostly been in rocks."

"Then you would have felt right at home in the cockpit for a while there."

The humor surprised her, touched her and actually lifted her spirits a bit. "Until I got out my rock hammer," she tried to joke back.

"I was sure ready to hammer something. I just didn't have time."

Finally, she said what she should have said hours ago, most especially sure it was true and she should have been grateful rather than angry as she had been initially. "Thanks for getting us down in one piece."

"You can thank me when we're all safely out of here."

"No, I don't think so."

He shifted a little. "What do you mean?" He actually sounded uncomfortable.

"Whether we get out of here or not, there wouldn't even be a question of survival if you weren't a damn good pilot. So thanks for giving me the opportunity to worry some more."

"Sure. I think."

"I'm serious."

"I know." Again that uncomfortable shifting. "So what's the story with Cait? Has she been sick for long?"

"She got nonaggressive NHL a few years back and they managed to put her into remission. The stats are actually pretty good for that."

"But it's aggressive now?"

Rory had to swallow before she could speak. Her throat was tightening up again, and she hoped he couldn't hear it. She didn't want to seem weak. "Yeah. Very. And since her husband left her when she got sick again, I don't think she wants to live."

He swore quietly. "Well, that sure as hell complicates things, doesn't it?"

"A whole lot."

"And there's an experimental treatment in Minnesota?"

"Yeah. She was sinking so fast it was hard to get her in."

"And now this."

"Now this."

He muttered another curse. "I'm sorry, Rory."

"It's not your fault. At first I was mad, sure you must have done something wrong, but from what you've told me, it sounds like some mechanic did something wrong. At least we're all okay. And somehow we'll get out of this."

"Because we have to."

She noted that he said it as if it was all the reason he needed. Just *have to*. Well, there'd been plenty of times in her own life when forced to take action had been all that had kept her going and moving mountains. This was just another mountain, more frightening and intimidating than most, but still just a mountain.

"You must be scared," he said, surprising her.

"I am." It was easy enough to admit. "The treatment might not work. I know that. Not at this stage. But I think it'd have a whole lot better chance if she *wanted* to live."

"Well, of course. I don't suppose there's any chance her husband will come to his senses?"

"I doubt it. He moved in with one of his graduate students. I really don't think Cait would want him back now anyway."

"Probably not. I wouldn't, in her shoes. And I've been in her shoes, sort of."

The admission surprised her. "Really? You? The hunky flying ace?"

A startled but quiet laugh escaped him. "Try living with a navy pilot. Gone six months at a stretch. Sometimes flying in dangerous parts of the world. Looks good until you have to live it. And there's a lot of temptation around a base when your significant other is gone. Besides, I never got far enough that I felt I had an exclusive claim."

"I take it you've been on the curb more than once."

"More than once," he said frankly. "Which leads me to believe I'm not easy to get along with anyway. And maybe I wasn't back then. There's a sort of cockiness that goes with the job, I admit."

"And now?"

"If I have any cockiness left, I haven't noticed it recently. Flying a taxi kind of puts you in your place, don't you think?"

"Depends on who's hiring you." She rolled her head a bit, surveying the glow from the cabin, trying to see his face and being rewarded with a view of his chin. "You don't like what you're doing now?"

"What I like is flying. I've always loved it. And I've

discovered that I don't have to be in dogfights, or pull five Gs in a roll to enjoy it. So these days I think of myself as carrying eggs."

"Eggs?" she chuckled.

"Eggs," he repeated. "Raw eggs. And my job is to give them such a smooth ride their shells remain intact. That's not always easy flying over the mountains." He shifted a bit, and somehow he was holding her a little closer. "I guess it's all a matter of attitude."

She nodded against his shoulder, agreeing. Warmth had permeated every corner of her body, even her toes, and now that the cold was no longer a threat she was noticing other things, things she hadn't paid attention to in a long time now.

Like how good a man could smell—especially this one. She felt guilty for letting herself grow aware of him. For God's sake, Cait was in the cabin, so sick… Guilt started to rise in a nauseating wave. Then she realized something. Right now she couldn't do even the least thing for Cait. Nothing. Wendy was sitting out there, a trained and experienced nurse. Better care, no doubt, than she herself could provide.

So what was wrong with letting go for just a few minutes? Nothing. Maybe she needed it for her sanity after the last few weeks, a few minutes of escape into fantasy.

Because it was pure fantasy. When they got out of here, she'd be headed to Minnesota and would never see this man again.

That thought made it even more tempting to indulge the images that had begun to dance around the edges of her mind. He continued to rub her back, but she imagined her sweater vanished. She knew how his palm felt already, warm and dry, and it was easy to imagine it running up and down her back, skin on skin.

She felt her nipples pebble with hunger, and as they did so, a shaft of longing speared straight to her loins. Wow. It seemed like forever since she had responded to nothing but a few stray thoughts. Given her job, she'd carved sex right out of her life. She couldn't afford to have her subordinates gossiping and certainly not the roughnecks she worked with. Becoming asexual had seemed like a necessary protective mechanism.

But she didn't need that protection right now, and long-buried needs struggled within her for recognition.

He smelled good. He felt good against her. Knowing absolutely nothing could happen right now made her feel safe, too. With eyes closed, her senses filled with him, she let the fantasy train roll out of the station.

She hovered on the cusp of anticipation, caught on a needlepoint of longing as she imagined him transgressing beyond the gentle backrub. What if he slipped his hand around and cupped her breast? An electric shock zapped through her at the mere idea of how it would feel to have him touch her there, even through layers of clothing. Between her legs, a weight grew, heavy and hungry, and began to throb damply.

So far so fast, she thought with amazement. One little wisp of fantasy and she was as ready as she had ever been in her life. She bit her lower lip, tensing inwardly against the yearning that might cause her to make a betraying move. Thank goodness he couldn't read her mind. That privacy was precious, and she didn't want to reveal her thoughts by slipping and moving in some revealing way.

But oh, she wished she could. Her heart sped a bit and she bit her lip harder. If only this were the time and place, she'd gladly indulge in a quick, meaningless mating just to satisfy the hunger and carry a memory of it with her.

Memories served her well when she was far from home, and a stash of them that involved having hot, impatient sex with Chase seemed worth putting in her mental photo album.

It would be so easy. All she had to do was lean a little closer, roll just enough to throw her leg over his, and the invitation would be unmistakable.

Then, a few minor adjustments of clothing. They wouldn't even need to disrobe completely. Quick, hot... and frankly more like something you'd get on a street corner in many of the towns she'd seen.

A sigh almost slipped out of her as the fantasy popped, leaving her feeling disappointed and frustrated. That wasn't her—rough and ready, mating with a stranger. What was wrong with her? But that's exactly the urge he'd awakened in her, however briefly.

Stress, she told herself. Too much stress and worry. She was losing it.

Then he astonished her by the simple expedient of stroking her hair back from her forehead. She kept her hair relatively short because washing it wasn't easy in some of the places she worked, and it had been a long time since anyone had seemed interested in running their fingers through it.

But he did, combing the soft curls with his fingers, then once again slowly running his hand down her neck and her back. A shiver trickled through her, and it was not the cold.

"Sleep," he whispered. "Wendy will call you if Cait needs you. But you need to sleep."

So did he, she thought. Then, unconsciously, she

snuggled closer, letting him make her feel safe and wanted, illusion though it was, and this time when she closed her eyes, no tears fell and sleep came quietly.

Chapter 5

"Rory?"

She woke from a sleep so dreamless and deep that she almost felt drugged. Chase was still holding her, but it was his voice that had called to her.

"Mmm?" Her eyelids felt heavier than lead.

"Cait's asking for you."

All of a sudden, the lead vanished from her eyes and the sleep from her body. She sat up so fast she almost banged her head on the curving fuselage beside her.

"Whoa," Chase said. "Don't hurt yourself. That's a complication none of us needs."

Even as he spoke, though, he was sliding out of the bed, pulling the covers back so she could climb out. At once she noted how chilly the air felt after the warm cocoon Chase had made for her. No time for that now.

Except Chase figured there was time. "Get your boots on," he said. "You can't afford to get cold."

He was probably right about that. Between time and the risk of hypothermia, this plane wasn't as cozy as it might seem. Cozier than being totally exposed, but hardly a safe haven.

She jammed her feet into her boots, then reached for the laces as the light brightened and she realized that someone had brought a candle into the room. She glanced up long enough to see that it was Chase.

"It's not an emergency," he said, reassuring her. "She just asked for you. Wendy doesn't seem worried."

"Right." As if she'd take anyone else's word for that, except a doctor, and then only a doctor who had a chance to get to know all details of Cait's medical history. Nothing against Wendy, but she hadn't even known Cait twenty-four hours yet, and had no medical records to refer to. Those had all been faxed ahead.

She finished tying her boots then stood, reaching for her parka. Chase moved out of the way so she could stride quickly into the cabin as she pulled her jacket on.

She found Cait bundled in the same seat. Wendy had evidently lowered the back for her at some point, nearly making it flat, although she'd kept Cait's torso elevated by a few inches.

Rory squatted beside her and laid her hand on Cait's shoulder. "How are you doing, sweetie?"

"Okay." Cait's eyes fluttered with weariness, but she managed a faint smile. "They didn't have to wake you."

"They knew I'd want them to. Nobody risks my wrath."

Cait's smile deepened a shade. "Not even when we were little."

"Not even then," Rory agreed. "Are you hungry? How about something to drink? Something hot?"

"Wendy's been taking good care of me. Just sit with me?"

"Sure." Moving carefully, Rory stepped over her sister to the adjoining seat next to the window. All the blinds had been pulled down—not that it mattered. There was probably not a thing to see out there except snow.

She smiled at Wendy. "Your turn to get some sleep."

"I'm not going to pass on that offer. Billy Joe?"

He poked his head out of the cockpit. "Yo?"

"It's our turn for bed."

"Damn that sounds good."

Rory watched the Yumas work their way to the back of the plane and slipped her hand under blankets until she found Cait's hand and was able to hold it. She was grateful to discover that her sister's fingers didn't feel icy.

Chase moved around the cabin, replacing some old candles with new ones, and even added a few more to hold back the cold. The cabin wasn't freezing, by any means, but it wasn't toasty, either. Blankets and lots of clothing were necessary.

But it *was* warmer than the bedroom, and Rory was grateful that they had moved Cait out here. As sick as she was, she didn't have the stamina to withstand the cold, or much in the way of stressors. If they had to try to carry her out of here in order to save her life, they'd be risking it, as well.

Suddenly Cait's fingers tightened around hers. "Rory? Don't worry so much about me. It's in God's hands."

"That's the part I'm having trouble with."

"You always have." Cait's voice grew fainter, as if speaking were an effort. But her eyes remained open, looking at Rory. Then, slowly, they tracked to Chase. "You're the pilot, right?"

Chase slid into the seat facing her. "That's right, ma'am. Blame it all on me."

"I think you're a good pilot. We're still alive." A smile flickered around Cait's pale lips. "What's that saying?"

"A good landing," he replied, "is any landing you can walk away from."

"That's it. Very true." Then her eyelids sagged and she slipped again into sleep.

Rory turned her attention to Chase and found him frowning at Cait. He seemed to sense her attention, because he looked at her. "We'll get her to that hospital," he said quietly. "If I have to carry her out of here on my back."

Rory nodded, her throat tightening, even though she knew that might be too much for Cait. But if there was no alternative…

Ah, she couldn't think about that now. One foot in front of the other. How many times in life had she needed to do that? It ought to be a lesson well-learned.

"Rory?" Cait had apparently only been dozing lightly.

"Hmm?"

"Remember Mom and Dad?"

"Of course."

"I never told you, but I wanted to be like them. I shouldn't have gotten married…." Then she trailed off as she fell back to sleep.

That was surely one of the saddest statements she'd ever heard her sister make, enough to clamp a vice around her chest. Rory looked over and found Chase's eyes questioning her. She needed a moment to find the breath to respond.

"Our parents were both doctors. Once we grew up, they started working in underdeveloped countries with an international organization."

"That's impressive."

"Yeah. Except it killed them."

His brows drew together. "How?"

"They both caught a rare hemorrhagic fever and died. Five years ago. Right before Cait started to get sick."

"I'm sorry."

"That's life." Her mantra, although it was getting harder to say of late. *Life is unfair,* she reminded herself for the hundredth time. "They knew the risks, we discussed them, I was proud of what they wanted to do. And they weren't the only people who died in that outbreak. Lots of other grieving families."

"Does it help to think of it that way?"

Rory shrugged one shoulder. "Not always. But Cait is all I have left to call family. She loved her husband. I can't tell you how it hurts to hear her say she should never have married. That bastard deserves some come-uppance."

"From you?"

She shook her head. "No. I don't deal in vengeance. Which is not to say I wouldn't like to—I just don't do it. It would bring me down to his level."

"And you're better than that?"

"I wouldn't say that. But I try to be."

Chase nodded. "That's the key, I think. Trying to be better people." Then he gave her a crooked smile as if to lighten the mood. "I have the skinned knees and elbows to show for my attempts."

It worked. She felt herself smiling back a little. Just a little. Cait's hand within hers stirred a bit, then quieted. Still warm.

"So your parents were medical missionaries?"

"No, not like that. They worked for a private foundation, purely secular. They paid their own travel and living expenses and worked as volunteers. Sometimes, I guess, they even bought medicine and equipment."

"Pretty noble. Interesting that Cait mentioned that now."

Rory thought so, too. She looked at Cait and wondered if her younger sister had always harbored such a desire, and falling in love had simply gotten in the way, or if this was something new. Rory had moved on to jobs far away by the time Cait got married, and had been in touch with her sister mostly during holidays while Cait was still in high school. Neither of them had been good correspondents, satisfied to send a single line of email, and Cait had been awfully busy, too. Friends, school activities, a very full social calendar.

"She was a lot more outgoing than me," Rory said, still watching her sister, remembering. "I was more of a nerd, always buried in a book or a project. My idea of a great summer was hiking around some mountains and mapping things."

"Not looking for oil?"

"Not always. Sometimes I just enjoyed the rocks, and figuring out how things had come to be. Oil became my business later." She looked at him. "What about you?"

"Well, I can't remember a time when I didn't want to fly. I don't think I left room for much else. If flying required being good at math, then I'd be good at math. That was the way I thought. For a while I had a thing for fast cars, but that got in the way of what I needed to do to get into the academy so I gave it up."

"You're an academy grad?"

"Ring-knocker, that's me."

"I'm impressed."

He winked. "You'll get over it."

"Probably," she admitted, smiling. "Where did that term come from anyway?"

"Academy class rings. I think it was a derogatory way of saying those who graduated from the academies never let it be forgotten. It's an old term, though. I haven't heard it in a while." He shook his head a little, appearing amused. "I'm sure they've come up with better ones."

"People usually do when they resent something. I hear the academy is rough."

"Mostly in the first year. Then it gets better."

He didn't seem to want to go into it, so she didn't press him anymore. Heck, it wasn't as if she wanted to sit here and reminisce about *her* college days. She looked at Cait, glad to see that her sister appeared to be sleeping comfortably.

College seemed like an awfully long time ago now. The thought was almost wistful. "Things were so much simpler back then," she murmured. "In college, I mean. I had so much hope, everything seemed possible."

"Yeah."

"Funny how we don't often appreciate things until we're past them. All those big, important things that concerned me back then? I'd switch them for the problems right now in a heartbeat."

"I think a lot of us would. Maybe it says something that our view of what's a problem changes as we get older."

A sigh escaped her. "Too true. They do seem to get bigger and harder."

Cait murmured quietly and turned a little toward Rory. The movement made Rory's heart squeeze. How long did she have left with Cait? A few hours, a few days, a few weeks? Not long unless the experimental treatment worked. Not long before she might lose the last of her family on this earth.

She had to look away for fear that Chase would see the tears that had begun to sting her eyes. Didn't want him to guess how afraid she was, or that for the last few weeks she'd been so angry that she could barely stand herself.

But apparently she hadn't looked away fast enough, because she heard Chase move, and the next thing she knew he had captured her free hand in both of his. Reluctantly, she looked at him.

"We're going to get her out of here if there's any way humanly possible. I swear it."

She managed a nod. Then she admitted something she hadn't said out loud, not once. "I hate myself."

"Why?"

"Because I wasn't here. Because I was bouncing around the world doing my thing, and I lost all that time with my sister. I've hardly been back to see her since she was sick last time, and before that...not much better."

He stayed quiet for a while, not replying. But maybe there was nothing anyone could say. She'd screwed up. She'd gone off to live her own life without considering just how short life could be, especially so for her kid sister. Even after the last round, once Cait was in remission, she'd taken off again. She had promised herself she'd come home to visit every few months, but she hadn't. She had failed to learn the lesson.

"I'm stupid," she said. "How many times do I need to be beaten over the head? Our parents died, then Cait got sick, and what do I do? As soon as the docs said Cait was in remission I went back to my old globe-trotting ways."

"What were you supposed to do?" he asked. "Stop living your own life and move in next door?"

"No, but I should have come back more often. I should have gotten the message that tomorrows aren't guaranteed."

"No, they're not. But most of us couldn't survive if we believed that. Counting on tomorrow is what keeps us going. And you had your own life, Rory. You were entitled to that. You didn't do anything wrong."

"I think I did."

"Okay. But look at you now. You've dropped everything. I'm assuming that doing that has messed with your career a bit, since most people can't just drop out of their jobs for weeks on end. I know I couldn't. If I did what you're doing, I'd practically have to rebuild my business from the ground up."

"It's not quite that bad."

"*Quite,* huh. That tells me it is. But you didn't hesitate, you came home to take care of your sister, and you're not counting the cost. I can tell that from the fact that you hired me to get you halfway across the country to get her an experimental treatment. A lot of people wouldn't do that. So quit beating yourself up. You're here when she needs you."

"Late, but yeah." He was making sense, but the sense wasn't reaching her heart. She *did* appreciate the way he held her hand, though, and inevitably thought back to the time they had spent bundled in the bunk while he warmed her up. Her cheeks burned a bit as she remembered her burgeoning fantasies about him, and then it struck her that he was a generous man. He hadn't hesitated to offer his body heat when he surely must have been more comfortable in his own bunk than holding a stiff, shivering woman. And while that might be simply a matter of survival imperative, he hadn't been required to move over her way and take her hand when he sensed her emotional distress. Hell, most of the men she knew ran like sprinters from that sort of thing.

In fact, in her job she'd had to become "one of the guys," so much so that she never showed any emotion other than anger or humor. It almost surprised her to realize the tenderhearted part of her still existed.

It surprised her almost as much to realize that she wasn't exactly comfortable with it anymore, either. She wanted to fight for Cait with everything she had. She found it easy to get angry at the illness, easy to swing into action to reach for a last straw. What was not easy any longer was feeling the aching love for her sister, her fears, her pain.

Her job had warped her, she guessed, but she wasn't sure that was a bad thing. However it turned out with Cait, at some point she was going back to those oil fields and the world of machismo.

She drew a deep breath, not exactly a sigh, and waited for her internal landscape to resettle into more familiar contours. She couldn't afford to let herself fall apart. Not now, for Cait's sake. Later, for her own.

With effort, she removed her hand from Chase's clasp, regretting the loss of contact immediately, but steeling herself against it. She leaned back a little in her chair, and he read her reaction accurately. At once he leaned back in his own seat, and the gulf between them widened.

"Sleep if you want," he said to her. "I can keep an eye on things."

"You need sleep, too," she said. "We need you in top form. I'm no survivalist." A logical explanation when in truth she just didn't want to be unfair or selfish. They were supposed to share these watches.

He nodded. "Call me if you need anything." Then he rose and went to the cockpit.

Leaving her feeling alone all of a sudden.

Don't, she told herself. *Don't go there.* Given the circumstances, for all she knew she was experiencing some variant of the Stockholm syndrome, where hostages become attached to their captors. What did she know about this guy, anyway? That he had a military background? That the Yumas had been his friends for a long time? That under these circumstances he could be generous? What about the rest of the time?

He had already admitted that he didn't succeed at long-term relationships, that he was often, if not always, dumped. That should be a red flag.

Yet as she looked at herself she saw the same experience. She hadn't had anything approaching a long-term relationship since college, and in retrospect she could see that it had been motivated more by raging hormones than anything else.

Her life now didn't leave room for the long term. She traveled too much, and spent most of her life in places where she couldn't establish a relationship that wouldn't interfere with her job, or the perception of her workers.

In her experience, too, she seemed to intimidate a lot of men. High drive and career preoccupation, not to mention being home only a few weeks a year, didn't seem to appeal to the kinds of men who wanted more than a quick roll in the hay.

So who was she to think Chase's track record meant he was somehow defective? Thinking about it, she could easily see that, being gone for such long periods, he'd be leaving behind girlfriends who would face a lot of temptation around military bases. Guys who were actually there. Unless the relationship evolved into something strong and permanent, it would be unlikely to survive.

As for him having been cocky, well, she could imagine that might almost be a prerequisite for a military pilot. What else would make you take those chances again and again?

She smothered a sigh and looked at Cait, acknowledging that thinking about who Chase was or wasn't was a form of escape from her worry and fear. Much easier to ponder the characteristics of a near stranger than to actually think about how her sister's life was hanging by a thread.

A thread made all the thinner because she seemed to have given up.

Sometimes Rory almost wanted to shake Cait, to tell her there was a life apart from Hal. But she didn't have the right to do that. She couldn't even address it from experience. She had no personal knowledge of what it was like to love a man enough to marry him and devote your life to him. To be dumped by him when you'd given him everything, all because you were sick. To be abandoned by love at the moment when you most needed it.

Maybe she should get a voodoo doll of Hal and stick pins in it.

Impotent anger seemed to ride her constantly and

she hated it. At work she could solve nearly any problem. Now she was facing one she might not be able to do a damn thing about.

The experimental treatment had been a slim straw. Now that straw was slipping away as they sat mired in a blizzard inside a crashed plane. It seemed as if life knew no mercy.

Was she becoming bitter, too?

But reality was looking ugly right now. Her parents had devoted their lives to doing good for the less fortunate, and had died because of it. Now her sister, who had devoted her life to a man, and dreams of a family with him, had been abandoned in her hour of need.

Where was the good stuff? Did everything you reached for only turn to pain and loss?

Yeah, she understood that bad things happened to good people. She wasn't naïve. Her sister, and millions of others like her, didn't deserve to get hit with such serious illness. Stuff like that just happened, governed by the randomness of fate. She got that. It wasn't about what you deserved.

Meteors fell from the sky, too, and once in a while they hit a person. Maybe the amazing thing was that they didn't hit more people.

But sometimes, if you turned that pattern of random events around in your mind and looked at it from another angle, it didn't look quite so random, and so you started asking the unanswerable cosmic question: *Why?*

Her mother had talked to her about that once when she was in high school, and the words had stayed with her. She could hear it as if her mother were sitting right beside her:

Honey, bad things happen to everyone. It's what we

learn from them that determines whether we become better people or worse people.

Was she in danger of becoming worse? Because she didn't feel like she was especially good as it was. Nor could she ignore that very bitter rat now gnawing around the edges of her thoughts.

She stopped another sigh, looked at Cait's pale, small face. Her sister had become a mere shadow of herself, looking almost waiflike in her weakness. So fragile she reminded Rory of a dandelion puff, something a mere breath of air could scatter and carry away.

It shocked her.

Working around roughnecks in oil fields had taught her just how tough the human body was, how much resilience it truly possessed. It took a lot to actually kill a man.

Then this. Her sister exemplified the opposite side of the coin—displaying just how fragile life really could be. How frighteningly frail.

Just as morbid thoughts threatened to consume her, the plane jerked and let out a groan like a dying giant.

Rory froze, looking quickly at Cait, but Cait barely stirred. *My God, what was that?*

At once Chase emerged from the cockpit and started reaching for his outerwear. An instant later, Wendy and Yuma joined them.

"What was that?" Rory asked

"I think we just moved. I need to check it out." Chase pulled on his jacket impatiently.

"I'll go with you," Yuma said instantly. "You shouldn't go alone."

"No, you stay. You're the only other one of us with survival experience in these mountains, plus you know your way around the GPS and beacon controls. If both you and I go out there we could endanger everyone."

"I'll go," Rory said. "Yuma's right. In these conditions no one should go out alone." She looked at Wendy. "You know where Cait's meds are?"

Wendy nodded. "I saw."

Even as she yanked on her outerwear, Rory wondered if she was doing the right thing. She hated to leave Cait in someone else's care, but it would be foolhardy for Chase to go into this blizzard alone. And if someone could take care of Cait, it was certainly Wendy.

They couldn't afford to risk losing anyone to this storm, but a long career of making hard-eyed risk assessments told her that she was the most expendable of the lot. Another uncomfortable thought, but an honest one.

She felt a flicker of dark amusement. Funny how coming up against life and death made you realize just how puny and unimportant you were.

As soon as they were tightly buttoned up in their cold-weather gear, she and Chase both grabbed flashlights. Getting the door open seemed a little harder, as if the metal of the plane had twisted more, but with a couple of shoves it opened.

Outside the weather had grown savage. Rory felt the wind try to grab her and snatch her as she crawled over the badly angled stairs for the deepening snow outside. At last she stood beside Chase, their flashlights bouncing off wildly swirling snow, and then watched him close up their steel cocoon.

If Mother Nature had temper tantrums, this seemed like one of them. Even inside her snorkel hood the wind tried to steal her breath, and icy needles of flying snow stung her briefly before melting.

"What do you think it was?" she asked again, just as the wind keened forlornly around some obstacle.

"We're going to find out. Grab on to my jacket somewhere and hang on. We don't want to get separated."

No, they didn't. Rory estimated the whiteout conditions were limiting visibility to maybe five feet. She grabbed the bottom hem of Chase's jacket and hung on tight.

Dry though it was, the snow didn't help their footing at all. Obstacles had become invisible, and the ground offered plenty of them, for this was a mountainside—not pavement. Rocks, tree limbs, dips and unexpected hills all made the going tough, as did the wind itself. At times it slapped her so hard she felt like a sail in a gale.

Chase stayed close to the plane, moving slowly, shining his flashlight all over it, from the top of the fuselage, which was almost invisible, to the ground on which it sat.

As they rounded the tail, the plane itself blocked the wind, at least briefly.

"We must have shifted," he said, leaning his head close to hers so she could hear.

"The wind?"

"In part, probably. But you know what happens when ice gets compressed."

"It liquefies."

"Exactly. There was snow here before we came down. I'm guessing that the weight of the plane is melting it. By now we're probably sitting on a layer of ice and water."

That didn't sound very hopeful, but she just nodded her acknowledgment.

"We shouldn't be able to slide too far," he said reassuringly.

She hoped he was right. But she wondered just how much more stress the fuselage could take before it cracked like an eggshell. She imagined it must have been built to endure forces not so very different from the ones she dealt with drilling for oil. All those take-offs and landings, all the buffeting…it was undoubtedly strong. But no one could guess how much metal fatigue it had suffered in this landing.

They worked their way slowly around the other side. He seemed to be looking for worrisome signs of some kind. Perhaps additional buckling that appeared too sharp. The kind of thing that might expose them to the elements. The wing still had airspace beneath it, and she wondered if that was good. The wind must be gusting at least forty miles an hour, not enough for real lift. He was right about that. But maybe enough to move them from time to time.

They eased around the wing, staying close together, and worked their way toward the craft's nose. It was still mostly buried in snow, as it had been from the beginning, but more of the windscreen was visible now. The wind was steadily unburying it. What did that mean?

To her surprise, Chase began to dig away some of the snow with his free hand, revealing more of the nose cone. It looked a bit rumpled but not bad, considering that it had plowed its way through snow and debris. After examining the bit he could see, he patted it, almost fondly, as if pleased with how well it had withstood the landing.

A sudden *whop* caused them both to turn and look

back at the wing. Flying snow almost entirely hid it from view.

"The wing flexed," he said with a certainty that indicated he'd heard that sound before.

"That's not good. It could move us—that much energy."

"I know. Let's move farther forward."

She followed him into the maelstrom, hanging on to the hem of his jacket, noting that he didn't place them right in front of the plane. So he was indeed afraid that it might move.

Well, she was, too. They made their way forward until the nose was almost lost in the snow blowing behind them.

"You stand here," he said. "Keep your flashlight pointed in my direction so I can find my way back. I want to be sure of what exactly is in front of us."

"Okay."

Even inside her snorkel hood, the wind sounded loud, as did the swishing of snow as it snaked drily across the surface. Each time the wind twisted around and pushed at her, she could hear icy crystals pelt the nylon of her jacket.

Damn, it was cold and dry, and in no time at all she could tell where Chase was only by the insistent glow of his flashlight. The snow caught the light and tossed it around, making it unreliable, but still illuminating his general direction. It didn't exactly swallow the light, but it might as well have the way the flakes shattered the light everywhere in tiny, gleaming pinpricks.

She staggered a bit as the wind hit her back hard. This was not a great night to be out. The elements were having their way with everything, and she felt smaller just then than she ever had. Around her loomed a forest she couldn't see, a night that was full of threat.

The thought of animals didn't unnerve her. Little that lived unnerved her after some of the places she had been, but no animal with any wisdom would be prowling in this storm. No, it was the storm she feared, and how it could worsen their situation.

While the blizzard raged, threatening the plane, inside that plane her sister clung weakly to life. Time and the elements were conspiring, and she had to fight an urge to throw her head back and scream her fear, frustration and fury into the howling storm. As if the elements might heed it.

Almost unbearable tension coiled her muscles, and she'd have given almost anything to have the power to set this all to rights. Never, ever, had she felt so utterly helpless, except perhaps during the mere minutes before that well blew. Oh, hell, that didn't even come close. At least *then* she'd been able to get most of her people away in time.

An eternity seemed to pass, though she was sure it couldn't have been more than ten or fifteen minutes, before Chase began once again to emerge from the swirling snow. First his flashlight, then his vague outline, dark against the whiter snow.

"We can't move far," he told her as he reached her. "Even if there's a ravine up there buried in the snow, we'd probably slide right over it if we skate because it's so narrow."

"But if we don't?"

"Then we're going to be walking uphill inside the plane."

"Could it withstand that?"

"Ordinarily, I'd say yes, but after all this, I honestly don't know."

Icy fingers, icier than the needles of snow that stung her face, gripped her heart. "Can we do anything to prevent it?"

He waved in the general direction of the plane. "What do you think? That bird is heavy."

True. She lowered her head a bit, biting her lip, thinking about all the other dangers that might still get them. No, they couldn't prevent that massive, crippled plane from moving if it decided to. "Beyond the ravine?"

"Woods. They'd stop us for sure. How much damage we'd have would depend on how much momentum we built on a slide."

She turned from him and looked back toward the nearly invisible plane. A lot of momentum, if those tons of aluminum started moving. They wouldn't have to move fast. Hard as it was, they were going to have to trust that the plane would stay put because there wasn't a damn thing they could do to prevent it from moving. "I wish we could do something about the wings."

"Me, too. I don't think they're getting much lift at all, but evidently it's enough to cause them to flex. More metal fatigue."

"Yeah." That was one thing she knew a little about. "I guess we're just going to have to ignore the groans and moans." Not at all comforting, that thought.

"I can't see any other answer."

She'd been out here too long, she realized. Some inner clock was ticking, and it was pushing her to get back to Cait, to make sure she was still all right.

Chase took her elbow this time as they struggled back up alongside the plane. Funny, she hadn't noticed the slope on the way down, but now she felt the climb back up. Maybe they were at a high enough altitude to notice the thinness of the air.

The wing ahead of them flapped again, a strange sort of hollow, metallic sound, followed by a banshee moan. Before Rory even realized what was happening, she had been shoved to the side. The next thing she knew, she was lying on her back in the snow with Chase half over her.

The terrible screech of metal continued.

"Don't lift your head!" Chase shouted.

Eyes wide, protected from the wind by the snorkel hood, she watched in horror as the wing, lit from beneath by their flashlights slid over them, starting and stopping several times.

"Oh, my God," she whispered. "Oh, my God!"

The snow was so deep beneath her that she could have reached up and touched the wing as it jerked its way over her. Then, with a visible shudder, everything froze.

Chase's weight held her pinned in the snow, and she had no desire to move. Staring straight up at that wing, she waited for it to move again.

"We're going to crawl now," he said, leaning close to her ear. "Turn over, crawl straight under the wing."

For an instant after he levered off her, she wondered if she was going to be able to move at all. Then, with effort, hating to take her eyes off that potentially dangerous wing, she rolled over. Chase tugged her arm up the slope. Only at the last instant did she remember to grab her flashlight.

She hadn't realized how big that wing was. The journey beneath it, crab-crawling because she was afraid to lift herself, went on forever.

"Okay," Chase said. "Okay. You can sit up."

She did, twisting to look at the wing that now lay in the snow behind them, the front edge now nearly buried, the tunnels they had made crawling out rapidly filling.

"Everything's okay," Chase said, standing, his voice loud now to be heard over the wind. "Nothing's any worse. Maybe it's even better."

"Better?" Losing the last of her fear that somehow the weight of that wing was going to fall on her, she scrambled to her feet. "Better how?"

"The wing is buried at the front edge now. We'll get less movement."

Until the snow blew away. "How did that happen?"

"Apparently, when the plane slid forward, it tipped more."

"I don't know if that's good."

"Rory," he said, "at this minute I'm grabbing every straw."

He was right, she realized. There was no point in looking at negatives unless you could do something about them.

"We need to get back inside and reassure everyone. That slide must have worried them."

That was also true. She hoped it hadn't awakened Cait. Whether it had or not, those in the cabin must be wondering about whether more was coming and whether she and Chase were all right.

Once again they struggled into the wind and the upslope to round the rear of the plane. At moments like these, Rory appreciated just how big this jet was.

In her business she flew this way only as someone's guest. She preferred to be far more penurious with her travel expenses, and this kind of luxury had always struck her as unnecessary unless you had some kind of important work to do that you couldn't on a commercial flight—work that couldn't wait.

Cait couldn't wait, however, and she certainly couldn't travel by commercial airliner. Not in her weakened condition with her compromised immune system. This time, cost was the last thing Rory had considered.

But it was a huge plane.

When they reached the far side again, and the door, they discovered that the forward slippage had moved the plane so the door was blocked by deep snow.

"Hell," Chase said, then bent and started scooping snow with his hands.

Rory joined him. "You have everything else. How did you overlook a snow shovel?"

She thought she heard him snort, but the wind left her unsure.

"The best-laid plans," he quoted, scooping rapidly. "I think we may have lost our fire pit, too."

Rory glanced around, but as heavy as the snow was she doubted she could have made out the metal box. Why hadn't they thought to bring it inside? "We can make another one, right?"

"I hope. Mainly I hope we can get this door open. Then we'll worry about everything else."

She joined him in digging, growing hot inside her insulated clothing, but glad she no longer felt cold. She even started to perspire a bit and once again she noticed that she couldn't seem to get quite enough air.

"Stop." Chase reached out and gripped her arm. "You don't want to be breathing like that out here."

"Why not?"

"Altitude. And the air is extremely dry. You could get pulmonary edema."

"What about you?"

"I didn't come from sea level. This change isn't as big for me as it is for you."

She obeyed him, hating to feel useless, but his hands were big and strong, and even bigger inside gloves. Plus, the snow's dryness seemed to aid him, blowing away most of what he scooped to make a drift elsewhere.

"There," he said finally. The exit door was mostly unburied. He banged hard on it, and moments later they could hear banging from the inside. Yuma, and perhaps Wendy, were trying to shove the door open.

Chase worked his fingers into the crack on one side, and Rory immediately worked hers into the opening on the other side. Together they tugged, and at last the door began to swing down.

When they at last clambered inside, Rory threw back her hood but left her jacket on and unzipped. The cabin was warmer than outside, of course, but even though she had warmed up from her exertions, she could feel that it was still chilly inside. Perhaps too chilly.

She wanted to hurry back to Cait, but over the seats she could see her sister sitting up, holding a mug of something hot in her hands.

Cait's expression at once revealed that she had been terrified. "I was so scared for you," she said, her voice louder than Rory had heard it since coming home.

"We're fine," Rory assured her, easing past the others to reach her sister and sit beside her. "How are you doing?"

"I'm okay." Which was what Cait usually said.

"What happened?" Yuma asked.

Chase answered. "The plane slid forward about fifteen feet. Nothing seems to be any worse, though."

Wendy spoke. "We all just about panicked for you

two. Thank God you weren't right in front of this behemoth."

"We had to duck so the wing missed us, but it may have been a good thing. The leading edge is buried in the snow now. That'll help hold us in place."

"We tipped a little," Yuma remarked, "but not much. The really horrifying part was wondering about the two of you."

"Yeah," said Wendy an amused note in her voice. "The candles didn't even slide. We were fine in here."

"Thank God for that," Chase said.

Cait managed to lean forward and put her mug of broth on the table. Then she tugged her hand from beneath the blanket and reached out to grasp Rory's. "I'm glad you're okay," she murmured. Then her eyes fluttered closed, the last of her energy once again drained.

"Okay," Wendy announced. "The two of *you* go get some sleep. I think we're all going to be basically catnapping until we get out of here. I know I'm too wide awake to sleep now."

But Rory wasn't, she realized. The cold and the effort outside, plus the altitude made her wearier than she could remember being in a long time. Her eyelids seemed to be weighted in lead, and her limbs felt heavy. She could have slept right there. But even as she thought of lying down and sleeping, the desire for a bed grew even stronger. She gently drew her hand from Cait's slackened grip but hesitated, feeling guilty. Finally she gathered herself, needing to stretch out, needing the relative darkness, needing the comfort of a pillow to make sleep seem possible and right.

Odd, clinging to such a little notion in the midst of this mess. But God, she needed sleep or she was going to be worse than useless to her sister and everyone else.

At last she pushed herself to her feet and started to the back of the plane.

"Thanks for watching Cait," she said to Wendy.

"It's easy," Wendy assured her. "When I start to crash, I'll wake you, so don't worry."

"Thank you."

She doffed her jacket, snowpants and boots, this time keeping the felt boot liners on so her feet wouldn't get cold. It was definitely much chillier in the back of the plane than in the cabin, and she argued with herself for all of ten seconds about trying to sleep in the cabin before giving in to the lure of a very comfortable bed.

A short time after she stretched out on her side, she felt the blankets lift as Chase slipped in behind her, wrapping his arm around her waist.

"Warmth," he said.

She couldn't disagree. All of a sudden the small room didn't feel so cold, nor did she feel quite so alone.

"Thanks for saving me out there," she said.

"No problem. Not like I was going to stand by while that wing took off your head or broke your neck."

A little shiver ran through her as she remembered those moments. She had been so close to death or serious injury.

The shiver was misinterpreted. Chase immediately wrapped himself tighter around her and rubbed her arm gently.

"Sleep," he said. "God knows we're going to need clear heads before long."

Sleepy as she had been, now she felt wide awake to every nerve ending in her body. Her nipples had swollen, and each breath caused them to brush against the fabric of her bra, each time causing a pleasant tingle. She remained perfectly still, afraid of betraying how she felt, as syrupy desire steadily filled her. How was this possible? With all that was going on, how could she even be feeling this?

But the attempted guilt trip died as her body begged for more intimate touches, more intimate knowledge of the man who shared his warmth with her.

He shifted a little, and grew still.

Asleep? she wondered. But no, his breathing seemed more rapid, not the deep slow rhythms of sleep. Could he be feeling the same things? The same aching desire?

In spite of every voice in her head that screamed warnings, she wiggled a little back against him.

And felt it. Chase was as hard as a rock against her rear, as hungry for her as she was for him.

More objections popped up, thoughts about how she didn't know him, how her sister was in the next cabin at death's door, what a dangerous situation they were in. All the logical things that should be standing between her and these unwanted feelings.

But her body didn't agree. The desire that had begun to flame in her burned away all those rational objections, leaving her damp, hungry and needier than she could ever remember feeling.

And then it totally betrayed her, her hips arching back toward him.

She heard him catch his breath. He knew. She wanted to feel shame, but couldn't.

Then a shiver ripped through her as his hot lips found the nape of her neck, almost tentatively, in a soft kiss.

A whisper of breath escaped her, just a tiny bit—too quiet to be a moan. No sound. No sound, because there were people on the other side of an accordion door. Silence.

He kissed her again and she trembled.

She heard him whisper, "Oh, hell, you're going to hate me."

At that moment she couldn't believe it would ever be possible to hate Chase Dakota, unless he pulled away right then.

But he didn't pull away. His lips trailed to her ear, and she felt his hot breath in her ear. She shivered again and this time clasped his hand, holding onto it for dear life, giving consent. Maybe even begging.

"You are so sexy," he whispered in her ear, his breath causing her to shiver with longing again. "So sexy."

That was the last thing either of them said.

His hand tugged free of hers, slipping up beneath layers of clothing to find her naked breast, already aching for his touch. He brushed his thumb over her nipple, driving her insane with need, causing her to feel damp between her legs.

Over and over he teased that nipple, causing shocks of pleasure to tear through her as if on wings. His lips left moist patches on her neck, on her cheeks that grew cold as soon as he moved on. The contrast excited her even more.

Slowly, her hips pressed back against him, feeling his stiffness, thrilled by it. Little by little she began to rock in the rhythm of love, not caring how or when, knowing only that she was helpless to stop this now. The longing he evoked left her mindless.

She retained only enough sense to hold back her moans, and it wasn't easy. She wasn't a normally noisy lover, but he made her want to cry out over and over.

Then suddenly his hand slipped downward. He didn't even unfasten her pants. He cupped her hard, almost forcing a groan from her. She rocked into that pressure, needing it and more. Then his hips met the rhythm of hers, pressing into her bottom in time with the squeezing, rubbing motion of his hand.

She felt surrounded by desire, claimed as she'd never been claimed before. Aching, needing, helpless, trapped between his hands and his hips in deepening desire.

A slave to the feelings he awoke in her, and glad to be right there, right then.

His ministrations continued, somehow unbearably sexy, sexier than if he'd stripped the clothes from her body. It felt deliciously illicit, and her hunger discovered new heights.

Squeezing and rubbing, pressing himself against her from the other side, he created a rope of passion that bound her to him as tightly as if he had entered her.

At the very pinnacle, she thought she would shatter. She had to bite her lip to keep herself from screaming, literally.

As clenching waves of satisfaction ripped through her, she felt him stiffen, then shudder. He had found his completion, too.

Chapter 6

He never took his hand away from her, but continued to hold her tightly, making her feel claimed and oddly safe. As sleep fought to take her, she found it easier to let it. He had drained all the tension from her, leaving her soft, tired and so relaxed.

When she awoke, Chase was rolling away from her.

"Wendy says she's having trouble keeping her eyes open."

At once Rory sprang to her feet. She felt the need to wash, to change, but even changing into something from her carry-on needed to wait. Cait first.

Chase was out of the bedroom almost before her feet hit the floor. She smiled rather grimly. He probably wanted a postmortem about as much as she did, which was to say not at all.

Their unorthodox sex needed to be confined to some dustbin at the back of their memories for many good reasons. If the memory of those moments wouldn't leave her alone, then she'd remind herself of every single one of them.

It had been good, it had probably been born of adrenaline, their unusual circumstances and some crazy need to affirm life in the face of all the danger they faced. Better to forget it than dwell on it.

Maybe someday, when she was an old lady, she could drag the memory out and remember the brief period when she'd tossed out every inhibition to be with a stranger. Old ladies could safely indulge those memories, and maybe even cackle over them with glee. If she looked too closely at it right now, she might wonder if she had lost her mind.

Well, she had, she thought as she slipped her jacket and boots on again, then headed up front to Cait. She'd gone nuts for fifteen or twenty glorious minutes, if that long.

It was okay to go nuts sometimes. It happened. Over the last few weeks, plenty had been pushing her in that direction.

Cait was still sleeping, but a touch found her cheek warm, and her breathing seemed regular, if a bit shallow.

"I got her to cough some more," Wendy said. "And she had another cup of sweet tea. She seems fine right now."

Fine. Not exactly the word Rory would apply, but she understood Wendy's meaning. "Thank you."

Wendy squeezed her arm, then disappeared into the bedroom with her husband.

"This is a fractured night," Chase remarked. He glanced at his watch. "Close to endless, too. Coffee? Soup?"

"Coffee." She straightened and started to follow him to the galley, but he waved her back.

"Sit with your sister. I can make coffee."

He also probably didn't want to be too close to her. That might be a good idea right now. Pretend it didn't happen, and don't give either of them a chance to talk about it. Sometimes silence was wise, and Rory felt this was one of them.

But wise or not, she couldn't help remembering. Judging by her response to the memory, her body wanted a rerun even if her mind warned her it would be dangerous and maybe even stupid. Even with her sister sleeping right beside her. God, was she losing her mind?

It was as if this crash and her sister's illness had unleashed a whole bunch of stuff inside her that she'd been keeping under for too long. The side of Aurora Campbell that she never let anyone see: the woman.

Twenty minutes later Chase returned with steaming mugs and put one on the table in front of her. Then he sat across from her and Cait. Some part of her was surprised that he hadn't sought the solitude of the cockpit.

But he didn't seem to be avoiding her, and that made her feel a bit better. Damn, she was a tangle of emotions right now, acting in a way she wouldn't ordinarily act, having feelings that seemed to come out of nowhere and didn't resemble anything remotely logical.

Why would she have felt bad if he had avoided her? Wasn't that basically what she was advocating by trying to pretend that nothing had happened?

She sighed quietly and sipped her coffee, looking again at Cait. No, she couldn't do a damn thing for her sister right now except sit here and worry. What good was that? So she turned back to Chase.

"Do you have enough insurance to get another plane?"

"Of course. I'm covered for everything. But I doubt I'm going to need it. We had a mechanical failure on the first flight after a major overhaul."

She nodded. "But you're out of business for a while."

"Yeah, but I can make it. What's going to tick me off is losing regular customers unless I can rent something in the meantime."

"That would be tough. Believe me, I know."

"Are you losing customers right now?" he asked bluntly.

"Not yet. But it could happen if I don't get back on the job soon enough. For the moment my clients are understanding." That was something she refused to worry about right now. At this moment in time, Cait was unquestionably more important than a mere business. Even though it had taken her years to build.

"They should be. Some things come before business."

"Not always."

"No," he agreed. He sipped his coffee and put his mug on the table.

She tried another tack. "So what's the likelihood that the storm is interfering with the GPS?"

"I can't give you percentages. All radio transmissions can be disrupted by atmospheric conditions, and the GPS is trying to reach a satellite. That's usually more reliable than other line-of-sight methods, which is why I have it, but things can affect it. Ionization in the upper atmosphere, for example. For all I know the aurora is active right now. Then there's the moisture in the air column. This is a really bad storm, which means lots of moisture at the upper levels, so that could be interrupting the signal. When it starts to pass, we'll know for sure."

She looked at the table in front of her. "I'm not good at being helpless."

"Me, neither. But that's where we are until later today or early tomorrow. I don't want to muck around with wiring too much until I'm sure it's not just the storm. I might break something that isn't broken."

A quiet, humorless laugh escaped her. "I second that."

He was silent for a minute then said, "You shouldn't feel so guilty. It's not your fault that your sister is sick, and you're doing everything you can."

She felt a spark of anger. "That doesn't help."

"I know it doesn't. Chalk it to something I just needed to say. Cait's lucky to have you. Too many people have no one at all."

There was no argument against that. She had tightened her lips, but now she let them relax. What was the point? Life was what it was, and sometimes it was a bitch.

Then she caught a possible subtext in what he had said. "Do you have someone?"

"I have friends. No family. Only child."

"Your parents?"

He nodded. "My dad was a pilot, too. Unfortunately, he had a small single-engine plane of his own. Well, I guess I shouldn't say *unfortunately.* He got a lot of pleasure out of it. But two years after I graduated from the academy, they took a trip in Alaska and went down in the mountains."

"I'm very sorry." It struck her that the current situation must be reminding him of that, stirring all kinds of emotional echoes for him. But she didn't know how to broach the subject. What right did she have to pry? A brief experience of sex didn't make them any less strangers.

He looked around the nearly dark cabin. "We were damn lucky," he said.

"We had a bigger plane and apparently an outstanding pilot."

"Size *does* make a difference," he said. Then he startled her by winking.

"You didn't just say that!" She had to bite back the most unexpected giggle.

He cocked a brow. "The air was getting heavy. The situation is heavy enough."

"No denying that," she agreed. Amazing how he had just lightened her mood. Then he surprised her again by leaning over and opening a small drawer under the table. He tossed a pack of cards between them. "Name your poison."

How many hours had she spent in oil fields playing cards with her coworkers? More than she could count. She reached for the pack, opened it and pulled the jokers out of the deck. "Seven-card stud," she said.

He had some poker chips, too, and soon they were deep in the game. A good form of distraction, and an equally good excuse not to get personal.

She just wished she knew whether to be grateful for that or not.

"So," she said, "tell me about Wendy and Billy Joe." That seemed safe enough. "Wendy told me a little. They're an interesting pair."

"More interesting than most of us realize. I was young at the time they got together, and too busy with other things to really pay attention to the rumor mill. It did create a stir because he was so much older and folks pretty much had him figured as a permanent loner."

"Because of his PTSD?"

"Partly, I guess. Like I said, it wasn't really on my radar. But I got the impression that our old sheriff, Wendy's dad, was on the horns of a real dilemma."

"How so?"

"Yuma was his friend, and Wendy was his daughter, and he didn't want either of them getting hurt." He chuckled quietly. "From what I know of her dad, he probably warned them both off the other. He's never been a man to mince his words if his dander gets up, and I bet his dander was up about this one."

"But age isn't necessarily a determining factor."

"Most of the time I'd agree. But you can imagine where he was coming from. Yuma was a vet with some issues, and Wendy was his little girl. He probably saw disaster written all over it for both of them."

"Evidently he would have been wrong."

"Evidently. They've been married a long time now." He smiled, his eyes crinkling. "Your deal."

Chase was finding it hard to accept that just a few hours ago he had acted like a randy teenager in the back of a car with Rory. The intensity of wanting her had overwhelmed him, especially when he had sensed that she might be feeling the same way.

He wanted to put it all down to their situation—if anyone knew how danger could heighten the sex drive, it was him—but he couldn't quite.

Rory wasn't just a stranger to him, even though they hadn't known each other twenty-four hours yet. Situations like this compressed emotional time, and you got to know important things about people when so much was on the line. However, he warned himself to be careful because she was going to be flying on to Minnesota with her sister, then back to Mexico.

A rueful thought struck him: Maybe all his girlfriend problems over the years had stemmed from his own choices. Maybe, at some level, he kept picking women he knew wouldn't stick.

He'd certainly picked one here.

But having watched Rory with her sister, he knew that while circumstance would carry her away from him, she was at heart a "sticker." Once she cared about someone, apparently there was no limit to her caring. Yes, people loved their families, but they also had limits. Cait was dying. He was sure insurance wasn't going to pay for this experimental treatment; it never did. And the cost of hiring him and his plane for this trip was exorbitant.

A lot of loving people, looking at this prognosis, and hearing that their loved one just wanted to give up, would, with great grief, give in. They would listen to doctors who said it was impossible to save Cait, to doctors who had evidently said Cait was in such a condition the treatment, already uncertain, probably wouldn't work. But here was a woman who was risking her career, spending a fortune, probably planning to pay for uncovered treatments that would leave her in debt for a long time to come…because she loved her sister.

That didn't make Rory one-of-a-kind, but it sure made her relatively rare in his experience.

They'd been playing in silence for about a half hour when he had to ask the question. "Did you have to fight to get Cait into this experimental treatment?"

She looked up, her face tightening. "Like a pit bull," she said finally.

"I wondered."

"You were right to wonder. She might skew their results because she's so weak, and that could affect the drug's evaluation."

"So how did you manage it?"

"I argued my way up the chain until I got to the guys who designed the drug and were having it tested. I managed to convince them that it would help them a whole lot if they got a good outcome with someone so far along. More than it would by only picking people who'd just gotten sick. And then I argued that they could quite easily list her as an outlier because of her condition, and use that as an excuse for removing her from their evaluation if it doesn't work."

One corner of his mouth lifted. "You really don't give up."

"Giving up has never gotten me anywhere. I might not be able to make it, when all is said and done, but if you give up, you never find out, do you?"

"Absolutely not." The quiet admiration he'd begun to feel for her despite his initial irritation at her pushiness, grew. "You know, I hope if I ever need someone in my corner, I get someone like you."

Thanks to the candle he had placed on the table so they could read the cards, he was able to see her blush. My God, Rory could blush. That tickled him somehow. He would have thought her long past it.

"Just doing what needs doing," she said quietly.

Exactly what most heroic people said, he thought. He was tempted to say so, but figured he'd embarrassed her enough.

She pushed her cards aside. "Enough of that."

"Sure." He started scooping them up into a neat pile. "Maybe more later."

He nodded, sensing that her mind had wandered off somewhere. Probably to the hours, perhaps days, ahead. He was with her in worry right now. But he could hardly tell her how furious and sickened he would feel if Cait were lost while in his care.

Because she *was* in his care. He was captain of this crashed ship, and her life was in his hands as surely as if he were one of her doctors. He had to get her out of here before her medicine ran out, before she came down with something else in her weakened state.

Nor was he the kind of man who could just shrug it off and say it wasn't his fault the plane crashed and that Cait was so ill.

No, he wasn't made that way. It was killing him that at the moment he could do so little to protect his passengers, especially Cait. He knew they could hang out for weeks in this plane. He had enough food, enough candles, and with the snow there'd be plenty of water. But none of that would help Cait if her drugs ran out. Four days. By the time the storm blew through, they'd be down to two. If the beacon wasn't working...

He didn't want to think about that. Sitting here waiting for rescue without a beacon, in a plane that would be invisible under the snow, might cost them Cait. So if they didn't get GPS back, how long could he afford to spend trying to fix things before they'd have to try to hike out, because waiting would ensure Cait's death?

He didn't like their odds.

He leaned back, closing his eyes for a moment. Cusswords floated through his mind, but they didn't help at all, especially since he held them in. A little swearing might ease his anger at this situation, but doing it silently inside his head just fueled his rage.

Some freaking mechanic somewhere was going to pay for this.

He looked at Rory. "People make mistakes."

"Yes, they do." Her look questioned him.

"But some people, given what rides on what they do, shouldn't make them."

"I agree. But, unfortunately, they do anyway. Even brain surgeons."

"I know."

"The point is?"

"Right now I'd like to strangle a mechanic."

"Ah." One corner of her mouth lifted. "I felt that way just recently about some roughnecks."

"I'm sure you did. I'm just really angry right now."

"So vent. I'm angry, too. I was going to be angry with you, until you explained what happened. I'll join you in thinking of horrible ways to deal with that mechanic, whoever he is."

"It had to be mechanical failure." He'd run over this in his mind a thousand times since the crash, but for some reason he needed to run over it again. "Something caused us to lose fuel fast—faster than a simple leak. And I can't think of anything except that something was wired poorly—or loose—something that caused us to just dump the fuel. It happened that fast, and I couldn't stop it."

She nodded. "Kinda like I felt when I realized those guys hadn't stopped drilling."

"Yeah." He shook his head, all of a sudden back in the cockpit in those minutes leading up to disaster. "Fuel jettison equipment was optional on this plane."

"You mean they don't all have it?"

"No. It depends on the structure. Some planes don't have to lighten their loads to land safely. This one had it as an option, and obviously I didn't buy it new. But I thought it was an advantage."

"Why?"

"Because the last thing you want in a crash is a lot of aviation fuel onboard. So I just felt it was better to have a plane with a jettison system than one without. Never occurred to me it might *cause* a crash."

"Do you suppose because it was optional somebody didn't check it out?"

"I don't know. I guess the NTSB will find out. If that's what happened. I'm just guessing that's the cause, but I suppose something else could have gone wrong."

"The more complex the equipment..." She let the thought dangle. He certainly didn't need her to finish it.

He closed his eyes again, envisioning the gauges as the whole flight went to hell. By the time he was sure what was happening and that he couldn't stop it, they were in deep trouble. That fast.

"Reliving it won't help," she said quietly.

His eyes snapped open. "You read minds?"

"Sometimes. No, it's just that I know. I replayed my orders to those roughnecks a thousand times. I wrote down my exact words and had a native Spanish speaker look them over. I hadn't misspoken in either language. Then I moved on to wondering what else I could have done."

"I'll get there, I suppose."

"Maybe not. You got us down in one piece. I don't know a whole lot about planes, but when the engines flamed out, a lot of other equipment probably stopped working, too."

"It did. And when I replace this plane, I'm getting one with a windmill, to generate power if the engines fail. We have some auxiliary power, but it's not a lot and it doesn't work for long. Shortly after the flame-out, I started to lose my hydraulic pumps. Mechanics alone weren't enough. The aux drains fast."

"I thought so. From my narrow knowledge base, I assumed most of the power was coming from the turbines."

"It does, because that's efficient. The engines do two jobs. If you think about it, it makes perfect sense. When do I need aux power? Just for the length of time it takes to board and get the engines going. Or long enough to run emergency lighting for evacuation. Why carry another generator?"

"I agree."

He shook his head, tired of his own internal hamster wheel. "The odds against this were incredible. No amount of planning would have conceived of this."

"Unlike my well disaster."

"Point taken."

She smiled faintly. "I wasn't trying to make any point. That was agreement."

He liked being able to talk to her, he realized. She understood what fascinated him in ways most people didn't. She might not be intimately acquainted with planes, but she could discuss aviation intelligently and she didn't give him the feeling that she was hiding boredom.

Another sign that he'd been selecting all the wrong women. "So flying is my life, and oil is yours."

She nodded. "For now. Someday I hope to have things built up enough that I can delegate more, maybe spend less time in the field. I actually feel pretty root-less now."

"At least I have a home base. Do you?"

She shook her head. "I don't keep an apartment or anything. My office is my computer and my cell phone. Soon I hope to be a little beyond that. With a real office. And not needing to be in the field quite so much."

She averted her gaze briefly. "I wasn't thinking about the really important issues. This situation has made me reconsider. A career isn't everything. I haven't even been good about visiting Cait. I just assumed she was happy with Hal and didn't need me."

"How could you know if she didn't tell you?"

"I know, but I still feel guilty. You take some things for granted until life rears up and reminds you that you might lose them."

"I think we all do that."

"I'm sure. But it doesn't make it right." She gave an-other little shake of her head, looked at her sister and then at him again. "I've been questioning myself a lot the last couple of weeks. About what's essential, and where I really want to be in ten or twenty years. Cait had the life she wanted all laid out in front of her, and now look. So what's life about, Chase? Have you ever figured that one out?"

He shifted a little, feeling a bit awkward. He wasn't used to discussions like this, at least not since his youth when cosmic questions had been hot topics. At twenty you thought of them, and believed you might figure them out. Then you got older and got way too busy to even wonder.

Yet what better time than now, stranded on a moun-tainside in a blizzard, in the company of a very sick woman? He could well understand why Rory was wondering, and if he were honest with himself, he probably should be wondering, too.

"I haven't been thinking about it," he admitted. "Flying is—was—my whole life. I expend most of my efforts to keep myself in the air. To grow my business enough that I don't have costly downtime. But…that's not enough, is it?"

"Are you asking me?"

"I'm asking myself, but I'll listen to answers."

"It's not enough," she said firmly. "It's not that I haven't been living, but I've been living with such an intense, single-minded focus. Cait's illness has forced me to think about the parts of life I've been neglecting. I'm not sure yet which ones I want, but one thing I'm fairly certain of is that my life is going to broaden after this. I can't be consumed with work and business, however adventurous it may seem."

"A lot of people would think you live a broad life already. Travel, other cultures, that sort of thing."

"But it's all about work. I don't put down roots—all my friends are in the business. I've been asking myself what I'll have left when that's gone. Not much."

"I know. I haven't been thinking about it, but you're making me." He felt emotions beginning to roil inside him, emotions he couldn't quite identify. It was as if he sensed a big change coming, but didn't know what it might be or if he would like it.

And for the last day, since the crash, he'd been looking at Wendy and Yuma. They were so close they seemed to communicate without words, to find comfort in each other's presence. To be a self-sustaining unit even in the midst of crisis. If he allowed himself to be honest, didn't he want the same kind of relationship? Eventually?

"It's easy," Rory said, "to push matters down the road. To tell yourself you'll get to it later. Well, time is passing, and how can I be sure there'll be a later?"

"Obvious question right now," he admitted.

Her gaze grew intense. "Let's be honest," she said. "We can't be sure we'll get out of this mess. There's no guarantee. Not just for Cait, but for any of us."

He didn't argue, because even though he believed they could make it, with the possible exception of Cait, the fact remained that he hadn't planned on a plane crash, either. What if he hadn't been able to bring them down in one piece?

"I don't think I'd like my own epitaph," he admitted. "What's it going to say? *He flew?*"

"Yeah. Mine wouldn't be much different. It's going to be an empty tombstone if I don't make some changes."

"Do you have any in mind?"

"I don't know," she said. "Cait wanted to have a family. She couldn't and they didn't discover why until they diagnosed her illness."

"You want a family?"

"I've begun thinking about it. I mean, what does it come down to, Chase? What is our legacy going to be? If we die in the next few days, what will it all have meant?"

"I don't know." But she was sure making him think about it. "You're right. It's easy to just push stuff down the road. And some of them…well, it's not as if you can just make them happen."

"True," she admitted. "Having a family means finding the right person to do it with. But there are other things. Other legacies. Other reasons for people to say I didn't just take up space. Kids aren't the only one."

"No. But maybe the one that matters is love. And if

that's the case, you're doing a damn fine job of it with your sister."

In the flickering candlelight, he saw her mouth curve into a faint smile. "Love? A man mentions love?"

Now he really *did* feel awkward. "Why not? You want to talk about the meaning of life and what matters, well, even a stupid guy like me can figure out that what matters is the lives you touch, and how you touch them."

"I'm sorry," she said instantly. "I guess I'm a little down on men at the moment. Cait's husband."

"And those guys who didn't listen to you about not drilling." But he appreciated her apology anyway. At least she wasn't the kind of woman who hated all men on principle. If he was going to be disliked, he wanted it to be for something he'd done. There's been ample reason in his life for that. Wasn't there for everyone? But a sense of discomfort began to niggle at him.

"I work with men all the time," she went on. "Most of the time, in fact. I really don't have anything against men in general. I don't know why that popped out."

"I do," he said with a quiet laugh. "Most guys *do* run like scared rabbits at the mention of love."

Her smile widened. "You're not talking about only that kind of love anyway."

"No, I'm not." Unaccustomed as he was to this kind of discussion, he found himself reluctant to drop it. The quiet intimacy growing between them in the near dark was satisfying something in him, just as their earlier sex had satisfied a need. Only this one seemed so much more profound.

So he looked for a way to continue it. "Yuma," he said finally.

"What about him?"

"He tried to walk away from life," Chase said thoughtfully.

"Wendy said something about that."

"Yeah, for years he lived in these mountains with a bunch of Vietnam vets who couldn't handle the rest of the world. I don't know a whole lot about post-traumatic stress disorder, but I guess if you live among triggers, it can get pretty bad."

"That's what I hear."

"So he hid for a while. Then he came down out of the mountains and started flying our medevac helicopter. The same kind of helicopter he'd flown in Vietnam."

"I can only imagine how hard that must have been," Rory observed.

"Me, too. Anyway, he never forgot the rest of the guys in the mountains. And every working day he does something important for really sick people. Long after he's gone, people in Conard County are going to remember him."

"Not everybody can have that kind of impact, though," Rory noted.

"No, but right now I'm flying tycoons around. It's a job that pays me to do what I love. That's not a legacy. That's a toy."

"Whoa!" She looked shocked. "Don't put yourself down like that. You said you had friends. Maybe you do a lot for them and don't even realize it."

"I don't know," he said ruefully.

"Man!" It almost sounded like a curse. "So what should I say? I run around finding oil for tycoons? Ouch."

"I didn't say anything about you."

"You didn't have to. The thing is, you're right. Obviously, we both do something that people are willing to pay us to do, but if that's all we do…" She trailed off, frowning.

Chase felt annoyed with himself. His own self-examination hadn't been intended to put her down, but he'd done just that.

As he began to wonder if she'd ever say another word to him, she spoke. "Clearly, at least I need to do something in addition to work. Just more food for thought."

At least she wasn't angry at him, but he was a bit angry at himself. He seemed to be finding maturity late, propelled by this woman's devotion to her sister. Things to which he hadn't given much thought gnawed at him now. He wasn't that old—thirty-six—but he ought to realize by now that in a few eyeblinks he'd wake up some morning and realize that he was forty. Then fifty. He was no longer the young turk who had graduated from the academy and leapt into a career of flying high-performance jets. If failing his flight physical hadn't gotten that through to him in an enduring way, this certainly had.

He'd merely transferred his passion, but he hadn't improved himself. Maybe this whole airline business of his was the emotional equivalent of a pacifier. Still flying, still busy and still very much the jock aviator.

"Damn," he said.

"What?"

"I guess I still have a lot of growing up to do."

She smiled, giving a quiet laugh. "I think we spend our entire lives trying to grow up. But I'm sure reevaluating."

He was, too. And, oddly, he felt more comfortable with it now. Maybe because they'd talked about it.

They fell silent then, Cait slumbering between them

almost like a human signpost, pointing out all the things he'd been ignoring. And maybe Rory, too.

He watched her fall into her own thoughts, and noted yet again how pretty she was, how very attractive. Her devotion to her sister only enhanced her magnetism.

He looked at the two women and finally admitted that there was a huge hole in his life. A crater, actually. One he hadn't even noticed before.

Chapter 7

Morning arrived at last. Rory had dozed fitfully in the seat beside her sister, waking at every little sound. She'd been aware of people moving around from time to time, of the exit door opening a little, briefly, to let in fresh air.

Then the sound of Cait's breathing caught her attention. She sat bolt upright and listened, seeing Chase in the seat across from her.

She knew it was morning only because he'd raised the window shade beside him, and faint light filtered in.

She turned her attention to Cait and heard him say, "I was just thinking about waking you. Her breathing changed just a few minutes ago."

Cait's breaths were shallow, but they rattled a bit, too. Rory felt the sting of panic.

"I'll get Wendy," Chase said.

Rory nodded, leaning over to wake Cait.

"Cait? Cait, sweetie, wake up. Please."

It took several attempts, but Cait's eyes at last opened. "I'm so tired," she whispered.

"I know, Cait. I know. Do you think you can cough?"

Cait tried but the effort was weak.

Then Wendy appeared, looking tousled but fully awake. She listened to Cait's chest with her ear, and Rory caught the look in her eyes, though it was quickly concealed. Wendy was worried.

"Okay," Wendy said. "We've got to humidify this air. Chase, more candles. Rory, get that thing you made for boiling water. I want it here on the table. And Chase, can you find anything I can use to tent her so she'll get the moisture?"

"I've got survival blankets."

"That'll do."

All of a sudden the plane was a beehive of activity. Yuma appeared, too, and as soon as they had the chafing dish heating in front of Cait, he and Chase announced that they were going out to build a fire and make some kind of breakfast.

Rory lifted the window blind beside her, and in the weak light outside could tell only that the blizzard was still raging. Hard to believe that they'd left Seattle less than a day ago. It felt like a lifetime.

When the plane's door opened, a blast of arctic air blew in, bringing a cloud of fine snow with it. Rory looked out again after they closed the door and saw the men disappear into the maelstrom of snow. Build a fire in this?

But that problem couldn't engage her attention. Cait was all she could think about. She helped Wendy spread a mylar blanket to make a tent to make sure Cait got all the steam from the water that had just begun to boil. She slipped under the tent with her sister to keep an eye on her.

"I'll get stuff together and make her a hot drink in the galley," Wendy said.

"Thanks." Rory found her sister's hand and held it. To her horror, it didn't feel cool. Too warm? She touched Cait's cheek gently and was mildly reassured to find that it wasn't hot. Not feverish. Not yet.

In their little cocoon, light from the candle reflected off the mylar and made it almost bright. Cait struggled back to wakefulness.

"Breathe, sweetie," Rory urged her sister. "The steam will help."

Cait surprised her with the shadow of a smile. "At least it's warm."

"Yeah. It is." The mylar was helping with that, too. "Wendy's making you something hot to drink. And you need to take your meds again, too."

One solitary tear rolled down Cait's cheek. "I'm sorry, Rory. I'm messing up your life."

"Don't be sorry. Whatever you do, don't apologize to me. I wish I could do more, not less."

"I'm lucky you're my sister."

Rory forced a smile. "I'm glad you're my sister, too."

Cait gave a little laugh, but it barely started to emerge before it vanished in a deep, barking cough.

"That's good," Wendy's voice said from outside the tent. "Get her to lean forward. I'm going to tap her back."

Tap? Rory thought. The way Wendy did it, it was more than a tap. But essential, too. Absolutely essential.

She wrapped her arm around Cait's front and bent

her forward, making sure she didn't get too close to the hot water and the candle. Then, Wendy pounded Cait's back.

After several tries, Cait coughed again. It still sounded tight, but at least a little seemed to loosen.

"Five more minutes," Wendy said. "Then we'll try again."

"I'm sorry I'm so tired," Cait whispered.

"Don't think about it. We're going to get you to that hospital, and on that new drug. You're going to get better." Maybe she was a fool, but she couldn't allow herself to consider anything else.

"I almost believe you," Cait sighed.

That was an improvement, Rory thought. Small but significant. Will to live, she believed, was as important as any pill or IV, and her greatest source of concern the last few weeks had been Cait's apparent desire to just give up.

It took a half hour, but they managed to loosen Cait's chest enough that her breathing sounded better. And after all that, she still had enough strength to drink some soup and take her pills.

Wendy had removed the tent, setting it aside, saying they'd use it again in a couple of hours. But she didn't take the chafing dish away. She added more water to it, humidifying the entire plane.

"It's hell out there" was Chase's pronouncement as he and Yuma finally returned to the cabin, having successfully managed to throw together a meal, a stew made of whatever foods they had onboard that they thought would go together reasonably well.

To Rory it tasted like ambrosia. It didn't matter what was in it, only that it was full of calories. They finished off with hot coffee, and even though she liked her coffee black, she added sugar for fuel.

They huddled close while they ate, and lit more candles for warmth. Under other circumstances it would have felt cozy.

But Rory's mental clock was ticking loudly again. Three more days of medicine for her sister, and now breathing problems for which they had no treatment but a jerry-rigged humidifier. The fear she had been feeling since she learned of her sister's illness ramped up again, agitating her, making it almost impossible for her to hold still.

But there wasn't a damn thing she could do.

"Maybe when this storm clears," Yuma said, "I can figure out where we are. I used to walk all over these mountains. I might recognize a landmark."

"That would help," Chase said. "Especially if I can get the radio to work. Then it won't matter so much if the GPS doesn't come back up."

Rory perked up a bit, feeling a ray of hope. "You mean we could find our own way out of here?"

"That'll depend," Yuma said.

"Well, obviously. It's just good to know there might be an option other than hoping the beacon works, and works soon enough."

"Not a great option," Chase warned her. "Getting down these mountains through fresh snowfall will be challenging."

Rory glanced over at Cait, sending a clear message. Cait's condition made it impossible for them to wait. The clock just kept ticking. In fact, it seemed to be accelerating, especially with Cait's new breathing problem.

But she knew now that everyone on this plane

cared about getting Cait out of here alive. If this had to happen, she couldn't have asked for a better group of companions.

After breakfast they tented Cait again while the guys went out to wash dishes over the fire in the snow. It was still blowing so hard that when Rory glanced out, she could barely see them, and the fire looked dim.

Another fifteen minutes of steam, and Cait began to cough hard. Rory felt another prick of fear, because there was no ignoring the fact that Cait was coughing way too much to be explained away simply by her being so exhausted and not breathing deeply enough.

Again she caught that look of concern in Wendy's gaze. Cait had no resistance left and was taking drugs that suppressed her immune system. If she was developing pneumonia, it would hit her fast and hard. Maybe too fast to get her out of here.

But Wendy laid her hand on Cait's forehead, then nodded. "No fever."

"But this congestion could cause serious problems, right?"

"If we don't keep on top of it. We'll keep at it, though. I promise."

Cait had fallen back to sleep as soon as she cleared her lungs, and apparently didn't hear their concern. Good. Rory figured her sister didn't need another complication, most especially another reason to give up hope. She feared Cait would do exactly that, too, after what she'd seen in her these past few weeks. Never in her worst imaginings had she thought Cait would just want to give up. It seemed so unlike the Cait she used to be, and was probably the best indicator of just how bad Cait felt.

Rory could hardly stand to think about it. Never had

she reached a point in her life where she might have wanted to die, but when she imagined how her sister must be feeling to want to give up this way, the pain became almost unendurable.

"We've got to get her to drink more," Wendy went on. "It's essential. Lots of sweet tea and soup. As much as we can get into her. She needs the calories and she needs the fluids to keep her chest loose. Every half hour if we can."

Rory nodded, adding another ticking clock to the one at the back of her mind. "I'll keep on it."

"We both will."

Time might be running out even faster than she had thought. She wasn't much of a praying woman, but lately she'd been praying a lot. Now she added another prayer, begging God for mercy for her sister.

Chase disappeared into the cockpit again, determined to see what he could do with the GPS and radio communication. He emerged a long time later, looking grim. In answer to their questioning looks, he shrugged.

"Nothing."

But the storm was still blowing heavily, rescue was out of the question until it passed, and maybe that was the only thing wrong with their communications. They couldn't be sure until the storm subsided.

That was an uncertainty she had to live with, like it or not. She loathed it.

"I think," Chase said, "that we need to take alternating naps throughout the day. None of us got enough sleep last night, and tonight we'll still have to keep watch." He paused. "From what I recall of this storm system, it should clear out sometime late tonight or early tomorrow morning. We need to be rested and ready to deal with whatever we have to do."

Rory didn't think she could sleep, so Wendy and Yuma agreed to take the first nap. Chase sat across from her again, and Rory noticed that he looked at Cait with real concern.

"We'll get her out of here," he said yet again. "One way or another if I have to carry her down this mountain on my back."

It didn't sound like bravado, but rather like real determination. Rory felt a rush of warmth toward him.

"I'm scared," she admitted, not an easy thing for her to do. Admitting mistakes was one thing; admitting fear entirely another. In her life she had to always keep her fear hidden, because there was a danger the men she worked with would see it as weakness. As a result, she'd come to see it as weakness, too. But she could no longer pretend it didn't exist. She was terrified of losing Cait.

His gray eyes settled on her. "Only a fool wouldn't be scared right now, and your sister's situation only makes it worse. But we'll get her out of here."

"You can't really promise that." Her voice broke, and she realized with horror that she was on the verge of tears. "Oh, God," she said quietly, her voice thickening. "I can't break down."

"Why not? Sometimes it helps. Cry if you need to. God knows, you've got plenty of reasons."

"I'm so worried."

He nodded. "I don't like that coughing, either. I'll help when you need to tent her again."

"Thanks."

He startled her by reaching across the table and clasping her hand. The warmth and contact felt good, so she turned hers over so they were palm to palm. He squeezed gently.

"Last night," he started to say.

She cut him off. "We don't have to discuss it. It happened."

He frowned. "Was it that bad?"

Her head jerked backward in surprise. "I didn't say that."

A slow, sexy smile came to his face. "Ah."

She felt her cheeks heat. "Chase, please. I don't know what came over me."

"I do. *I* did." His smile widened a shade. "Do you hate me for it?"

"Of course not!"

"Well, then. I wanted to hate myself for it, but I enjoyed it too much. You really are one sexy woman."

She gaped at him, then glanced quickly at Cait. Her sister still slept. "Me?" she said finally, quietly. "Not me. And certainly not now. I haven't showered since yesterday morning, I haven't changed my clothes, I feel like something that ought to be in the dustbin."

"Funny, that isn't turning me off at all."

She told herself he was just trying to distract her from her worries, and maybe he was. But no, the glint in his eyes said he meant every word.

"I just thought," he continued, "that since I took advantage of you last night instead of just keeping you warm, I ought to be a gentleman and tell you it was wonderful. And not at all meaningless."

"How could it mean anything? You don't know me." But she liked the part about it being wonderful. A trickle of warmth wended its way to her center.

"It meant something. I'm thirty-six years old, Rory.

I don't do that with just anyone. And I figured you had a right to know that. I'm not sixteen anymore."

Her cheeks grew hotter. Mainly because she was basically inexperienced with this kind of conversation. Only once since college had she made love with a man because she spent all her time making sure her conduct was professional and that nothing she did would make any man perceive her as a sexual being. That was particularly important in the places where she worked. Gossip could grow fast, and undermine her authority.

"As for not knowing you," he continued quietly, "I think you're wrong. I don't know all your historical details, but I've had the opportunity to watch you under tremendous pressure. Times like these show our real character, believe me."

He had a point, she admitted. In these conditions you either stepped up or you fell down. A lot could be learned.

In fact, thinking about it, she realized that she knew the truly important things about Chase now. Not just that he was a great pilot, but that he took care of the people in his charge. He was strong, determined and even kind.

Kind enough to promise to get Cait out of here if he had to carry her on his back. The kind of man you'd want at your side in hard times. That said a lot.

"Anyway," he said, "I just wanted you to know. Last night happened because you, not anybody else, make me hot enough to forget the niceties. No roses, no dinner, no champagne. Shoot, that'll have to wait for another day. In fact, I'm going to ask you right now for a date."

"A date?" She almost could have laughed, given their

circumstances, but she knew it would probably sound bitter.

"A date. The first one won't be much, sorry to say. But the second one, after we get out of here and take care of your sister...well, then I'll do all the special things. So, I guess I'm asking for two dates. Will you say yes?"

But she hesitated long enough to ask, "Why me?"

"Because of your love for your sister. And because you're so sexy. So, yes? No?"

"Yes," she said finally, telling herself he'd probably forget all about her as soon as they got out of here.

"Good. This first date, your sister is invited along. Let's have some hot drinks and see if we can't get some down her as well. And then I'm going to tell you what you made me realize about myself."

That instantly piqued her curiosity. He wouldn't let her help, but insisted on making coffee for them and tea for Cait. He also astonished her with a blueberry muffin.

"My weakness," he said as he put it in front of her on a napkin. "I never travel without them. I was saving them for dinner, but I think I have enough for us to have one now."

In spite of everything, she began to smile. When he brought the drinks, she woke Cait gently.

Chase pushed out of his seat and squatted beside Cait. "Hi, Cait. I'm Chase. I'm the guy who crashed the plane."

Cait blinked. Then she looked more closely at him, showing a spark of real interest that thrilled Rory. "I thought you saved us from crashing."

"Well, I couldn't exactly prevent it. But I wanted to ask your permission to date your sister."

At that a weak little laugh escaped Cait. Rory's heart swelled until she thought it would burst.

"Is that a yes?" Chase asked.

"Yes," Cait whispered. "If she agrees."

"I think she just did. Can you drink some tea? I made it special for you."

"Sure." Another whisper.

Chase reached for the cup on the table before Rory could, and brought it to Cait's lips. "You are one special lady," he said as Cait sipped.

"Me?" Cait looked surprised. "You don't know me."

"Ah, but we can judge people by those who care about them. Rory cares about you. A whole lot."

"I'm lucky."

"You're more than lucky. Lots of sisters don't like each other. So Rory's concern about you tells me all I need to know."

That elicited another smile from Cait. "I think I can hold the cup."

Rory helped her free her hands from the blankets and watched with easing tension as her sister drank. She was making an effort, and every effort she made was a commitment to live.

"Want to share my blueberry muffin?" Rory asked her. To Rory's great delight, Cait nodded.

Rory broke it into pieces and pushed the napkin over in front of Cait. Her sister put down her tea and picked up a small piece. "I'm so tired, but I'm getting hungry, too."

"That's good." Although it wasn't really. Cait had been on IV supplements that nobody had thought it was crucial to continue over the few hours it was supposed to have taken them to reach Minnesota. Of course she was getting hungry.

But Cait managed to consume nearly half the muffin and the whole cup of tea before coughing racked her again. Rory pounded her back the way Wendy had, and at last the coughing subsided, leaving Cait drained. Moments later she fell back to sleep.

Rory sat back, picked up her coffee mug and said with bitter frankness, "I hate myself."

"Why?"

"Because I wouldn't wait until I could hire an air ambulance. They'd have had IVs and all that stuff."

"Why didn't you wait?"

"No time." She shook her head, feeling a surge of frustration. "I had to get her there immediately or they wouldn't add her to the trial, because her doctors were saying she only had weeks left. I told you it was a hurdle to get her on this program. Well, the first air ambulance I could get wasn't for ten days. Nobody would bump another patient, one who was more likely to be saved by transport."

He nodded. "It's a hard calculus. I guess I'm used to it from the military."

"Triage. I get it. No one in Seattle held out any hope. So bumping some burn victim or desperately injured child wasn't going to happen. And I couldn't wait ten days because the researchers were flat-out frank about it. The longer the delay, the less they wanted her as a trial patient."

"More ugly calculus."

"Exactly. My sister's life was being weighed against the likelihood that anything might help her. I get it. I got it totally. So I asked what if I flew her on a private jet. None of the docs thought that was going to make anything worse. I've been wondering if that decision was solely because they considered her hopeless. Regardless, it was only supposed to be a few hours."

"Then don't hate yourself for not getting an ambulance. Dammit, Rory, what choice did you have?"

"I didn't think I had any."

"Well, you didn't. And if we hadn't crashed, she'd already be in the trial. How can you argue your decision now? You did the best you could under the circumstances."

"I know, I know. It's just that I'm looking at her now and thinking of all the things I wish I'd insisted on before we left. Like keeping her on IVs."

"I couldn't have transported her that way. So that would have taken you back to the ambulance solution. Which clearly would have prevented her from getting in the trial."

"I know." She bit her lip. "I know all of this logically."

"Then stop beating yourself up. Everything would have been just hunky-dory except for some lazy mechanic in Seattle who didn't do something right. Those are the kinds of things nobody can prepare for."

Rory drew a few deep breaths, fighting down her frustration. Being frustrated wouldn't change a thing. At last she let go of a long breath and tried to smile at Chase. "I thought this was supposed to be a date."

"It is. Who says you can't talk about things that upset you on a date? What kind of date would that be?"

"I don't know."

"Well, I do. It would be exactly the wrong kind. Exactly the kind of date I've gone on too often in my life. I said I was going to tell you something I'd realized about myself."

That completely captured her interest. "What's that?"

"That I got kicked to the curb a million times because I made a career out of picking the wrong kind of women. Over and over. And I think I did it on purpose."

"Meaning?"

"I had fighter-jock syndrome, for one thing. I looked at the outside of the package and made my selection from the unending deli of beauties who prowl the bars looking for guys like me. And then I picked the ones I knew wouldn't stick around."

"Why? Why would you do that?"

"I guess because I didn't want to get attached. I dunno. I'll have to think about that some. But watching you with Cait, I realized that you're the kind of person who will stick through thick and thin. That's what I wanted in my wingman. Why the hell wouldn't I want that in a woman?"

"Don't ask me. I have no idea. I know why I avoid involvement."

"Why's that?"

"Because it would lessen my authority if people are thinking about my sexuality. I'm already fighting an uphill battle."

"At least you understand why. I'm still working on it."

"Maybe you were just young and liked being foot-loose."

"And maybe I liked visiting the deli to try out a new sandwich." He gave a snort. "Don't think I'm proud of that."

"That doesn't make you unusual for a man."

"You might be right. Everyone I knew, with a few exceptions, was basically doing the same thing. Oh, they tried marriage, the operative word often being *tried*. Some found good relationships. A lot more wound up divorced. We're not very good marriage risks, navy pilots. Maybe it's different for the air force."

"That I wouldn't know."

"I don't have statistics to refer to," he admitted. "But watching you with Cait, I suddenly realized that I'd been getting exactly what I wanted from my girlfriends—desertion. And I don't think I want that anymore."

Her hand froze on her cup. Was he trying to tell her something? God, she hoped not. She had enough on her plate right now, and she didn't want to be another one of the women who kicked him to curb.

"Anyway," he said after a moment, "a little self-revelation. That's always good."

"I'm sure the women you're no longer blaming will be relieved."

He chuckled quietly. "I think they were playing by the same rules. I doubt a single one of them remembered me after I flew away."

"You make it sound like you were all counting coup."

"Maybe we were. Notches on the belt or something. More coffee?"

He refilled their mugs and poured some more water in the chafing dish that was still steaming on the table. "Do we need to tent her again?"

Rory glanced at her watch. "Another ten minutes or so."

"Okay."

He sat regarding Rory steadily. His stare made her a bit uncomfortable, especially since she was remembering how he had touched her the night before, and wishing he would do it again. The conflict between her worry for her sister and this unexpected sexual need jarred her, but there it was.

Two sides of her nature, both trying to take charge. Well, one side *had* to be in charge. No way around it.

Then it struck her that he hadn't asked her to say anything about last night. No, he'd simply told her something that she would need to know later: that he hadn't just taken advantage of her because of proximity.

Later, whatever happened, that would reassure her that she hadn't just been used. The kindness of that was almost enough to take her breath away.

But he'd asked for no reassurance for himself. Didn't he need it? Or maybe he didn't want to hear her answer, was afraid she might say she'd just been having an adrenaline reaction.

Maybe she had been. But she doubted it. Truth was, sitting here across from him now, she still felt his magnetism. She still wanted to have sex with him. Out of place or not, there was no denying that it was real and she wanted more. With him. Only with him.

She hadn't felt that in a long, long time.

But she was afraid to tell him so. Afraid of what that might mean. There could be no future for them. She had to take care of Cait, then she had to get back to her job. Where could anyone else fit into that? Nothing had really changed—her job would make the same demands, and there'd be no place once again for thoughts of marriage and family. She *had* to believe this was just a passing desire or how would she ever get back to her career?

"Have some muffin," he said, nudging the napkin toward her. "This is a date, remember?"

"Certainly a memorable one."

He smiled. "We aim to please."

He helped with tenting Cait as he had promised, and they got her to cough some more. They even got her to drink another cup of heavily sweetened tea.

"I thought you two were having a date," Cait said breathlessly as she sagged back in the seat.

"Shh," Rory said, holding the tea to her lips.

"No." Cait gave another small cough. "This is something I never thought I'd live to see. My sister on a date."

"In a crashed plane," Chase pointed out. "With the pilot who was at the helm. At least we have the candlelight to add to the romance, though."

Cait actually laughed. It dissolved into coughs, but when she caught her breath again she looked at Rory. "I think," she said faintly, "that I want to live."

Rory's heart cracked as surely as if it had been cleaved in two. Her throat grew so tight she couldn't answer.

"That's good news," Chase said gently. "We'll get you to Minnesota, Cait. We will."

Her sister looked at a man she didn't even know, and Rory saw the trust in her gaze. "I believe you."

"Then how about some more tea or muffin? Gotta keep your strength up."

But the clock just kept ticking, and to Rory it sounded like the heartbeat of horror: loud and echoing. Time kept running out like grains of sand in an hourglass, and more endless hours stretched ahead of them before they could do a damn thing.

Time, the cruelest taskmaster of all.

Chapter 8

The day outside brightened steadily, but the snow showed no evidence of abating. The plane rocked a little as afternoon arrived, and Rory guessed that the buried wing had been blown clear again.

Her nerves grew tighter, ready to shriek from the inactivity. God, she couldn't stand this. Cait might be worsening, to judge by her congestion, and Rory just wasn't built to sit around twiddling her thumbs, which was about all she could do right now.

Playing cards didn't distract her nearly enough, and even the funny stories Chase tried to tell about the military filled only small pieces of endless time.

Except time wasn't endless. It might feel like it right now, but it was short—shorter than she could stand to think about.

Every time she looked at her sister, she questioned her judgments and decisions. Not only about deciding to take a private flight to save time, but about how to handle this situation when the storm passed.

Should they wait if the GPS came up, assuming the beacon was undamaged? How much more might they risk by stumbling out into the snowy mountainside? Would the exposure put Cait at even greater risk?

There were no answers. None at all.

She had believed that she had learned to live by the maxim *Worry about the things you can fix, and not the things you can't.* Yeah, she could do that when it came to her job. She had a lot of control there, and when control was taken from her it was often by someone who employed her, and the problem then became theirs.

But this was different, so different from anything she had faced before. Her coping skills fell far short of having learned to wait.

"You need to nap," Chase told her.

Wendy and Yuma were in the galley, making more hot soup to be followed by tenting Cait again.

"I don't want to be alone." The bald admission startled Rory. She was *used* to being alone. She basically lived her life alone, relying only on herself. She thought of herself as strong, independent, a woman who could travel the world and work under nearly all conditions.

And now she was falling apart, feeling weak, frightened and afraid of failing. So unlike her. She wished she could snatch back the revealing words, but even if Chase hadn't been there to hear them, she *had*. Now she stared starkly at herself, at the facade she had created over the years, and realized there were other parts of her long unnourished. Parts she didn't want. Parts she wished she could sever.

"Okay," Chase said. "After we eat, I'll nap with you. You know Wendy can look after Cait."

In fact, Wendy had been far more useful in looking after Cait than Rory had been. She wouldn't have known how to handle her sister's growing congestion. Wouldn't have been able to listen to her sister's chest and judge the gravity of it.

"I guess we're lucky there was a nurse onboard," she said.

"Very." Chase gave her a half smile. "A damn fine nurse. She's dealt with a lot worse in emergencies."

Rory didn't want to imagine worse. This was certainly bad enough.

They chatted about nothing substantial during their meal, avoiding any discussion about the situation. Cait ate another full cup of soup, and then cleared her lungs again. Only when she at last slipped back into sleep did Rory feel that she could go nap herself.

But she wasn't at all sure she'd sleep. Wound as tight as a coiled spring, every muscle in her body was tense enough to ache. She slipped under the covers in the chilly aft cabin, and stared at the fuselage only inches away, almost invisible as only a little light reached the room from the candles in the main cabin.

She knew she needed to sleep. At any moment something could change, and the better rested she was, the better she would be able to handle it. Fitfully dozing last night had not left her feeling rested. But would anything?

A few minutes later, Chase entered the cabin. She heard him close the door, move around a bit, and then he slipped in behind her, wrapping his arms around her.

God, it felt good to be held. So good. How could she have forgotten the soothing power of a simple hug? It had been so long since she had allowed anyone to do this.

"Relax," he murmured. "We'll be the first to know if something happens."

That was true, and acceptance of that allowed her to uncoil just a bit. He helped by running his hand soothingly along the length of her side, from shoulder to knee. As if he were petting her.

With her head pillowed on his arm, his other hand stroking her gently, she closed her eyes and willed herself to relax.

The anxiety that had been winding her steadily tighter since she had learned of Cait's illness, and ever more rapidly since the crash, began to ease.

Surely it wouldn't be a crime to let go of worry for just a little while. Especially since she was helpless to do anything about it.

And as she relaxed, weariness began to rise. God, she was worn out. Worn out from the last few weeks, worn out from all her terrors and all her efforts, worn out from the last twenty-four hours and all the added complications.

"Chase?"

"Hmm?"

"She's all I have left."

"I gathered that."

"I don't know what I'll do." A tear rolled down her cheek, just one, hot against her cold skin. "Maybe it's stupid, but even after we lost Mom and Dad, Cait was always there in my mind. Like an anchor. I still had family."

He made a sound like agreement.

"I wish you'd met Cait when she was well."

"Was she like you?"

"That depends on what you mean."

"Feisty, determined, dedicated," he said.

"That's an overestimation of me."

"We can argue about it another time. Tell me about Cait."

"She's softhearted. I don't mean that in a bad way, either. Just that she was the one who'd bring home the stray cat or dog, who'd get upset even about killing a spider."

"Really?"

A choked laugh escaped Rory. "You will never know how many times I had to agree to try to capture bugs before I was allowed to step on them. We had a problem with pygmy rattlesnakes in our yard for a while, and what with the dogs she'd brought home, Mom and Dad were worried one of the dogs might get a snake-bite. But Cait would go out with a shovel and scoop them up and toss them back into the woods."

"So she *is* like you."

"I dunno. At that age I was all for killing them."

"But you didn't."

"No." She sighed. "I guess at some level I was glad she protected them. Yes, they were a threat, but if they could be safely removed, why kill them? As she was fond of saying, 'They're just being snakes doing snaky things.'"

"And when she got older?"

"Pretty much the same. Rescuing animals. Until she became sick, she worked for a rescue organization. She got married, talked about having four kids, and in the process of trying to find out why she couldn't get pregnant they discovered the lymphoma."

She sighed, and used a corner of the blanket to wipe away that stray tear. "She was all about helping. Helping people, helping animals. I couldn't even list all the charities she volunteered for. She's one of the last people this world can afford to lose. Me, I just went off to do my own thing because finding oil challenged me. I looked for the excitement, I guess. She looked for love."

"She sounds pretty special."

"She is."

"Here." He tugged her gently until she rolled over so that they were face-to-face. There was no light in the bedroom, except what seeped around the door from the candles in the main cabin. Even so, she could just make out his features.

"You've done everything humanly possible," he told her. "I admire that."

"What if I've failed?"

"It won't be for lack of trying. You can be proud of that. No one on this planet can promise you the outcome you want, so whatever happens, it's hardly failure."

"Maybe not." But her heart ached and she squeezed her eyes closed.

He tightened his arms around her. "Right now you have to let go. I swear, as soon as this storm passes, we'll figure out what's the best thing to do, and we'll do it. You're not alone in this, Rory. I promise. I'll help every way I can, every step of the way."

God, how long had it been since someone had said she wasn't alone with something? Maybe it was her own fault—her need to control—but she never relied on other people to do more than the bare minimum. That was a far cry from someone telling you that he'd be with you, that you weren't alone.

All of a sudden she felt frightened again, but for a very different reason. She realized that she had armored herself against needing anyone or anything, seeing it as a weakness. Mostly she had feared that others, who already wanted to put her down because she was a woman, would see it as weakness and try to take advantage of her.

Right now she felt that protective shell trying to crack open, and she was terrified that if it did she might never be able to put it back together.

"Rory? You're shaking."

But not from cold. Sheer terror gripped her, terror that she had been holding at bay for weeks now. She was out of her element, she was helpless and she was dependent on others. Something had at last risen up in her life to show her that, in the end, nobody could do it all alone.

No matter how tough she was, no matter how much in charge she was, no matter how she tried to wrest what she wanted or needed from the world around her, she couldn't always rely on her own determination, stubbornness, intelligence and strength. Sometimes she needed help.

She had always been a fighter. She had always gotten what she wanted, including getting Cait into this clinical trial, even though she didn't strictly fit the criteria. She fought, and she usually won, because she wouldn't quit, and because she could always find a way.

Not this time. Not in a crashed plane on a mountainside. There was nothing she could do to change this situation.

These past few weeks she had been trying to avoid facing this. She had tried to force a system to give Cait back her health, even though they all kept telling her they couldn't do anything. She had battled to get Cait into this clinical trial against all odds, and had succeeded. Then their plane crashed. Then they were lost on the side of a mountain with no assurance that they could get Cait out of here no matter what anyone did.

But of one thing she was certain: none of the traits she prided herself on would allow her to solve this alone.

Just as once she entered Cait in the trial it would be out of her hands.

She had refused to think about that. Refused to acknowledge that sooner or later she would become helpless to do more. She didn't allow herself such thoughts, ever.

But she couldn't escape them any longer.

"Rory?" His voice, pitched low, was gentle.

"I'm so scared," she admitted brokenly. "I can't fix anything. I can't do anything. I'm helpless."

He took a few moments before responding. "We're all pretty helpless right now. That's going to change during the night. Then we're all going to pull together, and you'll be able to do plenty. I'm counting on it."

She sighed, trying to release tension, and failing. "That's not exactly it."

"Then tell me."

"I'm used to being in control. One way or another, I deal with problems, and I solve them. And right now I can't do that, and when you said you'd help me, I realized how little help I've accepted or even wanted over the years, and it just...just..." She couldn't go on.

"I see." Again he pondered for a minute or two. "One of the things you learn in the military is that you're part of a team. Even a fighter jock doesn't get off the runway without a lot of support from the ground crew and the tower. Everyone plays a key role. Then when you get in the air, your life can depend on your wingman if there's trouble. I guess I'm used to relying on others."

She sighed again, trying to absorb what he was saying.

"You don't have to be alone. And right now we're all pretty helpless. We have to lean on each other. There's no other way to get through this, Rory. And that's not a sign of weakness."

She almost gasped. "How did you know I was thinking about that?"

"Maybe I read minds. I don't know. Maybe because I've known control freaks before. They only feel safe when they do everything themselves, and depend only on themselves."

"I am a control freak," she admitted. "I thought of it as being strong, but it's not that. I don't dare depend on others."

"And now you have to. We're all leaning on each right now. There's no weakness in that. In fact, it's how we become stronger, by working together."

"I've been part of teams," she argued.

"But I'll bet you were the boss."

"Usually," she admitted.

"This time there's no boss, except maybe Yuma. He knows these mountains and how to survive in these conditions better than anyone. But we'll still be pulling together once this storm passes and we figure out what we need to do."

She bit her lip, gnawing on it just as she was gnawing on the upheaval inside her. She'd always been afraid of leaning on others, because what if they failed? Yet here she was, unable to do anything else. Maybe, a little voice in her head said, she just needed to get over herself. Things were complicated enough without twisting herself into knots over needing help. And wasn't she proposing to lean on doctors in Minnesota? Sheesh, she wasn't making sense at all.

"I suppose," she said tremulously, "that I could call this a life lesson."

"Maybe. They always seem to hurt."

"Yeah."

He drew her a little closer, hugging her tighter. "One of the things I had to face was that I wasn't indestructible. I mean, you've gotta have a tremendous sense of invincibility to be a fighter jock. Then one day they tell you there's some little squiggle on your EKG, it's meaningless but hey, buddy, you can't fly those planes anymore."

"Ouch." She could easily imagine that, actually.

"Yeah, ouch is right. All of a sudden you're not invincible. The years are creeping up on you and you've just lost the thing you thought you were living for. It doesn't help when they tell you it happens to nearly everyone by your age, and that they're just being hypercautious. Doesn't help one bit."

"No, it wouldn't. I'm sorry, Chase."

"Thanks. But I've made the adjustment and I'm mostly content. Now *you're* making an adjustment. There are some things—important things—that you can't control. So we're going to be operating as a team."

His logic reached her brain, but her heart was struggling to accept it. She hated the weakness and helplessness she felt now, and yet he was telling her she was no more weak or helpless than any of them. Maybe he was right. Maybe it was time to grow up and face the fact that not everything in life would bend to her will or her expertise.

"I've been deluding myself," she said after a bit.

"How?"

"Thinking I needed no one. That I was a solitary pillar capable of shouldering any burden. Apparently I'm not."

"That's not a bad thing, because none of us are that strong."

"No." She drew a long breath. "I started thinking about this when I realized just how much it meant to me when you offered to stand by me. I can't remember the last time someone offered me that, and that's when I realized it's because I don't allow it."

"Maybe it's time to offer a little trust, and let someone help."

"I have no choice now."

She wished the words unspoken as soon as they left her mouth. She felt him stiffen and draw back a little. Amazing how much that small withdrawal pained her.

"That came out wrong," she said quickly. "I didn't mean it the way it sounded."

"Then how did you mean it?"

"That I think I have no choice but to learn a lesson I probably should have learned a long time ago."

She felt him relax and was more relieved than she cared to admit. She didn't want this man to pull away from her, not even a trifle. Nor did she want to think about why she felt that way. Just let it be. For now. If she could do that as necessary on her job, why not in personal matters? She put that question away for another time, too. She sensed, however, that somewhere in there was a key to her nature that needed some attention.

Odd that she felt so close to him, though. Not just physically, but emotionally. She never would have expected that when she boarded this plane, or even directly after the crash. Something about him, however, seemed engagingly open and inviting. She got the sense that he was long past playing games with himself or anyone else.

How did you get there, she wondered, because it had never been clearer to her that she had been playing her own game, pretending to need no one and nothing.

Hell, maybe she'd even been using memories of her sister, awareness that she still *had* a sister, all these years to keep herself from feeling totally adrift, even though she hadn't visited often enough.

No, she wasn't going to beat herself up about that now. Enough, already. She couldn't change the past— she could only resolve to do better from now on. She had a feeling, though, that earthquakes were going to be rattling through her psyche for a long time after this.

Sleep eluded her, though, as her mind tried to race in useless circles, worrying over the things she'd learned about herself, worrying about things beyond her control. Damn, she wished her brain had an off switch.

Apparently it did. As if he sensed her continued tension, Chase began rubbing her back gently. Instinctively, she moved closer, every other thought forgotten as she became instantly aroused.

How could he do that to her?

But she didn't care. At first she welcomed it as a relief from the places she'd been wandering, but it wasn't long before it went past welcome to hunger and need.

Nor was it just a means of escape, she realized just before his mouth settled over hers. In her deepest being, she was certain that she would have wanted him under any circumstances. Any circumstances at all.

And these weren't the best. A slim door to give them

privacy, a room that was too chilly, danger lurking…
and dammit, she wanted him.

She raised her arm to hug him back, and heard a
quiet murmur of approval from him. She didn't know
what they were doing, if they were making a mistake,
and she absolutely didn't care.

She wanted Chase, he wanted her, and that seemed
like the answer to nearly every question in the universe
right then.

He hadn't kissed her before, but he kissed her now as
if her mouth were all he wanted. He teased her tongue
with his, traced her lips with it, then dove in for a
deeper kiss. She was oh so ready for it, the rhythmic
movement of tongue against tongue, tasting faintly of
coffee. It seemed so right that in these endless, dangerous, helpless hours that they should seek to express
something beautiful, something life-affirming.

When she could welcome him no more deeply with
her mouth, he rolled them a bit, so that he rose over her
on one elbow.

"Stop me now," he murmured against her lip. "Now
or never."

"Don't stop," she whispered. "Oh, please, don't stop."

Given permission, he didn't hesitate. His hand
slipped up under her sweater, cold against her midriff.
She shivered with delight as much as with the cold
touch, but he was patient. He let his hand warm against
her while he trailed kissed across her cheeks, her throat,
her ear and then captured her mouth again.

Their tongues dueled as if they had been born for
this moment. Never had a kiss felt so right. Then his
hand stole upward.

He found the front clasp of her bra and set her free.

* * *

Cupping her breast, Chase felt the lightning bolt of heat shoot through him to his groin. She felt surprisingly full in his hand, and her nipple was as hard as a pebble. Feeling it against his palm nearly dragged a groan from him.

He squeezed gently, until she writhed against him, then he brushed her nipple with his thumb. A shiver passed through her and into him. Between his legs he felt hot and heavy, ready. More than ready.

But he didn't want to rush this. He had to battle an urge to just take her now, claim her now, make her his now, because he felt an equally strong urge to carry her every step of the way with him.

There was only one road to heaven at the moment, and this was it. He was going to make sure she came with him.

Besides, he was feeling unusually protective of her. He hadn't felt this way about a lover before. His partners in bed had always been experienced, always knowing what they were doing, and never wounded or hurt.

But he felt a deep hurt in Rory, one that went beyond her sister's illness. That hurt made her vulnerable, and he was determined that she not walk away from this time feeling used. No, he wanted her to feel worshipped. Adored. Cherished.

With the blood throbbing in his head and his body, he couldn't analyze those feelings now. They just were. When a soft moan escaped her and her body arched against his, he knew there would be no stopping. She was ready right now, but he wasn't going to allow this to be rough and graceless like last night. There might not be any roses or champagne, but they weren't what mattered anyway. What mattered was how he treated her now.

He took his time. He tormented her by holding back. And he almost chuckled when she pressed her breast harder into his hand, signaling her need unmistakably.

It was chilly in the cabin, but he suspected neither of them much cared right now. He pushed her sweater up, baring her breasts, wishing only that he could see their delights as well as feel them. A shudder ripped through her, and then again as he found her nipple with his mouth.

"Ahh…" It was little more than a sigh, but it told him enough. He sucked gently at first, teasing her nipple with his tongue, liking the contrast of its hardness compared to the softness of her breast. Liking the way it felt both soft and rough against his tongue.

She writhed, pressing harder against him from head to toe, and the ache within him grew to massive proportions.

It had been a long time since he'd come this close to losing control, but something about this woman put him on the very brink.

He paused just a moment, fighting down his own needs, determined to give her everything she could possibly want in these circumstances. Then he found her breast again, sucking even harder, as if he wanted to draw her inside him. A little nip for good measure and she arched so hard against him that he almost lost it.

God, she was sexy, and good and… Rational thought abandoned him.

Rory had never guessed how exquisitely sensitive her breasts could be, but Chase was rapidly teaching her that every other experience in her life had been pale by comparison.

It had been way too long since a man had touched her this way. Too long since she had even considered allowing it. It was as if pent-up years of self-denial were exploding all at once.

Her nipples were acutely sensitive, the one in his mouth responding to his ministrations, the other puckering in eagerness in the chilly air, the merest brush against it sending spikes of sheer desire to her very core.

She throbbed, she ached, she grew damp, and they'd barely started. She never wanted it to end.

Finally, he tore his mouth from her and trailed it up her chest, her throat, to give her another kiss. "It's cold in here," he whispered finally. "I don't want to go fast, but I don't want you to get chilled."

She didn't think that was possible. She was also in no mood to wait. Right now that was a luxury that didn't appeal to her at all.

"Hurry," she whispered back. "Oh, please, just hurry."

She hardly cared how cold the air felt when he rose, taking the blanket with him. She could hear him struggling to strip in the dark. Then his hands tugged at her clothing and she fought to help him. She wanted it all gone, every bit of it.

Wanted to know the delicious feeling of his skin pressed to hers from head to foot. Wanted to know everything about how he felt, and how he could make her feel.

As soon as he'd pulled her jeans and panties from her, he spread the blankets over her again. Then, surprising her, he burrowed in near her feet.

"Oh…" It was barely a breath as she felt him kiss the insteps of her feet, then her arches. Inch by inch he made his way up her legs, kissing and licking here and there. Making even that ordinary skin feel like an instrument of exquisite pleasure.

Anticipation built in her, a violent but steady drumbeat. Steadily, he moved upward, approaching that most secret of places, the part of her that felt as if it were expanding, opening, crying out silently for fullness.

Then he found her, dropping kisses on her swollen, moist petals. She bit back a groan, trying to hold still so that it would never stop, but her body betrayed her, tipping her hips up toward him.

At once he pressed his face hard against her, then a sharp shaft of pleasure-pain speared through her as his tongue found that exquisitely sensitive knot of nerves. It was almost too much to bear, and only some dim remaining sense kept her from screaming out at the sensation.

Never before…

None of this had ever happened before. He licked her again and it almost seemed as if something grabbed her, forcing her hips upward for more and more. She was afraid it would end. She feared she couldn't handle much more. So intense. So extreme. So utterly unimaginable…

Again, then again, and just as she thought she would shatter into a million billion flaming pieces in painful pleasure, he stopped. He left her hanging on the precipice.

But not for long. Not for long at all.

He slid up and over her, his staff seeking entrance. She reached down to help him, finding him sheathed in latex, knowing a momentary pang that there was something between them, however necessary.

And then he slipped into her, filling her, answering that ache for his swollen member. How could she have forgotten how good it felt to be filled and stretched this way? Had it *ever* felt this good?

His mouth clamped to her breast again, making her feel as she were one long wire of exquisite feeling, as if nothing existed but his hardness driving into her and his mouth tormenting her.

He plunged again and again, rotating gently in a way that caressed her swollen knot of nerves.

Higher and higher until…until everything vanished except the peak they strove for. Until nothing existed but the pleasure between them.

She sucked in a sharp breath, feeling it happen. Nerve endings exploded everywhere, a hard ache turning to incredible release that rolled through her like ocean wave after ocean wave.

Endlessly.

"Damn, Rory," he panted by her ear. "Damn."

She doubted that she could move a muscle. Talking seemed like way too much effort. "Something wrong?" she managed thickly.

"God, no! I've never…"

"Me, either," she mumbled.

He groaned. "Sorry."

She almost protested when he rolled off her. She didn't want him gone, but understood. She was growing cold. He had to take care of things….

It was the cold that brought her completely back. He found a candle on one of the shelves and lit it. By its dim flickering light, he untangled the heap of clothes on the floor and quickly started helping her to dress.

As soon as she was clothed again, he donned his own garments. Then he laid down with her and pulled the blankets over them, snuggling her close as warmth returned.

"You're amazing," he murmured, and kissed her.

"So are you. I've never…" She didn't want to say it, but she didn't need to.

She snuggled into his embrace, her head in the hollow of his shoulder. "Thank you for everything."

"I think you got that the wrong way around."

"I hope you think so."

He squeezed her and shifted a bit so that his leg lay between hers. "I really do want to date you after all this is cleared up."

"I'd like that."

"I mean, I realize it'll be tough with you a country away and all, but I *do* have wings."

"You'll need to persuade some of your clients to check out the oil biz in Mexico. All so that we can eat tortillas and drink tequila together."

"Oh, I think we'll do more than eat tortillas."

She smiled. "Probably."

"No probably about it. Now try to get some sleep, darlin'. We'll have plenty of time to talk later."

Now she didn't want to sleep for another reason. She wanted to savor the afterglow, to remember each detail of what had just happened so she could take it out and enjoy it again and again no matter what happened.

But she really hadn't had enough sleep, and despite her efforts to hold it off, it claimed her almost without warning.

* * *

Wendy and Yuma let them sleep until suppertime. When Rory emerged from the bedroom, having stepped in the bathroom to wash quickly with some paper towels and icy water, she found Cait awake and sipping another hot beverage. Playing cards were laid out, even in front of Cait.

"She's been playing rummy with us," Wendy said brightly.

Something in that bright tone alerted Rory. She took a second look at Wendy. "What?"

"Cait's a little more congested. We've been working on it."

That didn't sound good, but Rory didn't want to ask in front of Cait for fear of adding to her stress. "Should I tent her more often?"

"Yeah," Wendy said. "And if she starts to sound tight again, wake me, okay?"

That was not good. The last lingering bit of afterglow fled as she slid into a seat beside Cait. "Playing rummy, huh?"

Cait gave a little nod. "Sort of. They were helping me."

Rory studied her sister's face and didn't like what she saw. Cait's eyes appeared too bright, and her color, so pale for so long, had risen. Fever. She wanted to reach out and check, but again hesitated for fear of adding to Cait's concerns. She glanced up at Chase and saw him frowning.

"I'm going to go try the damn radio and GPS again," he said. "I'll be back shortly."

So he was worried enough to struggle with equipment, even though he knew it probably wouldn't work until the storm had passed. Or even then.

Because it was beginning to seem to Rory, although she was no expert, that the amount of atmospheric disturbance required to keep them totally out of touch this long was probably not normal.

And Chase's march into the cockpit seemed to substantiate that.

When he returned twenty minutes later, he gave her a shake of his head. "We need to eat."

A totally different topic. And now her fears had ratcheted up another notch, something she would have thought impossible. Guilt speared her, too. When she had gone to take her nap, Cait had actually seemed a little better, a little stronger. Now she could only kick herself for not being beside her sister when she was obviously getting sicker.

It was a stupid thought, as if she could have prevented this. Wendy had done everything possible while they were stuck in this trap. She didn't doubt it, so why beat herself up over it?

Yuma had apparently made dinner before waking them. Chase heated what was left over with candles. Cait stirred and agreed to another cup of tea.

It was so little to do for her sister, so very little. She felt the worst urge to indulge in a primal scream just to ease the tension.

Chase brought out more muffins, too. Rory ate without tasting, in between getting more sips of heavily sweetened tea into Cait, and encouraging her to eat some muffin.

"I never ate so much sweet stuff at one time," Cait whispered.

"Enjoy. They'll probably take it all away from you again at the hospital."

Cait managed a smile, then started coughing again. Rory definitely didn't like the sound of it.

"I'll get the tent," Chase said immediately.

Once again Rory huddled under the survival blanket while steam filled it from the chafing dish, holding her sister's hand and pounding her back every few minutes.

Cait's congestion had increased; Rory could hear it. Worse, her cough sounded tighter. *Pneumonia.* The dreaded word could no longer be pushed away.

Finally, exhaustion claimed Cait, taking her into slumber so deep it approached unconsciousness. Rory sat awhile longer, waving steam toward her sister's face, but no more coughs came.

At last she pushed away the blanket and looked at Chase. "We've got to get out of here."

"I know. But not in the dark. Not until the storm stops. It won't do anyone a damn bit of good—least of all Cait—if we go out there, get lost, break legs…"

"I know, I know. I just want some mercy. Just a little mercy." It sounded exactly like the plea it was: a cry straight from her soul.

He nodded, his mouth tightening.

But what could he say? Not a word. "Eat up," he said after a moment. "You need to pack in as many calories as you can. We may well be hiking out of here early."

She nodded. She didn't want to think of all the difficulties that would face them in these mountains. But if the plane wasn't sending out a locator signal, they couldn't afford to wait. Not now.

Her heart sank to her toes.

Chapter 9

It happened during the wee hours. Rory had refused to leave Cait's side even to sleep, so she was dozing beside her sister. A groan awoke her and for a few seconds she couldn't identify it.

She turned at once to Cait, who still slept, and noticed that her breathing sounded a little raspy, but not terrible. Evidently, she hadn't made that sound.

Then it came again. Chase, who had been slumbering across the aisle sat bolt upright. "Hell," he said.

"Chase?"

He didn't answer. He jumped up immediately and went to get Wendy and Yuma. A few minutes later they stumbled out of the back cabin, carrying their boots.

"Everybody get dressed. Everything you've got, as many layers as you can. Rory, if you have an extra set of thermal stuff, get it on Cait."

She did. Why she had an extra set, she didn't know.

At the time she'd bought it, she'd wondered, but for some reason had felt compelled. Maybe because she'd been worried about how cold she would get in Minnesota when she was used to Mexico.

Wendy helped her before finishing her own dressing. They dug out more survival blankets and tucked them along with every available blanket around Cait.

"What's happening?" Rory demanded even as she worked.

"I'm not sure, but I think we're about to move."

"Why?"

"Yeah," Yuma said. "Doesn't it usually get colder behind a storm?"

"I don't know," Chase said flatly. "I don't know. But I feel something…" He told them all to buckle into their seats.

Then he blew out the candles and they waited.

For a long time nothing happened. Then she heard another groan from the metal around them. Her heart slammed, because this time she thought she felt movement. It was hard to be sure, but her body seemed to have felt a slight slip, the smallest increase in pressure of her back against the seat.

She gripped the arms of her chair until her fingers ached, her heart rapidly pounding, and waited… waited…

The next few minutes felt like eternity. Just as she began to hope that nothing more would happen, it did.

There was a sudden slip, a shriek from metal, she knew a few moments of dizziness, a lurching feeling, and the next thing she was aware of was snow blowing in her face.

She opened her eyes, but could see nothing at all.

"Nobody move," Chase barked. "It might not be over."

He was right. Another lurch, another scream from the plane, more icy air and snow whipping about her.

Then she felt as if she were riding on one of those circular sleds, round and round like a top, only not as fast. A huge crunching sound rent the night, then it all came to a sudden halt that threw her sideways and made her seat belt tight.

Then nothing. For a long, long time, nothing except the cold and blowing snow. She felt as if she couldn't catch her breath.

A light snapped on. Chase had a flashlight. He was still belted into a seat and she could just make him out as he played the beam around the cabin.

She followed the light, gasping in horror as she saw that the fuselage had torn open. And somehow, impossibly, the very back of the plane seemed to have filled with snow.

"Don't anybody else move," Chase said. "I can't be sure it's over. Rory, make sure Cait's face is covered."

She leaned over, aided by his flashlight, and drew one of the blankets over Cait's face. Amazingly, Cait seemed to have slept through it all. Not good. In fact, terrible. No one should have been able to sleep through that. That frightened Rory so much she leaned over to make sure her sister was still breathing. Yes, she was, but it didn't sound good.

Chase shined the light on his watch. "Dawn in two hours. I think our options just grew more limited."

"I agree," Yuma said. "We just lost our shelter."

The protection the plane had provided was gone. They were exposed now, as exposed as if they had walked out into the storm.

"It doesn't seem to be blowing anywhere near as hard now," Chase remarked. "It must almost be over."

But the rest had only just begun.

They waited a long time before Chase was convinced that they were probably done moving, at least for a while. Rory jumped up when he said he was going out to see what had happened. She looked at Wendy, who nodded toward Cait, signaling that she would watch her.

Never built to just wait, Rory joined Chase and Yuma as they clambered through the cracked hull to examine what had happened.

The plane had turned around somehow as it slid, and had broken in two places: just forward of the port wing and at the tail. In fact, it looked as if the tail had been sheared off as it swung around and hit the trees that earlier had looked so far away.

"One of the wings must've lifted on the wind," Chase said. "Right as the plane started to slip."

They walked back upslope and surveyed the path of the slip. Clearly, the snow under the plane had turned into a sheet of ice. Combined with a few gusts of wind, that had been enough.

"I guess we're lucky it didn't happen sooner," Yuma remarked.

"I guess."

But Rory noticed something else. "The snow is stopping. The air feels warmer, or am I imagining it?"

Chase paused and lifted his face. "You're right."

"If it's been warming," Yuma said, "that would explain the slip. We were probably frozen in place until then."

"Maybe," Chase agreed. "Okay, we need to get it

together. We're going to have to leave. This isn't shelter anymore, it's just additional danger. So we've got to gather everything we possibly can, and we need to make a stretcher. Or find a way to tie Cait to my back like a papoose."

Rory didn't object. As sick as Cait was getting, she didn't want to wait. Plus, it seemed to her they'd all be warmer if they kept moving than they would be if they tried to sit it out now.

They'd lost their shelter. That didn't leave a whole lot of options.

Now that the storm was abating, Chase tried the radio and the GPS once more. Nothing. Somehow, some way, those devices were dead. If any beacon was still broadcasting, it would require homing in on.

"I figure that if they get anywhere close to the plane, they'll find us. I've got flares to signal if we see a search plane."

"Agreed," said Yuma, and Rory nodded.

Especially, she thought, since the wind kept blowing, and even from inside the remains of the cabin she could see that the plane was rapidly being buried once again.

At first light, they were ready to go. Rory put her own jacket on Cait, who was wrapped in layers of blankets, to protect her from the dry air and cold. For herself, she just piled on every other piece of clothing she had, and accepted Wendy's extra knit hat, scarf and gloves.

"Once we get into the woods," Yuma said, "there'll be a lot less wind." He stood outside for a few minutes, looking around as daylight revealed the terrain. It had stopped snowing completely, though the sky was still clouded and the snow on the ground kept blowing around.

"The clouds are good, right?" Rory said.

"They'll keep the temperature from dropping suddenly," Chase agreed. "At this time of the year, it usually gets colder when they clear out."

"Small blessings."

"I'll take every one I can get."

So would she.

"I think I know where we are," Yuma said. "If I'm right, and we head downhill, we should hit a county road."

He didn't say how long that would take, nor did Rory ask. She decided that for once she was better off not knowing some things.

There was a road out there. She made up her mind that they were going to reach it come hell or high water.

Amazing everyone, Chase dug some bungee cords out of one of the now-twisted overhead bins. "What?" he said when he realized that everyone was staring at him.

"Is there nothing you don't have on that plane?" Rory asked.

"These are handier than you would believe. I use them all the time. And now we can use them to secure Cait to my back. Maybe later to a stretcher if that seems like a good idea."

Pretty soon every pocket was stuffed with something, from food packs to lighters, and even a first-aid kit. Wendy and Yuma had been traveling with duffels and backpacks instead of suitcases, and those proved extremely handy.

By the time they took their first steps away from

the plane, Rory felt they had gathered everything they possibly could carry that might be of use.

She looked back once as they walked away from the plane. It had been good to them, she thought as she watched it get buried even deeper in blowing snow. It had saved their lives.

Now they had to save their own.

They reached the forest after only ten minutes, despite the deep snow. Once under the thick boughs, the wind nearly vanished, and the blanket of snow thinned appreciably.

Rory had only one concern. "No one could see us in the trees."

"It's okay," Chase said. "I have the flare gun. We hear a plane, we shoot."

"Okay."

"Then," said Yuma, "we hunt up a clearing. There are lots of them. But right now we can't afford the exposure of open ground, or the risk of avalanche."

Rory's heart skipped a beat. "I hadn't even thought about avalanches."

"The safest place to be is in thick woods," Yuma answered. "Take it off your worry list."

"I guess I do have a whole list."

Wendy patted her arm. "So would I, in your shoes."

Yuma led the way, heartening her with his confidence. He seemed to know where they were, and which was the best way to go. He did pick up a tall stick, though, and she watched him use it to test the ground ahead of him, looking for dips that might have been hidden beneath the snow.

Every so often, they paused and Rory checked on

Cait. Her hands remained warm, her face didn't feel chilled, but her breathing rattled.

She and Wendy pounded Cait's back without untying her from Chase, and managed to clear out her lungs a bit, but not enough.

"Another hour," Wendy said. "Another hour and we've got to tent her."

"Consider it done," Yuma answered. He picked up the pace.

Rory's mind scrambled around frantically. They had to ease Cait's breathing, but every stop to build a fire was going to slow their progress. For the first time she realized how fortunate they had been to have the plane's protection. All the frenzy she had felt to be on the move and seeking help had partially blinded her to their good fortune.

Now the threat was not the lymphoma—it was pneumonia. Her sister could die on this trek, no matter what they did. How had she ever thought hiking out of here would be better than waiting?

But they had no choice now. None. The plane had become dangerous as a shelter, open to the elements. They had to strive to make it to a road. They could do nothing else.

On another day, under other circumstances, she might have noticed the beauty of the woods around them, the evergreens and snow. So appropriate for the season. But she couldn't care less about the season, and had no sense of the beauty. All she knew was that they had to keep moving as quickly as possible.

She was so unaccustomed to the altitude that it fatigued her as much as the uneven terrain and the snow she had to wade through. She hated to admit it, but when they stopped to build a small fire, heat some food and tent Cait, she needed the rest nearly as much as her sister.

The tenting was more difficult now, as the wind managed to occasionally find them. They had untied Cait from Chase's back, then set her on Rory's lap.

"You're not used to the altitude," Wendy said. "You need the humidity almost as much as she does."

She held her sister on her crossed legs, making a chair for her, keeping her off the icy ground. Another survival blanket had been tucked beneath her for protection, but while she didn't get wet from the snow, it scarcely felt warm at first.

Chase had managed to pack the chafing dish and snow melted quickly in it over a very small fire. They propped the tent on some tree limbs, keeping it above the ground just enough to admit oxygen, but soon it grew almost cozy inside, and filled with steam that immediately began to bead on the silvery blanket.

Cait moaned softly and began to really awaken. "What's going on?"

Earlier she had been only half-awake, and quietly accepting, but now she seemed to become aware of the change in scenery.

"We're hiking down the mountain to help. And you need to cough," Rory said firmly. "No matter how tired you are, you *have* to cough. Please, Cait. Please."

"'Kay."

But it seemed like a long time before she even attempted it. Just as Rory's concern began to reach a fever pitch, she heard the first tight cough. A moment later came a small one that sounded looser.

At once the tent was removed from Rory's head and tucked between her and Cait.

"Let's go," Wendy said. "Lean her forward so I can reach her, or lean back yourself."

Rory wasn't sure Cait would remain upright if she took her arms from either side of her, so she urged her sister to lean forward. Wendy stuck one arm beneath the tent to keep Cait from tipping forward, and pounded almost mercilessly on her back.

Rory gasped.

"I have to," Wendy said. "Sometimes you just can't be gentle."

At last they found success. Even as she listened to the necessary coughing, though, Rory heard how bad it was. Her sister's congestion was worsening. From the sound of it, she might have begun to drown.

And all of this might be for naught.

Wendy kept at it, though, until Cait's breathing sounded clear. Rory could easily imagine that her sister's back must be bruised, but there was no other option.

At last Cait sagged back against her, and they were able to get her to drink some hot tea, which made her cough some more. This time the coughing sounded normal.

They all ate quickly, their food heated over a second fire. Cait even swallowed a few mouthfuls and asked for more tea. A good sign? God, Rory hoped so.

They packed up as quickly as they could, tying Cait once again to Chase with bungee cords. Rory offered to carry her, but he shook his head.

"I'm used to the altitude. I know Cait doesn't weigh much, but it might be too much for you right now. We don't need you to get pulmonary edema."

More hiking. More snowy stops. An occasional

clearing where the going became even harder with deeper snow.

Rory lost all sense of time, all sense of how far they had traveled. She had become an automaton, awakening from the daze only when Cait needed tending.

At some point she realized that the day was waning. The sun poked through a few times, and once, as they approached a clearing, she could see the lengthening shadows.

One more day of meds for Cait. And they might prove useless.

But she had wearied too much now to even feel the fear. Numbness took over and she let it.

It was a small blessing.

All of a sudden, when she was sure that night was close to overtaking them, Chase froze.

"Stop. Listen."

Rory obeyed, wondering what he wanted them to hear. At first she heard nothing at all except the stirring of the treetops in a wind that couldn't reach them down here. Not a bird call, not a snapping twig.

Then, slowly, she caught snatches of a humming sound. A plane? She hardly dared believe it.

Chase looked at Yuma. "Now?"

He nodded. "Let them know our general area. We'll have to press on a little longer in hopes of finding a clearing."

Rescue? Could it be? Rory almost collapsed to the ground, but found some last reserve of strength to keep herself upright.

Chase fumbled at a bag that had been hanging at his belt and brought out the flare gun. He loaded it with quick efficiency, then looked up for an opening.

There were plenty. The woods had thinned here for some reason. He waited.

"Why are you waiting?" Rory asked.

"Because we have a better chance of being seen if the plane is coming this way."

She hadn't thought of that. Despair started warring with hope inside her. What if it was some normal flight, and came no closer?

She listened as hard as she could. Chase kept turning his head this way and that as if trying to locate the sound.

Rory hoped she wasn't imagining it, but the engine seemed to be approaching them.

Suddenly, Chase lifted his arm and fired. Rory tipped her head back, watching the flare rise until it burst into bright red flame, then rise even higher. It seemed to hang in the air above their heads, high, but maybe not high enough. Then, all too soon, it began to fall, growing dimmer as it did so.

Oh, God, what if it hadn't been seen?

"Let's keep moving," Yuma said.

"But they'll know we're here," Rory protested.

"If they saw that flare, we're not going to get so far that they won't see the next one and locate us. We're going to need a clearing to be rescued anyway."

So they stumbled on, but more slowly this time. Rory was certain she wasn't the only one straining her ears, listening for the plane engine over the muffled sounds of their breathing and their footfalls.

Another personal eternity passed for her before Chase waved them all to a stop again.

Rory held her breath. Then she heard it. The engine's buzz was coming closer. "Oh, God," she breathed brokenly.

Chase took a couple of steps and fired another flare. Once again all their hopes rose with it.

Even as high as it went, she thought she could hear it hiss and sizzle. The plane engine was still at some distance.

And night was encroaching steadily. Too late. Oh, God, too late. Her heart fell to her shoes, and a tear leaked out to freeze on her cold cheek.

Then, like the cavalry in the last minutes of an old Western, the sound grew louder. Steadily. Closer and closer.

And then, to her amazement, through the treetops she saw a plane fly over, low, almost too low, and as it did it waggled its wings.

Yuma let out a loud, "Yeehaw! Those are our guys!"

Dulled by fatigue, Rory hardly dared believe it. "They found us?"

"They found us," Chase said. "But we still have to get through the night."

"Why?" God, she felt like a dullard. She suspected that she already knew the answer, but they wouldn't come. The cold had seeped into her brain.

"Because they can't come in the dark, and there are still too many trees. But they've marked where we are. We'll find a clearing, and they'll be back at first light."

"That's right," Yuma agreed. "First light. And they won't quit until they have us."

She stumbled forward to check on Cait again. What she heard made her wonder if morning would be soon enough.

Chapter 10

Yuma led them to a small clearing. It wasn't huge, but he judged it large enough.

They tucked Cait into the shelter of a huge boulder while they made a camp with the survival blankets. Once again, dull as she was feeling from the cold and altitude, she was amazed at the things Chase had stowed on his plane, things he had brought with them.

Duct tape joined the pieces of survival blanket and taped them to pine boughs to make a lean-to. A couple more of them made a groundcover.

"Why do you carry so many of these?" she asked him.

"In case. They fold up to almost nothing, so why shortchange myself? I always figured if I was in a situation like this with passengers, I'd hate myself for being cheesy."

"I'm glad you're not cheesy."

He flashed her a smile.

She had started to stumble, but refused to give in as she helped gather wood from the forest for a fire to keep them warm overnight. The lean-to arrangement with a fire at the mouth promised as much coziness as they could hope for, short of a cave, and she didn't think any of them were about to hunt for one.

Finally, Chase told her to climb under the shelter and take care of Cait.

At least he hadn't pointed out that, unlike the rest of them, her stamina seemed to be failing. She was ashamed of that, then told herself not to be silly. She wasn't used to the cold, she'd given her warmest clothes to her sister, and the altitude wasn't helping, either.

"How high are we?" she asked.

"Over six thousand feet. That's enough to make any flatlander weary. You need some liquids, hot ones, and some warmth. You'll come back quickly."

She hoped so. Falling apart at this stage seemed ludicrous.

This time they built a bigger fire. The tent captured its heat and reflected its light into a wonderful bright yellow glow. Cait awoke again as they started boiling water, and Rory used a pine bough to sweep the steam into the tent.

Soon Cait was coughing again—deep, racking coughs that frightened Rory as much as they relieved her. She gave Cait medicine, and more hot soup and tea, and even received a smile for her efforts.

Chase brought her soup of her own, and some warmed-up mash of ready-to-heat foods he'd had on the plane. Ambrosia.

They made cowboy coffee, too, in the chafing dish, and she ignored the occasional coffee ground.

"Adds body," Chase said to her with a wink.

Weary and worried though she was, she managed a small laugh in response.

Cait woke up again and seemed a little brighter. Considering that they were keeping hot water steaming just inside the lean-to, near the fire, Rory thought that might be helping her sister revive. More coughing, which was good, and then a request for more tea.

"We're going to get out of here in the morning," Rory told her as she helped her hold the cup. "They know where we are now. You'll be in a hospital soon."

Cait wrinkled her nose, and astonished her with a flash of humor. "That's *good* news?"

Rory obligingly laughed again, although she was terrified of the hours between now and then. Cait felt feverish—no mistaking it. She was far too warm for it to be explained by the heat in the lean-to. In fact, the lean-to was warm only by comparison with the dark world beyond it.

But at least her own earlobes felt as if they were thawing.

"Rory?"

She turned at once to her sister, who was now lying cocooned on the groundcover. "Yes?"

"I want you to know something."

"What's that?"

"I know I haven't been awake much. I know I upset you when I say I don't want to fight anymore." Cait paused, panting a bit, trying to get her breath. "But I want you to know…I know you've done all you can. More than most people would."

"Shh… You need your breath."

Cait gave a little shake of her head. "I know, Rory.

I want you to know that. I know how much…you love me. I love you, too."

Rory felt tears prick her eyes, even as dread squeezed her heart. Surely Cait wasn't trying to say goodbye? Cait couldn't possibly believe she'd be gone before morning. Every cell in Rory wanted to scream a fierce denial. *No, you're not taking her,* she shouted inwardly. *Not now, not after all of this.* God, the cruelty of it at this point would be beyond bearing. All this fight, all this struggle, all for naught? No way. *No way.*

Instead of giving voice to her terror and anger, she managed a calm response. "You can tell me all this once we get you to the hospital and you can breathe again, okay?"

"Okay." A sigh. Then so softly Rory almost missed it, "I *do* want to live."

They took watches again that night to keep the fire burning high while ensuring that it didn't burn their tent. Sleep wasn't easy, but it no longer mattered to Rory.

She wrapped herself around Cait on one side, and was touched when Chase wrapped himself around them both from the other side.

"A sandwich is warmer," he said, then reached for and held her hand. "You're cold."

"I'll be warm tomorrow."

"More coffee or tea?"

"When we next take care of Cait." Then she whispered, "One more night."

"We'll make it."

"I think we will, thanks to you and your Boy Scout motto. You were prepared for everything."

"Not quite." He sighed. "But maybe enough."

"Oh, definitely enough. All these survival blankets. Duct tape. Flare gun. Food, candles… Chase, if my portable office in Mexico was half as well-stocked as that plane, I'd brag."

"You don't fly. You're firmly planted on the ground. Besides, you're talking to a guy who was given survival training by his former employer. They taught me enough, setting me free with only what I could carry on a fighter with me. I developed quite a list of things that were portable and would make surviving easier."

"I can see that. Coffee even."

"Hey, nothing short of Armageddon can separate a navy flier from his coffee."

She smiled in the dark. "Thank you."

"Thank me when you get to Minnesota," he said gruffly.

"I will."

"Good. So are you going to stay with your sister during her treatment?"

"As much as I can. I'm hoping to be there for the whole thing, but business may rear up." At this point, though, business didn't seem to matter at all. Not even wild horses were going to drag her away until she knew Cait was getting better. Or until it was over. The last thought caught in her throat, tightening it. She swallowed hard and pushed the notion of failure away. She couldn't, wouldn't, allow herself to think of it.

"Yeah, business has a way of doing that, doesn't it? Well, don't be surprised if you find me standing outside your portable office one day. I got wings, lady. Or I will again soon."

Rory's chest ached with an impending sense of loss. Were they saying goodbye? It certainly sounded like it.

If so, she wanted it to be a good one. "I also need to thank you for teaching me some things."

"I didn't teach you a damn thing, darlin'."

"You did." She didn't feel like exposing herself right then, though. She was exhausted, worried and very much on edge. "You made me think some things through, and in the process I learned something about myself."

"I could say the same. Watching you with Cait...well, let's just say I know I've been missing something. And that I've been making bad choices. But I told you that."

"Yes." She fell silent then, lost in wandering thoughts, all of which came back to the same place. When she left here tomorrow for Minnesota, she was going to be leaving friends behind. Worse, she was going to be leaving Chase behind. She was sure he was teasing about showing up at her office someday. It was just a kind, joking thing to say to lighten this last awful night.

He'd done a lot of that, she realized. In a quiet, no-horn-tooting sort of way, he'd shouldered responsibilities, among them helping her to stay strong. He'd let her lean on him, and taught her that leaning was not necessarily a bad thing.

Her life was going to be poorer without him.

In fact, it was going to be downright empty. Saving her sister was paramount, of course. Top of the list, no question. But saying farewell to Chase was going to be extremely hard.

She truly wished she didn't have to.

Chase's thoughts were following a similar line: *no future in this*. He couldn't believe he'd tipped over the brink of caring in less than two days. He'd never let himself really care for a woman before. Ever.

Yet this one had somehow wormed her way into a special place. He guessed that made him a fool, because tomorrow or the next day she'd be on her way to Minnesota with her sister, and from there to Mexico. He might joke about having wings, but he knew better.

They'd shared an intense time, everything heightened because of the crash and Cait's condition. He wouldn't have believed it if she said she cared for him, and he couldn't believe his own lying heart.

But as the night hours dragged by on leaden feet, he knew that he was about to lose something. He wasn't exactly sure what, but he could sense the impending loss.

The best thing to do, he decided, was to make sure she left without feeling that she owed him anything. Make it clear that the last two days had created no ties that couldn't snap in an instant.

He had to let her go free of any sense of obligation or debt, because he didn't want her that way. He'd rather lose her than risk that. So he'd cut her loose tomorrow. If she chose to look him up later, that would be different, but for now he had to do what was best.

Best for *both* of them. God, he was going to hate himself come tomorrow.

Thoughts of separation didn't last long. A few hours later, Cait's breathing worsened noticeably. The rasping woke Rory from a doze.

"Chase? Wendy?"

In an instant, both were squatting over Cait.

"It sounds like she's drowning." Instinctively, Rory pulled Cait up into a sitting position. Never, ever in her life had she heard someone sound like this. Cait didn't even wake up, not even when jerked upright.

Chase swore. He went to get the dish full of steaming water and cussed again. "It's dry. I'll get some snow."

Yuma was up now, too, pulling on his boots. "I'll build up the fire."

Rory wrapped her arm around her sister and pounded her back. What else could she do?

"Stop for a second," Wendy said. She pulled away blankets, unzipped Cait's jacket and pressed her ear to the woman's chest. "She's filling up."

"Oh, God," Rory said faintly. "Oh, God."

Wendy didn't offer any false hope. Not a shred of it. "I need a hot, wet cloth," she said.

Rory didn't hesitate. She pulled off her sweater and crawled out into the snow. She pushed as much snow into the fabric as she could then crawled over to the fire. She didn't even feel the night air's bite.

As soon as the snow melted into the sweater and the fabric grew hot, she scooted over to Wendy.

Wendy took it and stuffed it inside Cait's jacket, covering her chest with it before rezipping the parka.

Then she pounded Cait's back again.

Cait's eyes fluttered opened. She drew a shallow, ragged, wet breath, then coughed. It almost sounded like a barking seal. "I'm sorry."

"Hush," Rory said sharply. "Just cough, dammit."

Cait tried again, but it sounded both weak and far too tight.

The light suddenly brightened and Rory turned her head to see Yuma throwing more dry pine branches on the fire. Chase was already hovering over the bowl of snow, and she could see steam starting to rise.

When it was good and hot, he grabbed it with his

gloved hands and brought it to them, duck-walking beneath their shelter. He didn't set it down but held it directly under Cait's chin.

"Breathe, Cait," Rory begged. "As deeply as you can."

Chase looked over his shoulder. "Yuma, get that other pot out of the duffel. Boil more water."

"You got it."

Cait's breathing was so shallow that Rory despaired that she could draw enough steam into her lungs. "Cait, please, try. Inhale it."

Cait opened her mouth and drew a breath. It was a little one, but Rory could see steam drifting toward and into her mouth.

"Another one, Cait."

Wendy pounded some more, but no cough emerged. She looked at Rory over Cait's head. "We're going to have to keep this up until the 'copter gets here."

"Then I will."

"No," said Chase. "*We* will."

"I must have fallen asleep," Rory said. "Oh, God, how could I have slept and not heard this?"

"Rory." Wendy's voice was firm. "Given her condition I told you this could be sudden. You probably heard it the minute it got worse. We've been getting her to cough regularly. It's all we could do then. Now we do what we can do nonstop until rescue gets here."

After a moment, Rory nodded. What else could she do?

Chase switched the steaming bowls. Wendy pulled the wet sweater out again and told Rory to reheat it.

Though it seemed like forever, probably a half hour passed before Cait had her first productive cough. Then she drew a deeper breath, though not deep enough, and sounded a bit looser.

"Good," said Wendy with evident satisfaction. "One of you guys get some sleep. We only need three of us to take care of this."

But nobody slept. Nobody even tried. The steaming-bowl brigade continued. Yuma took over heating the sweater for Rory, and in between times gathered more wood for the fire.

Little by little, Cait's breathing improved.

Rory looked at Wendy. "What about when she's on the chopper?"

"They can give her plenty of oxygen. They also have other stuff. Don't worry about that."

"Okay."

Never had she been more out of her element than in these long night hours. She barely felt it when Chase touched her shoulder, barely noticed that her lack of response caused him to draw back a bit.

Only one thing mattered: Cait.

Chase felt her withdrawal as rejection. All he'd tried to do was offer silent comfort, and she'd acted like he wasn't even there. Good. That would make his task easier.

In the meantime, he wanted nothing more than to ensure that Cait survived to be evacuated. He wanted it for Rory most of all, but he wanted it for himself, too.

Because there were some burdens that might be too heavy to carry. He wanted Cait to live. He didn't want to feel responsible for killing her.

And he would if they didn't get her out of here alive, and get her past the pneumonia.

The rest of the night he ferried water and listened

hopefully as Cait coughed and struggled to draw deeper breaths. Little by little, she seemed to improve.

And then, just before the first pale light of dawn began to overtake the fire's light, she had a coughing fit he thought might kill her all by itself.

When it passed, she sagged against her sister, and at long last drew a deep breath. And then another.

"Tea?" he asked.

Cait nodded weakly.

He went to the pot that was heating by the fire, made the tea with plenty of sugar, and passed the cup to Rory.

Then he rose and left the lean-to, to walk around the clearing's edge.

If God had any mercy, he thought, that woman would survive and get her trial on the new drug. And if any of that mercy was left over, he hoped he could find a way to cut the tie with Rory. For good.

Neither of them needed this. It was born of an artificial closeness. He gave himself another dozen or so arguments, absolutely none of which he believed, but what the hell.

It was going to hurt, but not for long. She hadn't been in his life for enough time to leave a permanent scar.

He only wished he believed that.

As soon as it was light enough for visual flight rules over these mountains, he heard a plane engine coming their way again. He stood in the middle of the clearing, flare gun ready.

"Build up that fire, Yuma?"

"I already am."

When it sounded close enough, Chase sent up his last flare. They damn well better see it.

Five breathless minutes later, the plane soared over them and waggled its wings. They had been sighted.

Now it would be only a matter of time before the chopper arrived.

Reluctantly, he turned back to the lean-to. Cait was still drinking tea. Rory looked at him, something he couldn't define in her gaze, then her attention slipped away.

He'd definitely been relegated to the forgotten. And he was going to make damn sure he stayed there somehow.

For both their sakes.

A half hour later the helicopter arrived, emblazoned with a red cross and blue lettering on white that identified it as a medical evacuation chopper. It hovered as low as it could without landing on the snow or clipping the trees, its roar deafening.

It lowered an EMT to them immediately, then lifted a bit, waiting. He greeted Wendy and Yuma with quick hugs while Wendy filled him in on Cait.

Within five minutes, after he spoke through his headset to the chopper, he was lifted again. Then down came a basket stretcher.

Her heart pounding madly, Rory helped settle Cait into it and strap her in. When Wendy was satisfied, she made a winding motion with her hand and the stretcher began to lift, swaying a bit, but far steadier than Rory would have believed possible.

Then Cait vanished into the door of the chopper.

Wendy leaned close to Rory. "They can take only one more person on this trip. They're sending down a harness for you."

"You should go," Rory said, panic stabbing at her. "You know how to navigate it all, get her help faster."

Wendy grabbed her forearm. "Hang in there. You know as much about her condition as I do, and when that thing lands at the hospital, there's going to be no hesitation in beginning treatment. Plus, you know her doctors, right?"

Rory nodded, looking up.

"You know more of the important stuff than I do, and there's an EMT onboard right now," Wendy said. "You don't need an extra one."

Only then did Rory admit that she didn't want to let her sister out of her sight. She was afraid something would happen and she wouldn't be there. She couldn't bear the thought.

She looked toward Chase. He nodded, his expression cool. "Good luck. I hope it all turns out well for you."

Woodenly, she allowed Wendy and Yuma to buckle her into the waiting harness. He hadn't even asked her to let him know how it came out.

She wondered if she could stand anymore, because her heart was cracking again, this time because of Chase.

Then a flicker of fury saved her. She read the farewell in his eyes, in the dismissive tone. In the way he wished her luck, and didn't say anything about seeing her later. She felt used. She looked him square in the eye and spoke coldly.

"Have a nice life."

Then the winch lifted her to whatever the future held.

The local hospital put her in a bed next to Cait's in the emergency room. The oxygen seemed to be brightening her color, and Rory hardly tore her gaze from her sister as people checked her out for exposure, pumped fluids into her, insisted that she eat.

Cait was unconscious again, but the E.R. personnel lifted the burden from Rory's shoulders. The E.R. doctors spoke to Cait's doctors in Seattle, and came in to tell Rory that a treatment plan had been made. They were going to treat the pneumonia immediately with powerful antibiotics and decongestants.

She watched again and again as they forced Cait to cough.

Then a nurse came to tell her that they had arranged medical transport to Minnesota the next day. Cait would still get into the trial as long as her pneumonia showed improvement by tomorrow or the next day.

By late afternoon, Cait's breathing improved. Hope alone was enough to allow Rory to lie back and give it all into the hands of the medical people. Not long after that, they released her and she followed Cait up to ICU, where she remained in a chair beside her sister's bed.

"How are you doing?"

Wendy's voice drew her out of numb preoccupation and she looked up. "Okay. She's breathing better."

"I can hear that."

"They say her tests show no organ damage, so that's good."

Wendy nodded. "I heard. And she's still going for the trial."

"Yes."

"Then we succeeded."

"Thanks to you and Yuma. And Chase." Chase who hadn't bothered to come by even once to see how Cait was doing, how *she* was doing.

Wendy hesitated. "You and Chase…"

"It was nothing. Forget it. I have."

And that was probably the biggest lie she had ever told.

Chapter 11

Rory was coming out of the hospital on a cold Minnesota afternoon, planning to get a decent meal somewhere besides the hospital cafeteria.

A familiar voice brought her up short.

"Howdy, stranger."

She turned slowly and saw Chase standing there on the sidewalk looking oddly awkward. At least for Chase. He smiled uncertainly.

All the pain she'd refused to allow herself to feel rose up in a tidal wave and transformed into anger. "What are you doing here? Not having a nice life?"

With that she turned and started to storm away. He'd hurt her worse than she had realized until later, and she wasn't going to let him hurt her again. No way.

But he caught up with her. "I wanted to see how Cait is doing."

She resisted answering him, but finally said shortly, "Much better."

"Really?"

She kept walking.

"Rory, look. I owe you a date."

"Like I care."

"Then call it lunch. I need to talk with you."

"No, you don't. You made that clear over the last couple of months."

"I was an ass. Does that help?"

"And you're not being one now?"

"God, I hope not."

Somehow that got through to her. She glanced at him, and realized that his face still had the power to tug at her heart. "Lunch," she finally agreed grudgingly. "Not a date."

"Fine." Another half smile. "Where?"

"There's a place up here that offers a better menu than the hospital cafeteria."

"Sounds perfect."

It wasn't an upscale restaurant by any means, basically a diner with a counter and booths and food that didn't try to match some dietitian's view of hell.

They slid into a booth facing each other, and said little until after they ordered.

"So she's really improving," Chase said when the waitress walked away.

"It's amazing," Rory said, and her voice cracked a bit. "For the first time since I came home, doctors are saying hopeful things to me. All I heard before was that I'd better prepare myself. That she only had weeks or at most a few months. Now I'm actually hearing references to when she finishes this treatment. There's a future again."

"Thank God." His words were clearly heartfelt, and despite herself she warmed a bit toward him. "Long term?"

"She'll probably never be cured. Few cancers really are, I guess. But she can have this treatment again if necessary. The doctors are thrilled by how she's responding. So am I. Chase, she's smiling again. Eating. Starting to talk about things she wants to do."

"That's wonderful. That must make you feel wonderful."

"It does, obviously. I hardly dared hope."

"I know. But you fought for her like a tiger."

She hesitated. "You helped."

"Not much. I'm the guy who brought us down on a mountainside."

"Safely," she reminded him. "Did you find out what happened?"

"A comedy of errors that almost wasn't a comedy, if you get my drift. A handful of things went wrong because mechanics missed something, or failed to do something exactly right. No single one of them would have been catastrophic, but put them all together that's what they became. Oh, and you'll love this."

"What?"

"The beacon wasn't working at all. That freaking expensive piece of equipment I had installed so our location could be pinpointed in a crash failed. I guess that wasn't installed right, either."

"Maybe you need to find a new mechanic."

"I'm not sure, but some heads are going to roll."

She nodded. "So you get your new plane?"

"I flew here on it."

"That was fast."

He shrugged. "That overhaul was done by the plane's

manufacturer. Once the preliminary report came from the NTSB, they couldn't give me a replacement fast enough."

"I'm glad you're back in business."

Silence fell again. Their sandwiches were served, both of them thick and meat-laden.

"How about your business?" he asked after they'd eaten a few mouthfuls.

"I'm managing it long-distance. Thank God for the telephone and the internet."

"That's good."

Another silence, this one more awkward. What was she doing here? This was worse than ripping a sticky bandage off a wound. She could feel barely formed scabs shrieking.

"Rory..." He hesitated. "I've had some time to think. I need some time with you. To talk. To figure out stuff. I didn't want to be a bastard, but I was. Please. Can you spare me some time?"

She hesitated, realizing that she wanted to hear what he had to say, regardless of how difficult it might be to hear. The way they had parted had given her no closure at all. She needed some closure on her episode with him, just so she could live with herself.

Especially now that the future existed once again, with Cait's improvement.

"All right," she said finally. "I'll go back to the hospital and tell Cait I'm going to be away for a while."

"Thank you."

They talked casually thereafter. He told her more about Wendy and Yuma, and how they were doing. "They wanted to come along to see Cait. I told them next trip."

Rory caught her breath. "You believed that strongly that she was going to get better?"

"If she's anything like her sister, I figured her for a fighter."

"She almost lost that fight."

"I know. Don't lose yours. Not for any reason."

What did he mean by that? she wondered as they walked back to the hospital. As they rounded a corner, the icy winter wind snatched at them and she almost lost her breath. He reached to hold her elbow, to steady her, and she didn't pull away.

Soon enough, she told herself, he'd be gone for good, and she could start growing the scabs again. Put the bandages back in place. Get on with life.

Cait waved at them through the glass that separated her from the world until her immune system was restored. When Rory said she was thinking about being away for a few hours, Cait waved a hand.

"Go. For heaven's sake, get out of here and breathe something that doesn't smell like iodine."

Chase laughed. "You *do* sound better."

"I am. Now go—both of you."

"Where are you staying?" Chase asked as they reached the lobby. "I don't really want to talk in public. It'll make me nervous."

"But it might keep me from yelling."

He gave her a smile that at once looked a bit pained, yet reached his eyes with real humor. "I deserve it. If you want to yell, I'll listen."

The cab ride was short, and soon they were in her hotel room, a nice enough place but nothing special. She only slept here and worked from a laptop on the table. There were two chairs, though, and once they'd doffed their jackets, they sat.

"Okay," she said. "I'm listening."

"First of all, maybe I'm an ass—actually, I know I am—but I felt you wouldn't want anything to continue between us."

"And you got that idea where?"

"From the way you acted in the last few hours. So I decided, given that everything that had happened occurred partly because we were under extreme pressure…" He paused. "Let me find another way to phrase that. I wanted us both to have space, to see if what happened meant anything."

"I might remind you," she said a bit sarcastically, "that you were the one who said you really got to know a person fast in those conditions."

"I did. And I still believe it. But that doesn't mean it's anything that can go past that."

She couldn't argue that, she supposed. They had been in a crucible, and while it might reveal their true characters, it didn't mean they could handle normal life together. Especially with both of them being at opposite ends of the world half the time. She sighed.

"I didn't want to hurt you," he said. "I was trying to be smart."

"Maybe you were." The words were heavy with reluctance, because as she looked at him now, she realized that she had feelings for him that had extended well beyond those few days.

He fell silent, a kind of sadness settling over his face. "Maybe so. Maybe that's how you feel. Maybe you're right."

"I didn't exactly say that." And she had just exposed herself. Clenching her hands, she waited for the bomb to drop.

"No, you didn't." He leaned forward, passed his hand

over his face. "Man, I could screw up falling off a log. Look. What I'm saying is, I've spent the last few months telling myself to forget you. I can't. I just can't. For the first time in my life, I can't just walk away. You'll have to send me away. And if you don't, I'm not going to be greedy. I'm just going to ask you to give us a chance."

"A chance for what?" But her heart was beating heavily now, rising with hope that only a few short weeks ago she had feared she would never feel again. Cait was improving. Now Chase was suggesting…suggesting what exactly?

"A chance to see if we can build something together. I want to date you. I don't care if I have to fly to the jungles of Mexico as often as I can manage and eat tortillas by candlelight while battling mosquitoes and other critters. I just want us to try. Is that possible?"

For the last few months she'd been telling herself that she wouldn't care if Chase Dakota fell off a cliff. She'd been telling herself lies. She knew that now, as tears pricked at her eyes, as her heart began to soar. Hope. So much hope. It overwhelmed her.

"Rory? If it's not possible just shake your head and tell me to go."

She'd walked away from him once. She didn't have the strength to do it again. She'd never be able to live with herself if she did.

"Stay," she said finally, a whisper.

He let out a whoop and jumped up. "Really?"

"Really."

Suddenly he was on his knees in front of her, cradling her face in his hands. "I admire everything I've seen of you. This whole time I've been beating myself up for not at least trying. I never before met a woman who reached the places you reach inside me. They've been cold, empty places for too long."

She knew exactly what he meant, but it was getting so hard to breathe. Emotions were overwhelming her, her protective shell was cracking, and it hurt worse than anything except her fear for Cait.

No more talk, she thought. "Shut up, Chase."

Then, as he started to pull back, she leaned in and kissed him.

An instant later his arms surrounded her, holding her so tightly it almost hurt. His tongue sought hers, instantly lifting her to that place only he had ever taken her.

The room spun, and she realized that he had lifted her and carried her to the bed. Then he laid her down, standing over her, smiling. Absolutely smiling, the most beautiful expression she had ever seen.

He looked so powerful. She wasn't used to seeing him without the bulk of winter clothing, and she liked what she saw. He was strong, lean, tall. And he was impatient. He pulled his clothes off as if they were still in the frigid plane, as if he couldn't risk getting cold before he dived into her warmth.

But he was gentler with her, far gentler. He unwrapped her as if she were a fragile gift, as if he wanted to delay the moment of discovery just a little longer.

She felt a fleeting shyness, because before they had made love in the dark, and this room was bright with winter light pouring in the window. But the way he looked at her drove that shyness away.

"You're beautiful," he said. "Perfect."

"No..."

"Oh, hush, just accept the compliment."

That startled a giggle out of her, and shyness took

flight. Then he took her on another flight with him. Lying beside her, the cold no longer a concern, he drank her in with his eyes, then studied her with his hands.

She could not long remain still. She turned toward him, reciprocating as she hadn't been able to before.

She found all his muscled hollows and hardness with her hands, memorizing the dry warmth of his skin, the way he flexed on her touches, loving it each time she drew a moan from him.

They didn't have to be quiet this time, and soon her moans were melding with his as they hungrily explored each other. No place was too secret to be discovered by hands or mouth.

The heat built in her, along with that wonderful ache. And when she felt that she couldn't bear to wait another minute, he made her wait longer.

Until, finally, his name was an imploring chant that emerged on moan after moan.

The world spun again, and she found herself straddling him, his staff hard against her most sensitive places. His eyes were heavy-lidded as he looked up at her, a smile at the corners of his mouth.

He reached up, cupping both her breasts at once, tormenting her nipples with his thumbs. Helpless, she leaned down until he could take one into his mouth. Each time he sucked strongly, she felt it throughout every inch of her body, and between her legs the throbbing ache grew.

She was in charge, the way she liked to be. The thought flitted across her mind, recognizing the gift he was giving her, but was immediately lost in the rising drumbeat of passion.

At last she reared up, and looked down to where their bodies almost joined. So close, yet so far.

"Wait," he managed huskily. He reached for the bed-side table. She saw the foil packets immediately and grabbed one, tearing it open.

Then she did something she had never done before: she rolled the protection onto his staff, finding it one of the sexiest things she had ever done, especially when he writhed in response and deep sounds of pleasure escaped him.

She discovered that she enjoyed teasing him, and making him wait. Then, almost euphoric in her plea-sure, she gave in to her body's demands. Rising, she impaled herself on his manhood. All the way. Deeply.

And as their centers met, she threw back her head and closed her eyes, savoring the fullness, loving the exquisite, intimate contact.

She didn't move immediately. No, she held them suspended that way, propping herself on her elbows and she came down onto his chest. With her mouth she found one of his small nipples, and discovered that teasing them and sucking them pleased him just as it pleased her when he did it to her.

Delight speared her, for now she had a new way to delight him.

But at last, at long last, she couldn't hold back the tide anymore.

Her hips moved in a helpless, ancient rhythm. She felt him grip her rear, keeping her close, his touch heightening her desire.

Together, all barriers gone, they climbed their way to the stars.

Later, much later, they showered together, then dressed.

"I need to go see Cait," she said.

"I'll go with you."

"I'd like that."

When they were just about ready to put on their outerwear, he stopped her, taking her hand. "I want you to consider something."

"What's that?"

"After Cait gets out of here…well, where is she going to go? You said her husband left her."

"I haven't gotten that far," she admitted.

"Then I have a suggestion. She can stay with me while you have to be in Mexico. We'll be a family."

Stunned, she plopped down on the messed-up bed. "Chase, do you know what you're saying?"

"I think so. Okay, she needs to see doctors. I can provide transport. I can keep her company when she has to be here and you're away."

"But…but that's a *commitment!*"

"I know. And I know how big it is."

"But you said…" Her mind was reeling. Her heart was leaping.

"I know what I said. Call it my wedge. What I really want is for us to do more than try. And I like your sister. I know exactly what I'm volunteering for here. Trust me. I've seen it."

She believed him. His generosity finally broke the dam, and tears began to roll down her cheeks.

"You'd feel better, wouldn't you, to know she's not alone when you're away. That someone who cares about you also is caring for her."

"My God…" She couldn't speak through her tight throat.

"I'm not just going to try, Rory. I'm going to do my damnedest to make this work for all three of us."

She stared mutely at him through blurry eyes.

"Rory? Did I say something wrong?"

"No." She swallowed. "Oh, no. You just said the most beautiful thing in the world."

He began to smile. "Then let me add, I'm pretty damn sure I'm in love with you. And on my honor, I've never ever said that to anyone before."

"I…I'm in love with you, too," she admitted.

He reached for her then, holding her close, murmuring in her ear. "We'll make it work," he vowed. "We will make it all work. I want marriage. I want Cait to live with us. Kids are negotiable, depending on how you feel about it. But one thing I swear, and that's that I can't live my life without you."

She hugged him back, squeezing her eyes against tears of joy. "I love you, too. I couldn't bear the thought that I'd never see you again. I couldn't."

"So start planning on permanence. I let you go once. I'm not going to do it again."

The joy that filled her became incandescent. "I want kids."

"Good. Put them on your calendar. You can even add a picket fence if you want."

The tears were still falling, but she laughed. It felt so good to laugh.

"I love you, Rory."

"I love you, Chase."

And an hour later, when they stood looking at Cait in her isolation room, they held up their linked hands.

Cait, who no longer looked as fragile as a dandelion puff, grinned. It was a wide, happy grin, and she applauded.

For the first time ever, Rory knew that life could be perfect. Oh, not always, but every now and then.

And right now it was pure perfection.

* * * * *

A sneaky peek at next month...

INTRIGUE...

BREATHTAKING ROMANTIC SUSPENSE

My wish list for next month's titles...

In stores from 20th January 2012:

☐ Wild Stallion — Delores Fossen

& Unforgettable — Cassie Miles

☐ Branded — BJ Daniels

& Lassoed — BJ Daniels

☐ The Secret Soldier — Jennifer Morey

& Under the Gun — HelenKay Dimon

☐ The Cowboy's Secret Twins — Carla Cassidy

Available at WHSmith, Tesco, Asda, Eason, Amazon and Apple

Just can't wait?

Visit us Online

You can buy our books online a month before they hit the shops! **www.millsandboon.co.uk**